T0369198

THE LAST STOP

Donald R. Nuss

iUniverse, Inc.
New York   Bloomington

The Last Stop

Copyright © 2009 Donald R. Nuss

All rights reserved. No part of this book may be used or reproduced by
any means, graphic, electronic, or mechanical, including photocopying,
recording, taping or by any information storage retrieval system
without the written permission of the publisher except in the case
of brief quotations embodied in critical articles and reviews.

This is a work of fiction. All of the characters, names, incidents,
organizations, and dialogue in this novel are either the products
of the author's imagination or are used fictitiously.

iUniverse books may be ordered through booksellers or by contacting:

iUniverse
1663 Liberty Drive
Bloomington, IN 47403
www.iuniverse.com
1-800-Authors (1-800-288-4677)

Because of the dynamic nature of the Internet, any Web addresses or
links contained in this book may have changed since publication and
may no longer be valid. The views expressed in this work are solely those
of the author and do not necessarily reflect the views of the publisher,
and the publisher hereby disclaims any responsibility for them.

ISBN: 978-1-4401-2214-9 (pbk)
ISBN: 978-1-4401-2215-6 (ebk)

Printed in the United States of America

iUniverse rev. date: 1/27/2009

Dedication

Diana Lycette and her husband, Bill, were the first couple my wife and I met at the Covington Retirement Community. They were attractive and interesting. Bill was a big, good-natured, funny teddy-bear, and Diana, well she was something special. Intelligence exploded from her eyes. She graduated cum laude from the University of Washington, was elected to Phi Beta Kappa, and had an IQ rating at the genius level. But her most endearing specialty was her wit. Every sentence she spoke or wrote was tinged with humor and brought a smile to the listener or reader.

Besides taking care of her husband Bill, she had three other passions. As a writer, she conducted writer's workshops, wrote and published stories for children and adults, won an award for her play, *Up with the Dragons*, and shortly before her death published a mystery novel, *All the Dead Little Dolls*.

As a social worker she volunteered for the Washington Association of Retired Citizens, was the leader of Campfire Girls and Cub Scouts, therapist for psychiatric patients in Seattle, and was an active member of the Daughters of the American Revolution.

She lovingly raised, with Bill's help, four children, two boys and two girls. Her five grandchildren also received her special love and care.

She encouraged me with my first novel, "To Do and Die" and graciously helped with character development and story lines.

Her generous work as chairman of various committees—rose garden developer, and Editor of the Chat, to name a few endeavors—was instrumental in elevating the pride and affection the residents have for the Covington.

Diana died on May 22, 2008 after bravely battling ovarian cancer for two years. Her husband and family, the Covington residents, all her friends, and I will greatly miss her wit, charm, and unselfish willingness to help others.

Acknowledgements

I am grateful for the support of the residents of the Covington, a retirement community, located in Also Viejo, California. I particularly am indebted to those with exceptional writing skills who allowed me to reproduce some of their prose and poetry in both the novel and its appendix, namely: Dee Leif, Ruth Cushingham, Diana Lycette, Betsy Schulman, and John Dilkes. Additional thanks is owed Mrs. Leif who discovered and corrected my many errors of grammar and punctuation.

Judge David Thomas, retired from the Superior Court of the State of California, Los Angeles County, graciously and with kind patience made sure that the protocol, language, and procedures of my two courtroom chapters were correct. Thank you, good friend.

"The Last Stop" tells the stories and describes the people who live in The Wind and Sea, a fictional retirement community located in Santa Barbara, California and with poetic license reflects the lives of the residents and events that happened at the Covington.

People in their seventies, eighties, and nineties who have moved to retirement communities, whether healthy or suffering from illness and infirmities, live in dignity, look forward each morning to another fulfilling day, and accept the verdict of the actuarial tables.

A more gifted writer than I am is required to truly describe and define the emotions and internal grace and strength of those who have lived through the Great Depression, World War II, the loss of mates, children, most of their friends, and have suffered through the depths of financial and health emergencies. "The Last Stop" is my best effort to portray those strengths, thanks to my friends at the Covington.

Prologue

March 12, 1979

For three weeks, the *Los Angeles Times* headlined the trial of the century. Deborah Farrell, Hollywood's leading lady and sex goddess, was on trial in L. A. County's Superior Court. The tedious voir dire and testimonies from minor witnesses had been completed. Now everyone eagerly anticipated today's critical testimony from the prosecution's key witness.

The bailiff stood and cleared his throat. "All rise please. The Superior Court of the State of California for Los Angeles County is now in session. The Honorable Roger Palmer presiding."

Judge Palmer strode through the door and to his chair behind the bench. His black gown billowed behind his tall frame. He bent his head first toward the prosecution and defense tables and then to the jury. In one quick motion, he swept his robe off his chair and sat. He was a worldly man whose bright, intelligent eyes had seen it all.

Judge Palmer pounded his gavel. "Is your next witness ready to testify, Mr. Armstrong?"

Joshua Armstrong put on his horn-rimmed glasses. "Yes, your honor." The middle-aged assistant district attorney shuffled his papers, then took his glasses off and held them in his right hand. "The prosecution calls Gerald Timson."

A heavyset man strolled to the witness chair and sat with a weary sigh.

"Please state your name," the clerk said.

The man raked his fingers through his gray hair. "Gerald H. Timson."

"Do you swear to tell the truth and nothing but the truth?" the clerk continued perfunctorily.

"I do."

Armstrong stroked his neatly trimmed beard and toyed with his glasses. With his bald head and dark, intense eyes he knew he looked like an Old Testament patriarch full of fury and ready to extract justice for his people. He practiced daily in front of a mirror to perform like one. He cleared his throat. "What is you occupation, Mr. Timson?"

"I'm a private investigator and a good one."

John Cummings, the defense attorney, jumped to his feet. "Motion to strike, your honor. Please instruct this witness to refrain from advertising and answer only the questions asked. The jury will decide if he's any good or not."

Judge Palmer hit his gavel. "Granted. The phrase 'and a good one' is stricken from the record."

Silence fell over the courtroom as everyone leaned forward, intent on hearing every word.

"Sometime prior to March 30, 1978 did the defendant, Deborah Farrell, employ you?" Armstrong asked.

"Yes," Timson replied.

"And what were you employed to do?"

"I conducted a surveillance of her husband, Mark Chambers, to determine if he was cheating on her."

Armstrong waved his glasses around. "In your investigation did you see Mr. Chambers in the company of Ginger O'Conner on the afternoon of Thursday, March 30, 1978?"

Without changing his bored expression Timson said, "Yes, I did."

"Where were they?"

"At the bar in the Sunset Tennis Club."

"And then what did you see and hear?" Armstrong the lion was moving in for the kill.

"They had two drinks at the bar, martinis for him and fruity rum drinks for her. At four-thirty, he drove her to the Hilton Hotel in Beverly Hills. I knew where they were going, so I took a shortcut, and was at the check-in desk before them to learn their room number."

Armstrong's stern expression became a smirk "How long did they stay?"

Timson shrugged. "Maybe for the night. I left after four hours."

Tension grew in the courtroom. *Why would a man married to a goddess want another woman?*

"Did they stop for dinner?"

Timson, realizing he was now center stage, gave the jury a cockeyed grin. "No, they didn't stop for anything."

The crowd in the courtroom tittered and laughed.

"Order in the courtroom," Judge Palmer thundered. "I will have the bailiff remove anyone who does that again."

Armstrong paced in front of the jury. With a knowing smile, he looked at Timson. "Is there any doubt what they were doing in the hotel room? Chess, maybe? Or gin rummy?"

"I listened several times at the door of room four twenty-two, registered to Mark Chambers, and no, they weren't playing checkers."

Judge Palmer's glare prevented any outburst.

"Mr. Timson, is it your testimony that you believe Mr. Chambers was having sex with Ms. O'Conner?"

Timson scratched his nose and cleared his throat to restrain the chuckle that threatened to escape. "Yes, Mr. Armstrong. From the grunts, squeals, and groans, it was sex. Room shaking sex. Supercharged."

"Motion to strike, your honor," Cummings said. "Mr. Timson is not a sex expert. He didn't see anything. Perhaps they were arm wrestling."

Laughter erupted, and Judge Palmer jumped to his feet. His elegant robe, tailored on Rodeo Drive in Beverly Hills, made him look taller. The spectators were circus lions and he was their trainer. He raised his right arm and they soon cowered back into respectable, compliant silence.

"One more time and I'll have an empty courtroom. Understood? The witness may answer the question simply 'yes' or 'no.'"

Timson glared at the defense attorney. "Yes, and I've seen and heard more sex than you ever will."

Armstrong was establishing a motive, an important part of the prosecutor's case. Cummings couldn't rebut the message, only the messenger. Also, Cummings knew the jury was sympathetic to his client. It was worth the risk of a judicial reprimand.

"You're a voyeur. All hotel dicks are voyeurs and probably sexually repressed. You hear someone grinding coffee beans and you presume sexual activity."

Judge Palmer rose. "In my chambers, now!" He nodded to the jury, and walked majestically from the courtroom.

Armstrong and Cummings sat in leather-covered, upholstered chairs facing the judge who stood behind a mahogany desk. Leather-bound books filled the library behind Judge Palmer. His private collection of first editions mingled with the legal volumes. A narcotic aroma of leather permeated the room. Cigarette or cigar smoke would be an abomination.

"You both know better. This is an important trial and you're acting like second-year law students conducting a moot trial." He relaxed, and his voice remained steady, but some of the color drained from his face. They had shamed his court. "Joshua, you can't or won't control your witness and John your comments are completely out of order."

Without giving them a chance to answer, Judge Palmer concluded, "Unless you comply with the standards I demand, either or both of you will be held in contempt, understood?"

Both attorneys nodded and all returned to the courtroom where Armstrong resumed questioning Timson. "Did you discover anything else for Ms. Farrell?"

Timson shifted in his chair. "Yes. She wanted all the joint accounts held with her husband studied. I hired an accountant, Thomas Warner, to check them. I believe he will be the next witness."

"Thank you, Mr. Timson." Armstrong smiled at the defense attorney. "You may cross-examine, Counsel."

"Mr. Timson," John Cummings began. "Hotel doors aren't what they used to be, are they? With the new plastic key cards, hotel dicks no longer have keyholes to peep through. Did you used to do that, Mr. Timson?"

Armstrong raised his hand. "Objection, your honor. He's badgering the witness."

"Sustained," Judge Palmer said..

"So without the keyhole you didn't see anything?" Cummings asked quickly.

"No, I didn't," Timson answered with a face that had lost all expression.

"All you heard were grunts, squeals, and groans, correct?"

"Yes," the witness replied.

"Mr. Timson, those are the exact sounds you hear in a gymnasium. I believe they rented the hotel room to do their daily calisthenics. No further questions for this witness."

Giggles and subdued laughter rolled through the courtroom, but Judge Palmer ignored the disturbance.

Armstrong rose, then took his glasses off again. "Your honor, the prosecution calls Thomas Warner."

After Warner was sworn-in Armstrong continued. "Mr. Warner, you were hired by Gerald Timson to check Deborah Farrell's accounts for fraud, correct?"

Warner straightened his tie, and wiped the sweat from his brow. "Yes."

"And what did you discover?"

"I found that Mr. Chambers had embezzled $100,000 from one of Ms. Farrell's investment accounts and charged $20,000 on a Visa card by forging Ms. Farrell's name."

"Thank you, Mr. Warner. Your witness, Counsel." The assistant district attorney was proud of himself, and gave the jury a big smile.

Cummings remained seated and flipped his hand at the witness. "No questions at this time, your honor."

Armstrong studied his files, then looked up at Judge Palmer. "Your honor, the State calls Soey Wong."

A small, Chinese-American gentlemen shuffled to the witness chair.

"What is you name and occupation?" Armstrong asked.

"Soey Wong, and I am chief of the Los Angeles Forensic Laboratory."

"Now, Mr. Wong." Armstrong pointed to the evidence table. "I show you a gun previously identified as Prosecution's Exhibit Number Two. Are you familiar with it?"

"Yes, that is my mark on the butt."

"Were there any fingerprints on it?" Armstrong asked.

"There was one on the barrel of the gun and it matched a print taken from the right forefinger of the defendant, Deborah Farrell."

"Thank you, Mr.Wong." Armstrong sat back down. "Your witness, Mr. Cummings."

Cummings walked over to the witness. "Mr. Wong, did you find a print on the trigger or the handle of the gun?"

"No, only the barrel."

"Only on the barrel, correct?" Cummings wanted the jury to hear this evidence twice.

"Yes, that is correct," Wong replied.

"No further questions, your honor."

Judge Palmer ordered a lunch recess until two p.m.

Promptly at two, Judge Palmer commenced the afternoon session by requesting the prosecution to seat another witness.

"The State calls Mr. William S. Matteson. He will be our last direct witness, your honor."

A well-conditioned man walked to the stand, favoring his right leg, and dropped his five-foot-ten-inch frame into the witness chair.

"Please state your name and occupation," Armstrong said, after the clerk had sworn him in.

"I'm a detective with the Los Angeles Police Department."

"And were you the lead detective in the investigation of the murder of Mark Chambers, the defendant's husband?" Armstrong pointed to Deborah Farrell, a tactical mistake. Her attorney had instructed her to wear a simple black dress, with no make-up, use a hair style of the sixties, and look as sedate as she could. She was a helpless waif flung out into the snow. As an actress she'd played this role several times and had perfected the look of a forlorn orphan.

Matteson's eyes darted to the ceiling, then down at his hands. "Yeah, I was."

"Now, Detective, I show you Prosecution's Exhibit Number Two—a gun. Do you recognize it?"

"Yes, sir, it's the murder weapon."

Armstrong turned to the jury. "Please note that Detective Matteson has identified a Smith and Wesson thirty-eight caliber revolver as the murder weapon." He then looked back at Matteson. "And what's this?" He pointed to a tag dangling from the trigger guard.

"That's my identification mark."

"Detective, how are you certain this is the murder weapon?"

Matteson leaned forward and rested his arms on the ledge. "The slug that killed Mr. Chambers was recovered from his brain, and the markings on it matched that of the one test fired from that gun."

"And, Detective, to whom is the gun registered?"

Matteson paused and cleared his throat. "The defendant, Ms. Farrell."

Armstrong beamed. He disliked all guns, and after gingerly setting it down, pressed ahead with his god-given task of righting wrong.

John Cummings listened, but his focus was on the jury. He studied how they reacted to the answers from this competent and likable detective. When his turn came he'd have to plant doubt in their mind, reasonable doubt.

"How about an alibi, Detective? Did Ms. Farrell have an alibi?" Armstrong moved closer to the witness.

"The murder happened at about three p.m. on Thursday, August 12, last year in the defendant and Mr. Chambers' home in Bel Air. I asked Ms. Farrell where she was at that time and she said with a friend, a Mrs. Hazel Sommers, who lived near her in Brentwood."

"Did you interview Mrs. Sommers?"

Matteson leaned back in his seat, then shifted uncomfortably. "Yes. She confirmed what Ms. Farrell had said, but then she disappeared into thin air." Matteson waved his arms. "Her friends and relatives haven't heard from her, but all of her clothing and jewelry remain at her house."

"When did she disappear?"

"Sometime between when I last saw her on August fifteenth and two days later."

"So, Detective, without this witness, Ms. Farrell has no alibi?"

"That's right, and we've searched diligently for Mrs. Sommers."

Removing his glasses and closing for the kill, Armstrong felt omnipotent. "Ms. Farrell had the means, her revolver. She knew her husband was cheating on her and stealing from her and she has no alibi, is that correct?" Armstrong looked at the jury and repeated the question.

Matteson rubbed his forehead. "Yes, Mr. Armstrong, I'm afraid so."

"Thank you. And the citizens of Los Angeles also thank you, Detective, for your excellent police work." Armstrong sat down. "Your witness, Counselor."

Cummings slammed both palms of his hands on the table and stood. "Objection. I'm sorry, your honor, but that was cheap theatrics by the assistant district attorney who is known for them."

Armstrong, full of self-righteousness, jumped up. "Objection your honor, slander."

Judge Palmer straightened his cuff links. "Both of your objections are sustained, sit down." He turned his attention to the defense table. "It's too late to start your cross, Mr. Cummings. We will adjourn until nine tomorrow morning." Judge Palmer banged his gavel, and for the first time smiled at the assembled.

* * * *

March had been a rainy month in Los Angeles but the last three days were bright and crisp. People began arriving at the courthouse at seven the next morning in hope of being a part of the Farrell trial. They supported the defendant, but yesterday's testimony from Detective Matteson disturbed them. They prayed her attorney, John Cummings, could mend the damage.

Sharply at nine the defense attorney sauntered over to the witness while smiling benignly to the jury. Cummings was young, thirty, and filled with vivacity and charisma. He'd never lost a case defending a celebrity in a criminal trial and he promised his client that this wouldn't be the first.

"Good morning, Detective, good work."

"Thank you, Counsel, I try."

"But it was all smoke and mirrors, wasn't it? Mere speculation, doesn't prove anything, let alone murder."

"Objection, Judge Palmer," Armstrong bellowed.

"Overruled."

"Thank you, your honor." Cummings sauntered back to his table. "Let's start with the gun. Ms. Farrell owns the murder weapon but she didn't have it at the time of the murder. You and the district attorney forgot to tell the jury that it was stolen in a robbery three months before. Why didn't you, Detective?"

Detective Matteson was a marine drill sergeant looking steely eyed at a recruit. "Because nobody asked me."

"Well, I'm asking you now. Was Ms. Farrell's gun reported stolen three months prior to the murder of Mr. Chambers?"

"Ms. Farrell reported the robbery and theft of the gun to the police immediately, and it was investigated by them. Jewelry and art objects were also stolen and none of those objects were recovered, only the gun."

"The police investigated this robbery and you've seen the report haven't you?" Cummings' smile changed to a grimace.

"Yes, Counsel."

"And where was the gun discovered?"

Matteson ran his hand through his sandy hair. "Under a potted plant in the defendant's living room."

"In her own living room, incredulous! Mr. Armstrong would have the jury believe Ms. Farrell planned this murder, removed the gun, used it, and then left it in her living room where any novice policeman would discover it. Unbelievable!" Cummings waved his arms. "Any one else would have taken it to the nearby golf course and thrown it into one of the lakes. You think this lovely woman is stupid, don't you?"

"No, Mr. Cummings, I don't think she's stupid at all."

"Detective, Mr. Wong testified that her fingerprint was on the barrel of the gun. I don't believe it's strange that her fingerprint would be on the barrel of a gun she owned. Do you?"

"No, I don't."

"And none was on the trigger?"

"No."

"So you believe she took the time to wipe off the trigger and butt but not the barrel?"

"I don't know."

"Isn't it logical that the perpetrator wiped his fingerprints off the trigger and butt, and then planted the gun where it could easily be found by the police?"

Before Matteson could answer, the bailiff raced to the bench and whispered to Judge Palmer, who jumped to his feet and in a trembling voice shouted, "We are adjourned, the jury is excused, and Counsel, I will see you both in my chambers."

A roar permeated the courtroom as everyone talked excitedly. The jury filed back to their room hoping for enlightenment.

After the attorneys had settled in chairs in his chambers, Judge Palmer said in a barely audible voice, "Gentlemen, the jury has been tampered with."

Both attorneys looked at each other. Armstrong's face turned ashen as Cummings heaved a big sigh.

"What are the circumstances, Judge?" Cummings asked.

"There are two—very troubling. Juror number three, a Helena Lopez, reported to the bailiff that a short, skinny man with a dark complexion and stringy hair approached her and offered twenty-five thousand dollars for an acquittal vote. Juror number eight, Paul Sanders, said he was offered the same deal."

"Where did this happen?" Cummings asked.

"The jury is not sequestered. The man approached Lopez as she walked from her car to her home and Sanders at his front door." Judge Palmer looked sternly into the defense lawyer's eyes. "Can you add anything?"

"No, your honor, this information disturbs me greatly. I know nothing about it."

"In addition, the court's investigator discovered that juror number eleven is a relative of yours, Mr. Armstrong." Judge Palmer looked at Armstrong. "His name is Kenneth Maxwell. Do you know him?"

The veins on the assistant district attorney's neck popped out as his face turned crimson. "As God is my witness, your honor, no."

"He is a second cousin on your mother's side and didn't reveal that relationship during voir dire. All jurors were asked if they were related or knew either of the attorneys. If he had answered 'yes' he would have been dismissed. He lied and committed perjury."

Cummings drummed his fingers on Judge Palmer's desk. "I move for a mistrial," he said in a steady voice.

Armstrong remained silent, knowing the trial couldn't continue with this cloud over it. The judge reached for a law book on the self behind his desk.

As he was reading, Cummings rose from his chair. "Furthermore, your honor, I ask that all charges against my client be dismissed."

Armstrong jumped out of his chair. "Ridiculous, your honor, the prosecution has a solid case against the defendant."

"Nothing but smoke and mirrors," Cummings answered.

"Gentlemen, I'll have preliminary arguments now. This matter has to be resolved. John, you first. "

Cummings cleared his throat and scooted up in his chair. "The prosecution presented their case in full; it has only three ingredients: the gun, the investigator's testimony, and the opportunity. First, the gun. It was stolen three months before the murder and was reported missing by the defendant immediately. The police investigated and found that besides the gun, a Rolex watch, belonging to Mark Chambers, two diamond earrings, and a pearl necklace were stolen. Only the gun has been recovered. It was an obvious plant in the defendant's home.

"Second, the witness testified that her husband was cheating on her and had stolen money from her. But Ms. Farrell knew he had a mistress and she had millions in other, private bank accounts. The money he took was pocket change to her.

"She'd filed for a divorce two months before the murder, and in California, a no-fault state, she would have gotten her divorce; she didn't need to kill him to get rid of him.

"Third, the opportunity. She had an alibi, from her friend, Hazel Sommers and Detective William Matteson had taken her statement. Mrs. Sommers subsequently disappeared. She either ran away with a lover, lost her memory and wandered off, or maybe she doesn't want anything to do with the police—for unknown reasons.

"Prosecution has no case, your honor. There's reasonable doubt written all over it. That's all they have and no jury will convict. Why waste the taxpayer's money?"

Armstrong rambled out of control for thirty minutes in response, repeating the testimonies of his witnesses. "Without Mrs. Sommers' testimony, Detective Matteson's assertion that she had confirmed Ms. Farrell's alibi is hearsay, not admissible. She has no alibi." At the end of his argument he was sweating and shaking. His glasses had slipped out of his hand and lay at his feet.

"Judge," Cummings said after Armstrong had calmed down. "Maybe the perpetrator knew there was more jewelry and cash in the victim's house and tried to rob it again. Unfortunately, Chambers was home alone and interrupted the robbery. The perp shot him and fearing the shot would be heard, got rid of the gun, and ran from the home. That's the defense's version and the jury will buy it."

After a few minutes, Judge Palmer said, "I will have these jury tampering instances investigated and if they are confirmed will declare a mistrial but will not grant a motion for acquittal. The district attorney will have to decide whether he has enough evidence to retry Ms. Farrell or not. I will have the jury called back, announce my decision, and discharge them."

A huge crowd gathered outside the courtroom. As Deborah and her attorney appeared, cheers and wishes of love exploded. Cummings made a short speech praising the judicial system as Deborah waved and blew kisses.

A few days later and with all the participants present, Judge Roger Palmer declared a mistrial and the news media responded.

"Mr. Cummings, will Deborah be retried," one reporter asked.

"That, of course, is up to the district attorney but I don't think so. They have no case against her, just speculation. He now knows that."

After finishing with Cummings, the reporters waited for Matteson. "How do you feel, Detective?" one asked.

"No comment."

The next question was a shocker. "What do you know about the Pink Daffodil?"

Matteson spun around and angrily answered, "No comment!"

"Her body was discovered two days after Mrs. Sommers went missing, and found just a few miles from the Sommers home. They're both white and about the same size."

Matteson wiped beads of sweat from his forehead. "That wasn't my case."

"Detective, why hasn't the murdered woman clutching the pink daffodil been identified?"

Matteson loosed his collar and took a deep breath. "Because her face was smashed to prevent dental identification and her fingers were dipped in acid to remove fingerprints. We don't know who she is."

Chapter 1

October 12, 1992

The Chairman

Sir Basil D. Rathbourn made the decision. "Santa Barbara," he said. "We'll exercise our option to purchase the *Los Campos de Sepulveda* property a mile south of the city and build our flagship, continuing care, retirement community. It's eighteen acres, on a knoll with a clear view of the ocean one mile away, with easy access to Highway 101." He clapped his hands together. "Perfect."

Chief financial officer, John Watts stroked his goatee. "Sir Basil, Santa Barbara is an expensive city. The labor cost for waiters and housekeepers will be too high. There are dozens of competing restaurants and hotels in town and their waiters receive generous tips from well-heeled customers. Elsewhere we get away with a dollar over minimum wage but here that won't compete for labor."

"John, John! I'm surprised at your negativism." Sir Basil paced the large conference room. "Santa Barbara has a large Hispanic population and we know how to keep our little brown friends happy, don't we? They'll love working for us."

"Not when they can make five dollars more an hour," John muttered to himself.

Sir Basil stopped pacing. "Did you say something, John?"

"No, Sir Basil, just clearing my throat."

John was correct. Santa Barbara was one of the most expensive cities in the U. S. It rested on a narrow shelf of land between the Santa Ynez mountains and the Pacific Ocean and traced its history back to the earliest settlement of the Spanish in 1602. Previously, the rich and famous had flocked to its white sandy beaches, red-tiled roof haciendas, and perfect weather for vacations. Now they and others, only slightly less affluent, built retirement homes in this romantic city. Carmel, Laguna Beach, and La Jolla are the princesses of California's resort cities but Santa Barbara is the queen.

Sir Basil thought back to when Queen Elizabeth had knighted him in 1963 for services to the crown. Now a real estate magnet, he owned choice properties on six continents and had options on many others in California and Mexico. His latest fixation was in his words, "providing comfortable homes for those approaching their twilight years," but in reality was the development of retirement communities. "Follow the sun" was his mantra.

Sir Basil looked out the window to the street fifty-stories below. "People want to live where it shines at least three hundred days a year. We'll provide their late-in-life nests in the warm sun."

His father, Lord Winston Rathbourn, had been a local squire and justice of the peace, and descended from a long line of landed gentry. Basil's ancestral home, Hollingscot in Yorkshire, included a stately thirty thousand square-foot mansion, one thousand acres of fallow, wooded land, a large lake, and stables. Claude Rathbourn, Sir Basil's grandfather formed Trafalgar Import Company in 1886 and began the family fortune by importing wine and exporting wool goods. Imports of tin from Malaysia and diamonds from India soon followed. Claude was named for a distant ancestor who was an officer with the invading army of William the Conqueror in 1066.

Sir Basil revered his English heritage, especially its language. The "loquacious one" was the sobriquet quietly used by his employees, and anyone who spoke or wrote incorrectly had to stand at attention for twenty minutes while he explored the proper use of English, which to him was the "mirror of the soul."

After graduating from Oxford and surviving as a Spitfire pilot in the British Air Force in the battle of Britain, he eventually decided on a career in real estate and let his younger brothers run Trafalgar.

Ten years later, he delegated trusted lieutenants to manage his commercial holdings in the world's major cities, and as chairman, Sir Basil concentrated on developing a new corporation, The Retirement Communities of the West. RCW owned a community in Scottsdale, Arizona, with others in Del Mar, Carlsbad, and Palm Springs, California. His option on the Santa Barbara property was nearing maturity but everyone knew he would exercise it. He bought the option to the property in 1985 for $50,000 when the price per acre was $400,000. In 1992 the land on the fringe of the city was worth $1,000,000 an acre.

Tall, thin and athletic, Sir Basil was the model for an upper-class Englishman. He brushed his light brown hair from his forehead, then turned back to the craggy Scotsman sitting at the conference table. He pulled out a chair and sat down. While he thought, he toyed with his luxuriant mustache that covered the space between his nose and upper lip from one corner of his mouth to the other. He'd started it in 1945 to cover a scar suffered in World War II.

"Santa Barbara will attract the richest and most demanding residents, John," the chairman continued. "They will expect the best and we will give it to them. And, we will set high standards. All will have to submit financial statements and those that want to be placed in the Independent Living building must present a letter from their doctors stating they are in good mental and physical health and ambulatory."

John was about to unload his substantial contrary arguments when Larry, Diggby and Goody joined them.

Sir Basil tapped his walking stick on the leg of the table. "Gentlemen, I intend to sign the Letter of Intent to Purchase tomorrow. Are there any questions or comments?"

John brought the three late comers up to date. The four whispered amongst themselves while Heather De Winter, Sir Basil's secretary slipped into the room and placed a tray of refreshments on the table.

Sir Basil placed his Scottish oak can across his lap, then ran his hand over the oval conference table's smooth surface. Made of black walnut, the twenty foot-long table carried the company's logo inlaid in its center—a marble blue dolphin,. Twenty leather-covered mahogany chairs surrounded the table. Sir Basil's downtown Los Angeles office was by far his favorite. He took a moment to admire the walls decorated with masterworks by the 16th and 17th Century English painters: Isaac Oliver, Sir Nathaniel Bacon, and John Hoskin. The piece de resistance was a portrait by Wilton Dobson bought at auction in London for $2,000,000.Overhead, hung a $2,000 Waterford, crystal chandelier.

Larry Turner cleared his throat. "Sir Basil?"

Sir Basil turned his attention to the burly engineer. "Yes, Larry?"

"I don't believe we should go ahead without a geological survey. How thick is the sand? What kind of bedrock lies underneath? And are there any earthquake faults nearby?" Turner flipped a page in his report. "Also, Santa Barbara has been plagued with severe drought and forest fires in the nearby Los Padres National Forest. Ojai is only twenty miles away and it nearly burnt down a few years ago. Insurance and water costs will be exorbitant."

"Larry, you're my chief engineering officer, but listen to me, this is not a seismic area; the nearest fault is fifty miles away. The five-story Hilton hotel is a mile away and has been standing undamaged for ten years."

Diggby Quinn tapped his pen on the table. "Sir Basil, fifty miles is not that far if a quake exceeds six on the Richter scale." He pointed the pen at John. "And I agree with John, this is an expensive area and labor will be costly." He put down his pen, then slid a folder across the table to Sir Basil. "According to this report, waiters and bartenders in the local hotels make an extra fifty to one hundred dollars a night in gratuities and tips; here they're forbidden. Also, new hotels will grab all the cleaning girls within ten miles. We should plan for a forty percent increase in hourly labor costs."

Sir Basil glanced at the personnel officer's report, then closed the folder and passed it to Goody. "Our labor costs will be high but so will our revenue. Diggs, the cliental here will pay more to live here, much more. Hollywood celebrities love Santa Barbara. Many will want to spend their golden years here with us."

Goodwin Oliver, president of RCW, looked up from the report. "The Episcopalians and the Presbyterians are expanding the number of retirement homes they operate. Do we know if they're planning to build in this area?"

Sir Basil poured himself a glass of water. "Goody, I'm surprised. Those not-for-profit homes can't compete with ours. Let them come and try."

Silence descended; the four men looked at one another.

Sir Basil sipped his water. "I assume we're in agreement?" he asked. "If there are no more suggestions, I'll sign tomorrow. Relax gentlemen and follow me. There *are* risks but my motto is 'the higher the risk, the greater the reward.' Let's move this project along as quickly as possible." Sir Basil set down his glass. "I'd like to have our grand opening in two years. Thanks for your unqualified support."

They gathered their papers as Sir Basil looked at them benignly. "Sir Basil," Diggby said.

"Yes, Diggs."

"Have you selected a name for this project?"

"Yes, I have. Considering the location I thought it should be dignified. 'The Santa Barbara Retirement Home for the Aged.' Do you like it?"

If Sir Basil had had the slightest knowledge of body language he would have known they hated it. They were on thin ice but they had to respond; the name was wrong, seriously wrong. Goodwin Oliver spoke quickly with his fingers crossed. "Sir Basil, the elderly know they're old and joke about it, but they resent being called old, elderly or aged. I recommend that we eliminate any reference to old age."

"Goody, how can we do that when we're building a home for the retired? I don't think there are many young people who are retired, are there?" Sir Basil asked with a self-congratulatory smile at his weak attempt at humor.

"Many retire in their sixties and they certainly don't think of themselves as aged," Larry added.

"You're absolutely right, Larry. I'm sixty-nine and I wake up every morning with a smile." Sir Basil grinned mischievously as he glanced at each man.

"Way to go, Sir Basil. With you in mind, how about 'The Santa Barbara Retirement Community for the Young at Heart?'"

Before Sir Basil could answer, Diggby said, "'Santa Barbara' is too formal. How about 'The Wind and Sea, a Retirement Community for the Young at Heart.'"

Sir Basil stroked his mustache. "Wind and Sea? I like it; go with it." He placed his bowler hat on his head, then strode to the door with his walking stick in hand. "Goodnight, boys."

"Have a save trip home, Sir Basil," Goody said. "Get a good night's sleep. We all have a lot of work to do if we want to open The Wind and Sea in two years."

Sir Basil waved his arm behind his head at the trio. "My door is always open, boys." With his hand on the doorknob, he turned around. "Except while I'm dictating to Ms. De Winter," he said with a wink.

"My God, he thinks he's Robert Redford," Larry remarked after Sir Basil left. "He's afraid of getting old and must remain forever healthy, virile, and rosy cheeked. He wants us to believe he's just one of the boys but we know his real persona: crusty, dictatorial, and sometimes downright unpleasant."

Goody collected the dirty glasses and returned them to the tray. "I like him. Inside I believe he is a decent man but is reluctant to reveal that side."

Larry stood up and pushed his chair in. "He called this venture his flagship. The White Steamship Company called the 'Titanic' its flagship and we all know what happened to it." Larry walked over to the window, muttering to himself. He gave the limousine below a malevolent smile as his fists opened and closed. *For once I'd like to hear him admit he's wrong. Self-righteous bastard.*

John Watts sighed. "He's either a genius or a very lucky man." He stuffed his files into his briefcase. "Just when one of his projects is about to tank, something fortuitous happens. Either a financial savior shows up on his doorstep or a local government agency floats a loan to help him or the demographics suddenly turn in his favor. He seldom if ever loses."

"I think his lucky streak is about to end," Larry muttered from the window. "I don't see how he can pull this investment out of the fire."

Chapter 2

The Beginning

September 10, 1996

The Wind and Sea Retirement Community for the Young at Heart had its grand opening on September 10, 1996, two years later than planned. The mayor of Santa Barbara, James Gallagher, cut the ribbon and retired Presbyterian minister, Glen Thompson, gave a lengthy blessing. Four hundred people, including 200 new residents, attended. After the ceremony the guests dined on champagne and a sumptuous assortment of hors d'oeuvres and desserts created by Pierre, the chef. A tour of the development—called the "campus" by the directors—followed the light meal.

The magnificent campus included eighteen acres of undulating land densely wooded with oak, cypress and elm trees. A stream, soon nicknamed the Amazon, rippled its way across the property from the north to the ocean. At low tide, the residents could wade and sunbathe on two hundred yards of crystal-white sand. Young surfers from the nearby University of California at Santa Barbara entertained them on most days as they challenged the six-foot waves in front of the campus.

Independent-living couples, widows and widowers unpacked their belongings in the Spanish-style main building of the complex. Five stories high, the U-shaped facility held three hundred, one and two-bedroom apartments. The large dining room—located on the fifth floor at the closed end of the U—presented a magnificent view of Santa Barbara to the north, the mountains to the east, and the vast expanse of the Pacific Ocean to the west. To the south were three buildings. One, with forty rooms was for those that needed temporary help named the Assisted Living unit for remedial rehabilitation. Another was the Intensive Care unit for those with serious health problems. The third was reserved for Alzheimer patients who stayed until death. It had thirty rooms.

Thirty cottages for independent residents surrounded the main building on the north.. Dotted between the main building and the cottages were a swimming pool, a concrete shuffle board, a putting green court, and a patio area complete with an awning, chairs and chaise lounges. Inside was a shallow pool designed for aerobic exercises.

The June 1996 issue of the AARP, American Association of Retired Persons, featured The Wind and Sea project with a four-page spread. "It is indeed the state of the art for retirement communities," it stated. "Its campus rivals those of the finest old private universities with resort living at its most elegant, capturing the flavor of Santa Barbara with thick stucco walls and red-tile roofs. It will become the model for future retirement communities."

Diggby Quinn, Larry Turner, and John Watts would stay temporarily with the project until it was up and running. Goodwin Oliver would return to headquarters in Los Angeles with Sir Basil.

Diggby, Larry, and John gathered on the patio and observed the group of sycophants surrounding Sir Basil.

Roger Palmer, now retired, raised his glass. "Congratulations, Sir Basil. I've reviewed retirement homes in the U. S., Mexico, and Europe and this one is the best, I now live in cottage number nine. Drop by for a drink later."

"This is what Sir Basil lives for," Diggby said. "Receiving accolades from an adoring crowd. I wonder how he'll explain the fifty million-dollar cost overrun in the next quarterly report to the stockholders."

John nervously sucked on his cigarette. "We tried to caution him on the possible—no, probable—problems we would discover in the construction." He blew a stream of smoke above his head. "Even that kiss-ass Goodwin offered a caution."

Larry shook his bald head. "Let me count some, but not all, of his majesty's mistakes." He held up a finger. "He hired an architect who had built a large retirement complex in Florida, with no experience in California, who didn't carefully examine the California and Santa Barbara earthquake codes, which resulted in new plans, a six-month delay, and an extra cost of five million." He held up a second finger. "Then after the foundation and first floor were in place, the inspectors discovered the plans were based on a four-story building instead of five, which was okay for Florida but not Santa Barbara; retrofitting cost ten million.

"And, he set the axis of the building wrong." Larry wiped a stream of sweat from his face. "Half the rooms get the blazing sun all day and the other half gets none.

"He made mistakes everywhere: The balconies are less than three feet wide— unusable. The exercise room and card rooms are too small. He didn't plan for a salad bar in the dining room, the make-fit one is too small, and there is no place for casual dining. The number of elevators is inadequate, and my favorite: there's no place for outside dining." Larry, baking in the hundred-degree heat, again wiped sweat from his face.

"The architect did his damage but the worst impact on the financial health of this institution is what we all told him it would be—labor cost," Diggby said. "With two shifts a day, seven days a week, we need one hundred waiters and busboys. Do you know how many trained ones we've hired so far—seven. An employment agency has filled the gap with temporary help at a cost of twenty dollars per hour, twice what we pay elsewhere. We'll have to depend on high school kids. There are only two schools nearby and their students drive BMWs to school."

Diggby set his empty champagne glass down on a nearby table. "They'll stay until trained and then go to the city's restaurants where they'll make twice what we can pay and won't work if they have a date, homework, or go to the nearby beach when the surf's up."

John took a final drag from his cigarette. "The University of California, Santa Barbara, is close and we advertised in their college paper—no replies. College kids can get better jobs in town."

Diggby eyed the college girls on the beach in their small, but efficient, bikinis. "Sir Basil said the residents will just have to pick up the extra costs— so he will stick it to them. The result, only a sixty percent occupancy in independent living, less in assisted. Not satisfactory." He nodded toward the girls. "He could have charged extra for this view."

With his active libido in charge, Diggby added, "Have you seen the new resident, Deborah Farrell? She has to be in her late sixties but she's still a knockout. Her face has a few wrinkles but her body remains as it was in the 1950s—beautiful legs and firm, full breasts—magnificent. I hope she has a complaint about the personnel and invites me to her room."

"Her face may not be as smooth as it once was but it's lovely and her golden hair swept back on the sides and gathered into a ponytail excites me," Larry said softly, looking at a distant sailboat. "And she doesn't walk; she glides through her number seven cottage. I wonder why she moved here."

John lit another cigarette. "I don't know, but she surely is an asset to The Wind and Sea. I've seen her movie, 'My Love Affair,' three times." He scratched his goatee. "It was made in the seventies, but remains popular today. That was her last movie, finished just before her actor husband, Mark Chambers, was murdered." John leaned on the patio railing. "That crime was never solved, was it?" He looked over his shoulder at his colleagues.

Diggby shook his head. "Neither was the Pink Daffodil case. Both murders remain as open files in the Hollywood Police Department." He walked over and joined John at the railing. "Do you believe she did it?"

John tapped his ashes off on the grass. "I don't know. The trial was terminated after jury tampering was discovered and so far the district attorney hasn't reopened it." He took a drag off his cigarette. "Her dark blue, sensual eyes are interesting, so sad, and so intense. They've seen much, maybe too much. If only they could talk." John sighed. "Anyway, do you believe it's just coincidence that both Deborah and the judge in her case, Roger Palmer, live here at The Wind and Sea?"

None of the three directors answered the hypothetical question John asked but continued to dissect and critique The Wind and Sea and a few of its residents. Lucky for them there weren't any hidden microphones nearby. Sir Basil wouldn't have approved of their comments.

Chapter 3

The Residents

The retirement community opened with fifty-five couples, sixty single women, and thirty single men with seventy-eight being the average age.

The Wind and Sea's location, facilities, and ambience attracted them. With a few exceptions, they were middle to upper-class people, executives of large corporations, successful entrepreneurs, writers, and entertainment celebrities that came from the four corners of the country. Some wanted to move closer to family members, others for the weather, advanced age, the fear of impending infirmities, or the need for new friends as death had taken most of their old ones. The intelligence, wealth, and social status of this group far exceeded that of any other retirement community in California.

The residents carefully read the contract between them and The Wind and Sea and knew their obligations and responsibilities as well as those promised by the provider both written and verbal. The quantity of the new residents was below expectations, but the quality and name recognition of many was exceptional. Of the two hundred and thirty persons residing at The Wind and Sea, twenty had been front-page news at one time or another.

Deborah Farrell set down her coffee cup and answered the phone. "Hello," the ex-actress said, smoking her first cigarette of the day.

"Good morning, Deborah, and I trust it has been a good morning. This is Carrie Boswell."

"Who? Do I know you?"

"Carrie Boswell, the writer."

Deborah searched her brain for any recollection of this person. "Oh yes, the writer of those trashy novels and contemptible biographies."

"The same, and guess what? I'm now writing one about you to be titled "Deborah Farrell, Goddess.""

Deborah took a sip of her coffee. "Why? I'm seventy-two— nobody's interested in me anymore."

"You're kidding. Queen of the fifties, sixties and seventies, star of thirty-three movies and five Broadway plays. Your retirement in 1978, after the murder of your fourth husband, broke the hearts of millions of men. People *do* want to know what happened to you and I'm going to tell them *all* about you. Besides, we both live here at The Wind and Sea. You're in cottage number seven and I'm in apartment 562—it'll be easy. I've written about three other famous people and no one has sued because I write only the truth. You're not afraid of the truth, are you?"

Deborah rolled her eyes. "I'm not interested. Please don't bother me again." Deborah slammed the phone and with shaking hands walked to a big hall mirror and stared at her still lovely face. "Not bad," she said to her reflection. "Let that bitch try to invade my privacy. I know all about her, too. That pathetic husband of hers, Arnold Myers, with no discernable muscles, poor eyesight, short and bald. She despises him and treats him like a servant; he must hate her. Why did she marry him? She's sixty and looks forty with that body of hers with face lifts, tummy tucks and breast implants— grotesque. Let her throw dirt. With thirty years of experience in Hollywood, I know how to handle these leeches."

Carrie walked to her computer and began composing. She wasn't interested in Farrell's movies or plays. Carrie would investigate— and expose—Deborah's four marriages, numerous liaisons with actors, playboys, and tennis pros, and the murder. Carrie stopped writing. *Who murdered her husband, Mark Chambers? Did she?*

After fifteen minutes she picked up The Wind and Sea's directory and dialed Steven Matteson's number.

"Hello," a male voice answered.

"Is this Steven Matteson, the detective?"

"Yes, but I've retired. Who's this?" he asked tentatively.

"Carrie Boswell, the writer." She kept her voice cheery and full of self-esteem.

"Oh yes, I've heard of you and your twenty trashy books. They're about sexual romps and I'm no expert in that sport."

He was abrupt and Carrie sensed he was ready to hang up. She'd have to revive his attention.

"We have a mutual acquaintance, Deborah Farrell. I'm writing her biography and I need your help, and by the way, it's *twenty-three well-read trashy novels*." She smiled, and sipped her second cup of coffee.

Steve cleared his throat. "Deborah Farrell? I don't seem to recall her and I'm not interested."

Carrie knew she was about to lose him and no one ever hung-up on her. "Come on, Steve, the trial in 1979. You moved to The Wind and Sea because she's here—so did I. You fled Los Angeles, changed your name from William S. Matteson and took you middle name, Steven, and became Santa Barbara's chief of detectives. But you haven't forgotten her, have you? You know she's guilty and it's eating you alive, isn't it?"

He hesitated. "It was long ago. I don't know how I can help."

She had him hooked and now she would reel him in. She lit a cigarette and crossed her legs. "We can help each other. I need to know what you know and I will tell you things you never imagined."

He'd dreaded the day when he would once again face his worst nightmare. But the chance to learn things about Deborah was too good to pass up. He ran his hands through his hair. "Okay, I'll meet you tomorrow at the coffee shop, Todd's, in the Plaza on State Street at ten." His heart was pounding and his hands shaking as he put down the phone.

*   *   *   *

The residents soon established a routine anchored by three daily meals. The routine began at 6:30 a.m. when the breakfast room, the Sand Castle, opened.

Seven energetic seniors, five men and two women, four Republicans and three Democrats, first served themselves juice or fruit, cereal, Danish, and coffee, then discussed the political issues of the day, their fellow residents, and the shortcomings of The Wind and Sea.

J. C. Wellington, age seventy-five, led the Breakfast Club. "Well, we now know where Clinton's brain is. I always knew it wasn't in his head. Doing it in the oval office where Roosevelt and Lincoln once sat. Unbelievable." J. C. shook his head, then stared at Mary Lee Hopkins. He knew the retired school teacher, an outspoken Democrat, would offer him an argument.

She laughed. "Just because you used to be a Wall Street investment banker doesn't give you the right to be hypocritical." She shrugged. "Besides, you never voted for Franklin, You hated him. Thought he was a communist, didn't you?"

Before J. C. could reply, retired Brigadier General, Frederick Sutherland interrupted. "I voted for him twice during the war. Thought we shouldn't change leaders during a war. But I was only a lieutenant then. What did I know?" Sutherland, even being shrunken with age and bent from osteoporosis, stood at six-foot two and towered over the other residents waiting in line. He wore a fatigue jacket with four rows of ribbons and one star. He was rarely seen without these ribbons.

Glen Thompson reached for a pastry. "I was an army chaplain during the Korean War. Stationed near the front lines, I prayed with the wounded." He had been with real heroes and the general's attempt to be one of them offended him. Glen kept his two Purple Heart ribbons and one bronze medal in a frame in his room and never discussed them.

"You don't like to be called Fred, do you General?" J. C. asked.

Sutherland placed a bowl of fruit on his tray. "No, I think it's belittling."

"How about Frederick the Great?"

The five men in the group, all having military experience, knew J. C. was saying it in derision. They knowingly looked at one another and shook their heads.

Sutherland hesitated, thinking hard. "Yes, I have been called that a few times by my men," he said solemnly.

Arnold Myers had hopes of being proclaimed the poet laureate of California during the Reagan years. After being ignored he became an associate professor of literature at Northridge State College. His wife moved with the in-crowd and he with other unrecognized professors and poor students who needed tutoring in English. Now retired, he became a groupie for any literary celebrity that happened to pass through Santa Barbara. He usually began the morning round of complaints. "I hope none of you had the rib-eye steak last night. I know it was horse meat." He adjusted his glasses, and inspected his glass of milk.

Rose Marie Dentz joined in the complaint game only to test her companion's credulity and understand their personalities. "I didn't eat the steak but I had a big bowl of the clam chowder. I couldn't believe my eyes," she said. "There were some strange creatures floating on top of my soup. Suddenly, they formed concentric circles doing a water ballet. First they would dive then spring up out of the liquid. It was beautiful." She liked to tease the general and Arnold because she believed both were mentally deficient. Only J. C. and Glen understood what she was doing.

Arnold pushed up his glasses. "Are you're kidding us, Marie?" He put the milk back.

"Would I try to kid any of you? As a psychologist, I'm a professional who deals only in facts," she answered with a dead-pan expression.

Glen Thompson suppressed a smile, then cleared his throat. "Well, we had a disaster last night. The waiter, I think his name was Fernando, took our order. My wife, Amy, and I finished our cocktails and waited and waited. After thirty minutes I complained to the hostess. She looked but Fernando he was nowhere to be found; he'd quit."

The general leaned forward. "He went AWOL? By God if he'd been in my army he'd been court marshaled. I didn't tolerate such behavior. My men had to shape up to pass my inspections. I was tough, but they were happy to follow me."

David Morris was the fifth male, an obstetrician/gynecologist, and married. He was best known for delivering—and aborting—the babies of many Hollywood stars. He was the least talkative of the group but most eloquent on certain subjects where his dry humor and specific use of four-letter words accentuated his message. He'd known many famous people and his stories about some of them titillated and amused the group.

The Breakfast Club continued in session until eight, dissecting the news, discussing politics with special emphasis on Clinton's dalliance with intern Monica, and local gossip. But with two Catholics, three Protestants, one Presbyterian, and one atheist in the group, religion was never discussed.

As they left one morning, Mary Hopkins asked, "Do any of you with Spanish-speaking maids have trouble getting through to them?"

Every member of the Breakfast Club nodded affirmatively.

J. C. put his hand on Mary's shoulder. "You need just one word, *limpia*. It means 'clean' in Spanish. Just point at whatever and say *limpia*. They'll understand."

"Don't condescend to them," the general shouted. "They're here and must learn English. Just look them in the eyes and say 'do it.' They'll understand. My men did."

Glen went his separate way, and Arnold rushed to intercept David. "David in the middle of the night, last night, I remembered where and when we first met. It was in your office on Wilshire Boulevard. My first wife, Gloria, was pregnant and you were her obstetrician. It was about twenty years ago."

"I'm sorry, Arnold, I've delivered more three thousand babies and I just don't remember hers." David tried to sidestep Arnold.

Arnold stepped in front of David. "Oh, I didn't expect you to. I remember one other thing, your daughter, Katherine, was in your office. My wife and I had a delightful talk with her while waiting for you. She was with her fiancé, a very personable and handsome young man. I don't remember his name."

David shook his head. "She had lots of flames. They came and went."

"I can understand that; she was a beautiful young woman. You should be a grandfather several times by now."

The veins in David's neck thickened as he looked away. He swallowed audibly. "Unfortunately not; she was killed in an automobile accident."

"I'm so sorry, David; I didn't know." Arnold patted David on his shoulder as he walked by and out the door.

Every morning, Enrico Di Donoto arrived at the breakfast room right before it closed at 9:30 a.m. He grabbed a couple of Danishes and took his coffee to go. He was a big man—not especially tall, only five foot, ten—but two hundred and ten pounds of muscle with big hands and size fourteen feet. He was clean shaven but his heavy blue-black beard was always present. That feature coupled with his black curly hair and intense dark eyes made his presence intimidating. *Obviously he was a successful business, financially secure, but had he received help from the Mafia?*

Little activity was planned for Mondays. On Tuesday, the "stretch and balance" class began at 10 a.m. and rubber bridge was set for 1:30 p.m. Wednesday was busy. In the morning one of the buses took a group sightseeing to museums, shows, and local places of interest. The other bus took residents to doctors, stores, or shopping malls. In the afternoon at 2:30 p.m., there was a "town hall" meeting, which wasn't a town hall meeting but only a director's report.

Either yoga or water aerobics was scheduled for Thursday mornings with "duplicate" bridge, for the more serious players, set for 1:30 p.m. and a movie planned for all at 7 p.m.

The main event for Friday was the popular "happy hour." Nearly everyone gathered in the "Great Room" at 4:30 p.m. Someone manned the CD player and for ninety minutes the joyous sound of the music of their youth filled the room: Tommy Dorsey, Frank Sinatra, Harry James, and the Andrew Sisters. Many emulated the "swing" dancing of the forties as nostalgia blanketed the room. Many of the women's faces were teary-eyed as they remembered being in the arms of their husbands dancing to "I'll Never Smile Again." The Wind and Sea provided a cheap wine and fair hors d'oeuvres and the necessary waiters.

On Saturday, the Walking Club, a fit and energetic group of elders, mounted the bus, which took them a distance away for their walk—either to a camp in the Los Padres National Forest, to the Santa Barbara waterfront, or to the historic and quaint town of Ojai, famous for its summer music festival.

At eleven on Sunday morning, Glen Thompson, The Wind and Sea's unofficial chaplain, conducted a nondenominational religious service. A few hymns were sung and Glen read bible passages. Special blessings were said for those who were sick or had family or other problems. If Glen was absent one of the more devout members stepped in for him.

There were many and ongoing criticisms of The Wind and Sea but the great majority of the "inmates," as they called themselves, was happy. All were newcomers, many were lonely. Everyone sought new friends to replace those of many years lost through death, crippling infirmities, or distance. "The people are great and I can stand the food and the other aggravations as long as my new friends are here," one said as others nodded. They were comrades united against a common foe—the management.

Simultaneously with the daily effort for enjoyment was the constant duel with mortality. Most of the residents were past the age of life expectancy. During the first four months, one person died suddenly, another fell and broke her hip; and one had a heart attack and was in intensive care. Two others were transferred to Assisted Living and a newcomer was diagnosed with liver cancer. Everyone knew the odds, the actuarial tables, but all faced them with happy, positive attitudes. "Hell, I'm going to live to be a hundred," one man declared as his friends applauded.

"This is my last stop. I will never have another home," Mary Lee Hopkins said. "Life is like a transcontinental flight. The takeoff strains every muscle of the pilot as he pushes the throttle to full power toward liftoff. The plane shutters and groans with the extra stress—birth. The increased velocity of the air across the wing foil lifts the plane to cruising altitude with the pilot, crew and engines still exerting near maximum energy— youth. At cruising altitude the pilot and crew relax, power is reduced, and the engines sigh with relief—middle age. With the flight nearing its end the pilot begins the descent. Everyone aboard begins to get nervous and wonders what awaits them at their destination. Will there be trouble with the landing? Will the baggage be there—old age. The plane lands and taxis to its gate and stops—death." She glanced around; everyone was looking at the sunset with grim faces.

"We've landed and are approaching our last stop. God bless us," someone said and received a chorus of amen.

Chapter 4

The Food Fiasco

Sir Basil selected Clive Huntington to be the executive director of The Wind and Sea with orders to make it the pinnacle of retirement communities. Clive was sixty, tall, gaunt, balding, and wore glasses. He dressed immaculately, but every Hollywood director would cast him as a funeral director. Care for the elderly was his career and for twenty-five years he had managed or directed several communities for the Episcopal and Presbyterian Homes.

Goodwin Oliver, the president of RCW, had studied Clive's resume, interviewed him once, but didn't ask for references from previous employers. He was impressed by what he read and saw, his appearance, and his insipidness, which was high on his list of desirable character traits. He always looked for a well-dressed "yes" man and knew he had found one.

Rose Marie Dentz took one look and shook her head. "Oh my God, that's our new leader?" Looking skyward, she plaintively prayed for help from any god present.

Mary Hopkins patted Rose on the arm. "Relax, honey. We'll give him a month's honeymoon before we make his life miserable."

Food was the key to success in man's ventures or adventures. If a woman could satisfy her husband's taste buds, the gods would allow her time to satisfy his other wants and needs and she had a good chance of gaining a long successful marriage. *The way to a man's heart is through his stomach* was still true.

Any general or admiral would confirm that successful military campaigns depended on a soldier's or sailor's morale and it went up or down depending on his acceptance of the food served. There was no group on the face of the earth more critical of food than the elderly at The Wind and Sea. Their days revolved around breakfast, lunch, and dinner. Anticipation for the next meal began shortly after their complaints about the last one ended. Age, infirmity, and melancholy made their days devoid of any desire for physical or mental activity. But food was the anticipation, the consummation, and the euphoria—their lives revolved around. Mutual complaints added the zest needed to make their existence bearable. They would forgive a stopped up toilet or leaky window, but not a disappointing meal.

The dining director, Eamon McConnell (Mac), was a tall, lean man with a full head of curly brown hair mixed with silver. The Irishman always carried a smile; and a poem, homily, or joke was never far from expression. Making people happy in *his* dining room was a life-long passion. He was the model by which they unfavorably compared the other directors. With their stomachs content, other contentions were ignored—for the time being.

Mac was the *maître d'hôtel par excellence*. Reservations were kept, tables sumptuously set, and waiters perfectly trained. The food was compared favorably to that of a five-star restaurant and servings were more than adequate. Chilean sea bass, wild ocean salmon not farm grown, Alaskan halibut flown in fresh, and all meat certified choice or prime were daily on the menu. Mac personally supervised receptions, birthdays and anniversaries, and often supplied his personal candelabras and silver serving plates for special events. He instantly resolved rare complaints. All the residents looked forward to mealtime—everyone gained weight.

Gunther Krause, a retired real estate developer and the chairman of the dining room committee, which consisted of ten residents, was Mac's counterpart. Gunther was a successful businessman, spoke English, Spanish, and German fluently and had many friends at The Wind and Sea. His German heritage imbued him with a hard work ethic, a belief in rules and regulations encapsulated in discipline. It also gave him a stout build with just the hint of a beer belly and gray hair, which he had cropped every two weeks in the first-floor hair salon. He was a tough workaholic who could destroy a competitor without a second thought, but a Liebelied by Schubert or a poem by Goethe brought him to tears.

Mac and Gunther were as opposite as two men could be, except for their mutual love of poetry and food. Strong friendship and mutual admiration developed between them immediately. Gunther held committee meetings monthly open to the residents. For the first four months the complaints were mild and often silly.

"Gunther, the dinner rolls are too hard. Why can't we have rye bread?"

"Gunther, the chef is cooking the vegetables with a different oil and it's making me constipated."

"Gunther, I noticed the new oil, too, but it's giving me diarrhea."

"Gunther, I believe there is sugar in our salt. Why can't we have sea salt?"

The chairman answered each complaint politely and at the end of the session all present went away happily awaiting the next meal.

In March 1997, with a voice full of tension, Mac asked Gunther to come to his office on the second floor of the high rise near the auditorium, known as the Great Hall.

Gunther arrived to this ten by twelve-foot room fifteen minutes later. "Mac, you look terrible. What happened?"

With his hands shaking and tears wetting his scrubby face, Mac said, "I've never been spoken to like this and treated like a novice. Twenty-six years in the business at some of finest restaurants and hotels. Always spoken to with respect, always cordial—now this."

Gunther couldn't bear to look at his friend in distress and gazed around the office. Photographs, mostly black and white, covered the walls. One showed Mac in a tuxedo, shaking hands with President Ronald Reagan while seated at a restaurant table. Another had Arnold Palmer's arm around Mac's neck with both men laughing in front of the 21 Club in New York. At least thirty photos, some brown with age, showed Mac with government officials, top athletes, and some notorious members of the underworld.

"Who jumped on you?"

Mac jerked his head, his intense dark eyes bore straight into those of the chairman. "That prissy new executive director, Clive Huntington, who wouldn't know the difference between a lamb chop and a slab of bacon."

"Okay, start from the beginning. What's this all about?" Gunther ran his hand over the top of his buzzed hair. "I'm sure we can straighten it out. Every problem has a solution; so what has caused you so much stress?"

"The food budget. Oh Mother of God please give me strength. Clive told me I was three hundred thousand dollars over budget."

"Well, are you?"

"Not according to my calculations."

Gunther held out his hand to Mac. "Let me see the budget he gave you."

"I can't find it. I don't think he gave me one. Sir Basil hired me away from the *Bahia de la Costa* where I was the *maitre'd* and told me to run a similar operation at The Wind and Sea, which I did."

Gunther pulled his sleeve down over his wrist, then crossed his arms. "Didn't you keep track of all of your purchases?"

"Of course, I know exactly what I spent. I know what my good friends here want and I bought it for them just like at *La Costa*, one million, two hundred thousand dollars for the first six months. Same amount of food for approximately the same number of people." Mac was now letting his natural Irish spirits take wing.

"Are you sure you didn't get a written budget?"

"Don't think so; can't find it. Just instructions to follow the same plan as at *La Costa*," Mac said firmly as he did a little Irish jig.

"Item for item, is the food cost the same as at *La Costa*?"

"No it's higher here. Extra distance and venders get more in this area."

"How much higher, percentage wise?" Gunther asked.

Mac scratched his head. "Oh, I guess about ten to fifteen percent."

"Damn it, Mac, you don't know exactly?"

A suddenly deflated Mac answered, "No."

"Okay, how about labor costs?"

"Oh, Mother of God. I told them how bad that would be but they wouldn't listen." Mac spread his arms.

Gunther started to talk but instead walked around the office. He peered at the pictures again, then strolled to get a drink of water at a nearby hallway fountain. Five minutes later he returned and after composing himself, asked, "How much higher are labor costs?"

Mac looked at a picture on the wall of himself and New York Mayor Koch. "Twenty percent for bus boys, twenty-five percent for waiters and hosts, and thirty for cooks."

"How about the chef?"

"Pierre? He came with me from *La Bahia de la Costa*. Same cost, $50,000 per year."

Gunther laughed. "Pierre! He looks Mexican to me."

Mac grinned in spite of the fear growing inside him. "He is Mexican, Jose Rodriquez, from Tijuana. He assumes the residents will appreciate the food more if they think he's French."

Gunther shook his head. "Huntington didn't do this alone. Who gave him orders?"

"Clive did mention President Oliver."

"Okay, it's just a warning. They're giving you another chance."

"Yes, John Watts is delivering next quarter's budget tomorrow. Please help me with it."

Gunther slapped the subdued man on his shoulders. "Of course I will. Call me when you get it."

The budget was in the dining director's interoffice mail box the next morning. An hour after receiving the news, Gunther closed the door behind him and told Mac to cut all phone calls.

Mac handed his friend the budget and after thirty minutes of study, Gunther said, "Let's get a cup of coffee and go sit on the patio. I want to smoke a cigar."

After his cup was drained and his cigar lit, the satisfied smoker asked, "Can you do it?"

"One third of the budget is for food. I can do that but the residents won't be happy. The rest is for labor and incidentals. Impossible. There's no way I can hire waiters for seven dollars an hour without tips. I've told them that before but they just won't accept the facts of life in Santa Barbara." Mac shrugged his shoulders and frowned.

"What are your options?" Gunther asked.

" Quit or eliminate the dining room manager's job, fire all of the experienced waiters and cooks making over nine dollars and replace them with inexperienced kids or worse, and reduce the waiter's staff by three people. The dining room will become a battlefield. The residents will be up in arms. What hurts the most is dismissing the workers that followed me here from *La Costa*."

"I've been in worse situations. Don't be too down on yourself. We'll try to talk to John Watts tomorrow," Gunther said, giving the despondent dining director a hug. "Want a cigar? They've helped me through tough times."

"No thanks, they'll stunt my growth." Mac managed a wry smile.

Two days later, the two men walked down the carpeted hallway, past the many pictures of Sir Basil shaking hands and drinking with notables from five continents. At the comptroller's office a secretary escorted them to a little adjoining conference room where John Watts presently joined them.

Watts' opening paragraph was short and succinct. "Mr. Krause, I know your intentions are good and you want to help, but the food problems are those of management. Residents should not and will not be involved."

Gunther gave Watts a cold stare of distain. "True, Mr. Watts, very true, but when I see a person slipping on ice and sliding toward a truck I grab and try to save him even though it's none of my business. What affects the dining room concerns the residents and unless you want to create a donnybrook that could destroy this fledgling enterprise, I suggest we sit and talk for awhile."

Watts looked at Mac. "Mac, will you please step outside? Mr. Krause and I have a private matter to discuss."

After the door closed behind Mac, Gunther said, "Listen, Mr. Watts—"

The comptroller raised his hand. "First, do I have your word that what's said in this room is between us will remain in this room?"

Gunther nodded.

"I know about your accomplishments and that your word is your bond. I'll trust you." Watts slid the budget report across the table. "The budget is stupid. There's no way it can be fulfilled. Mac will have to do the best he can and he will fail for two reasons. First because it is impossible and second because Mac doesn't know anything about money control. This budget came from Goodwin Oliver, the president. I can't do anything."

Gunther paused and looked around the room. Again, pictures of Sir Basil in various grandiose poses adorned the walls. Gunther's eye caught one of John Watts, his wife, and two children.

"Then there'll be chaos," Gunther noted.

"All inhabitants have deposited four hundred to six hundred thousand dollars as the entrance fee for their unit. The contract between the residents and The Wind and Sea stated that eighty percent of the deposit would be returned to the resident's estate on death or upon sale of the unit after approval of the buyer and the unit restored to its original condition." Watts stroked his goatee. "With the decline in food quality many wanted to move but they were in a box—stay or forfeit between sixty and one hundred thousand dollars."

"Has this contract ever been tested in court?" Gunther asked.

"Yes, unsuccessfully."

"Damn it!" Gunther exploded. "That's hard nosed and dirty. We residents don't deserve such treatment and some of us won't lie down. Your sales agent promised us the moon. 'The food would be equal to that of a fine restaurant and we would be served wine with our meals,' she said." Gunther jumped to his feet. "That may have been a verbal promise but it was a condition of agreement. Is Sir Basil now repudiating his own representative?"

Watts motioned for Gunther to sit down. "Sir Basil isn't involved in the local problems. He expects Goody Oliver to handle them, but yes, there is a powerful legal staff to back Goody. Don't even think of legal action. It'll eat you up—after it bankrupts you." Watts calmly studied Gunther. "I hope you don't challenge the mighty one too soon. Wait for the right openings and I believe you know how to spot them. But be careful. Oliver can be a most vindictive man. He loves inflicting pain—I know."

"Why are you confiding in me? Could be dangerous for you," Gunther asked nearly eye ball to eye ball with the slightly taller man.

"I have my reasons, substantial ones," John answered slowly with anxiety and fear clearly etched on his face.

"I don't believe God wants anything to do with this imbroglio, but we're going to need help from someone," Gunther replied. "Why don't you confide in me? Maybe I can help."

"Want a cup of coffee?"

"Yes, please."

Watts slowly poured two cups of coffee while debating with himself. After fidgeting with the cup and saucer, he began. "Ten years ago my wife and I owned, with the help of the bank, a small, thirty-room board and care facility in Del Mar California. We had one registered nurse, two aids, and five care-givers. Mostly our income came from Medicare for rehabilitation for hip replacements and broken bones, but we also provided care for elderly people with aging problems. After many years in the red we finally made a little profit and the future looked bright."

Watts took a sip of coffee. "One day Goodwin Oliver came to visit. He was very pleasant and complimentary. He said he was looking for a place for his aunt. I showed him our facility and even bought him lunch. He didn't mention he was associated with The Retirement Communities of the West.

"There was a ten-acre parcel of land about a mile away from our place. A month after his visit a large sign was erected on that property. 'Future Home of DEL MAR SHORES, a Continuing Care Facility for the Retired.' I check and discovered it would be one of Sir Basil's and that Oliver Goodwin was the president of his company, The Retirement Communities of the West.

"I couldn't compete and had to give everything my wife and I had worked so hard for back to the bank. Sir Basil found out about my predicament and offered me a job with his company. Oliver was the snake in the grass and I'll never forgive him— I vowed that someday I would get my revenge."

Watts stood and walked over to the window. Gunther followed and wrapped his arms around the stricken man. "Those kinds of men sooner or later receive their just reward. If I can help, please let me know."

"I will, and thanks for listening," John whispered as Krause walked toward the door.

Within a week everyone was aware of the changes. Several favorite waiters disappeared. Supper took over three hours to complete instead of the previous two. Some of the explanations Mac gave were "They're on sick leave," "They've moved," and "They need to spend more time at home." The food quality dropped precipitately. The meat was not choice but tough and stringy. Catfish was served four times a week. A tasteless mound simply called "white fish" replaced sea bass and albacore.

Meals, previously anticipated, were now avoided. In one month, despondent Mac lost fifteen pounds. All the directors were under siege. Many residents put their units on the market but none sold because the general public was now aware of the internal problems with food.

Dissatisfaction started slowly. They trusted Mac and believed he could regain control. However as the food quality continued to decline unrest turned physical. The wrong meals were served late, and cold. Reservations were mixed up and the residents argued and tussled for tables. They often had to get their own coffee, sometimes spilling it on themselves and others.

One night a tragedy was barely averted. Enrico Di Donoto ordered fish that arrived thirty minutes late and undercooked. He picked up his plate and rushed into the kitchen, cursing all the way. Two minutes later he ran out of the kitchen with a fat Mexican cook chasing him with a meat cleaver raised over his head.

During the height of this turmoil the president, Goodwin Oliver, added gasoline to red-hot coals. He discontinued the breakfast take-out policy.

A complimentary breakfast consisting of juice, Danish, hot and cold cereals, and coffee could be eaten in the Sand Castle Room by the residents or taken back to their units. Spouses took food to their mates; friends to those under the weather. Now the new edict stated, "Eat the breakfast where it's offered or pay five dollars to take it back to your room.'"

Gunther Krause heard the news just before the start of a food committee meeting. He looked at the fifteen angry people assembled. The color of his face changed from tan to ash gray. He raised his fist and crashed it onto the lantern. "Unconscionable, unacceptable! They're shoving our faces into the toilet. I'm sorry, but this meeting is adjourned."

Chapter 5

The Encounter

The Wind and Sea resident council was formed with two stated purposes: "To enhance the quality of life of the residents; and to communicate their needs, desires, and preferences to the administrators of The Wind and Sea." The unstated purpose was to challenge RCW's management when it violated the contract, curtailed or diminished the rights of the residents.

The resident council consisted of J. C. Wellington, president; Fredereick Sutherland, vice-president; Mary Hopkins, Secretary; Enrico Di Donoto, Treasurer; and David Morris, Parliamentarian. The residents elected them, and they met on the first Monday of each month to discuss policies and problems. On the second Monday, the members of the council discussed these and their possible solutions in an open meeting attended usually by about fifty residents.

The first order of business of each meeting was to read, and, if necessary, correct, the minutes of the previous meeting. First the "old" business was discussed, and then "new" business received attention. Residents now totaled hundred fifty. Nearly two hundred attended the June 1997 meeting because the new business was the food crisis. An angry mob was ready to voice their opinions and demands to the council.

"Enough is enough, Mr. President. Soon they'll be serving us hog food," a resident shouted, shaking with wrath.

"We are paying the prices of a five-star restaurant and getting one-star food," another shouted.

After ten minutes, J. C. raised both hands. "Complaints about the food deficiencies will take all day. We've all experienced them and know them well. Let's concentrate on our options. Generally speaking, we have two major complaints: the poor quality of food and the added fee for take-out at breakfast."

The general jumped up and raised one arm. He pointed to the horizon, emulating General Douglas MacArthur on his arrival back to the Philippians. "Let me talk to them. They'll soon learn we are about to counterattack and will be bringing our big guns."

"Sit down, Fred; you have no big guns."

The general turned and glared in the direction of the speaker, but after a moment slowly took his seat.

"Okay, J. C., the contract is on our side, how can we make them abide by it? Lawyer fees and court costs would be outrageous," Enrico Di Donato said.

"Right, Enrico, but there are organizations that have been established to help retirement communities—CALCRA, an organization made up of the residents of retirement homes, of which we are a member; an ombudsman organization that investigates complaints; the California Department of Social Services, which can bring legal support. The problem is if we get involved with one of these organizations it will take time to prepare our case and time for them to act—months. And we're not sure of the outcome."

Gunther shot to his feet. "Let's hurt them where it will really sting—their reputation; particularly that of Sir Basil's."

"How?" someone asked.

"By using the press. I know a reporter on the *Santa Barbara News Press*, Jeffrey Grainger. He's their investigative reporter and has been interested in the goings-on at The Wind and Sea."

"Careful, Gunther," J. C. cautioned. "The Press is interested in sensational coverage; their reporters can stir-up a hornet's nest. We don't want them to destroy our homes."

"I know. I have a plan, but I believe it would be best if only the executive council is privy to it at this time. There are too many residents present to discuss it now. 'The walls have ears,' as we said during the war. Could the council meet immediately after this meeting?"

*   *   *   *

The Wind and Sea's semi-annual meeting would be held the second Wednesday in November. Goodwin Oliver, president, would come from Los Angeles and preside. Diggby Quinn would talk about personnel matters; John Watts about finances; and Clive Huntington, The Wind and Sea's executive director, would give the welcoming speech. Afterwards champagne and hors d'oeuvres would be served. A past meeting had been a happy event and all of the officers looked forward to this one—they shouldn't have. It would be remembered fondly by succeeding residents as "The Geriatrics' War of Revenge."

Ten days before the meeting, Gunther drove into downtown Santa Barbara and met with Jeffrey Grainger. After introductions and the acceptance of coffee Gunther said, "Mr. Grainger—"

"Please call me Jeff, Gunther." His Cheshire-cat smile spread from ear to ear. He opened his notebook.

"Okay, Jeff. I'm a resident at The Wind and Sea Retirement Home. Would you care to write a human interest story on that institution?"

Jeff placed his pen beside his notebook. "Yes. But it would be more than a human interest story, wouldn't it? I believe you're having some serious problems there." When Gunther didn't answer, he continued. "You want to use the press to help you, don't you?"

Gunther was taken aback and paused. "Yes, but I don't want The Wind and Sea destroyed."

Jeff shook his head. "I have to report what I see and hear."

Gunther took a sip and leaned across the desk. "Of course, but language can be used to educate, to excite, or to destroy. Let me give you a more complete picture of what I want in confidence."

"It's off the record—for the time being." Jeff stood and poured both a second cup.

"A week from Wednesday at two p.m. we have our semi-annual meeting with the officers of The Wind and Sea. We're having a lot of trouble with the food mainly, but in many other areas also. Management has ignored our complaints so far and this meeting will be no different unless an outside agency such as the press is there. I believe I can get you an invitation from the executive director to attend and record the meeting. I guarantee you it will be interesting."

"I accept gladly, but there are conditions, aren't there?"

Gunther hesitated and scratched his head. "Yes, I don't want to be responsible for the ruin of what could be a wonderful home for those of us in our golden years, and the wrong kind of publicity would."

Jeff stood up and walked around the room. He returned to his desk, sat down and patted Gunther on his arm. "If you'll give me the exclusive on everything that happens at that club of yours, I'll let you read my report and make suggestions. I make no promises, but I'll try not to be destructive."

"I'm not in a position to promise you an exclusive but I surely can notify you first on everything that happens." Gunther sat back in his chair. "I've dealt with many men in my day and I believe I can trust you."

Two days later Gunther met secretly with John Watts.

"John, can this conversation be just between the two of us?" Gunther asked.

"Of course," John said with a beaming smile.

"And for your sake, I'm not going to give you the reasons why."

John wrinkled his forehead as his smile disappeared. "Go ahead."

"We want a reporter at the semi-annual meeting, but its management's meeting and we can't ask outsiders to attend." Gunther moved closer to John. "I have an idea."

"Okay, let it fly."

Gunther was ready. "Have our esteemed leader, Clive Huntington, invite Jeffrey Grainger of the *Santa Barbara News Press* to the semi-annual meeting. Tell him the publicity will be good for The Wind and Sea and he'll be the hero of the day when succeeding headlines proclaim the glory of our institution. Make him believe it's his idea."

"My brain tells me to ignore your request, but for now I'll go along. Clive will love the chance to take the credit." John paused with a smile spreading from ear to ear. "You're planning a trap, aren't you?" John put his hand up and shook his head. "No, don't answer that. I don't want to know."

"Thanks, John. Wish us luck." Gunther left the office and went whistling down the hall.

The anticipated day finally arrived. The Great Hall, festooned with flags from all of the countries anointed by Sir Basil, was filled to capacity—two hundred and fifty residents. The podium was center front with six chairs for the officers of the corporation to its left. The other directors sat in the first row center with four seats on the left aisle set aside for special residents or guests. J. C., as president of the resident council, sat in one. Jeffrey Grainger and his cameraman sat in the rear.

A nervous Clive Huntington was about to speak when in waltzed Deborah Farrell dressed in a form-fitting silk sheath. She seldom attended a resident meeting and all eyes were turned to admire this enchanting creature.

She acknowledged their admiration with a polite nod.

Roger Palmer quickly sat next to her. "Hello, Debby," he whispered as he gave her thigh a quick squeeze.

"Hi, Roge." She sighed as she patted his hand, then brushed it away.

Clive tapped on the mike. "RCW President Oliver, directors, officers, residents and guests, we are here today to celebrate the first year of The Wind and Sea Retirement Community." Clive paused while the residents applauded, then he continued. "It has had its problems, 'growing pains' as they say." He smiled at his metaphor. "But we have made progress. Let me mention a few accomplishments."

He droned on for fifteen minutes and would have continued but for a signal from President Oliver to cease. After the sporadic applause died, he said. "Now it is my pleasure to introduce our esteemed president, Goodwin Oliver."

Again only mild acclamation; the residents waited in ambush.

Oliver briefly stated he would return at the end of the meeting for questions and answers. John Watts, Larry Turner, and Diggby Quinn followed in turn to review their own department's difficulties and successes.

Ninety minutes later, Clive took the mike again and declared a recess for cake and coffee and the necessities. Roger Palmer and Ms. Farrell went outside for a brief smoke. All heads followed their steps.

After everyone was seated again Oliver asked, "Are there any questions or comments?"

Gunther jumped to his feet. "President Oliver, why are you deliberately violating our contract?"

Goodwin didn't handle confrontations well; Sir Basil always took care of those. "What is your name, sir?"

"Gunther Krause and I am chairman of the food committee. Your company is not honoring its commitments."

Loud applause rocked the room.

"Let me read from the contract signed by both your company and us, page thirty-four. Quote, 'The residents will be served thirty lunches or dinners per month in the dining room and a complimentary continental breakfast everyday,' unquote. Take-outs are allowed for lunch and dinner at no extra charge, but you initiated a five-dollar charge for breakfast. They were free for seven months then suddenly, in violation of the contract, you added this charge."

Oliver turned red as his hands shook. He turned to John Watts for help; John looked away.

"We asked our lawyers before we made this change and they said we were within our rights," Oliver said weakly. He picked up his copy of the contract and read. "Mr. Krause, if you will look on page nineteen, section B, rules and regulations quote, 'The management of The Wind and Sea may amend the rules and regulations from time to time,' And that's what we did."

"Oh my God. Where did you get your lawyers?" Gunther spread his arms and a fearful Oliver stepped back. "You're quoting from the resident handbook. Of course you can change the hours the swimming pool is open or when the bus leaves for shopping, but you can't touch the contract between us and it says we are to be given a continental breakfast and it doesn't say we have to eat it in the Sand Castle."

Everyone jumped to their feet and cheered. "Honor the contract, honor the contract," they chanted.

After five minutes, J. C. raced to the podium and held up his hands. "Okay, Mr. Oliver is our guest, let's act our age; we're not college kids anymore."

Beside himself with anxiety, Oliver silently pleaded to Watts and Quinn to take over; they refused.

Gunther now closed in for the kill. "Again I am quoting from the contract, page thirty. 'The residents are to be served healthy, balanced, satisfying meals in quantities needed and that are pleasing to their appetites and taste buds,' unquote. For the last five months we have been served cat and dog food. We know it; I, the food committee chairman knows it; and if you'd eat here you'd know it. Again, you are violating the contract and we demand that you comply with the agreement. Do you hear me, Mr. President?"

Jeff took notes while his cameraman snapped pictures— not so flattering ones of the president.

Oliver sat down and asked for a glass of water. After five minutes he resumed his stance at the podium.

Gunther sat down and Enrico Di Donoto stood. "Mr. Oliver, I'm Enrico Di Donoto, treasurer of the resident council. But you can call me Rico."

This remark encouraged a few giggles. Oliver smiled, believing the worst was over and Rico was a friendly Italian. Enrico, from sunny Italy, was not fun-loving.

"Mr. Oliver, we both signed a contract that states management can raise our monthly fee by a maximum of six percent." A menacing scowl replaced a friendly smile on Enrico's face. Oliver stepped back n fear "The contract is written to ensure that your company breaks even each year, doesn't go in the red and jeopardize our homes. I signed that contract believing you were honorable businessmen using generally accepted accounting practices—which I know very well—and that you were savvy in real estate operations." Oliver knew about Enrico's possible Mafia connections an began to worry about how much pain he could absorb.

"If you make a profit or break even there was to be no increase. But the way you keep books there'll always be a loss, won't there? You're *torto*. That's an Italian word, Mr. Oliver. Do you know what it means? It means your Retirement Communities of the West is crooked."

Life came back into the president. "Sir, I resent that. Sir Basil is respected all over the world. I demand an apology. Our accounting *is* according to generally accepted accounting principles."

"Bullshit—pardon me, ladies—but you place depreciation as an operating expense in the profit and loss statement. It has nothing to do with the profit or loss of this establishment. It should be placed after the profit or loss is calculated and only for the purpose of reducing taxable income. Your total cost of this project is $150,000,000, depreciated over forty years it's $3,750,000 per year that we have to cover, which is $15, 000 per resident."

Enrico walked to the podium and stood one foot from a fearful Oliver. "Your Sir Basil is *torto* because his accounting methods are *torto*. In addition, there are ten cottages and thirty apartments empty because they are obscenely overpriced. Your Sir Basil thinks he is smarter than the market. That's an average loss of revenue of $4,000 per month per unit totaling $160,000 per month or $1,920,000 a year. Add the depreciation and the total is $5,670,000 that the residents have to make up. Unacceptable!"

The audience shouted and shook their fists. Oliver staggered and stumbled to a chair beside John Watts who told Clive Huntington to take over.

"I believe you've had you say, Mr. Di Donoto. Please sit down," Clive said after reaching the podium.

"I will," Enrico said. "But not because you asked me to, only because I'm too angry to continue. I wouldn't want to grab you by your scrawny neck and wring it like a chicken's." He took a step toward the director who ran to the other officers.

General Sutherland, wearing a dress uniform with all of his ribbons, rose slowly to his full height; and with his right arm outstretched, he pointed at the officers. "You are all in dereliction of your sworn duties. You are hereby ordered to dig a latrine for each of us."

"Sit down, General. They're civilians and don't know how to shovel," someone in the rear shouted.

"By God, I'll teach them so they'll be good at something," the general answered proudly.

After a few laughs, the room quieted for a moment before ninety-year-old Maude Perkins stood. At four foot ten inches she barely could be seen, but everyone heard her. With her gray wig askew, she shouted, "We'll sue the bastards. Everyone who wants to file a class-action suit stand up."

Nearly everyone stood and chanted, "Sue the bastards." Soon a giant Congo line formed and slithered throughout the Great Hall. Maude was lifted by a big man and carried on his shoulders. She continued to direct the cheers until her wig fell off, revealing a billiard-ball head. The man placed it back on her head sideways. She didn't care; she was having the time of her life.

All of the officers were nervous and fearful—all except John Watts who secretly enjoyed the show. After the marchers tired and sat, the frenzy finally subsided and peace returned.

Oliver weaved back to the podium. "This meeting is adjourned. Thank you for coming."

John quickly walked outside and opened his cell phone. "Sir Basil, the meeting is over and it was a disaster." He then related imbroglio, chapter and verse.

Sir Basil, at the Hilton just five minutes away, answered, "Let them stew. What can they do except carp and complain?"

"Plenty," John said. "There was a reporter and cameraman here from the *Santa Barbara News Press* and he took notes of every comment and complaint; and the cameraman took pictures of residents waving their fists."

"For Christ's sake, why did you let a reporter in?" Sir Basil asked.

"I didn't. Clive Huntington invited him."

"That idiot; he's gone tomorrow. Why didn't Oliver take over and gain control?"

"He tried, but wasn't successful," Watts said, completely satisfied with himself.

*   *   *   *

Steve Matteson settled himself on Carrie Boswell's couch. "Did you see what I saw?"

"Deborah and Roger sitting next to each other?" Carrie asked.

"More than sitting next to each other. They held hands and rubbed shoulders. His hand was on her lap most of the time." Steve crossed his legs. "I sat in the second row directly behind them and there was a three-inch gap between their chairs. Hard not to miss his big hand flipping back and forth."

Carrie went over to her bar and mixed two stiff drinks. "They're lovers," she said with a knowing smile. "The judge and the Hollywood icon. Juicy stuff; I love it." She handed Steve his drink.

"He's married, isn't he?" He asked, taking a big swallow.

"I'll say. Victoria Crocker, the debutante of the year, 1970." Carrie stirred the ice around in her glass. "Did this affair between them begin before or after her trial?"

"If after, it's none of our business, but if before, it is. Maybe it explains why he so quickly dismissed the case." Steve, staring out of the window, suddenly became serious. "Did you know that they're going to exhume the Pink Daffodil's body for DNA?" He finished his drink in one swallow.

"That won't help unless they can find Hazel Sommers and compare the Daffodil's DNA with hers."

"Don't need to," Steve quickly said. "All they have to do is find a close relative, a parent or a sibling. And they've started the search." He set his empty glass on the coffee table.

"I wonder if our goddess knows." Carrie slowly sipped her drink, then lit a cigarette.

"I don't know, but I'm sure you'll tell her. I'm going to observe how Judge Palmer takes the news."

Chapter 6

The Pink Daffodil

Two weeks later, Woody Ferguson, a young detective with the L.A. police department, visited Steve Matteson. After a few polite words, Steve suggested they talk on the patio area outside the Sand Castle. "It's a nice day and there's plenty of good coffee and Danish," he said.

"We've found the younger sister of Hazel Sommers. She lives in Merced. That's up in the San Joaquin Valley about two hundred miles north of L.A." Woody rubbed his hands together "She's agreed to allow a sample of her DNA. We have a team flying up tomorrow to take it. We exhumed the Daffodil's body and have her DNA. If there is a match between these two, we may open the Mark Chambers murder case and I'll be in charge."

"So you want to pick my brain about the case? Okay, but evidently I didn't know enough to get a conviction or even get it to trial."

"You took that hard, didn't you?" the young detective asked.

Steve took a bite of a gooey roll and slowly washed it down before answering.

"I was devastated," he said finally. "I had to get out of L.A., change my name, everything. I had a fine reputation, years of service; Santa Barbara needed a new chief of detectives, and they accepted me."

Woody brushed a lock of red hair from his eyes. "If you don't mind, why did you move to The Wind and Sea?"

"My wife died years ago. I hate cooking, housework and gardening." Steve shrugged. "And I was lonely. I like it here; the people are friendly and the accommodations adequate."

"I heard the food stinks." Woody took a bite of his Danish; crumbs fell unnoticed onto his shirt.

"It does, but I think that will change. Gunther Krause, our dining committee chairman, and a local reporter have Sir Basil, the owner, by the balls," Steve said with a big smile.

"Did the presence of Deborah Farrell have anything to do with your decision?"

Steve fidgeted and searched for the right answer. "I'm not sure."

"And did you know Judge Roger Palmer lived here too?"

"Not until after I moved in."

"If there's a match between the sister of Sommers and the Daffodil, I'll need your help," Woody pleaded.

"I don't know how I could help, but I'll try."

Woody put down his cup, and placing his hands palm down on the table, looked directly into Steve's eyes. "Is she guilty?"

Steve rose and walked around the patio. "I don't know." He picked a red rose with a long stem that leaned against the balustrade. "Do you know how the Daffodil was killed?"

"By a .22 caliber gun—two slugs into her chest. And we haven't found the gun."

"A twenty-two? That's a woman's gun." Steve crossed his arms to steady his shaking hands. "But a woman surely couldn't have butchered her body the way it was done." He shook his head. "No, I take that back. I've seen them do worse."

Woody left after promising he would send the results of the Merced DNA test. He sauntered up to apartment number 562, and knocked on the door.

"It's open," a familiar female voice twittered.

Carrie Boswell stopped typing when she recognized her visitor. She stood up from her computer. "Want a cup of coffee?"

"Yes, please, maybe with just a splash of brandy."

Woody enjoyed visiting Carrie. She was more experienced and more knowledgeable, attractive in a used way, and certainly not the "girl next door" type. The energy exuding from every pour of her body excited him. He assumed she had no conscience and would do anything to get a story, but he didn't care. He wanted her to drain him, maybe to exhaust him but that pleasure would have to wait. He was on duty and she was a possible murder suspect.

She patted him on his shoulder. "Any news?"

"Yes, exciting. They've located Sommers' sister and will be taking her DNA soon." He took a big swig of hot coffee and choked. "You make your coffee strong and hot." He wiped his mouth with the back of his hand. "But I'm not complaining."

"Everything about me is strong and hot," she replied with a straight face.

Was that an invitation? He swallowed. *I'll ignore it for now.*

"Please, tell me more about DNA."

"Deoxyribonucleic acid is a nucleic acid found in all living things, animals as well as plants. The purpose of DNA is to guide its respective living organism in the way it develops and functions," Woody recited.

"These biological instructions are so specific that each individual person has a unique DNA that is responsible for the person's blood type, hair and eye color as well as organic strengths and weaknesses. And is the result of the two biological parents' DNA merging. In the case of identical twins the DNA is identical even though the fingerprints will be different. Siblings, not identical twins, will have DNAs that are very close. Criminal investigations and paternity testing are the most familiar uses of DNA testing." He took another drink of his coffee.

"DNA was first isolated in 1869 by the French but it took another 120 years for Sir Alec Jeffreys to develop today's standards of DNA testing,"

Carrie shook her head, and moved closer to him. "You're a regular encyclopedia."

"All detectives are trained thoroughly in DNA. It's the greatest tool we have for identification since the use of fingerprints," he explained as he began to perspire.

"So if the tests of the two women show similar DNA, the police will have a positive identification of the Daffodil?"

"Right," he gasped after draining his cup. "That's my news. Now tell me about Judge Palmer's wife, Victoria."

Victoria Crocker is immensely wealthy. Amazingly, she pursued the judge, not the other way around. But the judge is no slouch. He was at the top of his class at the Harvard Law School; a famous trial lawyer sought after by the movers and shakers of Southern California. And he was an outstanding jurist. President Reagan would have appointed him to the Supreme Court if he hadn't resigned. And he is a very handsome, virile man."

"Why would she move here?" Woody asked incredulously.

"She didn't. She visits the judge two or three times a month. I guess you could call them conjugal visits," she said with a suggestive smile. "She has a six thousand square-foot beach house in Santa Barbara and an apartment in New York, but her main residence is a mansion in upscale Hancock Park near downtown Los Angeles. She finished her education at either Vassar or Smith and is a busy woman: on the Board of the Los Angeles Philharmonic Society, chairman Los Angeles Museum of Contemporary Art, and director of the annual Los Angeles Flower Show at the Shrine Auditorium. I believe she's also involved with the Ojai Summer Music Festival. She never stops; she's smart and beautiful. The judge and her lead separate lives."

"Then why did the judge come here? If not the allure of Deborah Farrell's presence, what?" Woody asked.

Carrie shrugged. "I'm not sure, but I believe for peace and quiet; he's writing his memoirs. Also, he's a surfer and joins the college kids down on the beach many afternoons when the surf is up."

Woody waited for more information from this enchanting woman, but Carrie changed the subject.

"Why a pink daffodil; they're usually yellow, aren't they?"

Woody sighed and ran his hand through his hair. "Yeah, usually, but they can be white and orange too. Pink is the rarest, but it's available."

"Is there anything you don't know?" she inquired, moving closer to him.

"I've read a couple of your books and you know much more than I about the mating habits of the human species."

"I could teach you in one lesson—at your place." She rolled her tongue around her red lips.

Woody shifted positions in his overstuffed chair. "Enticing, a most desirable invitation, but for now I believe we should keep our relationship platonic and concentrate on solving the problem at hand. Maybe have a big celebration when that's accomplished."

Chapter 7

The Sting

Jeffrey Grainger called Gunther Krause. "I have the story ready; let's meet," he said.

"Okay," Gunther replied. "Not here or in your office. How about the Pierpont Inn on the Pacific Coast Highway tomorrow, Tuesday?"

Gunther asked J. C. Wellington and Enrico Di Donoto to join him, and all four met the next day at eight for breakfast. After the orange juice and coffee were served, Jeff asked. "Shall we wait until after we've finished, or proceed and hope we can keep our eggs off the papers?"

All indicated they wanted to begin immediately.

Jeff handed each man a copy of his story. "This is exactly what happened. No one is quoted out of context and I believe I've captured the anger and emotions of the residents. I promised Gunther that I would try to modify any part he thought was too, shall we say, 'stimulating.' Hopefully, he won't find much to edit."

For the next thirty minutes the three men read, then savored their food, then read some more. Gunther was the last to finish. "Great job, Jeff; you captured what happened. I'd like to be in Sir Basil's office when he reads this."

The others lifted their glasses in a toast to Jeff.

"This piece just may earn you a Pulitzer Prize," Enrico added.

"Jeff, could you call your office or smoke a cigar for about ten minutes? I have an idea I want to share with these gentlemen. It will be to your advantage," J. C. said.

"No problem. I don't smoke and I don't have to call, but there is another urgent matter that needs attention." Jeff said raced toward the restroom.

J. C. jerked to attention. "We have a rare opportunity. We have private knowledge, legal inside information. We can stick it to Sir Basil and at the same time make a fortune."

38

The other two men sat down their coffee cups and leaned forward. "How?" both asked.

"I was involved in a similar situation once before; I believe it was in 1972. But that time I took on a big risk. The Atherton Tool and Die Company was flying high. Stock was on an up trend and closed on a Tuesday at forty-five on the New York Stock Exchange. I received word from the assistant comptroller that the company's major customer owed it millions and was about to declare bankruptcy. It was a tightly held secret— nothing had been published. I told a small group of my closest associates and we immediately built a large, short position in the common stock using stock exchanges in Chicago, Los Angeles, Dallas, and London. By Friday night we had sold short nearly two million shares.

"The news of the bankruptcy flashed on the Dow Jones wire at seven Monday morning. We started buying back our shares when it had dropped to twenty. Our buying pushed the stock up and after we had covered our short position it closed at thirty-one. We netted nearly thirty million dollars in one day's trading. We had inside information and could have been in deep trouble, but the SEC in those days, didn't bother to investigate; it will now. The dissent at The Wind and Sea is common knowledge; we're just smart enough to use it to our advantage—nothing illegal."

"I'm in," Enrico said. "I have friends in New Jersey and Chicago who'll join me."

"Me too," Gunther said. "I can handle a few thousand shares."

J. C. stood and walked quickly to the public phone booth. "I'm going to call my broker to find out what their float is."

He returned five minutes later. "The Retirement Communities of the West, Inc., RCW, has twenty million shares authorized but only eight million actively traded. Can we manage twenty percent or one point six million shares? If we go over twenty percent the exchanges may stop trading in the stock and trigger an investigation. The stock right now is trading at twenty-two and a half—a new high. Twenty percent of the float would be $36,000,000. "How many shares do you want, Enrico?"

"It's going to take time and I don't believe we should ask Jeff to delay longer. We have a deal, don't we? It's just a matter of how big. Gunther, ask Jeff for seventy-two hours."

Gunther went and found Jeff drinking coffee with an attractive, young brunet, probably a University of California at Santa Barbara coed. "Okay, Jeff, please return."

After the four were reunited, Gunther began. "Jeff, you've written a perfect story. We don't want to change a word. You have our blessing, but we want you to delay publication for three days. If you will do that for us, I promise you a nice bonus."

Jeff's eyes sparkled, anticipating a few hundred dollars. "No other paper has bothered to cover The Wind and Sea rebellion and if we all can keep quiet about my article, I'll do what you want."

"I can assure you, Jeff, we won't say a word," all three said enthusiastically, shaking hands with the young man. "A suggestion, add to your story that the cost of the project was $55,000,000 over budget, is now only seventy percent occupied and is losing $2,000,000 per month."

"Thanks," Jeff said. "I will."

On Wednesday, Enrico received commitments for six hundred and twenty-five thousand shares from the secretary of the New Jersey longshoreman's union and a few of his friends on the East Coast. J. C. called his old Wall Street buddies and they pledged five hundred and fifty thousand. Gunther took the remaining twenty-five thousand shares.

It was agreed that J. C. would manage the attack. At two p.m., New York time, on Wednesday, he had a broker friend at Merrill Lynch short a few thousand shares at twenty-three. By the end of trading he had placed orders for fifty thousand shares. J. C. knew brokers in all the major U.S. cities and gave them explicit instructions on how to proceed. "After each up tick, short a thousand shares," he ordered.

On Thursday, the short orders were placed by his brokers on the west coast and in Dallas, Chicago and Atlanta. Only about twenty percent were placed on the New York Stock Exchange. By four p.m., closing time in New York, one million, two hundred thousand shares had been sold short and RCW closed at twenty-one.

"Tomorrow should be an interesting day," Enrico said. "I hope we figured this right. You guys may lose a little money, but I could be in big trouble." His smile was a little forced and his breathing heavy.

At 6:30 a.m. on Friday, the people in Santa Barbara and environs opened their morning paper. WIND AND SEA IN REBELLION, in bold twenty–four point headline, greeted them.

Jeff had captured perfectly the essence of the meeting's anguish; every statement was emboldened, every nuance accentuated. Glory, glory hallelujah, the army of the greatest generation was on the march. Sir Basil was in full retreat. Every wire service latched onto the story. At nine a.m. electronic tapes announced the story to the traders on Wall Street. Dow Jones and the N.Y. Times reporters bombarded Jeff's office with inquiries. He enjoyed his new status and embellished every answer. "Sir Basil would have been drawn and quartered if he'd been there," was used often. Late editions of all papers featured the story on page one.

RCW, which had opened at twenty-two, began to slide. By noon it traded at eighteen. At two, a block of twenty thousand shares sold at fifteen. J. C. had his brokers begin covering their shorts. The decline continued with an avalanche of sale orders. RCW closed at twelve and a quarter and all the shorted stock had been repurchased. Gunther, Enrico, J. C. and their friends netted eleven dollars a share for a total profit of nearly thirteen million dollars.

Jeff soon received a 1997 red Mustang for his help.

Variety, Hollywood's own tabloid, greeted one of their well-known playboys with Monday's headline: SIR BASIL LAYS A BIG EGG.

That esteemed gentlemen escaped in his private jet to one of his favorite hideaways in the Cayman Islands. His parting remarks to John Watts were, "Take over, John. Do what you can do to stem the flow of blood until I return. Try to determine who is leaking information from this office."

Christopher Fowler, a forty-year-old man who had received a graduate degree in Geriatrics and Retirement Home management, replaced Clive Huntington.

He's the opposite of Clive. Sir basil must have been in a panic when he hired Fowler, John Watts thought.

John invited Gunther to his office the next week. "You orchestrated last Friday's massacre, didn't you?" John wagged his forefinger.

"How could you think such a thought," Gunther answered with a smile. "But yes, I was involved."

"Congratulations. It was a splendid coup, but Sir Basil doesn't like to lose. He will hire detectives to discover who was behind it and then will come after you. He has friends in Washington who'll be asked to investigate your little conspiracy; watch out," John said. "He hates to lose."

"Thanks," Gunther replied. "But this time he may be overmatched. I'm associated with some real tough cookies. I mean dangerous."

"I'm temporarily in charge and want to keep you up-to-date," John said. "As you know Clive has been replaced. I hate to tell you this but Eamon McConnell will have to go. He can't keep within his budget. He's already $100,000 over."

"I know," Gunther interrupted. "I tried to help him but he's an artist not a businessman."

"I've signed a contract with the Smith Food Company. They'll purchase the food and run the kitchen; we'll staff the dining room. Smith Food does it now for several country clubs and other organizations. Also, we'll rescind that hated five-dollar fee for breakfast take-outs. The residents can eat that complimentary meal wherever they want. You've won a big victory. Enjoy, but watch one another's backs."

Chapter 8

The Golden Years

By September of 1998, the residents had experienced two years of The Wind and Sea. Clive Huntington's departure pleased them, but Mac's demise saddened them. Everyone loved him, his food, and his happy Irish demeanor. Louise Le Claire became The Wind and Sea's dining director. She was French, had a good sense of humor, and if the residents couldn't have Mac, then she was the next best thing.

The food crisis was over; Smith offered a varied and satisfying menu. Meal time became fun again. Everyone had special friends they preferred to share their dinners and lunches with and everyone was welcome at any table.

The hatred of management and its dismissive attitude diminished. The residents enjoyed one another, but continued to mutually join in the "us against them" attitude."

The Wind and Sea inmates were eighty percent Caucasian, but several minorities had representation. Their keepers—the derisive name used for the staff—were all white except for Chauncey Talbot, the black activities director.

Social activities increased. To not be involved in one took a conscientious effort. Nearly all of the couples and many of the single persons had cocktail parties in their units before dinner. The Di Donotos, Enrico—called Rico by his friends—and his wife, Francesca, facilitated the most get-togethers. Besides the usual cheese and dips, they offered many Italian delights: apricot prosciutto on skewers, meat balls polette, and sautéed olives, to name a few. Everyone liked this big, larger-than-life man and his beautiful wife with her dark hair, olive skin, flashing eyes, and sparkling teeth. *Could this charming man and his delightful wife be connected with the mob?* Nobody knew for sure and nobody cared. Life with them was fun and worth any possible danger.

Deborah Farrell entertained occasionally, but not in the intimate surroundings of her own cottage. She selected one of the special dining rooms and invited a few of her Wind and Sea friends on occasion. But most of her guests were from her old Hollywood days. To be invited was a special prize and rewarded the recipient to many envious questions: "What's she like?" "Has she had many face-lifts?" "Did you talk to any movie star?" Roger Palmer was never invited.

Bingo on Saturday and bunko on Sunday afternoons were added to the game menu, in addition to party bridge on Tuesdays and duplicate bridge on Thursdays. Also, there was a smoke-filled poker game scheduled for Monday evenings. Serious players avoided this because five of the seven regular players were women and the game degenerated with deuces wild and crazy high-low alternatives. The experienced played only five-card draw or stud poker and used their own smoke-filled apartments.

Generally, the residents were glad they had made the decision to retire to The Wind and Sea. Especially the married women who joyfully threw down their aprons, stomped on them and proclaimed, "I quit." No longer did they have to shop and cook for their husbands or friends. Housekeeping and worrying about the yard or house repairs were in the past. Their newspapers were delivered to the door each morning, mail was picked up and delivered to their boxes near the lobby, food was available on the fifth floor, and staff was ready to assist them for all legitimate needs. Nostalgia was ever present for the places where they had raised their children and for friends living far away. *But what the hell,* they thought, *life is a series of phases. We enjoyed our earlier ones and now we must accept and relish this one—our golden years.*

Viola Kushovich was an exception; she was not happy at The Wind and Sea. Her son, Robert, had forced her to move to the retirement home after the recent death of her husband.

At age seventy-six and in failing health, Robert knew she couldn't cope living alone; she didn't agree. She was a smallish woman, five foot two, one hundred and twenty pounds, not attractive, and a loner. Her fellow women residents tried to keep her busy with bridge sessions, projects in the craft room, and meal time camaraderie. She accepted these, but did not enjoy their kind entreaties and returned to her lonely room as soon as possible.

Within six months of her arrival at The Wind and Sea, everyone notice a decline in her mental acumen. She couldn't remember how to return to her room, didn't remember names, and was completely disoriented. Diggby Quinn notified Robert, and he decided, with the staff's help, to move Viola from independent living to assisted living.

Viola begged her son not to move her. He knew he had to and the decision was made to do it on the first of November. On Halloween, the residents amused themselves after dinner by traipsing through the halls, knocking on apartment doors, and yelling, "Trick or treat." Of course the treat they sought was not candy, but booze. It was a clear, crisp night.

By nine, the full moon bathed the campus in a blush of white light. Suddenly, a woman's voice came from outside, and many rushed to their windows. "Oh my God, there's a woman standing on the railing of the common area balcony at the end of the fifth floor," one woman said. "She's all in white, glowing in the moonlight, screaming something. Oh no, no!"

"What happened?" her husband asked.

"She dove off the balcony and crashed onto the sidewalk below," the woman said between sobs.

The security guards and 9-1-1 were called. At least fifty people rushed to the site, which the guards had enclosed with yellow crime scene tape. The women sobbed as the men looked aghast at this pitiful sight. Blood soaked Viola's beautiful white gown, but her matching shoes remained attached, ready for the first dance.

"She looks like an angel," someone said.

"How could she remain balanced on that inch-wide railing?" another asked.

"She didn't," a guard answered. "There was a step-stool next to the railing. She stood on that."

The crowd suddenly became reverently quiet as the investigators arrived and went to work. A rich baritone voice began the well-known strains of "Amazing Grace." Within two bars everyone held hands and joined in singing. This beloved melody ended with, "Amen, may she rest in peace."

*   *   *   *

The U. S. Food and Drug Administration authorized the sale of Viagra in March of 1998. By November some of the Wind and Sea men had tried this new drug and praised its miraculous achievements to their fellow inmates. "I thought that part of my life was over thirty years ago," one eighty-year-old said with a smile on his face, "I'm as good as ever."

"Any side effects?" Another asked.

"Everything was blue for about thirty minutes. That's all; it was worth it. Oh there was one other side effect—my wife makes my cocktails again and says she's proud of me. Doctors advise that one should have a strong heart to indulge. I guess mine's okay."

Since the retirement community opened, single men had asked single women to join them for meals and other events and many became steady companions. Afterward, they went their separate ways. Now, with the advent of the miracle drug, some departed together.

At their regular weekly poker game, the regular players often discussed this new phenomenon. "Has anyone tried Viagra yet?" J. C. asked. The silence that followed indicted they hadn't or were too embarrassed to admit indulgence.

"Have you?" Gunther asked.

J. C. drew a card. "Not yet, but thinking about it."

"Discussed it with your wife?" Gunther continued his inquisition.

J. C. shook his head and shrugged. "Why, it has nothing to do with her."

David Morris, the gynecologist, looked up from the hand just dealt to him. "There are a couple of women here who have aroused my itch; I may be in the market. That author, Carrie Boswell, looks and acts like she might be interested in some action."

"For Christ's sake, guys; quit fantasizing and play poker," Tom Jenkins said.

Tom Jenkins, an Ichabod Crane look alike, wore plaid suits and didn't own a tie. A high school dropout, he'd survived by being successful in poker at the Atlantic City casinos. Conning people was his forte, and managing a used car lot was a natural for his talents where he acquired the name "Slick." He was flamboyant and an endless source of jokes, most of which could not be told in mixed company. Slick usually won but he was an honest player according to Rico who was an expert at detecting hustlers.

David Morris' pale-green sweater stretched across his ample stomach. He sucked on his pipe. "It's your turn, Slick." David toyed with his beard, anticipating Slick's next move.

Carlos Sanchez had recently sold his chain of three Mexican restaurants to El Torito. He and his wife, Conchita, had worked hard and had saved their money. They were popular at The Wind and Sea as both had fine voices and Carlos expertly picked the strings on his guitar.

A bag of mixed characters made up this poker group. Besides Slick, David, and Carlos, J. C. Wellington, the retired Wall Street broker, attended regularly, along with Gunther Krause, the retired real estate developer, and Rico Di Donoto, who had worked in waste management.

The residents celebrated the end of 1998 with a New Year's Eve party. Garlands and balloons adorned The Great Hall. Champagne flowed; and the Smith Food Company provided a sumptuous meal.

J. C., as the resident council president, toasted the New Year. "My dear friends, this last year we suffered a tragedy and we lost several good friends, but we made some progress in our efforts to make The Wind and Sea the best 'last stop' in California. I promise you that in 1999, the last year of the Twentieth Century, we will surpass our highest expectations. Salute."

The five-piece band played *"Auld Lang Syne."* Glasses were raised, drained, quickly refilled as everyone kissed his or her neighbors. The revelers believed the worst was over, and that next year would be nirvana. They couldn't have been more wrong.

Chapter 9

The Goddess

Woody Ferguson, the L.A. detective, phoned Deborah Farrell. A breathless, young voice answered, "Ms. Farrell's residence, I'm Karen O'Brien, her secretary."

"Karen, I'm Detective Ferguson with the Los Angeles Police Force, Hollywood Division. I need to talk to Ms. Farrell."

"Just a minute, please," she said in her intimate, panting way. Two minutes later she returned. "Ms. Farrell will see you at three this afternoon. I hope to meet you; detectives are so exciting."

Woody blushed and stammered, "Thank Ms. Farrell and tell her I'll be there."

He was on time, and a pretty young woman met him at the door. *An Audrey Hepburn look alike,* he thought, Her small features, and dark hair cropped to fit her exquisite head, enhanced her beautiful smile. She eagerly grabbed him by the arm and led him into the living room.

"Good afternoon, Ms. Farrell, I'm Detective Ferguson."

"Thank you for coming, Detective. This is my attorney, Roger Palmer. You may leave, Karen."

A man sitting next to Deborah stood and extended his hand. *He's shorter and a little heavier than he was at the trial,* Ferguson thought.

"Would you care for coffee?" Ms. Farrell asked graciously.

Woody absorbed his hostess. A blue ribbon held her blond hair back in a ponytail. *She was a goddess.* Her dress, a simple pink smock, fell just below her knees. The diamonds and sapphires in her necklace sparkled in the sunlight. As she gracefully poured, Woody glanced around the room. Elegantly decorated, the plush, powder-blue carpeting matched the color of the walls, which held paintings by seventeenth-century French masters. The cherry wood furniture glistened, and the finest silversmiths obviously handcrafted the exquisite lamps. Ms. Farrell had scattered bowls of pink rose buds throughout the room.

After ten minutes of polite conversation Palmer asked, "Why are you here, Detective?"

This was the biggest case ever assigned to the young detective and he was nervous. "We've reopened the Mark Chambers murder case, Mr. Palmer."

"What has that to do with Ms. Farrell?" Roger asked.

"I'm afraid quite a lot. DNA gave the police a powerful new identification tool. For some time we've suspected that the Pink Daffodil could be Hazel Sommers, the missing witness for Ms. Farrell at her 1979 trial. At that time, with no dental records or fingerprints, there was no way to be sure, now there is. We found Mrs. Sommers' sister in Merced, a Thelma Foster, and obtained her DNA. We matched that against the DNA of the Pink Daffodil. The technicians in the coroner's office state positively that they are a sibling match. Mrs. Sommers had no other brothers or sisters."

Deborah stole a quick glance at Roger, but he remained fixed, boring a hole through the detective with his eyes.

"All this proves is that whoever killed the Pink Daffodil actually killed Hazel Sommers. I repeat, what does it have to do with Ms. Farrell?"

Woody ignored the question. "Mrs. Sommers was killed by two shots from a .22 caliber handgun. Ms. Farrell, do you own such a gun?"

Roger held up his hand and leaned over to whisper in Deborah's ear. He nodded and she answered, "No, Detective."

Woody opened his briefcase and removed a sheet of paper. "Let me refresh your memory, Ms. Farrell. In March of 1972, you purchased a Beretta twenty-two caliber handgun in New York City. You properly registered it with the authorities on that date."

"Oh my God, that was twenty-six years ago. Did you expect me to remember that far back? I don't even remember what I had for dinner last night," she answered with a derisive laugh.

"But now you do remember?" Woody asked.

"I didn't know that little thing was a twenty-two. My manager told me I should keep one in my bedroom. 'New York muggers are everywhere,' he'd said. He was with me when I bought it and put it in a drawer in my bedside night table." She shrugged. "I forgot it. Never touched again; it might still be there."

"And what hotel would that be, Ms. Farrell?"

"The Waldorf-Astoria, room532; I always stayed there. Is there anything else, Detective?"

Woody scribbled on his notepad. "Yes, could you tell me how you and Mr. Palmer met?"

"I'll answer that," Palmer quickly interjected. "After the trial and outside of the courtroom, I accidentally bumped into Ms. Farrell. She thanked me for the considerate way I had treated her and left. About a week later, my wife and I were dining at a Sunset Boulevard club—"

"It was the Tropicana," Deborah added.

"Yes, well as the hostess led us to our table, we passed Deborah and her escort, whom I knew." Palmer snapped his fingers. "I forget his name."

"Paul Andrews," Deborah said.

"That's it. Anyway, he invited us to join them at their table. About two months later Ms. Farrell had a legal problem and asked me to help. I had retired from the bench and agreed." Palmer stood up. "Detective, if there's nothing more . . . ."

"Just one thing, Judge. Would Ms. Farrell be so kind as to show me the den with all her memorabilia? I've heard it's a must see."

The judge hesitated, but Deborah replied, "Certainly, Detective."

It wasn't a large room, about fifteen by twenty feet. Pictures of her and other actors, politicians, famous athletes, and two presidents—Nixon and Reagan—hung on the walls. The floor was crammed with walnut tables loaded with prizes, two Oscars, trophies, and awards covered the floor. There were none of her husbands, but one of a little girl about nine years old stood out. Another showed an older man with his arms around her, and in another one, Deborah was holding hands with Palmer. Woody didn't ask about the girl or the man, but made a mental note to seek information elsewhere.

"Are you sure you don't want a cup of coffee or a cookie, Detective?" Deborah asked sweetly.

"No, thanks. You both have been very kind, but I must go. Thank you."

After Woody left, Palmer said, "A fishing expedition, but you are definitely a person of interest. I wonder why he wanted to see the den."

"Just curious, Roge. People like to drive by the homes of the rich and famous just to get a vicarious thrill and brag that they were there."

"Maybe, but he studied those pictures closely. We'll have to wait for them to make their next move. It's too bad you bought that damn revolver." He shook his head. "The murder of Mrs. Sommers has nothing to do with you anyway. She was your alibi. Why would you want to kill her?"

After leaving Farrell's cottage, Woody trotted over to Steve's apartment. "How about a drink? I have some news for you," Woody said after shaking hands with the retired L.A. detective. He brushed his hair out of his eyes, then revealed what had been discussed at the Farrell cottage. "The DNA part is public knowledge, but please don't say anything about the revolver. And do you know if Ms. Farrell had a daughter?"

"I don't, but the county recorder's office should have a copy of the birth certificate. I'll check. I may have some information for you soon. I'm working with Carrrie Boswell, the writer. She's writing a 'tell all' book about Ms. Farrell and as in all of her books, dirt is the main ingredient. She phoned and said she had some exciting news about Farrell and wants to see me. I'll only tell her about the DNA and will let you know what I learn."

*   *   *   *

Steve rang Carrie's doorbell and was surprised when Arnold Myers, her husband, opened the door. "Coming to help Carrie with her book on Farrell?" Arnold asked cheerfully.

"Yes, she said she had some news," Steve replied nervously.

Arnold adjusted his glasses. "She's in the living room. *Avanti, buon giorno*; I have to hurry for an important date."

Steve walked into the living room. *What a strange little man.* "Hello, Carrie. I met your husband at the door and he uttered a couple of foreign words; I think they were Italian," he said on entering the room where she was busy at her computer.

She laughed. "Arnold tries to impress people."

After pouring Steve a cup of coffee with a splash of brandy, Carrie began with excitement, "I've been busy on the Internet and with some friends in the media and police departments. They'll help me if I don't reveal some things I know about them." She winked at Steve.

"First, let me tell you my news," Steve interrupted. "The DNA of the Pink Daffodil closely matches Hazel Sommers' sister. The Pink Daffodil is Hazel."

"Oh my God," Carrie exploded. "'Murder is afoot,' as Sherlock Holmes would say. I always thought that was a possibility."

Steve reached and selected a doughnut from the nearby table. "'The plot thickens' is another Holmes quote."

"If it gets any thicker, I won't be able to stir the pot." Carrie laughed. "Actually, I'm a little afraid. There's something ominous about this place. Are the police sure that Viola's death was suicide, not murder? The presence of that stepstool bothers me. A friend of hers told me that she had a wooden stepstool different from the metal one found on the balcony. Could she have been propped up on that stool and pushed?"

"It's possible, but I doubt it. Someone owns that stool and will claim it sooner or later," he answered.

Carrie refilled both cups and paused while organizing her thoughts. "Farrell has had four husbands: Pietro Molineri, the Italian movie director; Randy Anderson, a tennis professional; Rajai Habibe, the prince of a royal family in Saudi Arabia; and Mark Chambers, the actor. Are you paying attention?"

"Yes, hanging on every word."

"Three of the four died unnaturally and suddenly," she said slowly, syllable by syllable.

Steve reached for a pencil and paper. "Go ahead."

"Debby dear met Pietro in the early fifties in Rome. She was just a beautiful Hollywood starlet who had fled to Italy after being dumped by a big star—I forget his name, maybe Cary Grant. Pietro became infatuated with her and they were an item in Rome's night spots and newspapers. Either Gena Lolabrigida, Sophia Loren, or another actress equally well endowed was dumped so he could star Farrell in his new movie *Amore, Amore, Amore,* which was shot in Italian with English sub-titles. That was lucky for her because at that time her stage voice was weak and too high pitched. The movie was a big hit on both sides of the Atlantic, and her career was born."

Carrie looked at Steve's impressive body. *He's more mature than Woody. Maybe he would be more receptive to my charms,* she thought.

"She moved in with him and made another not well received movie. Hollywood beckoned and Pietro and Debby moved to California, where after a month they married. It was a stormy marriage well noted in all the scandal-ridden newspapers and magazines. First a public fight, separation, then a passionate reuniting, a new movie together, love forever more, then a repeat of the scenario.

"Steve, My back is tense. Could we stop for a minute and would you please give it a little rub?" Steve obliged with a little tinge of irritation and after five minutes she continued.

" These well-publicized fights propelled her forward and other directors clamored for her services. Two years later, Pietro suffered a mild heart attack on a movie set and was rushed to a hospital. The heart specialist in charge said he was in no danger and would be discharged in a few days. But he died three days after admittance. The doctor signed the death certificate without comment and there was no investigation.

"Farrell wore black and gave a great performance of grief and unhappiness but within six months she was spending extra time holding hands with her tennis pro, Randy Anderson. It was a wild thing: escapes to Acapulco, nude bathing at Malibu and public nuisances in hotels and night clubs. That was in 1961 and she was at the height of her career, three top box office hits: 'I'll Remember you Forever,' 'Mind, Body, and Soul,' and 'Till You Return.'"

51

"I fell in love with her after seeing *'Mind, Body and Soul,'*" Steve remarked with a longing look on his face.

"Well, you're lucky your passion was never consummated. She married Randy after making *'Till You Return.'* He died in 1962. Killed in an automobile accident, ran off a cliff in Malibu. His body contained a large amount of Xanax, an anxiety medicine. An endocrinologist had prescribed Xanax so there was no further investigation—just another accidental death caused by an overdose.

"Several years later she married one of the world's richest men, Rajai Habibe. She didn't love him, just his money. He flew her around the world in his private jet and they played in Capri, Monte Carlo, Paris and the Swiss Alps. She was contented to live this life until he took her to Mecca during Ramadan. She viewed the lives that Arab women lived and they frightened her. 'He could kidnap me to Saudi Arabia and force me to live such a life, she thought.'

"As soon as they returned to New York, she divorced him. He was ready to try someone new and didn't object. He said, 'I divorce you,' three times and according to Arab custom he was divorced.

"What's he doing now?" Steve asked.

"Wooing young, beautiful women and flying around the world as far as I know. He's the only husband of Farrell's that escaped death. We all know what happened to her fourth husband, Mark Chambers, don't we?"

"Yes, but how could foul play be proved for Molineri and Anderson? The authorities could exhume the bodies, but what could they find— drugs. We know Randy took an excessive amount of Xanax and maybe they would find a strange drug in Molineri. So what? It's been too long, the trail is cold." Steve looked off into the distance.

Steve studied his notes. "I'm told that in her den she has a picture of a girl about nine and another of an older man. Do you know if she had a daughter and when her father died?"

"I don't know about her father, but I've heard rumors. I don't know anything for sure, I'll check. Isn't it strange that you, the detective on the murder case, and the trial judge all live here?"

"Yes, it could be coincidental or it could be planned," Steve answered. "In my case, I really don't know. How about you?"

"I was tired of keeping a house and was looking around. As soon as I heard she was moving here, I decided to join her. Maybe become friends," she said with an enigmatic smile.

"That will be the day." Steve gave Carrie a peck on her cheek and left.

Chapter 10

The Executive Council

The second Monday of April 1999 was rainy and cold. With little else to do, the residents crowded into the Great Hall for the council meeting. Promptly at two, President J. C. Wellington banged his gavel on the lectern. "Please come to order," he said three times before receiving recognition. "Will the secretary call the roll of the council members to determine if there is a quorum?" The council included the executive committee and the seven chairpersons of the seven standing committees. After an affirmative nod from Mary Hopkins, the secretary, J.C. continued. "Before beginning business I would like to recognize three new members to our Wind and Sea family. Please stand when I call your name. Paul and Yvonne Ostrow."

A short man in his sixties stood; his petite wife slowly followed. The right side of Paul's face and the top of his head were bandaged.

"Paul is recovering from a serious automobile accident and is getting attention in our rehab center," J. C. added.

The audience politely applauded

"And our third new resident is Mr. Francis Pisano."

A tall, thin man with a large mustache stood and gracefully bowed to the audience. "Pardon my English, but I am pleased to be associated with such a distinguished group."

Rico jumped up. "Calibria?"

"Si," Pisano said.

Rico ran to him and they hugged.

"His family came from the same area in Italy as mine did," Rico proudly announced. He didn't say that Calibria, the province at the toe of Italy, was ruled by Communists. Calibria completely ignored the government in Rome and disregarded the dictates of the Church.

J.C. banged his gavel again. "I am happy to report that communications with our new executive director, Christopher Fowler, are improving. We have instituted weekly discussions with him. I believe the he will be an advocate for us, the residents. We will work through him to get needed additional improvements to services and activities here at The Wind and Sea.

The minutes of the last meeting were read and J.C. asked if there were any corrections.

"Chauncey Talbot raised his hand. "Yes, Mr. President, the third paragraph should be removed or rewritten. It could possibly be perceived as a pejorative personal comment directed however inadvertently and without intention toward a member of the staff."

Chauncey, I know you were educated at Oxford. Please tell me if I interpreted you correctly. You believe this paragraph insults a member of the staff and you want it removed, correct?

"Yes, Mr. President. You precisely have identified my request."

J. C. then asked for the committee reports. Chauncey, as activities chairman, announced the arrival of a new treadmill. Gunther Krause reported that the food department was over budget and complained that people showed for the Easter buffet without reservations. The Landscape chairwoman begged all owners of female dogs to please have their pets "wet" in the designated area. "There are more brown spots than there is green grass," she admonished.

"The first item of 'old' business is the naming of the forthcoming monthly publication. Your executive council voted to call it 'Tattle.'" Then J. C. wrinkled into a rare smile. "Remember to close you curtains at night; the Tattle's reporters will be peeping."

After a brief discussion Tatttle was approved by a majority vote and J. C. continued.

"The last item of 'old' business is the most disturbing; the threat from Sir Basil that management will change its method of calculating our monthly fees. California law gives the provider, The Retirement Communities of the West, two options. Previously RCW chose Option A (iii) Section 1771.7 of the California Health and Safety Code quote: 'Fees shall not be increased in excess of a specified percentage over the preceding year,' unquote. We know that percentage is six.

"Now President Oliver wants to change and take Option B, quote: 'Changes in monthly care fees shall be based on projected costs, prior year per capita costs, and economic indicators.

"We're going to get screwed and tattooed. We all know the cost for water, food, and electricity is going up. The waiters, bus boys and maid's wages will rise to the market—a substantial amount. And the directors will get what they want—higher salaries. Management didn't realize how expensive this area is. Now they do and they're going to pass the shortfall on to us. Think ten percent."

The audience voiced their dislike for RCW organization. Many others also stood and spoke concern for their financial future if the fees were raised substantially. J. C. let them vent their frustration for five minutes before banging his gavel. "Our options are limited. To challenge them in court would be costly and probably futile, but there are other ways. The executive committee will begin to find them immediately after this meeting. I assure you that we will not surrender to their greed.

"Don't forget on the second Saturday of next month we will have our semi-annual talent show. In addition, there will be a silent auction and a raffle for donated door prizes. All monies received will be for the benefit of the help. To keep them, and keep them happy, we have to augment management's paltry wages. You've collected things all your life. You don't have room for them now so lighten up; donate them for door prizes. Or if you have some really nice things, place them in the silent action group. If you want to participate in the talent show come to the try-outs, next Monday at three here in the Great Hall. If you play an instrument, bring it and we'll help carry it if you're into tubas.

Sally will be at the baby grand piano. So if all you have is a voice, bring it too. Sally knows all the songs, Don't you Sally?"

"I know all the good songs, J. C.; especially those written between 1936 and 1950. But not those you guys sang in fraternity houses and in barracks," this short lady with thin hair and glasses said. "J. C. can play those. I understand he used to work in a bawdy house."

Some were shocked, others laughed. How could this prim, sedate, and elegant woman speak about let alone know about the amenities in the houses of ill repute? What was true of Sally applied to all of the other inhabitants of The Wind and Sea. "One can't tell a book by its cover," was an old cliché but a true statement. By looking at this quiet group of people one couldn't know what they had suffered or accomplished. Every one of them could tell a unique story. All had experienced seventy to ninety years of failure, triumph, tragedy, sadness, and euphoria

"Rico Di Donoto has generously offered to provide the liquor and he and I. will be the bartenders. Believe it or not management will supply the hors d' oeuvres. Oh, I forgot to tell you that Deborah Farrell will join the party."

"Heaven be praised, she will come down from on high and anoint us with her presence," someone yelled from the front row.

J. C. scowled at the person but decided to ignore the remark. "We will close in our usual way. Reverend Thompson will give the blessing for those of our fellow Wind and Sea friends who are ill or injured."

Glen was always upbeat with a big smile and a happy remark. His job was to make conditions seem better no matter how bad they were. Everyone liked him, and on Sunday, his little chapel on the first floor was filled for his non-denominational service.

"Dear friends," he began. "Please join me in a silent prayer for the soul of our good friend Fred Beakins, who passed away early this morning. As you know Fred's heart has been weakening and this morning it stopped."

Everyone bowed their heads for a minute until Glen spoke again.

Glen read off several more names of residents who were suffering from various maladies and closed with a short prayer, ending with, "God bless our country's president and all those in the armed forces far from home who are protecting us from those who would harm us. And, Lord, please give special attention to our friends and neighbors in this community who are suffering in body, mind, and spirit. In the name of the Father, the Son and Holy Ghost. Amen."

A booming amen answered Glen as the residents filed out of the Great Hall to pursue the next activity planned for their busy schedules.

Chapter 11

The Talent Show

Chauncey Talbot was in charge of the talent show. He was a big man who had lived with money all his life, but who never discussed how that money was obtained. He was educated at Harvard and Oxford, his clothes were tailor-made, and his manners were impeccable. To him anything less than perfection was unacceptable. His wife, Latisha, complemented him in every way.

Starting at four p.m. on Friday, he and a crew of five maintenance employees worked steadily for eight hours. Twenty round tables, seating ten each and covered with linen cloths and decorated with candles and party favors, replaced the rows of chairs. The stage was festooned with banners and flags, and a portable wooden dance floor was put in place in front of it. Dave Henry and his band of five, the Moon Dogs, would sit on the stage and provide the dance music. A bar was constructed to the left side of the stage with ten cases of bourbon, Scotch, gin, and vodka stacked on its floor. Another ten cases of Merlot and Chardonnay wine and Coors beer were placed adjacent to the bar. The microphone and podium were made ready for the master of ceremonies, Tom "Slick" Jenkins. The front and center table was reserved for Deborah Farrell and her guests.

Promptly at seven p.m. the residents, including Ms. Farrell, entered the Great Hall in a happy mood. Soon after being seated, the residents joined the line for drinks. The room was filled by seven-twenty and Slick grabbed the mike. "Good evening, fellow inmates. Are you ready to party?"

A cheer of encouragement followed.

"Rico has supplied the necessary ingredients, hasn't he?"

Another cheer followed as most raised their filled glasses.

"The Irish like to drink too and I have a joke about them for you."

"Oh no, Slick," someone yelled. "If you have to be humorous, talk about those cars you sell. They're all jokes."

Slick shook a finger at the speaker and then continued.

Patrick O'Hara went to the same bar down on State Street every day at four and ordered three beers. He had done this for two years before the bartender asked him. 'Pat why do you order three drinks at the same time, line them up in front of you, and then drink them one by one? Why not order one, drink it, and then order another?'

Jack, these three drinks are not just for me. The one on the left is for my brother, Sean, he's in Canada. The one in the middle is for my brother, Timothy, in Australia. The last one is for me.

Jack, the bartender told all of the other imbibers what Patrick had said. Two months later, Pat came into the bar and ordered two drinks, which he consumed one after the other. Jack and all the others were shocked. Something had happened to one of Pat's brothers, they thought. Jack patted Patrick on the arm. "I'm so sorry, Patrick. Did one of your brothers die?

Oh no, Jack. They're both fine. I've just decided to give up drinking.

Most of the revelers laughed but some hooted and shouted insults.

"Just getting started," Slick said. "Lots more to come. Please take your seats. We have to get the show going."

It took the crowd ten minutes before everyone was served and had found their seats. "Ladies and gentlemen," Slick began. "The Wind and Sea is proud to present their first annual talent show and silent auction. And to headline this spectacular may I present the one and only Brigadier General Frederick Sutherland reciting his favorite poem, Gunda Din."

"Slick, you forgot to say, 'the Great,'" someone at a back table shouted.

The general slowly ambled to the stage in his loose-jointed way. "I've decided to change my program. However, I will recite the famous last three lines of Gunga Din by Rudyard Kipling." He stood ramrod straight with a pained expression and stared over the audience.

Though I've belted you and flayed you,
By the living Gawd that made you.
You're a better man than I, Gunda Din.

"And I've had many a man under me who would do anything for me. Even take a bullet intended for me."

"That's why you're called the Great," a wag on the left yelled.

The general ignored the taunt. "I changed my program because the next one, by that same poet, reminds me of me and the problems I've dealt with all my life." He cleared his throat and from memory continued.

If you can keep your head when all about you
Are losing theirs and blaming it on you,
If you can trust yourself when all men doubt you,
But make allowance for their doubting too;
If you can wait and not be tired by waiting,
Or being lied about, don't deal in lies,
Or being hated, don't give way to hating,
And yet don't look too good, nor talk too wise;

Sutherland continued for three more stanzas, finishing with,

If you can fill the unforgiving minute,
With sixty seconds of distance run,
Yours is the Earth and every thing that's in it,
And—which is more—you'll be a Man my son.

"My father read that to me when I was a boy and I've tried to live up to every one of Mr. Kipling's admonitions." Sutherland bowed to the audience.

"Give the general a big hand. Without notes; wasn't that marvelous?"

Everyone clapped loudly and there were no caustic remarks. Slick quickly announced the next act. "And now ladies and gentlemen the singing bartenders, Rico and J.C."

They had consumed a few drinks along with the others and felt no pain as they ran onto the stage, grabbed the microphone, and immediately burst into song.

On the road to Mandalay,
Where the flying fishes play,
And the dawn comes up like thunder,
Out of China cross the bay.

The harmony wasn't great but it was loud; some of the notes were off key both flat and sharp. They didn't know the next stanza so they invited the crowd to sing along as they repeated the one everyone knew. Everyone cheered as they returned to the bar.

Slick took the mike. "The bartenders, fellow residents. Don't you just love them?"

More cheers followed as the two men bowed.

"Now we have a treat for you, a two-act play by a local playwright and for his protection, he shall remain nameless. Arnold Myers will play Sir Basil; Chauncey Talbot, President Goodwin Oliver, and Mary Lee Hopkins will be Sir Basil's sexy secretary, Heather De Winter."

As the red velvet drapes parted, Arnold talked to his president on the left side of the stage. He was padded to look thirty pounds heavier, wore a long, black, formal jacket, and had a monocle taped to his head. Chauncey wore a plaid jacket two sizes too small with the sleeves threes inches too short. His checkered pants were three inches above his ankles. Mary, now eighty, was seated on the right side behind a desk. She was dressed in a cheerleader's short skirt with a letterman's sweater and wore a long, blond wig. There was an imaginary wall and door between her and the men.

Sir Basil: "They're ungrateful, Goody; all they do is complain."

Oliver: "I know and you've been like a father to them."

Sir Basil: "They're children and will have to be punished. I'm going to turn off their water. Let them drink wine."

Oliver: "But it's your wine, Sir Basil. You agreed to honor the contract, remember. Go after the trouble makers, Wellington, Krause, and Di Donoto. They're Nazis."

Sir Basil: "But I liked the Nazis. *Heil* Hitler. What does *heil* mean?" He stuck out his arm with fingers pointed.

Oliver: "It means 'hail' like in 'hail Caesar.'"

Sir Basil: "Eureka, Goody. That's it. No one challenged Caesar did they? From now on when I enter a board or employee meeting, I want everyone to stand, stick out their arms, and say, 'heil Sir Basil.' I will dictate instructions to Heather."

Arnold waddled across the room, opened the invisible door, and greeted Mary.

Sir Basil: "And how is my little pumpkin this morning."

Heather: "Lousy. I was up all night; gas. It was that damned Mexican food you forced me to eat."

Sir Basil: "Let me kiss you and rub your poor little tummy. I have magic in my fingers."

Heather: "I'm not in the mood. What do you want?"

Sir Basil: "I want to dictate to you, my little sun flower."

Heather: "Okay but don't try anything funny. And remember to pause at least three seconds between each word and no word over six letters unless you have time to let me look it up in the dictionary."

Sir Basil slowly dictated his instructions as Heather pecked on the typewriter with her right forefinger. He then grabbed her and tried to plant a kiss on her mouth, but the wig slipped and his mouth found nylon fibers instead of lips. He continued searching for her mouth, but managed only to move the wig until it was backwards. The crowd howled as he walked into the imaginary door and dropped to his knees, straightened the monocle and pantomimed opening the door. The band played a waltz as he danced to the president who clicked his heels.

Oliver: "*Heil* Sir Basil." As he stretched his arm, his jacket split down the back seams.

Sir Basil: "Think, Oliver. How can we make the residents at The Wind and Sea treat me with the respect I deserve?"

Oliver: "Just thinking out loud but you could try being nicer to them."

Sir Basil: "Goody, haven't you learned anything? Being nice is for nuns and Salvation Army people. Successful business men are never nice. Come, Oliver, think. To get respect you must instill fear."

Oliver: "We can't touch the food contract with the Smith Food Company and we can't cut off their water so let's pollute their air. Bring in a truck full of skunks and dump them in the courtyard."

Sir Basil: "Now you're thinking, Oliver."

The drapes slowly closed as the two men talked and waved their arms. Two hundred people clapped, booed, and hissed.

"Only the first act, folks. Wait till you see the second," Slick announced. "It's intermission, time for the silent auction, and a chance to dance to the music of Dave Henry and the Moon Dogs. If they haven't consumed all the booze, Rico and J. C. are waiting for you at the bar.

"World renowned and our very own artist, Francesca Di Donoto, is donating four of her oil paintings, famous Italian scenes, for the auction. These would sell for hundreds maybe thousands of dollars at any art gallery so don't be stingy and embarrass yourself. Also, Deborah Farrell will personally autograph ten pictures of herself with her late husband, Mark Chambers, and their dog, Wags. The auctions sheets, Francesca's paintings and one of Ms. Farrell's pictures are displayed on the table by the north wall. The high bidder's names will be read at the end of the party and they can claim their prizes at Ms. Farrell's table. I'll be back in twenty minutes, enjoy."

A crowd quickly gathered around the silent auction exhibits. Francesca's paintings were fifteen by eighteen inches and enclosed in aluminum frames. The seaport village of Portofino, the Trevi Fountain in Rome, the famous Ponte Vecchio Bridge over the Arno River in Florence, and Saint Peter's Basilica were brilliantly reproduced. The black and white photograph of Ms. Farrell, her husband, and dog, displayed in a wooden frame, was about twenty-five years old. Her husband smiled at her, but she looked straight ahead at the photographer.

Most of the people studied the prizes, but several elderly couples danced to the melodies of their youth: "Blue Moon," the Frank Sinatra favorites "I'll Never Smile Again," and "When I Was Seventeen." They glided to the music nearly as smoothly as they did fifty years earlier but without the flips and swirls they once easily managed.

Twenty minutes later and after belting a couple of drinks with his pals, Slick returned to the stage. "Show time friends and as promised another of my sterling jokes. A chorus of boos bounced off the ceiling. He ignored them and began.

"A priest and a rabbi were standing at the edge of a street with a large, hand printed sign, 'THE END IS NEAR, TURN AROUND' A young motorist in a sport's car slammed on his brakes and skidded to a stop.

"You damned religious people are always trying to cram your crazy beliefs down our throats," he said. "Take that ridiculous sign and shove it." He then sped away and a few seconds later they heard a loud crash.

The priest shook his head and turned to the rabbi. "You know, rabbi, I think we should change the wording of the sign to: 'STOP, THE BRIDGE IS OUT.'

The audience was more friendly this time; the cheers outnumbered the boos. Slick imitated Al Jolson and said, "You ain't seen anything yet, folks," while shuffling his feet and spreading his arms. After a few catcalls he continued. "We now have a treat for you, friends. Dee Leif has had her poetry published in the 'Ladies Home Journal,' 'Cosmopolitan,' and other well-known magazines. She will now read for you several of her shorter ones. Written while here at The Wind and Sea. Please, you drunks at that back table, give her the courtesy of shutting up. Dee."

Dee, a small, attractive lady, wore a black bejeweled jacquard jacket embroidered with gold tone flowers. She walked sharply onto the stage and placed her papers on the lectern. With her matching black pants she was dressed to perform at Carnegie Hall before formally dressed swanky people not in front of dozing, slightly inebriated, oldsters. She was an octogenarian but looked years younger. "Thank you, Tom. You're too nice to be called Slick and I won't. I was saving these to read to my granddaughter but you asked me nicely so here goes. The first one is called:

SMALL AMUSEMENTS

Lettuce, cheese and crackers
Cookies stashed away.
Puzzles, games, and videos,
Near enough to play.
No one ever told me,
This much could be okay.

Polite applause followed until she held up her little hand.

THE ORGAN

Better than the anthem itself,
I think I love the silent throb
When the last blended tone
Hangs liquid in the air.
Before the choir sits down.

She paused for a few seconds and then continued.

THE SEVEN STAGES OF WHEELS

The jogging young mother
Pushes her baby ahead,
The leashed dog trotting behind.

The abandoned tricycle
On the front lawn.

The teenager in the red car races past
Braiding through three lanes ahead,
While drivers clutch their wheels in horror.

The newlyweds washing their first car
That only they could love.

The motorcyclist roaring along
The traffic-jammed commuters.
The gurney for the quick trip to the hospital.

And finally,
The comforting four wheels
On the walker that prevents the dreaded falls.

"Now dear friends, please excuse me for quoting you. Do these sound familiar?"

"Is it Tuesday or Wednesday?"
"Why did I come here?"
"I can't hear you; my battery's dead."
"Not catfish again tonight."
"Where did I put my glasses?"

Dee bowed, grasped her papers, and with a straight back and head held high, she walked off the stage as an appreciative crowd applauded.

"That's a tough act to follow but our next performer will give it a try. Ladies and gentlemen, welcome Michelle Woodhouse."

A large, heavy woman in her late sixties stood and walked to the stage.

"With Sally at the piano, Michelle will sing Muzetta's Waltz, that famous aria from the second act of Giuseppe Verdi's opera, *La Traviata.*"

Michelle stood in front of the piano and clasped her hands below her bosom. Her full soprano voice shook the walls. It was a trained voice; maybe not up to Metropolitan Opera standards, but close. After the last beautiful note, the audience stood and shouted, "Bravo, bravo." Michelle acknowledged their praise with two encores, Mimi's song from the first act of Puccini's opera La Boheme and a medley from "My Fair Lady."

"Have we got talent or haven't we?" A smiling Slick murmured into the mike as the audience cheered. "Now folks we'll have another intermission for you to inspect the items in the silent auction, buy raffle tickets, and drink, eat, or dance. Be back in thirty minutes for the last act of our play and the names of the high bidders and raffle winning numbers."

Everyone moved around going to the restrooms, visiting other tables, dancing, or standing in the drink line. All were happy and animated including the little old ladies who seldom left their apartments. A few of them danced with men not known to them and felt just a tinge of long forgotten romance.

Tonight they were young and beautiful; tomorrow their eighty-year-old bodies would ache. Tonight it was wine and tasty food; tomorrow it would be pills, prunes, and oatmeal.

Thirty minutes later Slick fondled the mike and was about to speak when the biggest man at The Wind and Sea rushed forward with a steak knife and grabbed Slick. "No more jokes, okay," he said, brandishing the knife.

Slick dropped to his knees and begged, "Not even one? I have a good one about a judge, a milk maid, and a sailor."

"No not even one or you're shark meat," Oscar said with a grimace before he raised his arms, bowed, and returned to his table.

"Oscar Weber, friends. The new definition for ham."

During the applause a man whispered to Slick, who then announced, "A slight change in plans, folks. We've lost Sir Basil. We were going to the have the second act but instead we'll have the high bidders and the winning raffle numbers now and the last act afterwards. Francesca, will you please come forward?

"Give Francesca a warm welcome. Her pictures raised over seventeen hundred dollars for the fund."

Francesca walked forward and presented her oils to the four winners who were applauded by the residents as they returned to their tables.

"Thank you, Francesca." Slick paused while she exited. "I now will read the names of the ten winners of the pictures of Ms. Farrell and her family. She raised over eight hundred dollars for the employees. Please give Ms. Farrell a big hand." After a prolonged period of cheers and applause, Slick read the names. "Winners go to her table and Ms. Farrell will autograph each picture."

She graciously asked for their names and then signed the picture, "To my good friend Betty, Fred or Homer with best wishes. Deborah Farrell." She was the grand goddess again, smiling graciously to everyone.

Slick then read the winning raffle numbers. Moon Dog played while some danced. Fifteen minutes later Slick announced, "We've located Sir Basil. He went to his room on the third floor for a smoke. He's on his way back. It's approaching nine o'clock folks, bedtime. But first, the final act. I'm sure they're ready backstage, curtain please."

The drapes remained closed as the room buzzed. "Is he drunk? Did he forget his lines?" After ten minutes several residents started to leave; it was past their bedtimes. Suddenly the doors burst open as Abhullah Kadaffy, one of the maintenance men, entered. *"Messieurs, Dames,* excuse me," he said, mixing English and French.

Slick rushed to him. "Abby, what is it?" After a moment of animated conversation, Slick explained to the crowd. "Abby said he found a body at the bottom of the second floor staircase and he thinks the man is dead."

Steven Matteson, who sat at a front table, raced to the mike. "I'm a retired policeman. Everyone please remain seated. This could be a crime scene. No one can leave until after being interviewed by a detective. Mary, call 9-1-1. I'm going to the body."

"Everyone please remain calm," Rico yelled over the cacophony. "The bar will remain open until further notice. The band can't leave and has agreed to continue to play for us."

Steve and Slick followed Abby to the scene.

"It's Arnold Myers, our Sir Basil," Steve said. "He must have fallen down the stairs. The forensic people will have to determine whether it was an accident or murder. Abby and I will remain here." Steve tiptoed around the body. "Slick, please try to keep everybody calm."

"Steve, I'll take the names of the really frail people and let them return to their apartments. They can't remain in the Great Hall indefinitely without being affected seriously."

"Okay; don't let them panic."

Slick returned to the Hall and solemnly walked onto the stage. "Please be quiet." He waited until the crowd quieted down. "Arnold Myers is dead. Please bow your head for a moment of silence."

Within ten minutes an ambulance and a fire engine with paramedics arrived. They checked the body and confirmed that indeed Arnold was dead. Two uniformed officers who had been patrolling nearby soon arrived, followed by a detective who was briefed by Steve Matteson.

Steve led the detective to the stage and gave him the mike. "I'm Detective Blake McGee with the Santa Barbara Police Department and will be in charge of this investigation," he announced. "We won't know if Arnold Myers' death was caused by an accident or foul play until after the coroner makes his examination tomorrow. The crime scene people will come soon, tape off the area and do their thing. Please stay away from that staircase.

"We will allow everyone who lives here at The Wind and Sea to return to their apartment or cottage. But first you'll have to register your names and room numbers with one of those two uniformed police standing by that desk in the rear." Detective McGee pointed to the back of the room. "I will interview all guests who were seated at the center table in front. It shouldn't take long."

Besides the band members, there were only Deborah Farrell's two guests—her niece, Denise Thomas, and her husband, Jack who lived in Pismo Beach.

Blake wrote down their information and what time they had arrived at the party. "After the coroner's report we may want to talk to you again," he said. "Don't leave Southern California."

As a courtesy, he interviewed Deborah so she wouldn't have to wait in line. "I always enjoyed your movies, Ms. Farrell. They were much better than the ones they make today. Is it alright if I come to your cottage tomorrow about ten for further information?"

"Sure, Detective McGee. I look forward to it. And thank you for your courtesies." She gave him a warm smile.

Chapter 12

The Investigation Begins

Detective Blake McGee took Steve Matteson with him to the coroner's office.

Jake Conroy, Santa Barbara County's coroner for twenty years, had seen too many violated and mutilated dead bodies to remain completely sober. It never showed; but his daily consumption of Jack Daniel's bourbon neared a fifth.

"Blake, I have the crime scene report. Before I review it with you, tell me what you know."

"Jake, this is Steve Matteson, a retired L.A. police detective, who was present at the time of the incident. He's working with me unofficially."

Jake and Steve shook hands as Blake continued. "Arnold Myers' body was stretched out on the second floor landing. There was blood on the staircase so I presumed he had fallen down the stairs. Slick Jenkins, the master of ceremonies for the talent show at the old people's home—"

"Home for the young in spirit, Blake," Steve corrected with a smile.

Blake nodded and continued. "Slick said Myers had gone to his apartment on the third floor for a smoke. So I, with his wife, Carrie Boswell, went there. Sure enough there was a filled ashtray on the little table on the balcony. He must have had his smoke, walked to the staircase and then fell or was pushed down it. However, his wife said he always took the elevator. Why did he decide to use the stairs that night?"

"Maybe it was quicker," Jake said.

"No," Blake answered. "The elevator is closer and with everybody at the party it would have responded to his call immediately. His wife said he hated to walk down stairs; he had poor eyesight."

"Maybe the elevator was out of service."

"I checked and it worked perfectly," Blake answered. "We are asking everybody if there had been an 'Out of Order' sign on it that night. So far, no one has reported seeing it, but if you say this was murder then I'll bet a sign exists."

"It was murder." Jake reached in a drawer and slipped out a bottle. "Want a slug?" He held the bottle out to Steve.

"Why not," Steve said. "This place gives me the creeps."

The two Santa Barbara men were completely different. They were about the same age and both had served with the marines in Vietnam. Blake was in great shape with a full head of brown hair, tan, with keen eyesight; quick and vigorous. The coroner, Jake, was bald, overweight, and limped from a war wound. Both shared one ingredient, competence in their jobs.

"We know the time of death," Jake said, opening a drawer of the morgue freezer and pulling out a shelf with a body on it. "He left the stage approximately at eight-fifty and was found dead at nine-fifteen. We know the cause of death."

"The fall down the stairs," Blake interjected.

"No. He was dead before his body hit the stairs. See this deep gash in the back of his head? It was caused by a blunt instrument." Jake pointed to an indentation in Arnold's skull.

Blake and Steve looked and nodded. "How do you know that wasn't caused by the fall?" Steve asked.

"His nose was smashed and a broken arm bone was sticking through his skin. There should have been a lot of blood, but the forensic people discovered little. Also he was stretched out at the landing. A living person would have rolled himself into a ball to protect his head. He positively was dead before he fell." Jake pushed the body back in the freezer. "So we know the time and how he was killed, but not the why or by whom. That's your job; I've done mine. Death by person or persons unknown." Jake shut the freezer door.

"What was the murder weapon?" Blake asked.

"Something short and heavy, like a piece of pipe or a rock."

"Why short?" Steve asked.

"Because the ceiling height there is only eight feet."

"Could a woman have done it?"

Jake thought for a moment. "She would have to be strong and agile. I doubt if any living at The Wind and Sea qualify. They're too old and frail.

"But there were two female guests at the party strong enough: the soprano, and the woman guest of Ms. Farrell."

"Were there any fingerprints lifted?" Blake asked.

"No, none on the second or third floor doors to the stairs and none on the stair railing."

"So it was premeditated. The perpetrator took gloves with him—first-degree murder," Steve added.

The phone on a nearby table rang. Jake grabbed his cane and limped slowly to it. After answering, he listened and then said, "Thank you."

He didn't say anything until he came back to them. "That was one of your men, Blake. They've found the Out of Order sign. It was on the bottom of a trash barrel in the parking basement."

After a moment of silence, Steve said, "We now know the killer's movements."

The other men paused and waited for the revelation.

"The killer left the party shortly after Myers did. He left the Great Hall on the second floor, walked up the stairs to the third and waited at the top landing where he could hide in a corner. Arnold opened the door and walked to the top of the stairs where the perpetrator hit him, crushed his skull, and pushed him down the stairs. He then calmly walked back to the elevator, removed the sign, rode it down to the basement, ditched the sign in the barrel, and took the elevator back to the party."

"And he could ride the elevator down to the basement, ditch the sign and take it back to the second floor in seventy seconds," Blake said. "I know because I did it. I knew that sign was somewhere."

"So how long was the killer absent from the party?" Steve asked.

"Arnold announced he was going to his apartment to smoke. How long does that take?" Blake asked.

Steve shrugged, but Jake answered, "Five to ten minutes."

"Okay," Blake said. "The murderer waited for five minutes then walked up to the third floor landing. Assuming Arnold came to the stairs in another five minutes, I say the killer was gone from the party less than fifteen minutes."

Steve pounded a nearby table with his fist. "By God! The killer was seated at one of the front middle tables." He rubbed his hand.

"How come?" Jake asked.

"There was a lot of noise in the room, and only persons seated at one of those tables could have heard Arnold make the announcement that he was going for a smoke. There were ten at each table so we have thirty suspects."

"We'll start with those, but anybody could have seen him leave and followed. He was very recognizable by his Sir Basil costume," Blake answered. "And how about those that didn't go to the party?"

Steve looked around the cold room. "That's true," he said. "But I believe anyone sitting at those tables deserves special attention."

"I agree," Blake said. "Before the meeting tomorrow, I'll have my people list all the residents who missed the big event; we'll contact them later."

The next morning, the party goers seated at the three front tables the night before were asked to sit in the same seats and to be in the Great Hall by ten a.m. Deborah came early and took her place at the middle table. The others at her table included Roger Palmer and his wife, Victoria; Deborah's niece, Denise, and her husband Jack; Deborah's secretary, Karen O'Brien and her date; Oscar Weber; plus the poetess, Dee Leif, and her husband, Vern.

The Breakfast Club sat at the table on her left. It included: J. C. Wellington and his wife, Virginia; Mary Lee Hopkins; General Sutherland and his wife, Lucille; Reverend Glen Thompson, and his wife, Amy; Doctor David Morris; and Carrie Boswell sat beside Arnold's empty chair.

The table on her right was reserved for the performers: Slick Jenkins and his wife, Gail; Chauncey Talbot and his wife, Latisha; Enrico Di Donoto and his wife, Francesca; the soprano, Michelle Woodhouse; Steve Matteson; Rose Marie Dentz; and Maude Perkins.

"Thank you for being on time," Detective McGee said as he mounted the stage. "I assume you are sitting as you were at the party, right?"

Everyone waved.

"We'll do this as quickly as we can. Please remain seated until your name is called—except for a visit to the restroom," he added with a big smile. "Coffee, tea or soft drinks are available on that table in front of you. My associate, Sergeant Malloy, and I will be at the two tables across the room. To save time, please fill out the form provided and bring it with you to the table. You may talk to one another but please keep the noise at an acceptable level. We will start with the table on the left and continue until everyone who was at the party is interviewed. Thank you."

Blake gave them ten minutes and then called, "Mr. and Mrs. Wellington, please."

J. C. and Virginia, dressed in country-club casual clothes, walked with confident strides to the detective. McGee glanced at the form, which included their names, addresses, phone numbers, and the time they arrived at the party. "Mrs. Wellington, please sit at the other table and talk to Sergeant Malloy. I caution you both to answer our questions fully. The slightest detail could be important."

They would be asked similar questions. Their answers would be compared and if identical, red flags would fly; if different, further inquiries would follow.

Blake reached for his pen. "Mr. Wellington, how well did you know the victim?"

"Not before coming here and since, only for breakfast. We're both early risers and we're part of the Breakfast Club that meets at six-thirty."

Blake glance through a stack of papers, then asked, "Did you talk with him at the party?"

"Yes, we both sat at the same table, but not near each other, and he was on the stage part of the time. He commented that he thought his poetry was superior to Mrs. Leif's."

Blake studied Wellington's body language. "Did you hear him say that he was taking a cigarette break?"

"Yes, loud and clear, right before I went back to tend the bar. And so did those seated at the other two front tables. He was excited about his role in the play and wanted to get praise from all the tables, I think," Wellington said laughingly.

Blake paused. "Do you know if he had any enemies?"

"No. He was such a little wimp. I can't imagine anyone bothering to take him seriously or to fear him."

"Think carefully now, Mr. Wellington. Did you at any time leave the Great Hall?"

J. C. looked around the room and stared at his wife. "Yes, twice, and that didn't take long. I know what I'm doing."

Blake acknowledged the joke and smiled. "Did you dance much?"

"Yes," J. C. said eagerly. "We love to dance. Our generation did, you know."

"Thank you, Mr. Wellington. If you remember anything else, please contact me." Blake stood up and handed a business card to J. C.

After that fifteen-minute interview, Bake continued calling those from the first table, then those from Ms. Farrell's and finally those from the table on the right. He asked the same questions and the answers were similar. None had known Arnold before moving to The Wind and Sea except David Morris.

"Arnold said that I was his wife's OB/GYN about twenty years ago," Morris said. "I've delivered about three thousand babies and didn't remember, but he did. First time fathers remember every detail so I guess I did meet him before."

When interviewed, Rose Marie Dentz said she was sorry she'd teased Arnold so much. "He was so dumb and had such an ego, I just had to. It made my day," she said.

Some of the women thought him creepy and all of the men considered him a wimp. Nearly everyone heard him say he was going for a smoke.

His wife, Carrie Boswell had little to add. She'd used the restroom once and had danced with other men. "He was a good husband," she said. "He didn't get in my way or object to anything I did and he was an excellent dancer; a competent escort."

Blake noted that the word "love" was not mentioned.

Afterward Blake and Malloy headed to their offices to study the list of those absent from the party. Outside, Blake threw Malloy the car keys. "What do you think, Sergeant?" Blake asked.

"We've interviewed everyone that was at the party. None of them knew Myers except those in the Breakfast Club. With one or two exceptions the women are too old, frail, and not mentally able to plan and execute a murder. The murderer has to be one of the men we talked to today unless we find a candidate on the list of those absent from the party."

"Do you have any favorite candidates, Sergeant," Blake asked.

"The only person that had a motive was Carrie Boswell. I believe she was glad to get rid of her husband. He was a big, fat zero and embarrassing to her."

"How about Sir Basil," a smiling Blake asked. "He has a big ego and maybe the skit sent him into a rage."

Malloy shrugged. "No. He'll forget the skit tomorrow; he wouldn't dirty his own hands."

Fifteen minutes later they arrived at Santa Barbara's police headquarters, a two-story stucco building on East Figueroa Street. It was a busy day and took them twenty minutes to answer questions from other officers and fight their way through the mob of drunks and the resort city's other flotsam and jetsam that were waiting to be charged with crimes and misdemeanors.

They studied the list of residents who had missed the party. There were six single men, twelve single women and five couples. Blake and Malloy divided the list and began making calls for appointments.

Two days later they compared notes. Three single men, two single women and two couples were visiting friends or families. These had been contacted and their visits confirmed. All the other men except one were old, weak and sickly. None of the women were considered physically capable and the couples said they were together at the time. The one exception was big, strong, relatively young, Gunther Krause.

Lieutenant McGee called, and he and Sergeant Malloy visited Gunther later that afternoon. He met them at his apartment door with a handkerchief in his hand. "Come in at your own risk, gentlemen." Gunther gave them a weak smile. "But I'm almost over it."

"Our visits usually entail more risk than catching a cold, Mr. Krause. We'll chance it," McGee replied.

After they were seated and sipping coffee, McGee looked around the apartment. It definitely was occupied by a single man with sturdy furniture and void of decorative frills. A full bookcase covered one wall. Pictures of people and exotic scenes, artifacts and souvenirs from around the world filled the opposite bookcase. There was one picture of an attractive young woman with two small children.

"Mr. Krause, where were you on the night of Saturday, May eighth, nineteen ninety-nine?" Blake asked.

"Lieutenant, I was right here. I hated to miss the party but I had the start of a bad cold and didn't want to pass it around."

"Is there anyone who can verify your presence here?"

"No. They were all at the party, I guess. I watched TV until about ten then went to bed."

"Did you know Arnold Myers, the victim?"

Gunther paused and then smiled. "Yes, I do remember him now. He was a most vocal food complainer; I had to set him down on several occasions. Once he said that he could taste mercury in the fish. He really was a pain in the ass." Krause's broad face erupted into a smile. "Everything was either too salty, bitter, or tough."

"Ever get angry with him?"

"Angry? No. Upset? Yes, but he was too much of a joke to worry about."

"Do you know his wife, Carrie Boswell?"

"Sure. I'll bet she's glad he's gone. A few of the old geeks here have their eye on her."

"How about you?" Blake asked.

"Maybe, she could be exciting. And we need excitement around here."

After another thirty minutes, Blake and Malloy stood and excused themselves.

"I hope your cold is better soon, Mr. Krause," Malloy said. "We'll be in touch."

"He's a person of interest," Blake said to Malloy as they drove back to headquarters. "Gunther's a successful businessman and the food complaints didn't bother him, but I think something about Myers did.

"Time to summarize," Blake continued. "I haven't eliminated anyone, but let's start with Krause. He had the means; I saw some large, solid glass objects in his room, and he had the opportunity. There's no discernable motive, but see what else you can discover about him. Myers' wife, Carrie, needs further attention. And don't forget about Sir Basil. It's a stretch, but he's an egotistical, vindictive bastard who doesn't like being ridiculed.

"Let's find out everything we can about Arnold Myers. If his first wife is alive, find her. We know he had at least one child by her, find him or her too. Mrs. Boswell can tell you where to start looking."

Chapter 13

The Counterattack

On October 1, 1999, Sir Basil had an emergency meeting with Goodwin Oliver at the corporation's office in Los Angeles. It was a hot, smoggy day and Sir Basil was in a foul mood.

"That bunch of old codgers at The Wind and Sea, who in the hell do they think they are. That skit about me and Ms. De Winter was disgusting. My reputation and hers are at stake and I won't stand for it."

Sir Basil poured himself a cup of coffee. "Christopher Fowler, the new executive director there, has ingratiated himself with the residents and I don't want him involved in the coming crackdown; keep him out of the loop. But check with the three directors, Jasck Wilkins, Harry Foster, and Boyd Harvey we sent to replace Watts, Quinn, and Turner. Maybe they have made friends with some of the residents."

Sir Basil's face turned beet-red. "We can't afford to let slander go unnoticed. Have our lawyers checked the contract to determine what we can and can't do?"

Goody swallowed before answering. "They're working on it, Sir Basil."

"And has our investigator fully vetted J. C. Wellington, Gunther Krause, and Enrico Di Donoto?" he asked, waving his arms.

Goody nodded. "Almost completed, Sir Basil."

Sir Basil wiped coffee from his moustache. "They have a file on Arnold Myers too but we won't need that now, will we? Someone else took care of him for us."

"Sir Basil, that's a murder case. We shouldn't joke about it. Someone may get the wrong idea."

Sir Basil turned a sharp eye on Goody. "Are you criticizing me, Goody?"

Goody held up his hands. "Oh no, Sir Basil; just running up some caution flags; don't want the police nosing around."

"Okay, Goody. I want those damned reports here in two weeks. Then set up an emergency meeting with Watts, Turner, and Quinn. Also give our mole at The Wind and Sea a bonus of a thousand dollars.

*   *   *   *

October weather was not kind to Southern California. This year the smoke from raging forest and brush fires added to the misery of heat and smog. The four corporate officers gathered in RCW's headquarters' boardroom were sticky and unhappy. Sir Basil's one-hour tirade against the fair residents of The Wind and Sea had ended finally. "Goody, bring in the lawyers, Frank and Stuart, and Omar, our private investigator," Sir Basil ordered. "Let's see what they've brought."

The three men who had been waiting in the outer office walked in, nodded to all, sat down, and opened their briefcases.

Sir Basil wasted no time. "Frank, is the SEC going to file a complaint?"

Frank Carter adjusted his glasses. "I received an answer yesterday, Sir Basil. I'll read it.

'Our insider trading division has investigated the stock trading activities of a J. C. Wellington, Gunther Krause, and Enrico Di Donoto from May 8 to 10 last year, 1998. We found there was an orchestrated effort to short the stock prior to a negative announcement from The Retirement Communities of the West about the corporation's problems at its new community, The Wind and Sea, in Santa Barbara California. These men were residents of this community at the time of the incident. Our investigation shows that the financial and other problems of this community were known to the residents and to the general public. There is no evidence that these men received any information from either the officers or directors of the RCW. Therefore we have concluded that the men in question did not get their information from sources within the RCW Corporation.

We have turned this matter over to our criminal division to determine if funds were illegally obtained from the Teamsters and Longshoremen's Unions by any of these investors.

Sincerely,
E. Jeffrey Knight, Assistant Director, Insider Trader Division'"

Sir Basil slammed his fist on the table. "Damn! I donated one hundred thousand dollars to this president's campaign; look what his administration delivered. Stuart, what about the union angle?"

Attorney Stuart Millheiser cleared his throat. "I'm sure Di Donoto gave them the tip, but he had nothing to do with investing the union's money."

"What about that newspaper reporter?"

"For Christ's sake, Sir Basil; you know better. He won't reveal his sources. They're protected by law."

Larry, Diggs, and John looked at one another.

Sir Basil paraded around the room, shaking his fist at the window while his face turned redder. "God damn it. They made millions off of my corporation and the government's minions won't help me."

"Sir Basil, calm down," Omar Ghosheh, Sir Basil's private investigator said. "Forget the SEC. I have information about these three men; nothing usable yet, but if there's something in their past, I'll find it."

Omar was a Lebanese refugee who fled to the United States during his country's civil war in the 1980s. He had served as an intelligence officer in the army and spoke Arabic, French, English, and Hebrew. He worked as a waiter in an up-scale New York French restaurant where Sir Basil ate. Omar's language skills impressed Sir Basil, and he hired him as an interpreter. Omar had said to him, "Sir Basil, the Lebanese are descendents of the Phoenicians, the first world traders. Every Lebanese-American family owns their own business. We have many skills; use mine."

Later, Sir Basil gave him the money to start his detective business with the provision that Omar attend to his benefactor's needs first.

Sir Basil stopped pacing and sat down. "All right, Omar. I hope this is good."

"Gunther Krause, as chairman of the food committee, has caused you problems. That short-selling deal was orchestrated by him. He invested the least but is the one that brought that reporter into the mix. He made millions in Southern California real estate but lost considerable when the Sequoia Savings and Loan bank went broke in 1984; he was the chairman of the board and president. Fraud and money laundering were suspected but never proved. Chronologically, I know where he was and what he did except for the years 1965 and 1966. He seems to have disappeared those years. Also, he immigrated to the United States from Germany in 1957."

"What can we do to him? I mean punish the bastard."

"Sir Basil, unless I discover malfeasance during those missing years: there's nothing else. The savings and loan thing is a dead issue and—"

"Damn it, Omar, find something. He went after me and I won't allow that to go unpunished."

Omar shrugged and looked at his notebook. "I forgot, an informant told me that the police consider him a person of interest in the Arnold Myers murder." He shut his notebook. "I'll stay close to that."

"Wouldn't that be poetic justice if he would be charged?" A smile crossed Sir Basil's face as he wiped his mouth.

"Enrico Di Donoto is a different story. He's been a police suspect for a long time but they can't get enough evidence to take him to court. He started as a foot soldier in the old New York Pallandini mob and worked his way up to be the Capo di Capi of the New Jersey Mafia. The FBI and the local authorities know all about him, but he's too clever for them. I hear, and this not to be repeated, one of the residents is a FBI informant keeping an eye on him. I'll bet his phone is bugged. We should stay clear; treat him like he has poison ivy. If we get in the way of the Feds, we'll be in big trouble."

"I know J. C. Wellington has operated his investment business in murky waters for a long time, but most of his dealings have run through the statute of limitations. These three have skeletons in their closets but government agencies haven't found them and I don't believe I can, but, Sir Basil, I'll keep trying."

John Watts, the company's chief financial officer, jumped into the conversation, "Sir Basil, respectfully, forget revenge. We have bigger problems. Our stock is stuck at fifteen largely because of our problems at The Wind and Sea. We're losing close to two million dollars a year and food, labor, utility and maintenance costs continue to rise. That loss is not much by Wall Street standards but if we can't manage our latest, then our signature, community investors will avoid the stock."

"Changing from using the fixed, six-percent rental increases to one using the actual increases over the previous year will help, but won't be enough and will probably bring a lawsuit from the residents."

"Bring it on, we'll squash it like a bug," an excited Sir Basil shouted. "Won't we, Frank?"

"I'm not sure, Sir Basil. The residents signed the contact based on the old method. It hasn't been tested in court as to whether we can now modify it. Also, they have an ombudsman, the California Retirement Community Agency, CALCRA, and the California legislatures, Social Services Department on their side, plus Roger Palmer, a very competent lawyer."

"Bring them on. God damn it, who do those old farts think they're dealing with?" Sir Basil now drooled out of both sides of his mouth. "Water, please," he gasped.

The six men settled in their seats. Three lit cigarettes while the lawyers whispered to each other. Five minutes later, John Watts spoke again. "Sir Basil, we've cut services as far as we can without violating the contract. The answer is to increase revenue. I have two suggestions: promote the bar, open a community store, and—"

"I have better ones, but I'll have to ask the two lawyers to leave," Omar said.

Frank folded his hands. "Want us to leave, Sir Basil?"

"Maybe you'd better, Frank."

Stuart and Frank slowly stood and left unhappily. "Be careful, Sir Basil. Losing money is one thing; jail time is another." Frank Carter pointed at Sir Basil, then closed the door.

After the lawyers left, Sir Basil said, "Okay, Omar, what have you got?"

"I guarantee we'll have no problems with the police," Omar replied. "They won't be able to trace these ventures back to you, Sir Basil. John's suggestions are good, but what will the two of them produce? Maybe fifty to a hundred thousand dollars a month."

John Watts stood. "This talk makes me nervous. I don't think I want to hear what you're going to say, Omar." John pushed his chair in. "As the chief financial officer, I'd have to testify about any revenue received." He paused and looked directly at his boss. "I'll do anything for you but commit perjury, Sir Basil. It's best for all if I join the Stuart and Frank."

"Sir Basil," Omar began after John left. "For complete success Larry and Diggs here need to know what I do for this corporation besides investigations."

"I agree, Omar, proceed."

"I came to New York about ten years ago and settled into a walk-up flat on the lower east side. One of my neighbors was the Kadaffy family with a young son named Abdullah. He was a good-looking, very intelligent boy and I became fond of him. He spoke French and Arabic and I taught him English, but his main skill was mechanics. He could take an automobile apart and put it back together; he fixed everything that wouldn't work in the building—electric wiring, toasters, stoves, furnaces, you name it. When Sir Basil asked me to work for him I brought Abdullah with me. We "shortened his name to Abby and he's now at The Wind and Sea and works for you, Diggby, in the maintenance department."

"Yes, I remember him. A good worker, but the girls can't keep their hands off him." Diggby Quinn said with a smile.

"Abby has two jobs. One is to fix things and the other is to spy for me. Everyone who works for the corporation is under his surveillance from the executive director to the lowest hourly employee."

"What does he report?" Diggby asked.

"Disloyalty, dissatisfaction, incompetence, dishonesty, anything that would affect the corporation. But it's not all negative; he's best at discovering opportunities," Omar answered.

"One of the men who works with him in the maintenance department, along with three illegal Mexicans, are growing cannabis, marijuana, in the Los Padres National Forest and has asked for his help."

He abruptly changed the subject. "Do you know how much they get for this stuff?" he asked in an excited voice. No one did. "Twenty-two dollars a gram and that, if my math is correct, is about six hundred dollars an ounce." Omar exhaled.

"Their problem is water. They only have a few plants and are transporting water in ten gallon cans. They asked Abby for help so he inspected the site and checked a geology map. The area is in a valley at the edge of the Santa Inez Mountains and the water table is only twenty feet deep; with alluvial soil, drilling is no problem.

"Abby said he could get an old Dodge truck engine and rent a portable drill and rig the two together. Unless he runs into a rock formation he could drill to the water in two to three days. They now produce about a half a pound a day with their five plants. That's five thousand dollars, imagine."

Sir Basil's eyes widened as he quickly calculated the investment return. "The best cannabis seeds come from Amsterdam. I checked with a friend there and he informed me there are three different kinds: White Widow, Big Bud, and Super Skunk. The market price varies between twenty and thirty dollars for ten seeds depending on quality." He stopped and sat down.

"What are you suggesting?" Diggby asked.

"We buy a hundred seeds, the engine, the drill, and take over the project."

"What about the Mexican boys?" Larry Turner asked.

"We'll take care of them but they're illegals and scared of deportation; they won't say anything," Sir Basil opined.

"Where is this gold mine located exactly?" Goodwin Oliver asked

Omar had recovered his voice and answered, "It's only about thirty minutes from The Wind and Sea. Abby said you take the 144 to the 152 and go east to the Rattlesnake Canyon Road. Turn right, north, to the East Camino Cielo Road and turn east for about a half mile and look for an old, dirt logging or mining trail that is bumpy, but usable. Proceed on this for about a mile. Aby said it was a beautiful area with tall Ponderosa Pines and scrub oak tress that provide the necessary shade for the plants, which flourish best in temperatures between sixty-five and seventy-five degrees. Also its elevation is only one thousand feet and only occasionally freezes; seldom gets below fifty in the winter."

"This is your plan for increasing revenue?" Sir Basil asked.

"Yes, and we have a captive customer base at The Wind and Sea. Most of this generation smoked pot in their youth and enjoyed it; about half would do it again. Except for some of the single women they're affluent and can afford the drug. Of course we'll get customers elsewhere too. We'll laundry the money through that new store that John was talking about." Omar pointed toward the door.

Sir Basil looked at Omar and smiled for the first time. "Omar, you surprise me. You know that I've never participated in anything illegal. I'll fight the authorities, come right to the edge of stepping over the line, but—"

"Boss, you wanted additional income. Here it is," Omar said.

"Thanks, Omar. You said you had another idea?"

"Yes. The Santa Ohlona Indian Tribe has a gambling casino seventy miles from The Wind and Sea. I know the manager and have talked to him. He'll give us one hundred dollars for every customer we bring to the casino."

"How can he afford to do that," an incredulous Larry Turner asked.

"Because the average gambler loses three hundred and twenty dollars," Omar quickly answered. "But, Sir Basil, you'll have to change your rules and allow the buses to take them there."

"Consider it done," Sir Basil said. "How many of our residents will go?"

"The biggest bus holds thirty and I believe conservatively it will be filled twice a week. That's six thousand dollars per week, three hundred thousand a year and we don't have to launder the money. Indian casino gambling is legal and accepting a commission is too as long as we declare it on the income tax statement. We won't tell the residents about the deal."

"Gentlemen, I have another meeting." Sir Basil stood and grabbed his walking stick. "I agree to the casino contact, but not to the marijuana operation. Come up with some more ideas for additional revenue and don't anyone suggest a house of ill repute. I move to adjourn."

Everyone left, but Omar remained and made a call on his cell phone. A few minutes later, Goodwin returned just as Omar completed his call.

"Omar, how are you going to distribute the grass?"

"That's the big bonus. Abby will set-up a sales organization and sell it throughout Santa Barbara, Ventura, Kern, and San Louis Obisbo counties. The profits, in the millions, will be deposited in off-shore banks."

"Can this operation be traced back to us?" Oliver asked.

"No. Abby will be incognito; he'll wear a wig and glasses and add padding. The salesmen will know him only as Joe, or Pete, or Sam. He'll be the only one that will know about us and I trust him with my life. He owes me; I saved his family from deportation and gave him the chance to survive in America. He won't lead anyone to us." Omar cocked his head at Goody. "Are you interested?"

"Yes. Sir Basil doesn't want it for The Wind and Sea, but I do for me and I believe Turner and Quinn will want in too."

"Do you seriously want to be involved?" An incredulous Omar asked.

"Yes. More than anything else I've ever wanted."

"Okay but there is one more thing. Only Abby and I will travel to our little plantation. The grass will be wrapped in Mexico City newspapers so the clients will believe that's where it came from. This is a dangerous business. We're dealing with drug criminals who would kill for information. You must never discuss this operation with anyone, not even your wife. Understood?"

Goody agreed and started to walk away, stopped and returned. "I have one more question; one of Abby's jobs is to inform on The Wind and Sea employees, right?" Omar nodded. "Does he also tattle on the residents?"

Omar hesitated. "No, someone else does that. A mole. No more questions, please."

Chapter 14

Things that Go Bump in the Night

In October 1999, the full moon came two weeks before Halloween. The bright, Santa Barbara moon hung in the cloudless sky. It bathed everything outside in an effervescent glow. It was a warm evening and many of the residents sat on their private balconies or on the bigger public ones at the end of each floor. They drank coffee or smoked cigarettes.

At nine o'clock, shouting and pointing started at the back of the U shaped building and like a tidal wave it escalated to the front. A white human figure, a woman, shimmered in the moonlight and marched in cadence with an unknown beat. She moved slowly from the back to the front of the courtyard.

"It's Viola," someone screamed. "Viola Kushovich and she's in her wedding dress. Her suicide gown."

"Help me," the ghostly figure shouted. "Help me, I demand justice. Won't anybody help me?" As she shouted, she waved her arms and the reflected light bounced off her dazzling white dress as bright as if they were small incandescent bulbs.

"She's come back from the dead to tell us she was murdered," a big man on the third floor bellowed.

The women were hysterical and the men stunned. Everyone froze in place. "Please, someone help me. I did not deserve to be dead," she cried.

"Who was it?" A man asked.

"The meanest person in the world. It was . . . ." As she shouted the name, a burst of wind blew her large headpiece down across her mouth and the name was indistinguishable.

"Who?" everyone shouted in unison.

When she reached the front of the courtyard, she turned and waved. "I'll be back, please bring me justice." She sprinted down the walkway.

Several men ran to overtake her but she disappeared into the moon-drenched landscape.

"We can see for a hundred yards, she couldn't just vanish," one of the men said.

"She could if she was a ghost," another answered, blessing himself.

A scream came from the direction of The Garden—the euphemism for the Alzheimer building. The men ran toward it and were met by an attendant. "One of our patients is hysterical," she said pointing to the building. "Sandra Garfield said she saw a ghost through the window; a woman in a shimmering white wedding dress pointed at her. Some of these Alzheimer patients are rational at times. Sandra was recently admitted, is not badly afflicted, and I believe her."

"I do, too, because I've seen this apparition," a nearly out of breath, tall man gasped.

Few of the residents went to bed at their usual time; they gathered in groups in the hallways and in the common rooms to discuss this nocturnal phenomenon. Had Viola returned from the dead to accuse her murderer? Or was it an early Halloween trick? Or was someone or something trying to prod the police into reopening the case? Suicide, murder, or mysticism was the question debated that night and the next morning at the Breakfast Club.

"I don't know what to believe. She was pronounced dead and I don't believe in ghosts or zombies; people that return to life," Reverend Glen Thompson said.

"How about Jesus? You believe in his resurrection, don't you?" Mary Lee Hopkins asked.

"Our Lord, Jesus the Christ, was unique. He was the Son of God, who lived with men, was crucified, resurrected, and now lives on the right hand of God Almighty. Mary, I know you are not a believer and I pray for your soul every night."

Mary swallowed the bite of muffin in her mouth. "Thank you, Glen, but you, the pope, and all of Christendom could pray around the clock for me and it wouldn't change anything. My survival is dependent on being in the right place at the right time."

J. C. plunked down his fork. "Come on, you two. Neither of you is going to change the other's belief. I'm worried about our single ladies here at The Wind and Sea; they're terrified. First the Arnold Myers murder now this; they're keeping their windows closed, bolting their doors, and not going anywhere except in groups of two and three. Many of them and some of the men are demanding additional security at the gate and on the campus. Sir Basil will agree and charge the extra cost back to us and it will be excessive."

J. C. picked his fork back up. "Let's all relax. The mystery of the lady in white will be resolved in time and the current panic will seem like a joke."

David Morris broke his silence. "This recent episode is nothing but a prank. Why someone in his or her eighties would want to do it is a topic for another discussion." He shoveled more scrambled eggs into his mouth. "Less than a month ago, Arnold Myers was killed, and Halloween is coming in two weeks. A perfect time to amuse the inmates."

"I disagree," Rose Marie Dentz said. "I don't know if these two events are connected, but something is afoot, as Sherlock Holmes would say. I predict there will be more nocturnal events. Viola is dead. That wasn't a ghost parading in a white dress—that was a human being, presumably a woman, and it wasn't Viola who was much smaller. She now has our attention and the second act should be interesting."

General Sutherland stood and tried to straighten his bent frame. "I recall a similar situation. I remember it well." He marched back and forth in front of the table with his hands behind his back. "It was in Japan." He stopped and scratched his head. "No, no, it was in Germany." He resumed marching. "I was a bird colonel then; must have been in the seventies, maybe the eighties. It was a winter's night and bitter cold." He stopped and stared out the window, prodding his memory. "Yes, yes, I remember now. Did I tell you it was cold and snowing, bitter cold?"

The general again marched, his feeble body creaking with each step. "Our brigade was bivouacked in two parallel rows of wooden shacks. I was in a smaller building at the head of the rows. In the middle of the night my aide knocked. I think his name was Gene Pollard." He stopped and scratched his head again. "No, it was Andy Hood. Andy was a wonderful soldier. He would have given his life for me." He paused and stared off into the distance. "Where was I?" he asked, looking around.

"In Japan, no, Germany, in the middle of a cold night, I mean cold. It was snowing and somebody knocked to bring you a hot cup of tea," Rose Marie jested.

"No, my aide knows I don't drink tea. I'm a coffee man; have been since I was a plebe at West Point. I never recommend a tea drinker for promotion."

"My God, he's lost it," J. C. whispered to David Morris. "He belongs in The Garden with that Sandra Garfield who saw the lady in white."

The general marched on, wobbling back and forth. "Major Hood tells me an enlisted man is running back and forth between the barracks dressed in white, our Alpine uniform, and screaming something. I calmly dress and proceed outside in the bitter cold to confront the man. As soon as he sees me he salutes smartly. I return his salute and ask him why he's outside running back and forth. He doesn't reply and his arm remains in the saluting position. He's frozen; a block of ice.

"Several men come with blankets and we carry him to the infirmary. He lay there, frozen on a table still saluting me. My God, how my men love me." Sutherland staggered and grabbed the back of a chair.

Everyone in the room ceased conversation and concentrated on the Breakfast Club. "He's left us," someone said. "He's in Germany in 1970."

"Sit down, General. Let me help you?" David Morris rushed to the stricken man with arms outstretched.

"No, no," Rose Marie screamed. "Don't frighten him, be gentle."

The general reacted as soon as Morris touched him. Taller than David, the general wrestled the doctor to the floor, landing a blow to the stomach before J. C. and Glen Thompson subdued him.

"I've suspected it for sometime and now I know," Rose Marie Dentz said. "He has Alzheimer's. If you treat these afflicted calmly and with kindness, they become happy children. Scare them, like you did, David, and they become violent. Find his wife; I'll comfort him until she arrives."

Rose Marie guided the general to a chair, sat down beside him, and held his hand. "You're home now, General; everything's all right."

He laid his head on her ample bosom and cried.

"I've known it for some time," Lucille said when she arrived. "He's completely lucid and normal about half the time but . . . ." She paused and heaved a long sigh. "It's getting worse. There's no cure is there?"

"No, I'm afraid not. Alzheimer's slowly deteriorates the mind. I'm so sorry." Rose Marie hugged Lucille.

The next day, the general was taken to a specialist who confirmed Alzheimer's. Sutherland was placed in room 10 in The Garden wing next to Sandra Garfield. In The Garden, residents were locked in their rooms at night.

*   *   *   *

There was no moon this year on Halloween. It was as dark as the inside of a coal mine. The mood was subdued but many of the residents continued the tradition of romping from apartment to apartment saying "Trick or Drink." In fact, this year, the drinks were stronger and more were consumed. J. C. Wellington and his wife, Virginia, Gunther Krause, and Mary Lee Hopkins were sipping brandies in the home of Rico and Francesca Di Donoto when a blast of eerie music emanated from the courtyard. Discordant organ cords started at high C, and ran down the scale a full octave, then escalated back up again.

"The opening of the Phantom of the Opera," Francesca said. "It gave me goose pimples when I first heard it on stage in New York."

"It still does, Francesca, every time I hear it played," Gunther said.

Lights came on in all of the units. People rushed to their balconies and pointed in all directions to where they thought the sound originated. The opening bars to the "Phantom" continued for four refrains, then stopped. Several men ran around the courtyard, searching in the thick shrubbery for a device. In complete darkness many tripped on sprinkler heads or water hoses; several crashed into one another. "Without any light, it's hopeless. Let's wait until morning," a self-appointed leader said.

Christopher Fowler, the new executive director, was beseeched by the terrified older, single women. "I can't sleep; I'm so afraid," one said. "I double bolt my door and hang a cow bell on the handle," another cried. "Mr. Fowler, you must do something."

"Ladies, I've done everything. There's extra security on the gate and grounds. All the doors automatically lock at nine and we have teams of security men roving the premises from nine until dawn. I assure you no one from the outside is getting in."

"Then get Father Francis from Saint Anthony's to exorcise this place. It's haunted by the devil and the Father knows how to deal with him," one resident suggested.

"Ladies, I will have a meeting tomorrow with Lieutenant Blake McGee of the Santa Barbara Police Department and our own Steve Matteson, a retired police officer. I assure you, you are in no danger. Whatever this is, it's just a prank of some kind—an extended Halloween trick."

"Well, we don't want what happened to poor Viola Kushovich to happen to us, do we?"

"Ladies, she committed suicide," Fowler said.

"Are you sure, Mr. Fowler?" a nervous widow asked.

The next morning, three maintenance employees searched the courtyard, the grounds between the two wings of the main building and found nothing. "Whoever it was hid the device after dark last night and retrieved it before dawn this morning," one of them said. "It has to be either a resident or an employee."

"How could it be an employee?" another asked. "There are only five of them: two nurses in the intensive care unit, another to man the phone in the main office, an emergency maintenance man, and a security guard. Their whereabouts could be checked easily."

Steve and Blake McGee met with Chris Fowler the following day at ten. They were relaxed, thought Chris was distraught and hadn't slept for two nights. "I thought this would be a relaxing job—looking after the needs of the elderly. Instead, it's turned into a nightmare—a chamber of horrors. First a murder; now spooks that roam freely," Chris complained.

"Relax," Blake said. "We'll solve the murder and the spook is just one of your residents reliving his college days."

"It's a her, detective. A woman trying to tell us something," a haggard director said.

"Explain your nighttime security procedures," Blake said.

Fowler ran his hands through his hair. "All the outside doors are locked at nine p.m. A resident living in the main building can exit any door but has to come back in only through the front door, and a person is on duty there. No one is admitted through the gate unless he identifies himself and checks in at the lobby."

"How about the ground floor windows? Couldn't a resident exit and enter through them?"

"No, they're electronically secured and if opened just a crack after nine p.m., an alarm goes off. It's protection against burglary. All the buildings are wired including the ones for assisted living, intensive care, and Alzheimer patients."

"By God, we've got a cat burglar living here," Steve said.

"And probably a murderer," a despondent director answered. "Are you sure that Mrs. Kushovich wasn't killed and then pushed off the balcony?"

"No, Chris, Forensics is sure that the fall killed her," Blake said.

"Correction, Blake. It wasn't the fall but the stop that killed her," Steve joked.

"Damn it, fellows. This is no laughing matter." Chris said, trying not to smile.

"I and others are working on the Myers case and your night prowler hasn't committed a crime so we can't get involved there. I suggest you hire an extra security guard to roam your premises at night. I'm sure your mystery woman will soon tire of her nocturnal jaunts," Blake said. "Is there a room that Steve and I could use?"

"Take this one. I have to meet with a group of hysterical women."

After Chris left, Blake looked around the office. The previous director's personal effects were gone and replaced with a picture of a beautiful woman, presumably Chris' wife, and another of the same woman and two little boys. "He seems like a nice young man," Blake said. "I hope he survives here."

Blake fumbled around in his briefcase. "A new angle has surfaced on the Myers murder, Arnold's gambling. He regularly caught The Wind and Sea's bus to the Pokuchunga Indian Gambling Casino near Avila about an hour and a half from here. He preferred Texas Roll'em, a poker game, but evidently he wasn't good at it. Another who played at the table with him was Omar Ghosheh, a henchman for Sir Basil."

Blake paused to let the impact of this revelation sink in.

"Well, I'll be damned," Steve shouted. "The old fox could be involved in the murder after all."

"Woody Ferguson is coming from L. A. in a few days. He said he had new information on the Mark Chambers' murder and needed to talk with Ms. Farrell," Blake continued. "I hope he'll tell us whatever he's bringing."

"Speaking of Woody, I remember him telling me that he studied numerous pictures on a wall in Ms. Farrell's den," Steve said. "In two of them she wore a wedding gown. Do you suppose she could be the ghost running around here as an altar-bound bride? I know she played that role in several of her movies."

"This is a strange place. Why do you believe all of these prominent, notorious, and wealthy people came here?" Blake asked.

"I think it's a refuge," Steve answered. "An escape hideout. They've all lived busy, frantic lives and came here to live their last years in peace and quiet. But they're not getting it, are they? And many of the old and frail ones are so nervous and fearful, they could suffer strokes. I hope you're more successful in solving these cases than I have been in resolving the death of Ms. Farrell's fourth husband."

A few days later, Mother Nature added to the misery of the residents at The Wind and Sea. A five point five, on the Richer Scale, earthquake erupted along the Baseline Fault near Santa Ynez and Lake Cuchuma and only twenty kilometers northwest of Santa Barbara. The Wind and Sea suffered no discernable structural damage, but nearly every resident had pictures fall from walls, artifacts break, or food cans dislodge from shelves in pantries. Eight calls were made to 9-1-1 for residents who had either fallen, fainted or suffered strokes. The collective tension mounted as four after shocks rattled the campus over the next week.

Glen Thompson held an ecumenical service asking for the Lord's help during a time of stress and danger. "It can't hurt," he told the non-believers.

Chapter 15

The Coffee Klatch

"That's what I miss most about living here—a fireplace," Deborah Farrell told her confidant and lover, Roger Palmer. It was late November and the weather had turned bitter cold for Southern California.

"It dropped into the twenties last night and that's bad news for the avocado growers," Roger replied.

"Roger, Woody Ferguson, the Los Angeles detective, called and wants to see me again. When can you be here?"

Roger leaned forward on the couch. "Damn it. He's young; this is his biggest case, and he won't let go." He looked at his watch. "Tell him three o'clock."

Woody was prompt. And after Karen squeezed his hand, she led him into the living room.

Deborah, dressed in a form-fitting pink velour pant-suit, graciously offered him coffee, "Thanks, coffee would be great. It's freezing outside."

After Karen delivered the hot coffee, Deborah sat next to him, but Palmer remained standing.

"You may go, Karen." Deborah waved her bejeweled hand.

"Detective Ferguson, Ms. Farrell has nothing further to say to the police. She has answered all of your questions and I will have to protest any further visits," Palmer said.

Ferguson smiled. "Future visits may be necessary, Mr. Palmer. There have been two new developments, one good and one troublesome. We asked the manager of the Waldorf-Astoria, in New York, if a revolver had been found in room five-three-two in March of 1972. He said all rooms were checked for lost items and a twenty-two handgun was found on the tenth of March, 1972. The records showed that you had not left a forwarding address so the gun was placed in their lost and found storage."

Woody unwrapped the package he'd brought. "And here it is, Ms. Farrell. Please sign for it and I strongly recommend that you find someone else to keep it for you. You did sign an agreement that your home would be weapon free, did you not?"

Deborah nodded. "Yes, I did."

Palmer grabbed and inspected the gun before handing it to Deborah.

"Do you remember it, Ms. Farrell?" Woody asked.

She stared at for a moment. "It's kind of ugly, isn't it? I hated it then and I hate it now."

"Is that a 'yes,' Ms. Farrell?"

"It is and I'll find someone to keep it for me."

"I assume you now know that Ms. Farrell had nothing to do with the death of her friend, Hazel Sommers," Judge Palmer said.

Ferguson hesitated then leaned forward and looked directly at Deborah. "Do you know a Holli Logan?"

"Maybe—should I?"

"It might help. Evidently Hazel Sommers did. Ms. Logan came into our office two days ago with some disturbing news. She said that Hazel Sommers told her the day before she disappeared that she had lied to Detective Matteson about your whereabouts at the time of your husband's death. Hazel told Holli Logan that you were not with her at the time of the murder. That she didn't know where you were."

Deborah stood in defiance. "She's lying, Detective. Why did she wait so long to reveal this outrageous fabrication?"

"Until she knew that Hazel Sommers was in fact the Pink Daffodil, she thought she was just missing for some reason and would return. But when she knew that her friend had been murdered, she realized the importance of Hazel's revelation."

Palmer raised his arm when Deborah started to talk. "Ms. Logan's statement has no validity in a court of law. It is pure hearsay. Mrs. Sommers is dead; we don't know what she said. It's only Ms. Logan's unsubstantiated word—meaningless. And it is slander. If the police use Ms. Logan's slanderous statement against Ms. Farrell, I assure you, Detective, I will seek retribution for her, to the full extent of the law," Palmer threatened in a voice full of Biblical fury.

Woody slowly pushed himself out of the soft upholstered chair. "Thank you for the coffee, Ms. Farrell. If I have any additional news, I will call."

Woody took a long look at this gorgeous creature and heaved a big sigh.

"Good-bye, Detective. Keep warm," she said as Palmer remained silent until after Ferguson left.

"Want to tell me where you were when Mark was killed?" he asked.

"I don't know this Holli Logan or what her motive is. I was at Hazel's house the entire day Mark was murdered; just like I told Detective Matteson."

"Don't worry about it. They know Logan's statement is inadmissible." Roger's features softened. "Congratulations, you made a big hit at the talent show. The residents knew you only as a cold icon; an impersonal grand dame. They discovered you could be warm and friendly, and many of them changed their opinion of you. Now you must build on that beginning. You need friends here, people who will be on your side if you need them, and I know you can do it. Just play one of your charming, tender, motherly roles," Palmer suggested.

"Exactly what do you propose?"

"Invite a group of ten or twelve women in for a little social, a coffee klatch."

Deborah sat down and crossed her legs. "How do I choose? The ones not invited will not be happy about the rejection."

"Select the leaders' wives, also the ones at your table, plus the performers. I'll help you." He leaned over and kissed her.

On December fifteenth, Deborah's cottage was immersed in Christmas decorations. A perfectly proportioned Oregon fir touched the eight-foot ceiling and flames from green and white candles danced throughout the living room. Numerous Christmas cards crowded on the tops of the mantle and the baby grand piano. A four-foot high, fully dressed Santa, stood in one corner with a bag of presents at his feet. Bowls of fresh pink daffodils were scattered throughout the room.

Karen O'Brien greeted each guest with a smile and hug. "Ms. Farrell is so pleased you could come," she said to each. All were decked out in clothes especially purchased for this affair. Separates were the big favorite. Amy Thompson's was a white chiffon big shirt with metallic-threaded dots and black wool-polyester pants. Rose Marie Dentz sparkled in a powder blue cardigan top featuring delicate sheer ribbon embroidery with pearl accents, beading and herringbone pants. Mary Lee Hopkins was an exception. She wore a crepe dress with a flirty hemline that skimmed the body with princess seaming. Latisha Talbot's ebony skin encased in an Artic white silk dress accessorized with a diamond necklace and bracelet made everyone stare with admiration.

Karen introduced the guests to Ms. Farrell as two of the Wind and Sea's waiters served champagne, coffee, or tea. "Ladies, I am so happy that you accepted my invitation." Deborah clapped her hands together. "I thought it was time to get to know one another and talk girl talk. Let the men worry about the food or management problems; let's enjoy one another. Later we will sit down and have my favorite soup, a salad, finger sandwiches, and Danish."

Was she playing a role or did she really feel so warm and friendly? She was the consummate actress and one never knew—today the part was that of a congenial hostess. She didn't want to upstage her guests and wore a separate outfit similar to theirs. However, the single strand of pink pearls and her golden, elegantly styled hair made her unique—everyone else's hair ranged from gray to white, and their jewelry more simple.

The women arranged themselves into groups of three to five to discuss the good things about their children and grandchildren and the bad things about their husbands. Deborah flitted from group to group, joining in the conversations and complimenting each guest on her appearance.

The banter was lighthearted until someone mentioned the murder and the ghost. "I believe the ghost is somebody's granddaughter having fun scaring the crutches off us old folks," Lucille Sutherland said.

"That's an interesting thought, Lucille," Virginia Wellington remarked. "But I think it's one of us trying to make a point about our lax security."

"Or it could be the soul of that poor woman who committed suicide endlessly wandering around seeking salvation," Michelle Woodhouse, the soprano, said.

"Oh my God," Mary Lee Hopkins said. "You Christians with your souls, saints, angels, devils, and Holy Ghosts; won't you ever rise above that medieval, mythology crap?"

"You atheists have a right to believe what you want, which is in nothing," Michelle said to Mary. "But I have a right to believe what the good book teaches."

Latisha set her teacup down. "Come on, you two; don't spoil Ms. Farrell's party. Nobody ever wins a debate on religion—argue it in private."

After a moment of silence, conversation resumed. This time the subject was where to spend their next vacation.

Michelle turned to Deborah. "Ms. Farrell?"

"Deborah, please."

Michelle blushed and fanned her face. "Deborah, please tell us about your infatuation with pink daffodils."

Deborah smiled demurely. "Pink always has been my favorite color and I like the daffodil for many reasons; its simple and its brave. You know it can live in frigid or hot climates. I just admire this spunky creation. They're usually yellow, but the combination of this flower with the color pink is irresistible for me."

Virginia Wellington dabbed the corner of her mouth with her napkin. "Deborah, what was your favorite role?"

Deborah thought for a moment. "Oh, there were so many, but maybe Laura, the poor seamstress in the movie 'Think about Tomorrow,' is my favorite. Now ladies," she announced in a loud voice. "Let's go to the table for a little lunch and tell all about ourselves. We're going to be living together for a long time. Shouldn't we know one another better?"

After the cilantro and spinach soup was served Deborah said, "I'll begin. I was born in 1924 in a farmhouse just outside Sioux City, Iowa. My parents christened me Daisy. Can you imagine going to school with a name like Daisy Klinger?"

Everyone tittered at her self-deprecating joke.

"Soon after my high school days, I fled to Chicago from the farm and Sioux City and worked in a Woolworth store. I hated the job and the weather and soon boarded the Santa Fe bound for California where Lady Luck finally found me. I was working as a salesgirl in the cosmetic department at the Broadway Department Store in Hollywood when a distinguished middle-aged man asked for my help. He sniffed about twenty fragrances before choosing Chanel Number 5—I assumed it was for his mistress. I was wearing a name tag, which he noticed and asked for my phone number. At the time I was only twenty, a farm girl from the sticks with no experience with suave, rich men, but eager to escape from the department store." Deborah shrugged. "So I gave it to him not knowing if soon he would be asking another salesgirl for her fragrance opinion.

"He called and told me he was a movie producer and asked if I would care to audition for a role in his new movie, 'The Prairie is Endless.' I won the part, a small role in a horrible film. For the next few years I had several small parts in equally forgettable movies. My career was going no place until I met Pietro Molineri in Italy where I was making a spaghetti western movie. It was 1950 and . . . ." She lit a cigarette and looked around the table with a big smile. Her performance had been flawless with fluttering hand gestures, frowns alternating with smiles perfectly timed—it was Oscar quality. "Pietro directed me in several movies in Italy and then we moved to Hollywood where we made big, successful films—one was nominated for an Oscar.

"This wonderful phase of my life sadly ended in 1960." She stopped again and brushed tears from the corners of her eyes. "Poor Pietro died of a massive heart attack."

A sympathetic sigh rose from those assembled while she drank a full glass of champagne and struggled to overcome her momentary grief.

"He was a wonderful man who taught me everything about making movies and about how to live. Well, as all of you know, one can't feel sorry for herself. You have to pick yourself up and shake your sorrows off. Life must go on."

They all nodded remembering their own losses.

"A year later I met Randy Anderson, the tennis pro at my club. He didn't have a brain in his head, but he was fun. We went everywhere, Acapulco, Las Vegas, Cancun, you name it. I don't know what he was taking, but he was tireless. I was ready to call it quits when he died from an accidental overdose of a drug he was taking for anxiety." Deborah looked around at the women seated at her table. "I'm sure I'm boring you. Shall I quit now and let someone else relive her life?"

A loud "no" erupted, as expected, and she continued her monologue. "I was through with marriage or any relationship with men; my career was all important, but then a real prince came along, Rajai Habibe. He was rich, handsome, and a prince in the royal family of Saudi Arabia. I lived a fairy tale life, a princess flying all around the world in a private jet with dozens of servants."

She drank another glass of champagne and looked again at her admirers. "The excitement diminished and became boring and I wanted to live in the good old United States with Americans speaking English. I asked him for a divorce and he agreed without comment. He had girls waiting on every continent—he was ready to move on.

"I met and married Mark Chambers in 1975." She stopped and wiped an infant tear from the corner of her right eye. "You all know how that marriage so tragically ended and I really don't want to talk about it, thank you." The ladies sitting on either side of Deborah patted her arms and whispered encouragement into her ears.

After a minute of silence, Rose Marie Dentz said, "I hope I'm not out of line, Deborah, but we're interested in why you didn't have any children."

Embarrassed and shocked, the other guests looked away from their hostess.

"It's Rose Marie, isn't it?" Deborah asked. "A reasonable question that I have been asked many times— the answer is simple. My first husband was too old and involved in making movies. My second would have made a lousy father and I didn't want my third to father a child who would be raised as an Arab. By the time I married Mark I was too old to be a mother."

"Thank you, Deborah, God bless you. You do have a niece though, don't you?" Rose Marie continued.

"Yes, dear Denise. She lives in Pismo Beach with her husband and is expecting a baby. She so wanted one and as she is now thirty-five it came just in time. I'm so happy for her. My poor sister, she would have loved to be a grandmother."

"What happened to her, Deborah?" Latisha Talbot asked.

"Janet was two years younger than I and was my only sibling. Soon after college she vacationed in Italy, loved everything about that delightful country and stayed. Eventually she met and married Eugenio and they had Denise, my niece."

She stopped and drank another glass of champagne. "I'm sorry everyone; I think of my sister often. When Denise was five, Eugenio and Janet were on holiday in Sicily where they were killed in an automobile accident. Things were very tough in Italy in those days and Eugenio's family allowed me to adopt Denise and bring her to America. Since then she has had a full and active life living with me, her family in Tuscany, and in the best schools in Europe and America."

"I saw Denise at the talent show. She was delightful, and she looks just like you, Deborah," Virginia Wellington said.

"Yes, and so did my sister, and we both looked like our mother, very strong genes," the hostess answered.

"And if I may say, they are extremely beautiful genes," Amy Thompson said to which everyone clapped.

"Well, thank you, ladies. Now, enough about me; tell us something about yourself, Amy."

Each of the ladies gave a brief description of her life, her husband's foibles, the number of children and grandchildren she had and best wishes for their future lives at The Wind and Sea.

An hour after the last guest had departed, Roger Palmer visited. "How did it go, Debby?"

"Fine. Everyone seemed to have a good time," she answered. She paused as her face changed from a smile to a frown. "Latisha Talbot took notes from time to time. You know her husband, Chauncey, worked in the Justice Department in Washington for a long time."

Roger rubbed Deborah's shoulder. "That's probably a hold-over from her duty as an aide to her husband in the nation's capitol. Did the subject of Denise come up?"

"Yes, she sat with these ladies at the talent show. I felt I had to acknowledge our relationship."

"I know the police are checking all of the guests at that party. Denise will get special attention because the Pink Daffodil has been identified. Maybe others will be checking too, but Italy is far away and that was long ago." He then kissed her and pushed her down on the sofa.

Chapter 16

The Ghost

Every Wednesday at three o'clock little ninety-year-old Gladys Paulson joined a bible study group at Amy Thompson's apartment. Afterward, she said good-bye to her good friends and began her journey back to her home with the aid of a hickory cane. She held her head high and her shoulders square. Even though she was one of the oldest residents, she had one of the best postures at The Wind and Sea.

One particular evening, the group studied some of the parables of Jesus, and on the way home, Gladys contemplated the one about the "Prodigal Son." At the end of the hall about fifty feet away, a white apparition drew her attention. As the figure moved closer, Gladys' eyes dilated and her breath quickened. She dropped to her knees, blessed herself and recited the rosary, "Hail, Holy Queen, Mother of Mercy . . . ."

The radiant figure extended her right arm and touched Gladys' head. "My daughter, I bless you."

"Dearest Mother, I have such a pain in my right leg. Could you ease my suffering?"

The white specter moved her arm and touched Gladys' leg. "The pain has been driven from your leg. Rise and go in peace," it murmured as it passed by the still supplicant woman and exited down a staircase.

Gladys jumped to her feet, waved her arms, and ran back to Amy's apartment. "The Virgin Mary, I saw her. She's here at The Wind and Sea," she shouted to her friend as the door opened.

Amy grabbed her and led her back to the living room where four other ladies were preparing to leave. "Now calmly tell us what happened, Gladys, after you left here," she asked of her now shaking friend.

After a drink of watered-down brandy, Gladys did. "I saw the Virgin. I really did. The Virgin Mary is here. She was dressed in white—a wedding dress; it shimmered in the hall lights. She had long dark hair and her face was ivory color. Just like the paintings I've seen. There's no doubt it was Jesus' mother. She's the most beautiful woman in the world and she touched my leg. The pain I've suffered for years is gone." Gladys collapsed on the sofa.

*   *   *   *

Gunther Krause had helped Gladys in many ways. She always called him first when she had a problem and he made sure that her dietary needs were answered. The next day she called and asked him to visit. As soon as he was seated in her apartment she reverently told him about the visit of the virgin mother and the miraculous cure.

"Her eyes were so sad. She has suffered so much and yet she made the effort to comfort me. You know, Gunther, I'm ninety and it won't be long before I will be with her in heaven forever."

Gunther was not a religious man but didn't want to diminish what Gladys was experiencing. "Yes, Gladys, the Virgin Mary was telling you that you are special and God is waiting for you with open arms."

"Oh, do you really think so, Gunther?"

"Of course, Gladys. Are you coming for lunch today? The chef has made that delicious bread pudding that you like so much."

The next night the white apparition made another visit to The Wind and Sea." "Nurse! Nurse, come quickly," Sandra Garfield yelled from the Alzheimer's ward.

Nurse Ruth Pickens was used to such screams from this ward, and therefore slowly strolled to Sandra's room. She looked though the little, oval window in the door and saw Sandra Garfield sitting up in bed. Normally, she ignored a patient's pleas unless he or she were in danger. Tonight Garfield looked different, at peace and normal. "All right, Sandra. What's the problem?"

"I had a visitor—Virgin Mary, the Mother of God. She talked to me; she touched my head and has cured me of my disease. I want to be released. Test me."

Abigail had heard of Gladys' visitation and cure, and being a Roman Catholic, she couldn't dismiss this event without further investigation. It was a slow, boring night so she had time to humor the patient.

"All right, Sandra, name as many presidents of the United States as you can."

"I can name all who served in the twentieth century: McKinley, Roosevelt, Taft, Harding, Coolidge—"

"Okay, okay, very good, Sandra. Let's try some geography questions."

For the next thirty minutes Abigail asked questions about mathematics, locations of countries, and current events. Sandra answered them all perfectly. "I'll call your doctor tomorrow and have him come and examine you," Abigail said.

Apprehension flooded Sandra's face. "No! No, not him. He's one of them. He conspired with two of my children to have me committed here. I was railroaded for my money. For my safety, don't tell anyone in my family. Please call my lawyer, Craig Henderson in Los Angeles. And don't tell your executive director. I don't trust him either."

Abigail looked at Sandra. This was a different woman. Not the frail, scared little, elderly female that was brought here. This Sandra was a strong woman of the world, able to take care of herself, but Abigail had never heard of an Alzheimer patient being healed. *Is it possible the Virgin Mary caused this miracle?*

Gunther had promised Jeffrey Grainger that he would tell him first about any newsworthy developments at The Wind and Sea. He, J. C. Wellington, and Enrico Di Donoto had made a handsome return on their short position in RCW stock with Jeff's help and he felt honor bound to keep his promise.

Gunther met with Jeff a few days later in a local coffee shop and told him about the white figure's visit on Halloween, the recent appearance of the white Mother of God, and the two miracles.

"Thanks, Gunther. I'm going to have some fun with this. The Wind and Sea will become as famous as the Lourdes' Grotto. The Virgin of Santa Barbara will become as well known as the Virgin of Guadalupe."

"She really should be known as the Virgin of The Wind and Sea—she ignored the rest of Santa Barbara."

"You want to cause some excitement there, don't you, Gunther?"

"Yes. Our old hearts need some stimulation. And, I'd like to see how Chris Fowler and Sir Basil handle whatever happens."

"The Virgin Visits The Wind and Sea" headlined the *Santa Barbara News Press* two days later. The two-column report started with the suicide of Viola Kushovich, continued with the visit of the woman dressed in a white wedding gown walking across the courtyard demanding justice, and concluded with the appearance of an apparition dressed in shimmering white and proclaiming to be the Mother of God.

The White Virgin waved her hand and the lon- standing pain in Gladys Paulson's leg disappeared. She rubbed Sandra Garfield's head and her Alzheimer's affliction evaporated. The Catholics living in the community will ask Father

Donald R. Nuss

O'Malley, Pastor of Saint Vincent's, to start the process of having Rome designate The Wind and Sea *as a sacred site.*

The major newspapers in Los Angeles and San Diego sent reporters to Santa Barbara. The major TV stations rushed camera crews and reporters there as well. The City of Santa Barbara gave them permission to park their motor homes on the street. Vendors rented lawn space on the neighbor's front yards to display and sell medallions of the Virgin in copper, plated silver, and pot medal, rosaries, and bibles. Soon tour buses stopped and allowed their passengers to take pictures or kneel and pray.

Chris Fowler, the executive director didn't allow any of the reporters or sightseers admittance but a few climbed over the six-foot fence and had to be chased and forcibly ejected by the extra security guards that had been hastily hired. The residents could not legally be restricted, but as soon as they stepped or drove outside of the gates, their cars were blocked and the mob trapped them. The Wind and Sea was under siege.

Sandra's lawyer instructed her to not talk to anyone about her experience, but Gladys walked to the gate and eagerly embellished her experience to anyone that would listen. "There is no doubt in my mind that it was the Virgin. I have seen paintings of her in Rome and elsewhere and she looked exactly like them. I can still feel the touch of God through her fingers. I have no pain in my leg and am twenty years younger," she said with a rapturous glow on her face. Within days, articles and pictures of her, The Wind and Sea, and a reverent crowd were printed in weekly news magazines and newspapers in cities in North and South America and Europe.

*   *   *   *

Sir Basil called an emergency meeting. Diggby Quinn, John Watts, Larry Turner, and Chris Fowler sat glumly at the conference table while the boss paced the floor. "How could you let it get so out of control, so quickly?" Sir Basil looked directly at Chris.

"I talked to the two ladies within hours of their experiences. They were calm and didn't want any publicity. I thought the best approach would be to keep a lid on the situation and that it would go away. It would have if that damned reporter hadn't put it into the Santa Barbara paper. Then all hell broke loose."

Sir Basil rubbed his moustache. "What's the reporter's name?"

"Jeffrey Grainger," Quinn answered.

Sir Basil stopped pacing and raised his right arm with a closed fist. He sighed, then lowered his arm. "Him! Isn't he's the same one that worked with

100

Krause, Di Donoto, and Wellington in that stock caper that cost us millions a few years ago?"

"Yes, Sir Basil," the three officers said in unison. "But that's what reporters do when they get an interesting story."

"Oh, I'm not criticizing him. I want to know how he got the story? That's what we have to discover."

Sir Basil sat at the table and thought for a minute. "Chris, Steve Matteson, the retired Los Angeles and Santa Barbara detective, lives there at The Wind and Sea. He was in charge of the Mark Chambers murder investigation." Sir Basil snapped his fingers. "Ask him to help us resolve this woman in white situation. She's not the Virgin or a ghost; she's a resident. I'll bet my prize hunting dog on it. Give him anything he wants. He might enjoy being on the hunt again. Also, of course, have him find out who alerted the reporter."

Steve Matteson accepted Sir Basil's offer. The Wind and Sea had three investigations in progress: the reemerging Mark Chambers case with Woody Ferguson from Los Angeles talking to Deborah Farrell and Roger Palmer and picking Steve's brain; the Arnold Myers murder with Santa Barbara detective Blake McGee in charge; the Lady in White mystery with Matteson trying to sort it out. Could two or all three of these cases be connected? At least one of the detectives believed they were.

Chapter 17

Life and Death

Everyone liked Carlos Sanchez. His Spanish guitar and rich baritone voice were always available upon request. He was a strong, robust man seemingly in good health when he went for his annual check-up. Tenderness in his abdomen impelled his doctor to order an MRI, which found a dark spot on his pancreas. "It could be a cyst, a shadow or . . . it could be cancer," his doctor said calmly. "There is one test that can decide—an upper endoscope. The nearest lab that does this procedure is in Los Angeles. Please call them for an appointment immediately."

Two weeks later, Carlos received news that it was the worst, inoperable cancer. Carlos started a strong chemo treatment, which caused the loss of his thick reddish-brown hair. A knitted cap was now worn everywhere, and he ate in his room. He was optimistic and upbeat. "I'll beat this damn thing," he proclaimed. He continued to socialize, play his guitar whenever asked, and never let his warm smile wane.

Three months later his wife, Conchita, announced that Carlos had died peaceably and that his last wishes were for a celebration of his life. The Great Hall filled to capacity. Margaritas and beer were served as well as delightful Mexican fajitas, tacos and enchiladas. A five-man Mariachi band played for three hours. The highlight was a video of Carlos singing a few Mexican songs: "South of the Border," "Maria Elena," and others. He also had a message, thanking everyone for being his friend. His final words were:

Don't weep for me; I enjoyed life to its fullest.
I lived, I played, I sang, and I loved. I had the
best wife a man could have, three wonderful
children, and all of you as friends.
Gracias,
Adios, y Vayan con Dios

This proud generation had suffered through the depression, World War II, and the tumultuous aftermath. Most had received little from their parents, but gave all to their children. They had scraped the bottom and soared to the top and experienced everything in between. They were indefatigable survivors in a lifeboat sailing to that nearby shore. They suffered the waves of sickness and deaths of loved ones, but relished those moments in between when the affection of fellow residents calmed the threatening water.

*   *   *   *

Detective Woody Ferguson rushed to Detective Steve Matteson's apartment to share his exciting news. Steve poured two German Beers and waited for the young man to begin.

"I've been so frustrated with every lead in the Mark Chambers case becoming a dead end. Finally a breakthrough, I hope." Woody took a long swallow and continued. "Denise Thomas is Ms. Farrell's niece. Remember she was seated at Deborah's table at that ill-fated talent show. Supposedly, she was born in Italy, to Ms. Farrell's sister, Janet, and her husband Eugenio Alioto. We've worked with the Italian national police before and have done a few favors for them. Our chief asked them to find what they could about the Alioto's death and about the birth of their daughter, Denise.

"They were glad to cooperate because a big embezzler of a Rome bank is in the United States; they think he's in Southern California, and want our help."

"Two days ago, the Italians phoned and told us what they had found. On February 10, 1969, Janet and Eugenio Alioto were killed in a car crash on an icy road near the base of Mount Etna. They were driving from Palermo to Seracusa. That checks with what Ms. Farrell told a group of ladies. However, there was no mention of a surviving child. Eugenio was an officer of a large Italian bank and often in the news. His obituary mentioned no children and the *polizia* can't find any birth documents for a Denise Alioto. Denise was five in 1969, so she was born in 1964 and is now thirty-five."

Steve held up his hand and shook his head. "Hold on. You're going too fast. How do you know she was five in 1969?" Steve asked.

"Because Carrie Boswell told me and she got the information from a lady who was at Farrell's luncheon when she discussed her niece." Woody was hyperventilating with excitement.

Steve stood and walked around the room. "Want another beer?"

Woody shook his head. "It's obvious, isn't it? Denise is Farrell's child. An unwanted baby, raised somewhere for five years and then adopted by Farrell."

"Have you checked for a birth certificate?" Steve asked.

"Only in Los Angeles County and negative there. We're checking all the other counties in California, but she could have been born in other states or in Europe; it's nearly impossible to find the truth. Denise has accepted the story that she is Farrell's niece and has no memory of her first five years. She's lived in schools in America and Europe and with Ms. Farrell and maybe with an Italian family that claimed a relationship with her father."

"Okay. I agree, she's probably Farrell's daughter; so what. How does that help you with your murder investigation?"

"Aha, my dear Watson. Suppose Mark found out about Denise and was going to expose it. Farrell is at the peak of her movie popularity and in those days an out-of-wedlock birth would have destroyed her career. She kills him."

"Enjoy your beer for a few minutes. I want to think about this situation," Steve grabbed a cigar and walked outside. He walked around the campus, and ten minutes later he returned. "You have to sit on this knowledge, Woody. At least until you have positive proof. We don't want her or Palmer on the alert, and whether Farrell is the mother or not doesn't affect the Mark Chambers case. Find out the date of Denise's birth and then trace back where Farrell was nine months earlier. Who is Denise's father and why hasn't he come forward?" Steve asked softly.

Woody finished his second beer and started to leave. "You know, Steve, if we could get DNA samples from Ms. Farrell and Denise, we could solve the maternity issue. But I can't force them to give samples. Could you get them somehow on the sly?"

Steve smiled. "It's possible."

Woody headed to Carrie Boswell's apartment. His heartbeat accelerated with anticipation. "Calm down," he told himself. "I have to keep this relationship on a professional basis."

She welcomed him with a lingering hug and he had an impulse to pick her up and carry her to the bedroom. "How's the book coming?" He asked after discussing his options with himself and deciding on caution.

"Couldn't be better. Deborah's been a naughty girl. Two miscarriages that were really abortions, cheating on her husbands, and betraying a friend."

"Do you know the exact date of Denise's birth; it's important," he asked.

"What do I get if I tell you?"

Woody turned red and didn't answer.

"Oh, all right. I forgot you're on duty." Carrie reached over and grabbed some papers from her desk. "I was interested in that event too and I found an article in the L.A. Times' back issue morgue. It was about the sixteenth birthday party for Denise Farrell held at the home of her aunt, Deborah Farrell, on February 20, 1980. So she was born on that date in 1964."

"Very good. Now if you can get the answer to the next question I don't know how I could deny you anything," he said, throwing caution to the wind.

"I believe an officer of the law never goes back on a promise. What's the question?"

"Where was Deborah nine months prior to the birth, during, let's say April, May, and June of 1963 and who was she with?" He asked, hoping she couldn't answer at that time because his knees suddenly became rubbery.

She jumped up and looked through her stack of notes. Finding nothing she studied two books and a calendar. "I know where I can get your answer. Come back tomorrow at this time, I have friends at MGM where she worked during that period. I'll have it tomorrow, and, Woody, don't plan anything for the remainder of the day."

Woody didn't sleep well that night. If he kept his promise to her, he would be fired if his straight-laced boss, Captain Milford, found out, but if he didn't he would lose a great source of information. If he could solve this case his future would be bright indeed.

At three p.m. the next day, Woody rang, hoping she'd been called away.

"Come in," Carried called.

Woody wiped the sweat from his face and opened the door.

Carrie, dressed in a flimsy chiffon dress, jumped from her desk and reached for his hands. Woody willed his sweat glands to stop pumping hot, salty water into his shirt. Carrie went back to her computer; Woody followed.

"Were you able to get that information, Carrie?"

"You doubted me?" She winked at Woody. "Farrell was in London during the spring and summer of 1963 playing the feminine lead in Noel Coward's 'Blithe Spirit.'" She put down her paper and pouted at Woody. "Did you think I would fail you?"

Woody loosened his tie. "Of course not. You always deliver what you promise."

"Ready to respond to any request, Woody?" She licked her lips.

His sweat glands reengaged as he changed the subject. "Farrell was at her peak in 1963. I'm sure the Times in London followed her everywhere and reported what she did and who she was with. We'll have our contact there study the April through July 1963 issues of that paper."

"Better sources for that type of information are the London tabloids: 'The Daily Star,' 'The Mirror,' and 'The Sun,'" she suggested.

He grabbed her hands. "You're the best, Carrie, thank you. My glorious plans for the afternoon will have to change. I need to go, but I'll return as soon as I can. One more favor, please, ask your source to discover where Deborah was from July 1963 to March 1964." His legs once again gave him solid support as he hugged Carrie good-bye.

His spirits soaring, he decided to visit Steve again and accept an offer for a drink of his twelve-year-old Scotch. He passed many of the residents attempting to stretch their muscles and get some sunshine. Some used canes, others walkers and few in wheelchairs were doing imaginary lifts." *Poor old folks. I hope I'll never wind up like them.*

Steve was receptive to the company, and soon Woody was bringing him up to date.

"Farrell was born in 1924 so in 1963 she was thirty-nine. That's pretty old for a woman to have a baby, isn't it?" Woody asked.

"It is and you can bet the farm it wasn't planned. She thought she was past her child-bearing years and got careless," Steve mused. "But sometimes women get careless on purpose if Mister Right is involved."

"You're not suggesting that our goddess, the actress everyone worshipped, would do that, are you?" Woody joked with a big smile.

"Yes, I would, but you're certainly in a good mood today, Woody. You're making progress, but you have a long road ahead. Don't get too high because disappointment will sink you too low."

"Believe it or not my mood today has nothing to do with this case. It's another problem which I have to solve. Fortunately, it's been delayed for a few days." Woody drained his glass.

"Well, I accepted a new task after the executive director here begged me to take it," Steve said. "Have you heard of the woman that has been wandering around these premises?"

"Yes." Woody raised his empty glass. "Lucky you."

"Some of the residents think she's the ghost of the poor woman who killed herself by jumping off the fifth floor balcony; her name was Viola Kushovich" Steve continued. "Others think she's the Virgin Mary. I believe she's one of the residents having some fun. But it's raising hell around here with tour buses daily and reporters pounding on the fence."

"How are you going to tackle the problem?"

"I don't know yet."

"I know a black woman who claims she's a zombie. She reads chicken bones and says she can find lost souls and bring them in touch with their loved ones. Want me to contact her; she's cheap?"

Chapter 18

Puzzles

A rookie officer helped Woody sort through the electronic clippings sent from London's papers. The English editors didn't scan through the papers to find any reference to Farrell; they sent every page of their Society and Entertainment sections for the four months requested.

After four hours with many interruptions, the bristles on the back of Woody's neck erected. "Well, I'll be damned."

"What is it, Lieutenant?" the rookie asked.

"What we've been looking for. Here, read this from the Times."

Last night, Buckingham Castle was made festive indeed. It was bedecked for Queen Elizabeth II's annual Awards Dinner and Ball. The elite of Britain were there as were especially chosen dignitaries from around the world. Crown Prince William, the Duke and Duchess of Kent, Lord and Lady Chamberlain, and Lord and Lady Sheffield assisted the Queen with this time-esteemed ceremony honoring four gentlemen and one lady.

Pamela Louise Lasetor received praise from the Queen for her exquisite coloratura soprano voice and became Dame Pamela. Scientist Perry Lowry was knighted for his work in guided missiles and is now Sir Perry. Doctor Andrew Neall is now Sir Andrew for his discovery of a new medication for breast cancer. Doctor Robert Rostagno was knighted for his super human effort in trying to halt the spread of Aids in Africa.

Basil Rathbourn has received many awards for his humanitarian effort. Last night, the Queen elevated him for his leadership in the reconstruction of war-damaged London. "Arise, Sir Basil," the queen said as she tapped his shoulder with the ceremonial sword. "You did it in ten years—a remarkable achievement."

"Now skip the next three paragraphs. Read the last one."

In attendance at this gala event was the glamorous actress, Deborah Farrell, dressed in a magnificent Pierre of Paris' creation. Ms. Farrell is now appearing as Elvira in Noel Coward's 'Blithe Spirit' currently playing at the Savoy. It didn't take newly knighted Sir Basil long to notice Ms. Farrell. They were the most elegant couple on the dance floor and after several waltzes, fox trots, and sambas held hands at a table for two.

"Lieutenant, I don't understand why a homicide detective is interested in an American actress meeting an Englishman in London," the rookie asked.

"Twenty years ago Ms. Farrell was involved in the murder of her husband, Mark Chambers. Supposedly, she raised her niece, Denise, her sister, Janet's, baby, but we have found no evidence that Janet had a child. The child was born on February 20, 1964, conceived in the spring of 1963 when Deborah was in London. If Denise is Farrell's child, why did she deny it? And if her fourth husband, Mark Chambers discovered her secret and was blackmailing her—that's a motive for murder. One other piece of the puzzle: Ms. Farrell now lives in a retirement community owned by Sir Basil."

"The captain asked me to report to him as soon as I was through here, Lieutenant."

"Fine, thanks for your help, Rookie."

After she left, Woody paced around his office. His brain spun; questions tumbled around in his brain. Why would she want this foreigner to father her child? She'd just met him. She was at the peak of her career in Hollywood and she was not comfortable in the company of the stuffy upper-class Englishmen. And if not Sir Basil, who? In 1963, both Pietro and Anderson were dead, and she hadn't met the prince yet. What, if anything, did Judge Roger Palmer have to do with this puzzle and was Steve Matteson holding something back?

Woody knew Deborah's sister, Janet, and her Italian husband did not produce Denise. The Italian papers and the recording offices of all the big cities in Italy had been asked to check their files and a request was made to the Vatican to determine if a child of this couple had been baptized—all reported negatively. But where was Denise born and who was the obstetrician? Deborah returned to the United States in July of 1963. Where did she hide while she was getting fatter and fatter. Oh my God, I asked Carrie to find the answer? That means I have to see her again.

He stopped abruptly and a big grin spread across his face. "Yes, of course, that's it. Woody, you're a dummy." He snapped his fingers. *She used her maiden name. What the hell was it? We have to start all over again.*

*   *   *   *

J. C. sat across from Mary Lee Hopkins at breakfast one morning. "Mary, what was your opinion of Ms. Farrell?"

"She was a most gracious hostess, very friendly and open about her past life. Did you know her real name is Daisy Klinger and she was born in Sioux City, Iowa? She's been married four times to an odd mixture of men: an older movie director, a tennis bum, an Arab prince, and an actor. She and Rita Hayward were much alike. No children of her own but she adopted her sister's child, Denise."

"What happened to the sister?"

"Killed in an auto accident in Sicily."

The other members of the club had selected their juices, rolls and cereals and joined in the conversation.

"It was rehearsed," Rose Marie Dentz said. "Poor little girl from the sticks, trapped in a meaningless job in the big city, gets a break, meets the right man, and makes it big in Hollywood." Rose Marie rolled her eyes. "Heard it all before. Right on cue she cried when talking about the husband who got himself murdered. I could tell from her body movements that she playing a role in a movie. She'd done it all before."

Mary took a few bites of her eggs before speaking again. "I miss the general and Arnold. They were so much fun to tease. I wonder how the general is doing."

"I hear he's completely out of it," Glen said. "But a spark of his past must remain in his brain because I hear he marches around his room and gives orders to the walls. And at least once every hour he stands in front of his mirror and salutes himself."

"Speaking of Deborah Farrell, did you know she was becoming a substantial benefactor of The Wind and Sea?" J. C. asked.

"No. What did she give, more pictures of herself?" Rose Marie snorted.

J. C. turned and glared. "Why are you always so bitter, so acrimonious? Isn't there a drop of goodwill in you? For anybody?"

"My body is a tank full of the milk of kindness. My hand is on the spigot ready to let it flow on a worthy human being." She looked around the room. "Show me one."

J. C. ignored her. "She doesn't want publicity; her gifts are granted in private. I know she's paid the monthly fees for two of the single women who are in financial difficulty, and she's established and funded a scholarship fund for employee's children. She didn't have to do these nice things; no one asked her to, she just did them."

Rose Marie snorted again. "J. C., you're naïve. That woman doesn't do anything for nothing. She wants our goodwill; she's planning ahead."

Chapter 19

One Answer

Executive Director Chris Fowler slept so poorly and his wife complained so much, that he decided to temporarily move from his home in Dana Point to one of the guest rooms at The Wind and Sea. He knew how to operate a retirement community, felt comfortable with older people, and was satisfied with his staff and the amenities at The Wind and Sea, but that wasn't what he'd been doing. Instead of making them comfortable and happy he had to protect them from the hordes camped outside of the gate and fence. Two tour buses visited daily, the police patrolled the area, and reporters interviewed spectators, embellished their statements, and reported to the public on the nightly news.

Yesterday he wasted half a day with Monsignor Telford Duncan, a special envoy from the Santa Barbara Catholic Archdiocese. After Fowler explained Viola Kushovich's suicide and the two visits of the Lady in White in great detail, the monsignor asked only one question, "Were either Gladys Paulson or Sandra Garfield Roman Catholics?"

"No, Monsignor Duncan. Gladys was a Presbyterian and Sandra a Baptist."

"Thank you for your time, Mr. Fowler. I believe I have all I need."

Steve Matteson, after a week's delay, said he would attempt to solve the mystery. "I must work alone and I will discuss this problem only with you," he said to Chris. "Please tell no one about my involvement."

Chris accepted the terms and then timidly asked. "Detective, there is another problem. Perhaps you could help with that one too."

Steve nodded and listened impatiently as the director continued. "We have a very busy kleptomaniac living with us. Numerous items and cash have been stolen. Could you help me catch this geriatric thief?"

Steve burst into laughter. All the tension bottled inside him for months came tumbling out. Finally he shook his head. "No, Chris, I'll find your ghost. Have some of your security people round up your quick-fingered lady. It will be a woman, you know. Ninety-five percent of all kleptomaniacs are women."

After leaving Fowler's office, Steve decided to stroll around the campus, following the paths used by the nocturnal visitor dressed in white. It was a cold, crisp, late December day but his heavy, wool sweater gave him perfect protection against the near freezing weather. Most of the trees were bare but the pines and firs were full and brilliantly green.

Credit had to be given to Sir Basil, Steve thought. He did not stint on landscaping or know the names of all the plants, but did recognize the multi-colored roses, and the calla lilies, poinsettias, mums, and daises. Ono Watanabe, a Japanese gardener working nearby, would have explained to him that he also was looking at gardenias, tulips, amaryllis, and hellebores.

He took a good look at the campus for the first time. "It's lovely," he whispered to a small squirrel that peered at him while nibbling a pine nut. Steve sat at one of the benches placed every hundred feet along the path and reviewed the ghost's visits.

He concentrated on her movements. The first visit was during a full moon two weeks before Halloween. She started on the west side of the complex, the closed end side, and walked to the other end saying something like, "I want justice." She then walked across the road to the assisted living and Alzheimer's units, talked to a Sandra Garfield, an Alzheimer's patient, and disappeared.

Various scenarios tumbled around in Steve's brain. The second time, she was on the fourth floor of the independent living building walking down the hallway and scared Gladys Paulson who had visited a friend. She spoke to Gladys and cured a pain in her leg. She then passed her and exited down a staircase. A few minutes later she startled Sandra Garfield in the Alzheimer's unit and cured her of her affliction and disappeared.

Conclusion: unless she was escaping over a six-foot fence, she lived in either the assisted living or Alzheimer's unit. But Alzheimer patients were mentally incapable of planning and executing such an exploit so she must be in the assisted living unit, but they were physically impaired.

There was nothing he could do until she decided to visit again. *I'll be ready. I don't know where she'll start but I know where she will end.*

New Year's Eve 1999 was cold; frost covered the ground. But the mood was warm and happy; even Sir Basil would have been greeted with a hug. Chauncey Talbot and his activities committee had worked hard to plan a fun-filled gala party for all the residents. Geriatric merrymakers filled the Great

Hall. Some arrived with walkers; a few proudly propelled their wheelchairs, but most moved around without any support. A few coupled danced to the melodies of the forties and fifties played by Moon Dogs. The single women listened to the music, but thought of their youth, college love affairs, and long departed husbands.

At seven, J. C. Wellington walked onto the stage. With the mike in his right hand and a drink in his left, he made an announcement. "A Wind and Sea toast's to the new year—to baby boy, year 2000, to the beginning of a new millennium. May you grow to be a strong mankind to your parents and grandparents. Salute."

Everyone rose, lifted their glasses and drank.

J. C. continued, "My dear friends, may—"

The lights went out and the eerie chords of the Phantom of the Opera filled the Great Hall. "Don't forget me" a woman's voice said. "It's cold outside, but I must endure it in my search for justice."

Most of the elders remained seated, but a few men ran out the door, down the hall, and to an exit. "There she is," one man shouted. He pointed to the east where a feminine figure dressed in white was disappearing across the street toward the Alzheimer's unit.

She was opening a window when a big, strong man grabbed her. He ripped off the veil she wore and peered into her face, illuminated by the pale moonlight. "Sandra Garfield, you'll catch your death of cold out here. Why don't we go in the door?"

"I don't have the key. This is the only way in," she said calmly, but in a voice quivering with cold.

"Okay," he said as he assisted her over the sill, lifting himself in afterward. "Get into bed and pull the blankets over you and tell me what this is all about. I'm Steve Matteson, a fellow resident and a retired detective."

"What it's about, Detective, is vindication and retribution. My two daughters, aided and abetted by a greedy and sadistic doctor, forced me into the Alzheimer's unit against my will and without cause. I'm saner than every one of them. They wanted to be appointed conservators of my estate and bleed it dry."

Steve's heart went out to this spunky, small, eighty-five-year-old woman who had suffered the worst calamity that could be inflicted on parents—betrayal by their children. He admired her and wanted to help. "I thought all the ground floor windows were wired so an alarm would sound if opened," he said.

She laughed. "My late husband was an electrical contractor. I worked in his office and knew all about alarm wiring. I just shunted around the window."

"And it was easy for you to use the CDs and set a timing device to turn off the lights?"

"Very, so easy I could even teach you, Detective," she said with a big smile.

"Sandra, why did you take those nocturnal strolls in the moonlight in a white wedding dress?"

"Come on, Detective, that should be apparent. I wanted attention. No Alzheimer patient could have done what I did. It took skill and planning. I knew someone would catch me and I'm glad it was you because you know I don't have any kind of dementia."

He nodded in agreement. "Do you have any other children?"

"Yes, but he's a colonel in the marines, overseas and didn't know about my plight, no one told him and I couldn't. He would have stopped them and he's going to get all my money."

Steve sat down next to the bed. "Why didn't you put up a fight?" He asked.

"My damn doctor doped me. I was a zombie. I didn't know who or where I was until I recovered here. I could have tried to convince the nurses, but they're trained to ignore patient talk."

Steve looked around Sandra's small, white room and shook his head. "What are you going to do now, Sandra?"

"Sue! My two daughters, the doctor, and The Wind and Sea. That stupid executive director they had here then, Clive Huntington, could have helped. He could have investigated before agreeing with them, but instead he turned a blind eye to what was happening to me. I gave my attorney's name and phone number to the night nurse, Abigail Pickens and asked her to have him call. Would you make sure she does? His name is Craig Henderson. Please help me."

"I will, Sandra; I'll make sure he knows all about what happened. One more question. How did you hide that white dress?"

She thought for a moment. "I'll tell you, Detective, but let's keep it our secret; I want them to go crazy wondering about that, okay."

Steve nodded. "Okay, I'm on your side."

They brought my chest-of-drawers over here with me. It has a secret drawer where I kept my wedding dress. Can you spot it?"

Steve walked over to the chest and studied it for a few minutes. "No, I can't."

"I'll just keep it my secret for a while longer," she said with a far away look on her face, remembering the long ago date when she wore that beautiful dress at her wedding. It's best if you don't know for now."

"How do you feel?" he asked.

Sandra smiled. "Wonderful, never better."

"Do any of the residents know you?"

"No, I don't think so, only the nurses here."

"Want to go to a party?" he asked with a mischievous look. "Do you have a nice party dress in your things?"

"Yes to both questions. What do you have in mind?"

"Get changed. Wear your hair differently, put on some lipstick and makeup and we'll go to a New Year's Eve party. I don't have a date and you'll be it. I'll tell everyone you're my mother's sister visiting from Omaha."

She froze and a big smile spread across her ole but lovely face..

"Afterwards, I'll put you in a nearby hotel, and tomorrow I'll call your attorney. You need protection. We don't know what could happen to you here after your daughters and doctor find out about tonight. You could be in serious danger. As an officer of the law it's my sworn duty to see that you get that protection."

"Detective, do you remember Viola Kushovich, the one that committed suicide?"

"Yes, some of your fellow residents believe she might have been murdered," he answered.

She shook her head. "No, she killed herself. She was very unhappy with her son, Robert. He was forcing her to move from her apartment in the independent living building where she had some friends and move to the assisted living one where she had none. Why are some of our children so cruel to us during the last years of our lives?"

"I don't know, Sandra. It's sad that they abandon their parents, very sad."

"Please turn around, Detective. I want to get dressed and go to a party. It's been a long time since I've undressed with a man in the room."

She giggled like a teenager, and he laughed. "Don't worry, Sandra. My mother taught me to be a perfect gentleman."

Within two days, Jeff Grainger received the news. "The Wind and Sea White Angel is Grounded" greeted his morning readers the next morning. The crowds, the tour buses, and the police vanished. Everything disappeared— everything but the trash.

Chapter 20

Consequences

A convenience store on La Cumbre Avenue near the I-5 Freeway was robbed at two a.m. on the night of January 22, 2000. A silent alarm was triggered and the Santa Barbara police responded in time to catch the lone perpetrator, Juan Hernandez. When the identity of the twenty-two caliber gun was established, Lieutenant Blake McGee was assigned to the case. Immediately, he called Lieutenant Woodrow Ferguson of the Hollywood Division of the Los Angeles Police Department.

Juan was a young, good-looking Mexican-American man, five foot ten, one hundred and fifty pounds. Black hair covered his head and curled under his collar.

McGee pulled out a chair in the interrogation room. "Juan, you've never been in trouble before. Why now?"

"Señor McGee, my girlfriend is pregnant and I have no insurance for her. She is sick and needs help. I have only a little money so I did a dumb thing. I'm sorry; I wouldn't hurt anyone."

McGee studied this frightened boy and sympathized with him. "But, Juan, you had a gun and that makes this crime a felony." He shook his finger. "Very serious."

"I know, Señor McGee, but it wasn't loaded. Please help me." A tear rolled down Juan's cheek.

"No one was hurt and nothing was stolen," McGee said. "If you tell me the truth and the whole truth, I think I can help you."

"I will, I will. I'll tell you everything." Juan reached for the policeman's hand.

"Was anyone else involved with you in any way?"

"No, Señor. I planned it, studied the store and tried to rob it all by myself."

Blake thought for a moment, then leaned over the table and looked directly into the scared young man's eyes. "Juan, where did you get the gun?"

"I stole it, Señor McGee. I took it from a room at The Wind and Sea, a retirement community where I've worked since it opened."

Blake jumped up and walked around the room. "Do you remember which room?"

Juan scratched his head. "No, I'm sorry. Maria and I deep-clean each apartment and cottage every six months. I have been in every one of them at least five times. It takes a full day to deep-clean a unit; everything is moved and detailed and we don't even notice what unit we're in. We just spot, clean, dust, and vacuum. I saw the gun in one of the units and took it. None of the cleaning crews were questioned so I don't believe the theft was reported."

Blake's blood pressure soared sky high. The gun in question was a Browning .22 C Mark Contour Lite. The results of a test firing had been broadcast across the country and the Hollywood Division had responded immediately. This was the gun that killed the Pink Daffodil—Hazel Sommers.

"Juan, Sergeant Malloy and I will take you to The Wind and Sea and we'll walk through the place. Try real hard to remember where you found the gun," McGee implored.

They drove to the retirement community in silence. "All right now, Juan, don't be afraid; we'll casually walk through the place. We can't go inside the units, but if you see something that jogs your memory, let me know," Blake spoke softly.

After they had strolled about fifty feet, Juan stopped. "Señor McGee, I remember something."

With excitement in his voice the lieutenant responded, "What?"

"*La casa*—sorry Señor McGee, the home had many framed photos on the walls."

"Was it owned by a man or a woman?"

"I don't know. We have pass keys and most people stay away during deep cleaning; no one was home."

Two hours later, they returned to their car and drove back to the Santa Barbara police station. Juan couldn't remember where he stole the gun. "I'm sorry, Señor McGee. It was two years ago and the units all look alike."

"Okay Juan, you tried. Maybe you'll remember something later."

After he had poured himself a cup of coffee, Blake phoned Lieutenant Ferguson in Hollywood. "Woody, I didn't learn anything. Juan couldn't remember and I believe him."

"Thanks for the effort, Blake, but you *did* learn two very important facts."

Blake nearly choked on his coffee. "I did?"

"Yes, very important. The Pink Daffodil, Hazel Sommers,' murderer lives at The Wind and Sea and in a unit with many pictures on the walls," Woody answered.

"Discount that last item. These are old people and their walls are full of pictures of their children and grandchildren and snapshots of family get-togethers and vacations," McGee said.

"Not all of them. Some like to display paintings or decorative art works. Many of the units can be eliminated. We can't legally search those rooms so you'll have to work with the director there and get one of your policewomen hired as a cleaning girl. If the gun owner had one gun, he probably has two or three. Have her try to find them and the units with pictures on the wall. All the residents signed an agreement that their homes would be weapon free. And, by the way, I've been in Deborah Farrell's unit and her walls are loaded with pictures.

"I'll be driving to your lovely city next week on Tuesday. Let's have a meeting in your office and invite Steve Matteson. Say ten o'clock. Bring me up to date on the Arnold Myers murder, if you have anything. I believe Mark Chambers' murder may be connected to these others," Woody suggested.

*   *   *   *

The three police officers were alike but different met in McGee's office. All were proud men dedicated to their profession. Two wore their uniforms neatly, the third, Matteson, dressed casually in a Hawaiian shirt. He was the oldest with the most experience, but jaded by what he'd witnessed and knowing that the battle against the underworld would never be won completely. Woody, the youngest, was eager to win the ever-going war against crime. He would find a way to crack every case no matter how intractable. McGee had a master's degree in criminology from Stanford University and was working toward becoming a lawyer; Attorney General of the Justice Department was his goal.

They liked one another and for nearly an hour *bonhomie* and bad jokes prevailed. Finally, Steve asked Blake about the Myers case.

"We interviewed Wind and Sea residents. With a few exceptions they reported that a change had come over Myers; lately he'd become despondent and jittery. His wife, Carrie Boswell, said nightmares interrupted his short sleeping hours and that he wasn't eating much," Blake reported.

"When did this personality change take place?" Woody asked.

"Their stories varied but I believe the consensus was about a year ago, maybe less."

Steve laughed. "Maybe he was having trouble with a woman on the side."

The others appreciated his joke and after a moment Blake continued. "Three people, who sat at his table on the night of the talent show, told me something I think is important. He was on the stage most of the time, but when he was at the table he was jovial and seemed happy, then after the intermission he became nervous and irritable and badly needed that fatal smoke."

"What happened during the intermission?" Steve inquired.

"I asked that question," Blake said. "The Moon Dogs played music and several couples danced, there was a silent auction where people studied the paintings and other items and Deborah Farrell autographed her pictures."

"Did anyone observe what Arnold was doing?" Woody asked.

"Only that he bought one of Ms. Farrell's signed pictures."

Steve crossed his arms. "What was the subject matter of the picture."

"It was a black and white photo of Ms. Farrell and her husband, Mark Chambers."

Woody jumped out of his chair. "That's it. I don't know why but something in that picture triggered something in his brain that scared him. Something that caused his death. Chambers' and these murders are connected.

"He had other problems." Blake held up his hand to calm Woody down. "He had an ex-wife and a daughter living in Oakland in the Bay area—I interviewed the wife. It seems that while they were married he had serious gambling and drinking problems. Her name is Gloria and she said he reneged on paying his betting losses and received threats by phone and that he was severely beaten once. His daughter, Donna, now in her twenties, hated him and once threatened to kill him if he came near her mother again. I asked Donna why she hated him but she refused to answer; said it was too horrible to talk about."

Woody interrupted. "I believe we can forget the wife and daughter scenario, but not the gambling. We believe there are at least two Mafia members now residing in The Wind and Sea—none bigger than Enrico Di Donoto. Paul Ostrow and his wife, Yvonne, moved there recently and Paul's the one who came with his face in bandages. An FBI agent put a trace on him and found no past history. The agent claims he wasn't in an accident and that a plastic surgeon gave him a new face. The agent doesn't know for sure, but believes Paul is in a witness protection program. Retirement communities are a great place to hide these people. We have to get his fingerprints if they haven't been burned off. See what you can do, Blake."

"We have an agent inside now. I'll give her this new assignment."

Lieutenant McGee related the story about the gun and Juan. "I like the young man and want to help him. He made a mistake; he didn't want to hurt anyone. The gun he used wasn't loaded. I don't want his life destroyed."

"Then he has to be moved away from here," Woody said. "Whoever had that gun is a murderer and Juan is a threat to him—something could trigger Juan's memory and the killer can't take that chance."

"What do you suggest, Woody?" Blake asked.

"I met Sir Basil once. I believe if I ask him for a police favor, he'll move Juan to another of his communities. Far away, like his development in Del Mar, where he'll be available for any further interrogation or as a witness. He has to marry his girl friend so she'll be covered under the company's medical insurance."

"Did Gunther Krause have many pictures on his walls, Blake?" Steve asked.

"I really don't remember. I was too busy looking for a murder weapon the only time I was in his apartment."

Blake turned to Woody. "But doesn't Farrell have pictures on all walls, especially in her den?"

"She wouldn't be dumb enough to keep the gun, especially with Roger Palmer protecting her. Besides, I saw how she reacted to the gun I returned to her from the hotel. And why murder Hazel Sommers? She was her best friend who provided her with an alibi," Woody said.

Blake tapped his pen on the table. "We know two facts for sure," he started. "The killer or killers of Hazel Sommers and Arnold Myers live here at The Wind and Sea and quite possibly Mark Chambers' murderer does, too. Is it one person, two, or three?"

Woody thought for a moment before answering. "My gut, which has been right two out of three times, tells me that it's two. Arnold saw something in that photograph that got him killed and that picture was of Mark Chambers and Deborah. I don't know how Hazel's murder fits in, but I believe it does with a different perpetrator."

"How many residents live at The Wind and Sea, Steve?" Blake asked.

Steve, without turning his gaze from the window, said, "I anticipated your thoughts, Blake, and checked with the office. As of yesterday there were twelve in the Alzheimer's unit, thirty-five in assisted living, and two hundred and thirty-four in independent living, making a grand total of two hundred and eighty-one residents."

Blake cleared this throat. "The latest murder, Myers', took place in my jurisdiction. Sommers' murder weapon was also found in it so I'm assuming command of this inquiry. Any complaints, Woody?"

"Not for the time being. Maybe later, if we catch Sommers' killer here."

McGee nodded and then continued. "I believe we can eliminate the Alzheimer's and assisted living people all of whom have mental or physical deficiencies. I checked with the nurses in those units and none of their patients were physically able to commit the murders. In independent living, we can eliminate all the men above eighty years old and the women above seventy, agree?"

Woody folded his arms. "Yes, for the time being."

"In addition, fifty of the men below eighty have physical problems that eliminate them. Those that couldn't leave the party, race to the third floor, put a sign on the elevator, wait, overpower Arnold, and return to the party in fifteen minutes. Subtracting all of these categories we are left with eleven women and twenty-eight men as suspects, totaling thirty-nine resident suspects."

"Am I on that list, Blake?" Steve asked looking directly at the Santa Barbara detective.

Blake darted a look at Woody before answering. "Yes, Steve. This is an embarrassing situation for me, but you live here, are in the suspect group, and have no official capacity. I hope, though, you will continue to assist us with any information you may get."

"Of course I will, and you're absolutely correct in making me a person of interest."

McGee placed a piece of chart paper on the table. "Take those thirty-nine, add Denise and her husband, who were guests at the show, and we have a total of forty-one suspects. I'll write those names down the left side of this chart and name the columns across the top: (1) Know Sommers: (2) Know Myers; (3) Motive Sommers; (4) Motive Myers; (5) Opportunity Sommers; (6) Pictures on wall. Woody and I will have to interview these forty-one again and plot their answers on the chart."

"You missed 'Opportunity Sommers.'" Steve said.

McGee blinked several times. "Steve, don't you remember, we don't know exactly when she was killed."

Steve gave Blake a weak smile. "That's right, I forgot." He ran his hands through his hair. "That wasn't my case. I was busy with the Chambers murder and didn't follow it closely."

Chapter 21

The Town Hall Meeting

Sir Basil was scheduled to make one of his rare appearances to deliver an announcement of great importance at the next town hall meeting. Many past meetings had turned nasty when complaints and some off-the-wall comments from the residents got out-of-hand. The executive director, Chris Fowler, prayed that with the promise of champagne and desserts, today would not be one of those.

The residents were divided into two camps. One was fearful that Sir Basil would up the fees, eliminate the bus service, cheapen the food, or even close the facilities. The other camp readied to make an all-out attack.

Chris shook Sir Basil's hand when he arrived. "I don't believe it's a good time to deliver your announcement, Sir Basil."

"Nonsense," he replied. "I'll have them eating out of my hands."

"Then I suggest you stay out of the Hall until it's your turn."

"No, Fowler. I'll unobtrusively sit in the rear and listen. I'm sure it will be educational to hear my tenants' remarks and maybe I'll be able to help them understand management's problems."

"I'm sure you will, Sir Basil." Fear churned inside Chris as he stepped through the door.

"Welcome everyone," Chris Fowler began. "I will withhold my remarks until the end of the program when I introduce the chairman of The Retirement Communities of the West, Sir Basil Rathbourn. But first, we'll quickly have the directors' reports. Susan, will you please take the mike?"

Louise Le Claire grabbed the mike and began her report. "So far we've had a great month, only fifty complaints." She waited for the laughs and applause to stop. "I'm sorry, Mrs. Perkins, but my sources don't carry rutabagas and the turnips were too small; maybe next month."

Maude Perkins, with her wig on crooked and her glasses slipping down her nose, stood up and waved from the front row.

Knowing she had the audience's good-will, Susan slipped into another subject." We almost lost Chef Pierre last Tuesday. He almost walked out and we don't want that to happen, do we?"

"Nooo, what happened?" the audience bellowed.

"Chef Pierre is proud of his lamb stew. On Tuesday night, one table complained it was too salty, another said it wasn't salty enough. Another table grumbled it was too hot, another said it was too cold, and yet a third table growled it was both too bland and too spicy. When I arrived, he had taken an anxiety pill and was lying down before quitting. He said he would never make lamb stew again. Please fill out a comment card and beg him to make his delicious stew again.

"I know the dining room service is too slow, but we're working on it. We're advertising in the local papers, checking with the schools, and giving these young people thorough training. Please be patient. Thank you."

"Susan," Gunther Krause, chairman of the dining committee, stood up in the rear row of seats.

She recognized her friend.

"How much does it cost to advertise, fingerprint, vet through the police department, and train a new waiter?" he asked.

"About eight hundred dollars, Gunther."

"And how long do they stay with us?"

She paused and rolled her eyes upward. "About four weeks."

"Susan, Susan, a successful businessman first identifies the problem then solves it. Your problem is not finding or training these young people; it's turnover. The answer is to eliminate the undependable kids and hire older, more stable people, and pay them more."

Susan shrugged.

"I know, it's not your fault," Gunther continued. "Those geniuses in the head office won't let you, will they? They think that high school students are the answer and they're going to prove it no matter how much money they waste."

"I'm finished. Thank you." She looked directly at Sir Basil, waved to the audience, and rushed off the stage. The other directors hurriedly made their reports without making any controversial remarks. Normally, it took an hour for these reports; today only twenty minutes.

"Thank you, directors," Chris said after the last director left the stage. "Now it's time for our 'Question and Answer' segment. Let's do it quickly because I know we're all anxious to hear what our chairman, Sir Basil, has to say."

Maude Perkins stood again and waved her frail arm.

"Yes, Maude," Chris said. "Wait until Jean brings you the portable mike."

"My eyes are so bad I can't read the newspapers anymore and I've heard so many conflicting stories," she began. "Would you please tell me what happened to that sweet lady in white that blessed us with her presence a couple of times? Some say she was the virgin mother of Jesus."

"Maude, the lady in the white dress was Sandra Garfield, a patient in the Alzheimer's ward," the director calmly answered hoping that would settle the matter.

"But, Mr. Fowler, I thought that people who suffered from Alzheimer's were mentally and physically incapable of doing the clever things that she did."

"Mrs. Garfield actually was not suffering from that dreaded disease. She was in the Alzheimer's ward by mistake."

Maude suddenly filled with indignation. She stood on her tiptoes and shook her tiny fist. "That's horrible, Mr. Fowler. That poor woman; I hope she sues."

"She has, Mrs. Perkins, she has."

Chris knew he had made a mistake as soon as the words left his mouth and in panic tried to find another waving arm.

"How much?" one man shouted.

"I heard it was one million dollars," another thundered.

"Will the residents get stuck with it?" a third man asked.

Sir Basil stood and waved to Chris.

"Please be quiet," Fowler shouted. "Sir Basil will answer your questions."

At six foot two and dressed in a two thousand-dollar suit, Sir Basil was impressive looking. "Yes, ladies and gentlemen, Mrs. Garfield has sued but the suit is completely without merit. And we will resist it in court with our outstanding legal department. Her family and doctor had her incarcerated in the Alzheimer's ward; we had nothing to do with it." Sir Basil held up his hand. "Thank you."

"But, what if you lose?' another man barked.

"Not to worry, we are experienced in these situations, and I don't intend to lose." The Chairman waved and sat down.

The residents immediately became quiet and Fowler called on another woman. "Yes, Mrs. Leif."

"It may be my imagination but everything in my apartment is being moved around, my clothes, bric-a-brac, everything. Nothing is missing, just shoved here and there. I wonder if others have had this experience?"

A third of the women in the room raised their hands and agreed.

"The cleaning crews are doing exceptional work. We've hired some exceptional people lately," Chris advised.

"You may be right; the cleaning has been exceptionally good." Mrs. Leif sat back down.

Just when Chris thought the questions had ended, Oscar Weber jumped up. "Mister Fowler, what are you going to do about our very own kleptomaniac who is taking everything not nailed down?"

"I'm aware of the situation and have someone working on it, Oscar."

"He'd better catch the crook before I do," another shouted. "I'll kill him. I've worked for four months on my beefsteak tomato vines, fertilizing, trimming, and killing those god damn worms. Finally the tomatoes were big enough to pick and this demented person stole all eight of them. I dreamt about eating those big, ripe, mouth-watering tomatoes and I'm mad as hell."

Gunther jumped to his feet. "And she's stealing most of the hard boiled eggs from the Sand Castle. The cook puts about two dozen in a bowl and when no one is looking they disappear. She's not carrying them out in a bag; she must be putting them in her bra."

"Lumpy breasts; she should see a doctor," someone shouted and everyone laughed including Sir Basil.

"So that's where they come from," Gladys Paulson said. "Someone leaves a dozen eggs by my door every Friday. I change them into deviled eggs and bring them to the "Happy Hour" at four-thirty. I never asked, I just thought it was one of the party people—they love them and I like making them."

"Make some for me," a woman yelled.

Laughter rolled through the room.

"It isn't funny, damn it," J. C. Wellington bellowed. "I loaned our poker group my ivory chips. We decided to take a break and get a drink in the bar. When we returned twenty minutes later, they were gone. Fortunately we took our money with us."

"You're lucky," Mary Lee Hopkins said. "Everyone in the Tuesday bridge group puts a dollar in the pot for the eventual winners. It's left in the middle of the room. Last week someone stole the pot and the money while we were playing. Twenty-eight dollars."

Chris held up his hand. "I know The Wind and Sea has lost decorated bowls, artifacts, and even small pieces of furniture. Retired detective, Steve Matteson says that ninety-five percent of kleptomaniacs are women. Stopping this predator is high on my priority list; I promise you she'll be caught. Are there anymore questions or comments?"

Francis Pisano, one of the new members raised his hand. "Yes, Mr.—" the director stumbled.

"Pisano."

"Yes, of course, Mr. Pisano. What is your concern?" the embarrassed director asked.

"When I was young, like most of us here, I used to enjoy a joint now and then. Haven't smelt marijuana in a long time but once you've smelled it you'll never forget its sweet, pungent odor. The last couple of weeks I've smelled it in the halls of this building. What's going on? Is someone passing out samples?"

A buzz enveloped the hall. Some of the residents laughed, others frowning with disapproval.

"I don't know anything about this. Has anyone else smelled marijuana?" Fowler asked.

"Walk down the third floor at ten-thirty. Breathe deep and you'll get high," a big man in the rear shouted.

After the laughter subsided, Fowler continued. "Marijuana is an illegal narcotic. The police could close us down if this practice continues. Fair warning, anyone caught using this substance will be asked to leave The Wind and Sea."

"But Chris, it's legal in California with a doctor's prescription," someone hollered.

"That's right," several others yelled in support, with one wag adding, "And I'm seeing my doctor tomorrow."

"I will meet with our legal and medical people as soon as possible to determine how we should proceed." Chris paused and held up his arms. "That is all the time we have. Sir Basil has been waiting patiently and now it is my pleasure to introduce our chairman, Sir Basil Rathbourn. Please give him a big Wind and Sea greeting."

The applause was adequate, but not overwhelming .Except for Deborah Farrell who was most enthusiastic.

Sir Basil commanded their attention immediately, and the room became as quiet as an empty church. "Ladies and gentlemen," he began. "I am most happy to be here. Although apart, you have been in my heart and mind constantly. We, together, have suffered severe growing pains, but I can see from today's meeting that you know how to identify your problems, and with our help you will be able to solve them. I am as close as your phone; please don't hesitate to call. You are family. Each and every one of you is as dear to me as my brothers and sisters."

It wasn't said aloud but many murmured, "Bullshit."

"Your facility is the finest in our company. Congratulations; and the best is yet to come."

The applause this time was enthusiastic.

"This meeting has been long and I know the chairs are hard so I will cut to the purpose of my visit. You are living with one of the fine ladies of the twentieth century. Not only is she charming and beautiful, she is imbued with world-class talent, thirty-three successful movies to her credit plus five important Broadway plays. Most of the top leading men in Hollywood and New York fought to play roles with her.

"Twenty-two years ago she retired from acting, but that career has been replaced with another philanthropy. This lady, without any fanfare or publicity, endows acting schools in New York and California to help young, struggling actors and actresses learn their trade. She has set-up a trust fund to provide grants to children's hospitals in Los Angeles, Chicago and Dallas. Any actor or actress down on their luck gets a helping hand from the "Break a Leg Society" completely funded by this wonderful person.

"She loves living with you in this beautiful community and wants to help it reach its potential by improving your quality of life. Mr. Fowler, would you ask someone to help you mount the exhibit?"

Chris and a resident walked backstage and lifted a three-by-five-foot piece of cardboard. On it was a facsimile of a bank check. Everyone gasped; it was for $500,000, made out to The Wind and Sea, and signed by Deborah Farrell. The residents stood and applauded for five minutes. Several of the women raced over to Ms. Farrell and hugged and kissed her.

Sir Basil held a piece of white paper in his—hand. "This is the agreement, which Ms. Farrell and I have signed. May I read it to you?" They became silent and everyone listened intently to the chairman. "It is titled 'Charter Agreement for the Residents of The Wind and Sea.'"

I hereby grant in perpetuity the sum of $300,000, hereinafter The Fund, to be used to enhance "the quality of life" for the residents of The Wind and Sea.

It will be administered by a board consisting of a designee from Merrill Lynch, one from the music department of the University of California at Santa Barbara, one from Santa Barbara Department of Fine Arts and two selected by the residents of The Wind and Sea who will serve for two years. The Board's reasonable expenses will be paid by The Fund, which will be invested by Merrill Lynch in safe securities that pay the highest rate of interest. Additional sums will be added to The Fund from time to time to maintain its viability.

The purpose of The Fund is to make brighter—and happier in every way— the daily lives of the residents of The Wind and Sea.

Deborah Farrell

"This document is signed by Ms. Farrell and is dated February 17, 2000," Sir Basil concluded.

Everyone stood and applauded for several minutes. Deborah stood, and with her hands demurely clamped together, slowly walked to the stage. Sir Basil greeted her with a hug and a kiss on her cheek. She was beautiful and looked to be in her forties. Her golden hair dropped in wavelets to her shoulder. The blue in her eyes danced and matched one of the many rainbow colors in her multi-layered silk dress.

Sir Basil clasped his hands high like a fighter after a victory. He then handed her the mike as the crowd became quiet and she began to speak in her full stage voice.

"My dear friends and fellow residents, life is short and full of peril and unhappiness. Each of us in our own way tries to lighten the load carried by his fellow man. This agreement and fund is my contribution. It will allow you to hear the finest soloists, quartets, choirs, and small orchestras. Stimulating speakers will enthrall you with stories of their adventures and discoveries. If you want to hear and see a comedian or a magician, just ask. This fund is to be used to improve your quality of life. Maybe the addition of a soft ice cream machine or an espresso coffee maker would make you happy, ask The Fund's board and more than likely it will be yours.

"Life has been very good to me; I have been extremely fortunate and I want to share my blessings with you. Thank you for accepting me in your family and becoming my good friends."

It was a glorious climax; the women cried, the men cheered—it was an euphoric occasion. She remained seated as many of the residents walked by her chair to express gratitude and best wishes.

Sir Basil waited until all others had passed. "Deborah dear, may I escort you to your cottage?"

"I would be delighted. I hope you can stay awhile to reminisce about those long ago days. How many years has it been?" she asked.

He grabbed her hand and brought it to his mouth. "Thirty-six years, eight months, and fourteen days of longing and heartache."

All but two people had left the Great Hall. Roger Palmer started to leave, but when he saw Deborah with Sir Basil his legs became weak and he was forced to sit as his face turned ashen gray. He watched them leave, and pushing his mounting anger aside, he stood and slowly walked behind them. Another man remained until the room was empty. He then left by a side door and followed Palmer.

Chapter 22

Reminisces

Karen O'Brien greeted Deborah at the door, was introduced to Sir Basil, and then dismissed. "Take the rest of the day off, Karen, go to the beach and enjoy the sun," her boss said.

Sir Basil gave an approving glance as she departed. "I hope you won't be alone. That would be tragic," he said with a smile.

"Thank you for your concern, Sir Basil, but don't worry, I have someone anxiously waiting for me with a blanket and a beer." She waved and returned the smile.

Sir Basil sighed. "Ah, to be young."

"We were once, remember," Deborah reflected.

"Every minute," he replied. "Why did you leave without a word to me?" he asked.

She sighed and changed the subject. "Do you remember that lovely day in May 1963, when you took me in your sailboat across the lake on your Yorkshire estate?"

His face wrinkled into a big smile. "Yes, there was little wind and I rowed most of the way to a green, wooded glen on the side opposite Hollingscot. The muscles in my arms were so sore, I asked you to rub them."

"I was amazed at how strong you were. Let me see if you still have them."

He took off his suit jacket and shirt and showed her. "Next we opened that basket and filled two glasses with martinis from the flask we brought with us."

"I have a bottle of Beefeater's gin. Let's repeat the occasion."

"Do you remember how I like it?" he asked.

"Two ice cubes, gin and just a splash of vermouth." She winked and went to the bar.

"After we finished our drinks we stretched on the soft grass and let the warm breeze splash over our bodies," he said.

"And then you began to unbutton my blouse."

Sir Basil then stood, went to her chair, lifted her out of it, and carried her to the bedroom where laid her on the bed. He rolled her over and unfastened her exquisite silk dress, which he flung over the back of a nearby chair. Her bra quickly followed the dress. She quivered but did not restrict his exploration.

"My God, you haven't changed; you're as lovely as you were those many years ago." He continued to gaze at this beautiful creature while he removed his shoes and the rest of his clothes.

While kissing her passionately he removed her panties. His mouth and tongue first ravished her nipples, then inched further down until they reached her pubic hair. His hands gently rubbed the inside of her legs, caressing the most private part of her body She gasped with pleasure. He then entered her and began a rhythmic motion thrusting deeper and deeper into her. She moaned and whispered yes with each thrust. The whispers became louder and louder until he again covered her mouth with his.

They climaxed simultaneously and remained intertwined for several glorious moments, until exhausted, they rolled onto their backs.

"Just as it was then." She sighed. "You haven't aged a bit."

Sir Basil drew her close. "I never forgot; how could I? It was perfect then, it was now. We had a month of exquisite fulfillment. Why did you leave so suddenly without even saying good-bye?"

Deborah toyed with his chest hair. "For many reasons, but primarily your mother."

He waited for her to continue. After a few seconds, she did.

"She represented the type of woman she wanted you to marry. A regal English woman from the landed gentry. From a rich, powerful family that mixed with royalty and the movers and shakers of the realm. She knew you would never be happy with a showgirl from Hollywood of all places, and your father would not have approved either. The men folk in your family had married such women for three hundred years. You couldn't be allowed to break with that tradition."

"But I would have made that decision, not they."

"No, you are a victim of tradition buried deep inside you, in your genes. At the end, you would have agreed with them. Your wife had to be a regal, handsome and graceful woman. Every bone in her body made to be the wife of a Rathbourn. Always dressed perfectly for any occasion, hair set in the latest style, educated at the finest schools, using the Kings English, never uttering the wrong word. I was born on a farm in Iowa and didn't even finish high school. The make-up people on the sets taught me all I know about clothes.

I could have been your mistress, but never your wife. What we had and have is wonderful, but that would have faded as man and wife and you would be sorry you married me."

She stayed in bed with a sheet over her as he quietly dressed. "May I see you again?" he asked plaintively. "I must, you know."

She nodded. "I would like that and I want you to meet my niece. She's married and expecting a child. She lives near here in Pismo beach. I'll arrange a dinner party for the two of us and her and her husband, Jack. Would you come?"

"Yes, I would like to meet her very much."

"And Basil, you are the main reason I moved here. I hoped you would visit me sometime. What took you so long?"

"I wanted to, but the way we parted, I was afraid you didn't want to see me."

"Well now that ice is broken, you know I do."

He laughed. "We didn't break the ice, we melted it."

Cottage number seven was the last one on The Wind and Sea's property. Its bedroom windows had an uninterrupted view of the ocean. Deborah never drew the shades in this room. One man knew this and was in position when Sir Basil carried Deborah and laid her on the bed.

*   *   *   *

A cold and rainy in March, Deborah scheduled the dinner party. Sir Basil arrived with his signature tweed jacket protected by a Savile Row tailored overcoat, his signature bowler hat, and a dozen pink roses.

Karen greeted the Englishman. "I've seen those hats in the movies, but this is the first I've ever touched one. It's cute. They're all in the living room around the fireplace. Please follow me."

Deborah hurried toward him, grabbed his arm and waltzed him through the room. "Denise, Jack, this is my friend, Basil Rathbourn, known by everyone Sir Basil. I first met Sir Basil over thirty years go in England. Basil, this is my niece and her husband."

Sir Basil greeted both of them, then handed the flowers to Deborah. "I remembered that this was your favorite color."

"They're lovely, Basil. Thank you." She buried her face into their soft buds. "We waited for you to have our first cocktail."

Deborah passed the bouquet to Karen. "Would you please bring a martini with Beefeaters and a splash of vermouth to our guest, Scotch on the rocks for Jack, and glasses of Chardonnay for Denise and me."

"This is London weather. I thought Southern California was always sunny and dry," Sir Basil said as he studied Denise. She was a lovely young lady, so much like her aunt. Her four-month pregnancy did not diminish the charm of her small ears and dimpled chin. Her hair was styled differently from that of Deborah's, but it was as golden as her aunt's and the texture was the same. Take away those extra pounds and their statures were identical with Denise being two inches taller.

Sir Basil directed his attention to Denise's husband. "Why Pismo Beach, Jack? There's not much there."

Jack accepted his Scotch from Karen. "It's a delightful beach, completely unspoiled. My father used to take me there to dig for those huge Pismo Beach clams. They're gone now, but the fish and California lobsters remain. I'm in charge of an oil storage and shipping facility in Avila, which isn't far away."

"Sounds like a perfect place for a retirement community. What do you think, Deborah?" Basil enquired.

"Perfect, except it's isolated and finding sufficient help would be difficult," she answered.

After two cocktails, the group went to the dining room where the conversation continued.

"When did you first meet my aunt?" Denise asked Sir Basil.

"Over thirty years ago. Deborah was playing the lead in a revival of Noel Coward's play 'Blithe Spirit' in London. I attended with a friend and was awestruck by your aunt's talent and beauty. After the last act, I went backstage and introduced myself. She graciously accepted my invitation to dinner and we became good friends. What year was that, Debby?"

Without hesitation, the hostess answered, "The spring of 1963."

Denise thought for a moment. "Thirty-seven years ago; a year before I was born."

No one spoke for a moment until Deborah asked the two waiters, provided by The Wind and Sea, to serve the dessert. After the final course, they retired around the fireplace.

Sir Basil looked at Deborah. "It's not raining and I'm so full, I need a walk. Would you care to join me, Debby?"

"Yes, I need some exercise too," she replied.

They retrieved their overcoats and hats from the hall closet and braced themselves for the weather. After walking for five minutes on the path that circumscribed the development, Sir Basil stopped and grabbed her hand. "She's mine, isn't she?"

Deborah turned and looked directly into his eyes. "Yes." She closed her eyes and sighed. "I wanted to tell you, but I couldn't."

"That's the real reason why you left so suddenly, wasn't it?"

She nodded. "I told my staff and people in Hollywood that I was exhausted and desperately needed a vacation on doctor's orders. I used my maiden name, Daisy Klinger, and booked a flight to New York where I boarded another plane to Omaha, Nebraska and then a bus to Sioux City, Iowa. My mother welcomed me with open arms and I stayed with her until I had fully recovered after the birth. I called the studio once in a while and told them I was at a resort in Colorado." She reached for Sir Basil's hand. "I was afraid that if you knew you would have wanted me to abort. I couldn't do that to a child of yours.

"The publicity of a child out of wedlock in those days would have ruined my career. My sister, Janet, couldn't conceive and she and her husband were glad to adopt Denise. I traveled to Europe often to spend time with my child. I had her with me when they were killed in that automobile accident. I adopted her and brought her home as my niece."

He wrapped his arms around her and held her close. "I'll soon be a grandfather," he shouted to the darkened sky. "Does Denise suspect?"

"She's never asked, but I don't believe the news will surprise her."

"Shall we tell her now? I want to get to know my daughter and new grandchild as soon as possible."

Deborah smiled through her tears. "Yes, now is as good a time as any and I have some champagne on ice."

It rained and they arrived home wet, but with happiness exploding from every fiber of their bodies.

"That must have been a good joke," Jack said as he observed their smiling faces.

"Not a joke, but rather good news," Deborah answered. "Karen, you and the waiters may leave as soon as the dishes are in the washer, and thank you."

After they left, Deborah retrieved the glasses and filled them with the bubbly. She'd played many roles, but none quite like this one. She struggled to control her emotions and her voice.

Denise and Jack remained quiet, knowing something important was about to be spoken.

Deborah set down her champagne glass. "Denise, my most happy moments have been spent with you. You are the joy of my life. I've waited patiently for many years for the right moment to make this announcement." She hesitated and gathered inner strength. "I'm your mother—I hope you don't hate me for lying to you."

Denise rushed to her mother and threw her arms around her. "All of my prayers have been answered. I've always hoped that you were my mother.

Someday, but not now, you must tell me why you couldn't acknowledge me sooner; I know you had good reasons. I am so happy."

"Before you raise your glasses, I have one other announcement. Denise, meet your father, Sir Basil Rathbourn."

Stunned, no one moved.

Sir Basil's heart nearly stopped with what he considered a rejection.

"Perfect," Denise said finally. "Every girl's dream is to have a tall, handsome, rich father."

Basil stood and hugged his crying daughter. "I just found out too. I wish I had known you from the day of your birth. You will not be disappointed in me; I promise. Give me a chance to prove myself, daughter dearest."

The first bottle of champagne was emptied and another popped. Jack didn't say anything, but enjoyed the happiness that floated throughout the room.

"We must keep this news secret until we know exactly how we want it handled. The newspaper and TV reporters will be camped outside your doors, Denise and Basil, and leaning on the gate to this community.

Fear lined her lovely face. Her long held secret now was known to her family and soon would be to the public. How would it accept it? How would their lives be changed?

"The Mark Chambers murder is being reinvestigated and the police will be wondering how this mother-daughter relationship changes their previous conclusions. Our lives will be turned upside down if this information becomes public. It's none of their business," Deborah said. "Please don't say a word."

They all agreed to her cautionary request and finished the second bottle of champagne. Denise and Jack used Deborah's extra bedroom for the night, but Sir Basil had to return to Los Angeles.

While they celebrated in the living room, one of the waiters, who had stayed behind, secretly collected useful items. In the bottom of a large trash bag he carefully placed the glasses, napkins, and silverware used by Deborah, Denise, and Basil. From the hall closet, which was hidden from the living room, he vigorously rubbed a tissue on the inside surface of the bowler and lady's hats, and from the powder room he collected used tissues and hairs from brushes and combs. No one in the party saw him leave.

A happy Sir Basil retrieved his Mercedes from the guest parking area near cottage number seven. Within fifteen minutes he entered the south bound on-ramp and joined the light traffic on Highway 101, the Pacific Coast Highway. A large, dark-colored car soon joined him and stayed about two hundred feet behind. For the next thirty miles, through the towns of Summerland and Carpinteria, the highway widened and straightened. Near the Ventura County line, however, it was no longer carefree and uninteresting;

it became a driver's nightmare with a slick, 90-degree turn around the edge of a beautiful bay.

As Sir Basil entered this big turn, straining to see and fighting the wet road, the dark car accelerated, came alongside his, and rammed it from the side. Sir Basil lost control, and the Mercedes broke through the wooden guard rail and plunged fifteen feet down a rocky slope into the pounding surf of the Pacific Ocean.

Chapter 23

Love and Busy Fingers

A retirement community was a small town with all its blessings and faults. Everyone knew everyone and each person was concerned for the health and well-being of the others. Factual news and false rumors traveled from one end of the community to the other at the speed of light. Nothing was broadcast quicker and with more enthusiasm than suspected romances.

It had been the wisdom of the ages that physical attraction and romance between the sexes slowed at about age forty and stopped completely somewhere around seventy. Except for the occasional death of one spouse or the other, the couples at The Wind and Sea remained stable and predictable. There were no divorces or wife swapping. However, with Hollywood's influence, women's liberation, and the advent of Viagra, that old adage was no longer valid with the single men and women. With few exceptions, the healthy, viable, and ambulatory females were not content to spend the rest of their lives alone. The males, except for a few, did not pursue their counterparts with the vigor and aptitude that they did in their twenties, but if healthy, they did pick up on any vibes sent to their antennas.

Joe Larsen and Carol Staszak were both in their late seventies and neither had been married. Both were shy, quiet individuals who enjoyed their own company. He played the piano and took long walks; she had her collection of antiques. They didn't join any activity group nor have regular dinner partners. They sauntered back to their units alone as soon as any meeting or meal was completed. Everyone believed they just wanted to be alone and ignored them. Why were they so isolated? Were they always like this or was a rejection in high school, or college, or the work place so painful that they decided not to chance being scorned again? Or did a love affair end so badly, they were making sure another romance would never get started?

At first, the other residents tried to integrate them into the ongoing social activities, but they refused to join. They wanted to be alone,and soon the others acquiesced to their wishes. When it started, no one knew, perhaps they didn't either. But in the third year, they ate dinner together and they were seen walking back to her unit. There wasn't an announcement, but everyone knew they were going to get married. And they did, by a justice of the peace. The marriage probably did not make Guinness Book of Records but the marriage of two people, never married before and nearly eighty should have had at least an honorable mention. Joe and Carol waited a long time to find a perfect mate, and at their ages they had a good chance of honoring their mutual promises of "Until death do us part."

Cynthia Thompson and Richard Kramer had an unusual story-book romance. They were in love when both were students at the University of Southern California in 1942. During the war, they drifted apart, he into the navy and she into war production. Both married other partners and had children, but they never forgot each other. She wore a necklace he had given her and he kept a picture in a photo album of them together.

After long marriages, both of their mates died and memories of their long-lost romance resurfaced to both of them. His sister found her picture, made enquires, and traced her to The Wind and Sea. His subsequent phone call stunned them both. She'd believed he was killed in the war and he thought she was happily married and beyond reach. He was living in Michigan and she in Southern California, but distance was no handicap. A whirlwind, long-distance romance reignited a fifty-year-old romance and they were married by The Wind and Sea chaplain.

The Wind and Sea had an unofficial cadre of hosts to escort the single, elderly ladies to meetings, parties, and dinners. It was an interesting phenomenon to watch. Chester Hemingway was the leader. He first chose first the most attractive and stimulating female. Then the other three men made their choices. Chester would escort this woman to all the events plus meals for about four months, which seemed to be the average limit. After four months, everyone would notice that the two were not together, but rather sitting with different group. Gossip about them permeated dinner conversations. A month after the separation, Chester would choose again and the other three men would adjust their couplings. With Chester's current lady of choice becoming the heartthrob of the next in line. Chester's leadership was to be admired. It gave an orderly process to geriatric courting.

Bart Bradley was a maverick. He tried to relive his college days when his fraternity brothers stood in awe of his ability to bed the coeds at will. "It's simple," he told them. "Just ask if you can go to bed with them. I get slapped a lot but it's worth it. One out of three will smile and lead the way."

Now widowed and at eighty-two he tried to relive his youth. At the end of a dinner or social event, he would lead his female partner aside and state his proposition, "You are lovely. I like you very much, and I would like to make love to you."

He didn't get slapped, only a curt "good night" and sometimes a door slammed in his face. His many rejections only increased his ardor until the rising number of complaints forced Chris Fowler to contact Bart's son, William.

"Mr. Bradley, your father's behavior is so outrageous, I have to ask you to take him to another retirement community," Chris said.

"I know." The son looked down at his hands. "Yours is the third place. I don't know what to do. The man has a libido of a twenty-year-old and he wants to repeat the fun he had in college while he can."

"Your father is a lot of fun; everyone likes him. The men cheer him on and most of the women like the attention and compliments, but they can't openly accept his rather direct approach. May I suggest a remedy?" Chris smiled as he thought about his idea. "Salt peter was used in the old navy. I'm sure there's a better product now. Why don't you check at your local navy recruiting office?"

Other couples should be noted: Gunther Krause was Rose Marie Dentz' steady escort. Gunther started wearing a tie and jacket with his traditional long-sleeved shirt to dinner. Mary Lee Hopkins, the atheist ex-school teacher, was seen with Francis Pisano, the newcomer from Calabria, Italy. Much of their time together was used studying the proper use of the English language. Being Italian, Francis reserved some of the time to study the subject of *amore*.

*   *   *   *

Kleptomania at The Wind and Sea was now a serious problem. Everyday something disappeared. Chris once again appealed to Steve Matteson for help.

"I'm desperate, please help," he beseeched.

"I won't do the sleuthing," Steve said. "But if you will get a group together I will tell them all I know about this subject."

A week later, all the directors, security guards, and a few residents assembled in the executive director's private conference room to hear Steve's dissertation. "Kleptomania is an affliction, a disease, just like gambling and alcoholism. Objects are not stolen because they are needed. The theft of anything is a fix. It satisfies a need the same as a drink, a bet, or a shot of cocaine. The theft can be anything from a pin to a diamond ring. The value of an object is unimportant. Many kleptomaniacs are wealthy people, often celebrities. It's the thrill of a successful theft that satisfies the need, not its value."

"Are there any tell-tale identifying features?" one director asked.

"Only one. They will be female: young, old, short, tall, wealthy, poor, and they will be clever and crafty."

"I can attest to that," another director said. "My family owned a small store—kind of like the old-fashioned five and dime with small items. The sewing notions counter was loaded with thirty colors of thread, buttons, needles and zippers of all lengths. And the shoe counter had shoe lace, polishes, heels and so forth. Our inventories were always short. In the retail business, that's called shrinkage.

"We noticed this small elderly woman at these counters and suspected she was the thief. She wore an over-sized coat and her hands were like lightening. They never stopped moving over the top of the merchandize. We carefully inventoried the counters each morning before she came into the store and again after she left. She would pay for one or two items but five or six would be missing. Our only alternative was to prohibit her entrance to the store."

Steve thought for a moment. "Did she go to any of the other counters?"

"No."

"Then she was just a clever thief; she had a need for those particular items. She was probably a seamstress and in the shoe repair business. Kleptomaniacs don't steal from a need. They do it for the thrill of outsmarting the owners. I suggest setting up traps to catch her in the act or find where she is hiding her cache."

"There are hundreds of items she could steal in this building. We can't be everywhere," a director said. "How can we catch her?"

"Use her ego. Since that last town hall meeting she realizes we know about her activities. She wants to show her superior intellect. Her next theft will be gutsy," Steve concluded.

Chris Fowler jumped to his feet. "The Wind and Sea will give one hundred dollars to the person who catches this cat burglar."

All in the room cheered his remark.

Oscar Weber jumped up. "She won't steal my tomatoes again."

Pedro Martinez, one of the security guards, raised his hand. "Mr. Fowler, my girlfriend is one of the cleaning girls. Will you let her work with me?"

"Sure, Pedro, if she can keep her mouth closed," the director answered.

On Tuesday over the following three weeks, Pedro delivered the coffee and cookies to the bridge players in the card room where the money was stolen, and also the Happy Hour group in the same room on Thursdays where the deviled eggs were served. He'd worked at The Wind and Sea for three years and knew all but a few of those residents present at these two gatherings; he soon learned the other names. He discovered that three of the people attended both events, two were women.

Pedro asked his girlfriend to search both women's apartments. "Here's what I want you to look for," he said as he showed her a pencil sketch. "My family lived in a tough part of East Los Angeles. This is where they kept their valuables."

The kleptomaniac was inactive during the six weeks after the search for her began.

"She's wily and is waiting for us to relax," Steve advised Chris as he walked into the director's office. "She'll strike soon."

Pedro and Oscar were waiting in the office to speak to Chris and jumped to their feet. "No, she won't. I know who she is," Pedro boomed with glee.

"And so do I," Oscar exploded.

"Let's go to her apartment and I'll show you," a now calm Pedro said.

"We can't go into her place without her permission," Fowler explained.

"Yes, we can; she's not there. She's in the hospital." Oscar crossed his arms over his ample chest and grinned.

An exasperated director walked around his table with a scowl. "How do you know that?"

"Because I put her there."

"You'd better explain," Chris demanded.

The proud resident explained. "Eight more of my tomatoes are juicy ripe. I knew she would steal them so I injected each with a tomato herbicide that kills those god damn worms."

"You could have killed her. You damn fool."

"Naw, relax. She would have had to eat all eight at one seating. One would just give her stomach cramps. They were stolen yesterday and I noticed today on the bulletin board that Maude Perkins was taken to the hospital with stomach cramps."

"Yes!" Pedro snapped his fingers. "She's the one—the kleptomaniac."

Steve wrinkled his forehead. "The short, ninety-year-old lady? The one that worried about the 'White Ghost?'"

"Come, I'll show you in her apartment," an excited Pedro said.

The three quickly walked to Mrs. Perkins' unit and Chris opened the door with his key. "Here in the second bedroom," Pedro said, leading the way. "Help me remove the sheets off this king-size bed."

Five minute later, they placed the mattress against the wall. An identically shaped object that looked like a second mattress, and covered with a mattress cover, was on the bedstead. After ripping off the cover, they discovered not a second mattress, but a wooden box.

"A Mexican vault," a happy Pedro shouted.

It was hinged; and Pedro flipped the lid back. Inside was Maude's treasure—all the stolen items.

"You both get a hundred dollars," a happy Chris said as he slapped both men on the back.

Chapter 24

Sir Basil Recovers

"Downtown Los Angeles is ugly, isn't it?" Diggby Quinn mused as he looked out a window on the fiftieth floor.

"Yes, it is," Frank Carter said, without looking up from his notes.

"It's getting better," Larry Turner added. "You should have seen it thirty years ago. The thirteen-story City Hall was the tallest in the city and it was surrounded by relics of a sorry past."

"But it has some of the most exciting suburbs in the world." John Watts counted on his fingers. "Hollywood, Beverly Hills, Century City, and the Wilshire District. Los Angeles is one of the three most important cities in the world. California has the fifth strongest economy in the world and Los Angeles controls it."

Omar appeared in the doorway, pushing their leader in a wheelchair. Sir Basil was a mess. His left arm was in a sling, his right leg in a cast and the back of his head bandaged.

Goody rushed to Sir Basil's side. "Are you sure you should be out of bed?"

He raised his right arm and smiled. "I'm fine. But my nurse misses me and wants me back soon, so let's get started. Here's my agenda. Frank, why don't you be our leader." Sir Basil handed a sheet of paper to Frank Carter, the corporation's lead attorney.

Carter adjusted his glasses and began to read. "The first item concerns your accident, Sir Basil. Tell us about it."

The chairman moved around in the wheelchair, trying to get comfortable "The police are calling it a hit-and-run, but it wasn't. It was attempted murder. Someone in a big, dark car followed me from The Wind and Sea and waited until we were on the most dangerous stretch of highway. He then rammed into the side of my car, forcing me off the road. I was traveling at about seventy miles per hour and the car's momentum carried me through the guardrail, down an embankment, and into the ocean. Fortunately, another driver had a cell phone, saw the incident, and called the highway patrol. They arrived in about ten minutes. I was lucky. It was low tide and the water was only a foot high where I landed. I was unconscious and lying on the seat. At high tide the water is four feet high and I would have drowned."

Goody handed Sir Basil a glass of water. "Why would anyone want to kill you, Sir Basil?"

"I've been thinking about that for a week now and have drawn a blank."

"What happened at The Wind and Sea and why were you there?" Omar asked.

"Actually, I've been there twice in the past few days. The first time was to tell the residents about the marvelous, half-million-dollar grant that Ms. Farrell donated to The Wind and Sea. I arrived just before the start of one of their town hall meetings and sat through it." He shrugged. "The usual complaints and concerns, nothing important."

Omar scratched his head and hesitated. "After the meeting ended, what did you do?"

"I escorted Ms. Farrell back to her cottage and we talked about old times. I knew her in London many years ago."

"And when did you leave to return home?"

Sir Basil's answer was short and conclusive. "I didn't; I spent the night."

Omar had received the signal and knew when to change his line of questioning.

"Sir Basil, what about the second time?"

"Ms. Farrell asked me back to meet her niece and husband. I arrived at one, had drinks and food, left at six, and was rammed around seven o'clock."

Omar churned inside but knew his every word was dangerous. "Then these two trips were Ms. Farrell oriented. You contacted no other person or conducted any additional business?"

Sir Basil nodded and Omar continued. "Ms. Farrell is the link, the nexus. Someone is either afraid or jealous of your relationship with her."

Pain ripped through his arms and legs. His brain was on fire. He now knew the why of the accident but not who did it.

Omar tucked his pencil behind his ear and flipped open his notebook. "The man who saw the attempt on you life could only tell the police that the car had a California license plate and had something stuck on its back window. The driver's car must be damaged on its front, right fender. We're checking all the body repair shops in the area. But several days elapsed before we started and the minor damage caused could have been repaired and repainted in a day." Omar closed his notebook.

"Also we've checked all the cars at The Wind and Sea and found nothing. One is missing; Judge Roger Palmer and his car seem to have disappeared. I'm told he goes to one of his wife's houses often; we're checking."

"Thanks, Omar; keep at it." Sir Basil took a sip of water. "Now, to another subject, marijuana; some of the residents are using it. A few months ago, Omar, you told us about the nearness of a little plantation of marijuana. You thought we could make money by developing it. I said it was illegal and to forget it. Is this company involved in anyway?" Sir Basil stared directly at his investigator as Quinn, Turner, and Oliver began to sweat.

"No, Sir Basil. Not in any way." Omar shook his head.

The others looked away, secretly admiring Omar's ability to lie. *He could beat a polygraph machine.* But he wasn't lying; he was privy to recent information they didn't have. As of yesterday the marijuana process and sales operation had been hijacked by the gray Mafia.

Abby Kadaffy, Omar's protégé, sold a few joints to Enrico Di Donoto. With the promise of a big order, Rico seduced the young man to tell him more about the operation. Rico knew that Abby worked at The Wind and Sea and followed him one night after work to the marijuana patch. The next night Di Donoto, Francis Pisano and three armed, hired hands, all with guns, surrounded Abby and the three Mexican boys who worked the plants. Rico gave them a choice, switch their allegiance to them or die. After they agreed, their wages were doubled and everyone was satisfied.

Tearfully, Abby told Omar about the coup. The investigator forgave the boy, knowing he had no choice. Secretly, Omar was happy to be rid of the weed patch because his relationship with Sir Basil was in jeopardy. Lying to him was dangerous and would cost him his career, at least, if caught. Abby agreed to continue to snitch on the foibles of The Wind and Sea employees and residents.

Sir Basil shifted in his wheelchair. "Except under a doctor's supervision, the use of marijuana is illegal and we must find a way to eliminate its use in the building. Its odor offends people and sooner or later someone will report it to the police. Do something about it, Omar."

Omar knew exactly what to do. Discuss it with Di Donoto and reach a mutually satisfactory resolution.

"Now, to this lawsuit by Sandra Garfield. How culpable are we, Frank?"

"Her family and the doctor were responsible for wrongly putting her in the Alzheimer's unit. They may claim entrapment, but they'll lose. A civil court will come down big on her side. They might even be criminally responsible. Clive Huntington, the executive director at the time, acquiesced without doing any investigation, but I'm not sure he was required to." Frank looked up at Sir Basil over the rim of his glasses. "But, Sir Basil, we don't want our corporate name connected to this suit. I think we'd win but we don't need the bad publicity. Without admitting guilt, we should settle with her for a hundred thousand dollars."

After agreeing, Sir Basil wanted to return to his home in Beverly Hills, but before he could call for adjournment, Omar had one more problem to discuss.

"Sir Basil, you are in danger. Someone wants you dead. He or she tried once and will try again. I'm convinced that somehow you are involved in the tragic events surrounding Ms. Farrell. The murder of her husband, Mark Chambers, the murder of the Pink Daffodil, Hazel Sommers, and possibly the murder of that man who lived where she does, Arnold Myers. I have a contact inside the L. A. Police Department and they've uncovered new evidence that may involve Ms. Farrell. You must stay away from her and you must have a bodyguard."

Sir Basil churned inside; he could think of nothing else. He desperately wanted to be with Deborah and he needed to see his daughter again. It would beat least three weeks before he could travel to Santa Barbara and Pismo Beach. A bodyguard wouldn't be too intrusive at his mansion in Beverly Hills. "I agree, Omar. Send one to my home as soon as possible, and Goodwin, please have my secretary send a dozen pink roses to Ms. Farrell."

The meeting was adjourned and Sir Basil was wheeled to his car where his driver was waiting. "Henry, take me home, please, and there's no hurry."

That was an unnecessary remark because at six p.m. Los Angeles traffic was the slowest in the Western World. The hour it would take to get home was perfect for Sir Basil's brain to review his situation and consider his options. A smile covered his face as his sleepy mind meandered back to the beginning—spring 1963.

His affair with Deborah had been short, only two months, but he remembered every day. It was a benchmark, the pinnacle of happiness. When she so suddenly departed, he plunged himself into a life of drug use, drunkenness, and whoring with the lowest prostitutes he could find. His parents hijacked him to Switzerland and gave him to the tender mercies of the Boris Adler Institute, an institution noted for harsh methods, but also for its success rate in rehabilitating members of Europe's royal families and the progeny of the rich and powerful.

Six months later, Basil was released and escorted back to his family home, Hollingscot, in Yorkshire. His business acumen soon returned and he began to squire the daughters of London's finest families. As soon as he bedded them, he lost interest. Lord and Lady Rathbourn pleaded with him to marry.

He wanted to please them, but none of the women could eclipse the memory of Deborah.

In 1972, he met Pamela, the daughter of the Duke and Duchess of Kent. They were married at Saint Paul's in London. It was the social event of 1973. She died the following year without producing an heir to Sir Basil's fortune.

If Deborah will have me, I'll ask her to marry me, was the last decision Sir Basil made before drifting off to sleep.

Chapter 25

The Gun

With apprehension, Woody Ferguson knocked on Captain Milford's door. A summons to his office usually meant a criticism was forthcoming.

"Good news, Woody," the captain cheerfully said. "The new equipment at the local FBI office was able to read the serial numbers on the Browning .22 that killed Mrs. Sommers. It was registered to a Charles Sommers at 2508 Verdugo Avenue in San Diego on December 5, 1967. He must be the victim's husband."

Woody Ferguson damn near exploded with relief that the captain wasn't angry with him and that progress was made on his case. "Do we have a current address for him?" Woody asked.

"Yes, in 1977 he moved to Studio City in the San Fernando Valley from Brentwood. Here's his address and phone number."

Woody rushed back to his office and dialed the number. He couldn't believe his good luck when a male voice answered.

"Mr. Sommers?" he asked anxiously.

"Yes, but I don't want any, whatever it is."

"I'm not selling, Mr. Sommers. I'm from the police."

"Damn it, I paid that traffic ticket last week and I wasn't even speeding," an agitated citizen screamed.

"Relax, Mr. Sommers, my name is Woodrow Ferguson, and I need to talk to you about a gun you bought back in 1975, a .22 Browning."

"I don't have it. I gave it to my wife, Hazel, before our divorce in 1976."

"Fine, Mr. Sommers, but I need to come by and get a statement from you. It was involved in a murder. How about this afternoon?"

Mr. Sommers sucked in his breath, then gave a timid response. "Would four o'clock be okay?"

"Perfect, I'll see you then, and thank you." Woody quickly ran back to his desk to review the Pink Daffodil file.

At four, Woody rang the doorbell on this little California bungalow, circa 1940. An older man answered the door, his bare feet encased in muddy Nikes. He wore a dirty undershirt and his pudgy stomach hung over the top of torn blue-jeans. "Come in, please," he muttered, rubbing the stubbles on his chin.

Woody did and was immediately sorry. A stale cigar odor nearly gagged him. Poker chips and overflowing ashtrays loaded down a card table in the middle of the room.

"Sorry for the mess," Charles said. "I had my poker group over last night and it was too late to pick up."

It was obvious this was a bachelor's pad—any woman would faint upon entering. Newspapers were everywhere. Someone had slept on the sofa and left a blanket and a pajama top on it. Dirty dishes and soiled napkins piled on the dining room table. To enter the kitchen was to enter the city dump. Dirty dishes and opened cans covered the counters and filled the two sinks. Someone had spilled beans down the front of the oven and the floor was littered with beer bottles.

Sommers took magazines off the one upholstered chair and after pushing crumbs off it with his hand said, "Sit down, and let's talk."

"Tell me about the Browning .22 you bought in San Diego," Woody began.

"There had been a burglary near our house in San Diego and my wife, Hazel, said we should get a gun for protection. So I did and had it registered." He beamed with pride.

"When did you and your wife move to Brentwood?"

"When I opened the E. F. Hutton office on Wilshire Boulevard in 1970," Charles answered.

"And brought the gun with you?"

"Oh yes, Hazel was fond of that gun."

"You moved here after the divorce and left the gun with your ex-wife?"

"Yes, gave her the gun, gave her the house, and everything else I owned. Moving to Brentwood was the worst mistake of my life. Moved right into a snake-pit of dykes," an agitated man explained.

"Dykes, Mr. Sommers?"

"Lesbians, the neighborhood and the tennis club were full of them. Are you married, Lieutenant?"

Woody shook his head. "No."

"It's the worst thing in the world. To find out you're married to a damned homosexual. For five years I thought I was satisfying my wife. All the time she was bored with me and getting her pleasure from that bitch, Holli Logan, and maybe that goddess, Deborah Farrell."

Woody jumped up. His heart raced. He walked to the table and inspected the single lightbulb hanging from a frazzled cord. "Are you telling me that your wife was having a lesbian relationship with Ms. Farrell and Ms. Logan.?"

"I'm not sure about Farrell, but for sure with Logan. Hazel threw it in my face."

"Tell me about Ms. Farrell." Sweat rolled down Woody's neck.

"They were good friends, tennis partners at the club. She used to visit here, but Hazel never went over to Farrell's house. But she often went to Logan's. Dumb me; I never suspected."

"What do you know about your wife's murder, Mr. Sommers?"

"Please call me Charlie. Not much, only what I read in the papers. Someone told me she had disappeared, but I thought she's just gone off with one of her lesbian lovers. It was only lately that I found out she'd been murdered, the Pink Daffodil she was called."

Woody hoped that he was asking the right questions. "What did you do when you knew that your wife was the Pink Daffodil and was murdered," Woody moved closer.

"Nothing, that was twenty years ago. I tried very hard to forget her."

"Did the police question you after they knew that the Pink Daffodil was in fact your wife?"

"Oh yes. She was killed in the middle of August 1978. I was at a conference of Hutton people from August tenth through August eighteen in New York City. Why would I want to kill her? I was rid of her and happily married to another woman."

"May I ask? What happened to that marriage?"

"I lost my job when Hutton was bought by another brokerage. She left soon after that. It was a friendly divorce; she let me have this beautiful home. At least it was about money, not sex." He shook his head. "I'll never forget that bitch, Holli Logan. If you ever meet her, watch out."

"Actually, I have to see her next. May I use your phone?"

Ferguson had brought the Sommers file with Logan's number in it. He dialed and once again was surprised when a human voice answered. "Ms. Logan, this is Lieutenant Ferguson. Remember we talked several months ago about the Sommers murder. There has been a new development and we must talk again. Either you'll have to come into the Hollywood office or I can come to your house this afternoon."

Logan hesitated and Woody could hear her fingernails tapping on the phone. "Is it absolutely necessary, Lieutenant? I'm very busy."

"Yes, I'm sorry it is."

"How soon can you be here, Lieutenant?"

Woody hurriedly calculated the distance between Studio City and Brentwood via the San Diego Freeway. "Forty minutes," he said.

As he was leaving he turned toward Sommers and asked, "Do you know where your wife, Hazel, kept the .22?"

"I assume where she always kept it; in the top drawer of the lamp stand next to the table in the living room."

"One more question. Do you know who inherited that Brentwood house after Hazel was killed?"

"Yeah," Charlie said. "Hazel's nephew, he lives in Chicago. He seldom uses it; only a few weeks in the winter. I have his address and phone number here somewhere."

Woody was a happy man and hummed his favorite tunes on the drive. Traffic was light and he arrived ten minutes early. Holli's house was different from the Sommers house. It was a large mansion with beautiful landscaping, everything neat and tidy. After ringing the doorbell, he became apprehensive—he'd never interviewed a lesbian before. The first time didn't count; he didn't know she was a lesbian then. He remembered her, in her sixties, attractive with a trim body, little makeup, and dark hair tied into a ponytail.

"Coffee, Lieutenant?" she asked immediately after opening the door.

He looked around the living room before answering; it was breathtaking. Large pictures covered the wall; one was a Picasso and two were Jackson Pollards. The upholstered pieces and the carpeting were white, the chairs made of metal, and the table tops were thick glass. Every item in the room made a statement. *How could anyone live in a room like this?*

"Yes, please. You have a lovely home, Ms. Logan."

"Thank you. My late significant other was very generous."

Woody was not educated in the vernacular of the hip crowd, but assumed that Ms. Logan meant that she had been the beneficiary of someone other than a husband. *A male or female lover?*

They sat at a little table in a nook off the kitchen. After a few sips, during which she looked at him intently, he began. "Ms. Logan, after the Pink Daffodil's body had been identified as that of Mrs. Sommers, you voluntarily came to my office and said that Hazel Sommers had told you that Ms. Farrell had asked Hazel to testify for her, to say that they were together on the day that Mark Chambers was murdered, namely August 12, 1978. But your statement to me was that Mrs. Sommers was with you on that date."

Woody paused. The wheels in his brain spun. There were several ways to question this woman.. Which was correct?

"That statement is in direct conflict with the testimony of Detective Steven Matteson. He said that Mrs. Sommers told him that Ms. Farrell was with her on that date. Can you think of any reason for this discrepancy? And this is important, Ms. Logan, because that case may be retried and you will be forced to testify. So if you can spread any light on this conundrum please do it now?"

Holli lit a cigarette and put it in a long holder. "Yes, Lieutenant. I followed that court case and was surprised at the detective's testimony."

Woody noticed her nervousness and was ready to take advantage of it.

"I'm glad you came today; my conscience has been bothering me. I lied to you." Without waiting for him to speak, she continued. "After I knew that Hazel was dead and not just missing, I felt I had to correct Matteson's testimony, but I didn't want to get involved and I didn't want Ms. Farrell's reputation damaged because of my sexual orientation. So I told you a fact, but not how I knew it. Hazel did not tell me that Ms. Farrell had asked her to lie, but Lieutenant, Hazel Sommers could not have been with Ms. Farrell on August 12, 1978 because she was with me all day."

"Ms. Logan, you were sexually active with Hazel Sommers but not with Deborah Farrell, is that correct?"

"Yes, Deborah is very male oriented. She'd be the last one I would proposition. Also, Lieutenant, Deborah was with Hazel most of day on August 11, 1978, the day before. And I can prove it. Hazel brought her calendar with her on the twelfth; she left it and I put it in a drawer and forgot to return it. Let me show you."

She rummaged through an island of drawers in the middle of the kitchen. "Here's her calendar," she said finally.

It was a 1978, ten-by-twelve calendar, opened on August. On the eleventh was the notation:

Deborah Farrell 10 a. m. to 4 p.m.
To plan a fund raising event for
The Children's Hospital

And on the twelfth:

Going to Holli Logan's at 9 a. m.
Tennis Tournament planning . . . Party time.

"I hate to do this to Deborah, but I'm not going to commit perjury in a murder case." She pulled on her ponytail.

"Let me see if I have this straight," Woody said. "You wanted us to know that Farrell was not with Sommers on the twelfth so you lied and quoted Sommers as saying they weren't together on that date as Detective Matteson had testified. The calendar shows that Farrell was with Hazel on the eleventh but not on the date of the murder, the twelfth. How can you prove this calendar belonged to Sommers?"

"Look through it, Lieutenant. There are several meetings that only Hazel would know about and there are notes from other people."

"Unsigned notes could have been forged," he argued.

"But Lieutenant, Detective Matteson testified that Hazel told him that Farrell was at her house all day on the twelfth. Why would she say that when she was with me?"

"For two reasons. One, she was confused and mistook the twelfth for the eleventh or she wanted to give Farrell an alibi."

"ieutenant, you are so dense. What do you think 'party time' means? There were two other women here, the wife of a prominent politician and a well-known Hollywood party girl. I'll deny saying this and I won't reveal their names. Under oath my memory will fail me. Hazel was here."

Ferguson now knew this was not a woman to have as an enemy. "My head is spinning," he said, slumping in his chair.

"Want a drink, Lieutenant? I promise I won't make a pass."

"You've been very nice, but no thanks. I have to put all this down on paper and try to solve this puzzle. Charlie Sommers said some nasty things about you, but you're a good citizen, thanks."

Thank you again, Ms. Logan. We'll be in touch." He started to leave, then paused. "There is one other question, Ms. Logan. Did you know that Mrs. Sommers had a gun?"

"Yes," she said with a lingering leer. "Hazel was proud of it. She said she kept it to shoot a man, you know where, if he tried to rape her."

"Did Ms. Farrell know about the gun?"

"Oh my, yes; we all did. Good luck, Lieutenant."

Los Angeles streets, including its freeways, became parking lots during the evening hours when workers returned home. Woody was anxious to get back to his office and review the crime scene report on the Pink Daffodil homicide after it was known that the body was Hazel Sommers.

An hour later he studied the two reports. The original, twenty-two years old and ten pages long, he compared against the latest only a few months ago, one page long. The first was thorough. The body was found on August 17, 1978; the victim had been killed by two slugs from a .22 caliber gun, was murdered in the last twenty-four to thirty-six hours, and was killed where the body was found.

The second report was compiled after the identity of the victim was known. It identified the crime scene crew and detailed how they had searched the Sommers house in Brentwood. Their conclusion was that it was devoid of any evidence linking it to the murder of Hazel Sommers.

That was a sloppy job. They didn't want to find anything that would be contrary to their conclusion made twenty years earlier.

After reading it twice, Woody knocked on Captain Milford's door. "Captain, I believe the crime scene people may have missed something in the Sommers house. I would like to go over it myself."

"Okay, get permission from the owner or a court order."

It's only nine o'clock in Chicago. He should be home. Woody deciphered what Charlie had scribbled and rang Hazel's nephew. "Hello, my name is Woodrow Ferguson and I'm with the Los Angeles police."

"It's about my aunt's death again, isn't it?"

"Yes, there is new evidence and we have to look through your Brentwood house again. We need either your permission or a court order. Yours would be easier."

"No problem, the key is under the second geranium pot to the right of the door. Please return it."

Woody didn't sleep well that night. He was getting close, it was just beyond his reach, tomorrow would be the day that all would be revealed. He asked Sergeant Sean Murphy to join him, and they arrived at Sommers' Brentwood house about ten a. m. It was a large, two-story house with the living room, den, dining room, powder room and kitchen, opening to a three car garage on the ground floor. A sweeping circular staircase exited on a hallway on the second floor and led to the master bedroom and three guest bedrooms, each with its own bathroom.

A cleaning service cleaned the empty home every two weeks, so it was immaculate. "We'll inspect every square inch of this house even if it takes us all day," Woody said. "We'll start in the living room. You take the left side and I'll do the right. We're looking for something that doesn't fit, that seems odd."

The living room and den were furnished with Ethan Allen furniture, the early American style that was so popular in the sixties and seventies. "My wife loves this kind of furniture," Sean said. "I wish I could afford it."

Woody didn't answer; he was too immersed in his work. By noon they had completed the first floor and were halfway up the staircase. So far they had drawn a blank.

"Time for lunch, maybe we'll have better luck this afternoon." They locked up and found a local Denny's.

An hour later they were back at it and by four they were finished and disappointed in their efforts. They both collapsed on one of the beds. Ten minutes later, Woody sprang off the bed. "Something's not right in the den; let's take another look." After a quick trip to that room Woody exploded. "My mother used to have this type of furniture. It's always accompanied with heavy, braided rugs made out of rags. My grandmother used to make them just like the early American settlers. Look, there's one under the dining table, one by the fireplace, and one near the entrance, but there's none under this card table in the den." He bent over and closely inspected the floor. "Look, Sean, you can see an outline where a five-by-seven foot oval rug was. I wonder why it was removed."

"I saw an oval braided rag rug in the garage," Sean said. "It was folded over a wicker patio table."

Woody could have broken the Olympic record racing toward the garage. "Where?" he shouted.

"Over here," Sean said, standing by the rug.

They carried it to the den, removed the card table, and placed the rug on the floor. It matched the five-by-seven fade marks on the floor perfectly. "All the other furniture is exactly as it should be except this rug. Why?" Woody put his hands on his hips.

"Because," the young Irish policeman answered. "Whatever was on it or in it would have been noticed here in the den and overlooked in the garage."

"This goes immediately to the crime lab. Let's roll it up and put it in the trunk of the car," an excited Woody said.

Three days later, the doctor in charge of the lab delivered his report to Woody.

This rug was taken somewhere, probably outside in back of the garage, and washed. Traces of Clorox remain. I believe it was then put where you found it. Faint traces of two types of blood were found; much more Type O than Type A. The victim, Hazel Sommers, was Type O. Your perpetrator is Type A. We are sending the evidence to our DNA lab, but believe the samples of blood are too old and have deteriorated too much to get a conclusion. We believe Mrs. Sommers was murdered in her home and then carried to where she was found.

Sincerely,
Amos Fillmore, M.D.

Woody immediately called Lieutenant Blake McGee in Santa Barbara. "How many shells have been fired from that Browning .22?" he asked.

Blake checked his notes then said, "Three."

"Two hit the victim and one hit the killer," Woody explained.

"It could have been fired after the murder," Blake suggested.

"No, it wasn't, I guarantee you. That gun was sequestered until your boy, Juan, found it," Woody proudly announced. "Blake, I wish I could buy you a drink. This has been a good day."

It would turn out to be a better day than Woody could have imagined because soon after his phone call to McGee an envelope was delivered to him. It was from the DNA lab. After reading its contents, he let out a loud yell. "Well, I'll be damned."

The first three paragraphs described the procedure and interpretations; the last encapsulated the lab's conclusion. He read it again:

The samples of DNA taken from the glasses, flatware, brushes and tissues, clearly indicate with a ninety-five percent certainty that the female identified as Denise is the daughter of Deborah Farrell and Sir Basil Rathbourn.

He now had answers to some of his questions. Deborah Farrell, née Daisy Klinger, went to her home, Sioux City, Iowa, in February of 1964 to give birth to a daughter, Denise. A local doctor assisted, and Basil Rathbourn was the father.

I have to tell Captain Milford these facts, but for now no one else should know. Why did she deny for so long that she was the mother of Denise? Who was her local OB/GYN? Carrie Boswell stated that Deborah had two abortions. Did this local OB/GYN perform them? The Mark Chambers and Hazel Sommers cases are connected. Is the Arnold Myers homicide also connected to these two?

He knew who would have one of the answers and reached for his phone. "Hello, Carrie, how's the book coming?"

"Great, but you don't really care do you?"

""Of course I do. I have some information for you." It was easy for him to trace Farrell's activity in Sioux City once he knew the date and her maiden name. She didn't know the date and he needed to throw her a bone. "Dear Deborah gave birth to Denise in Sioux City, Iowa in February 1964."

There was a pause. "Wow, are you sure?" she purred into her phone. "I wonder who the father was. Surely not some Iowa farmer."

"I'm positive about the birth but haven't a clue who daddy is. Carrie dear, I need an answer and I'm sure you know it. What was the name of Farrell's OB/GYN?"

"That's easy. All the Hollywood stars used the same one including her, Dr. David Morris, and he lives here in The Wind and Sea. He either by phone instructed a local doctor or flew back o Iowa. Some of the starlets paid him off with favors. I wonder how Deborah took care of him.

Before she could phone seduce him he ended the call. "Thanks, Carrie, I owe you. Good-bye."

Chapter 26

Suspects et al

It was nearly six when Detective Ferguson arrived at his office. He studied the messages on his phone recorder and answered a few. He closed his door, poured himself a cup of coffee, retrieved two stale doughnuts from his top drawer, and placed Lieutenant McGee's interview sheets in front of him.

Gunther Ludwig Krause
5/11/99—4:00 p.m.—W&S

McGee: *Place and date of birth?*

Krause: *March 6, 1919—Hamburg, Germany*

McGee: *Date of entry into the U. S. and date of citizenship if any?*

Krause: *June 1, 1957 and September 12, 1963*

McGee: *What were you doing before the war?*

Krause: *I was enrolled at the University of Heidelberg, a junior.*

McGee: *What did you do during the war?*

Krause: *I spoke three languages and was an interpreter for the army at the second battalion's headquarters in Munich.*

McGee: *Itemize what you have done from June 1, 1957 to the present?*

Krause: *From June 1, 1957 until February of 1965, I worked for the First Bank of New York in New York City. I then took a leave of absence and spent the next two years traveling mostly in South America looking for investment opportunities. Upon my return in March of 1966, I moved west and began my own real estate business in Southern California.*

McGee: *Have you ever been married?*

Krause: *Briefly in Germany; it didn't work out. We had no children.*

McGee: *Did you know the victim, Arnold Myers?*
Krause: *Only here at The Wind and Sea, slightly.*
McGee: *How about Mark Chambers and Hazel Sommers?*
Krause: *Never met them.*
McGee: *Where were you on the night and at the time Arnold Myers was murdered?*
Krause: *Here in my apartment sick and alone.*

Comments

Krause was straight forward, never hesitated, but I believe his time in South America should be investigated. I don't believe his answers about his marital status were truthful. I noticed that he always wore long sleeve shirts even when the weather was in the nineties.

Ferguson then read the report on J. C. Wellington and his wife, Virginia. Neither had met Sommers or Chambers and only knew Myers at The Wind and Sea. McGee believed they were not suspects and neither did he.

The next sheet was on Roger Palmer and it was brief.

Roger O. Palmer
Comments

Mr. Palmer was not available for an interview. His monthly rent check was sent by first-class mail with a New York City return address. It is assumed he's living with his wife in her New York City apartment. He first met Ms. Farrell when he was the judge at her 1979 trial. Palmer owns a cottage at The Wind and Sea and is believed to be close friends with Ms. Farrell.

He knew Myers casually and never met Hazel Sommers. He is no longer a person of interest.

Steve eagerly looked forward to reading the next report.

Enrico Giuseppe Di Donoto
5/9/99—11:00 a. m.—W&S

McGee: *I am investigating the murder of Arnold Myers. You knew him and were here at the time of his death. You may know something about it. I am not interested in your past or what you are engaged in now.*

	If you would prefer not answering a question, please say so, but please be truthful in any answer given. When and where were you born?
Enrico:	*July 8, 1924; New York City*
McGee:	*Your education, how much. Where?*
Enrico:	*New York City public schools to the tenth grade*
McGee:	*I know you were a soldier in the Pallandini gang. You worked your way up to be the capo of one of the New Jersey gangs. You were in the trucking and waste management businesses and secretary of Longshoreman's Union on the Jersey docks. Correct?*
Enrico:	*You left out a few things but got most of it right.*
McGee:	*Did you know Myers?*
Enrico:	*Only as a resident at The Wind and Sea.*
McGee:	*Where were you on the night of his murder?*
Enrico:	*Watching that talent show. Never left, not even to take a pee.*
McGee:	*Do you know anything that could help us solve this murder?*
Enrico:	*It was done by an amateur. It wasn't clean and there were too many possible witnesses. Myers was a scared little rabbit especially afraid of Gunther Krause, and Paul Ostrow and his wife Yvonne, also Rose Marie Dentz. He avoided them and cringed when they were near.*
McGee:	*Paul Ostrow is the man with the bandaged face, isn't he?*
Enrico:	*Yes. It surely is healing slowly.*

Woody quickly leafed through the reports to find the one on Ostrow.

Paul David Ostrow
5/9/99—10:30 a.m.—W &S

Comments

Paul Ostrow had never spoken to Myers, nor met Chambers or Sommers. He knew Farrell only as a fellow resident. I put his fingerprints through the system but they didn't show up in the military, police, or driver license files. His past history is suspect. He said he and his wife lived in Chicago but could give no address. He said he had a stock brokers license and worked for Dean Witter but again no time or address.

His account of the accident that caused his head injury is bogus. He either is in a witness protection program, hiding from someone or something, or has a hidden agenda. He has a slight accent but says he has an American passport. He's lying but I have no reason to question him further. He had no answer as to why Myers should be afraid of him. He is not a suspect but definitely is a person of interest.

It was now eight o'clock; Woody was tired and hungry. He should go home, have a good meal and a full night's sleep, but his mind was spinning and he knew he couldn't sleep. "Rookie," he hollered. "Send one of the office clerks out for a pizza, medium size with three toppings. I don't care what kind. Thanks."

After talking with a few of his fellow officers, he returned to his office and drank coffee until the pizza arrived. Six reports remained: Francis Pisano's, Chauncey Talbot's, David Morris,' Steve Matteson's, Tom (Slick) Jenkins', and Carlos Sanchez'. He glanced at them and discovered that there was nothing of importance in Talbot's, Pisano's, or Sanchez' interviews or comments. Jenkins had one interesting item. When he was a new car salesman Slick had sold a Cadillac to Deborah Farrell. McGee had dismissed them and so would he. Matteson's and Morris' were set aside until after he had enjoyed the pizza.

After swallowing his last bite of pizza and pushing it down with a swig of Coca-Cola, Woody studied Steve Matteson's interview.

William Steven Matteson
5/9/99—2:00 p.m.—W&S

McGee:	Date of birth?
Steve:	July 20, 1925
McGee:	Education?
Steve:	Los Angeles High School; California State, San Diego
McGee:	Military?
Steve:	Two years navy; ordinary seaman
McGee:	Professional career?
Steve:	From 1949 to 1979: Lieutenant at the Hollywood Division; 1979 to 1990: captain in the Santa Barbara Police Department.
McGee:	Marital status
Steve:	Married for a short time, many years ago; no children
McGee:	You were the investigating officer in the Mark Chambers murder. What did you do?
Steve:	Chambers was murdered on August 12, 1978. I interviewed his wife, Deborah Farrell, on the 13th of August, again on the 19th, and several other times before and during her trial. You can get my complete report.
McGee:	Farrell said she was at a Mrs. Sommers house on the twelfth. Did you interview Sommers?
Steve:	Yes, on August 15 at eleven a.m. She was confused but confirmed Farrell's alibi for the twelfth.

McGee: *Did you ever talk to Sommers again?*

Steve: *On the sixteenth she phoned and left a message for me to call. Upon returning to the office late in the afternoon, I did. There was no answer and a body was discovered on the seventeenth that, with DNA twenty years later, turned out to be hers. I wasn't connected to the Pink Daffodil case, but I believe the detective in charge of that case blew it. He should have made the connection between the discovery of the body and the disappearance of Sommers, who was obviously killed in her home and taken to where she was found.*

McGee: *Why do you assume that?*

Steve: *Because it was staged, a grand opera production. The ground was raked; the body was perfectly laid out with the daffodil in her hands. The crime scene investigators found no tooth fragments on the ground or acid stains on her dress. It was a work of art done elsewhere. It was hallowed ground desecrated by cops, news people, and sightseers. Hazel Sommers deserved better.*

McGee: *Did you know Arnold Myers?*

Steve: *Met him once, then saw him again on the stage playing Sir Basil.*

Comments

Matteson's comments about Sommers' body blew me away. Thinking about it put him into a trance. He was a high priest handling the Holy Eucharist. A team is scouring her home for fragments or acid stains; so far nothing.

Woody jumped to his feet and rushed to the water cooler. Three glasses of the cool liquid didn't reduce the body temperature rising to the top of his head. *No, no, it can't be. Impossible. My God, what have I got into?*

He couldn't concentrate on David Morris' sheet. It would have to wait until the next day.

After a restless and sleepless night, he dragged himself back to the station. "Woody, you look terrible; go home and get some rest," several of his fellow officers told him. He drank a cup of bad coffee and ate a stale doughnut. Refusing to look at Matteson's report again, he picked up the last one.

David Phillip Morris, M. D.
5/9/99—10:00 a. m.—W&S

McGee: *Date of Birth, where?*

Morris:	November 11, 1920; Baltimore Maryland.
McGee:	Education?
Morris:	University of Maryland, B.S; John Hopkins, M.D. in OB/GYN
McGee:	Military service?
Morris:	None
McGee:	Did you know Mark Chambers or Hazel Sommers?
Morris:	Never met Sommers. I belonged to the same tennis club as did Mark and Deborah. Met casually in tournaments and banquets.
McGee:	How well did you know Arnold Myers?
Morris:	At The Wind and Sea's Breakfast Club and other social events. He says we met about twenty years ago in my office. Evidently I was the obstetrician for the birth of his daughter—I've assisted in about three thousand births. I don't remember him or his daughter but he says my daughter, Katherine, was present with her boyfriend one time when Myers brought his wife in for an examination.
McGee:	Were there any problems with the birth of his daughter?
Morris:	No.
McGee:	Where is your daughter now?
Morris:	She died in a car accident.
McGee:	How old was she?
Morris:	Twenty, beautiful and in the prime of life.
McGee:	Did you ever perform an abortion for Ms. Farrell?
Morris:	That's privileged information.

Comments

His only contact with Myers was outside of The Wind and Sea and was over twenty years earlier. There were no complications with the birth of Myers' child, so Myers had no complaint with the doctor. Katherine was Morris' only child. Tears filled his eyes when he talked about her.

Lieutenant Ferguson reread several of the interview sheets and then put them in a folder. He reached for his phone and called operator. "Yes, operator. I'd like the phone number of the Shore Breeze Retirement Community in Del Mar, please." A few minutes later he thanked the operator and dialed a number; it was answered after three rings. "I'm Lieutenant Woodrow Ferguson of the Los Angeles Police Department and I would like to speak to a Juan Hernandez. I believe he is a waiter in your dining room, thank you."

Chapter 27

All the Usual Suspects

Detective Ferguson had an appointment with Blake McGee at the Santa Barbara police headquarters, but decided to talk to Steve Matteson first. He had experienced a most rewarding week but it ended on a disappointment. The blood samples on the crocheted rag rug taken from Sommers' house were too old, weak and deteriorated for a definitive DNA identification. Knowing that Sommers' blood was Type O and the other person's, probably the killer, was Type A was great but a DNA positive report would have been better.

Steve was glad to see him and offered his friend a beer, which was refused. For a bachelor, the retired detective maintained a neat, clean apartment. It was not professionally decorated but the few pictures on the wall and the California modern furniture were tastefully selected.

"Do you remember Ms. Farrell's blood type, Steve?" Woody asked.

"I remember everything about her and that case. It was Type A, why?"

"I'm reviewing the case and couldn't find the blood data."

That's strange," Steve said looking dubiously at the other man. "Usually it's stamped on the first page of the profile report." Steve became defensive and Woody knew the older man didn't believe him, but he wasn't going to share his new knowledge with anyone.

"Say hello to Blake for me. I haven't seen him for awhile. I hope he has completed that chart he designed," Steve said without any enthusiasm.

"That's why I'm seeing him. We have to get Myers' case moving or I'll be a sergeant again."

Woody started to leave, then stopped. "I came here to ask you about your testimony and almost forgot to ask." He shook his head. "I'm getting old."

"It's all on the record," Steve muttered between clenched lips.

Without acknowledging his friend's irritation, Woody continued. "Would you please repeat your first conversation with the suspect, Deborah Farrell?"

Steve glared at the young, detective from Los Angeles who had taken over the Mark Chambers' murder investigation. "Chambers was killed on the afternoon of August 12, 1978. Farrell wouldn't talk to anyone on that day, but I talked to her at ten the next day, August thirteenth, at her home in Bel Air. I asked her where she was at the time of the murder. She said she was with a Hazel Sommers, an old neighborhood friend, at her home in Brentwood, which was about a mile from hers. She was there all day planning a fundraiser for the Children's Hospital."

Steve settled back in his chair and dialed his memory bank. "Hazel couldn't see me on the fourteenth, but said she was available on the fifteenth. I arrived at eleven at her home, which was smaller than Farrell's. Many of these older homes were bought for location and then torn down.

"I accepted her offer of coffee and we sat at a table in her den. I asked if Deborah Farrell had been with her at her house on August twelfth. She said 'yes' immediately and then two minutes later she said she was sure it was the twelfth but wanted to look at her calendar. She said the last two weeks had been very busy and she had been to many events and seen many people. She walked to the kitchen and rummaged through several drawers. Upon returning she said she couldn't find her calendar and didn't remember where she had put it, but she was certain that Ms. Farrell had been at her house on the twelfth. I left soon after that because she said she was late for a meeting and practically threw me out the door."

"Steve, do you remember how the house was decorated," Woody asked.

"Yes, as a matter of fact I do. My mother liked the period, Early American with Ethan Allen furniture," Matteson answered.

"Did you happen to notice the crocheted rag rugs?" he asked, looking into the distance.

"Yes, there were several in the house. They must take a lot of time to make."

"Was there one under that den table?"

Steve thought for a moment. "Yes, I believe there was, but why do you ask?"

"I'm thinking about redecorating my pad. I like them and might ask the present owner if they're for sale."

Woody started to leave and then changed his mind again. "May I use your phone? I want to call Farrell and to ask if she'll see me now."

She was home, but the conversation was brief. "She can't see me now but can at four this afternoon after my meeting with Blake McGee." Woody waved to Steve and walked to the door.

Santa Barbara was lovely in early February if it wasn't raining. The nearby hills were green, the quaint little Spanish town looked clean and alive and the distant mountains were strikingly beautiful. His drive was less than thirty minutes and Woody enjoyed every minute of it.

Lieutenant McGee was waiting for him with his charts and sheets of notes.

"Any conclusions?" Woody asked.

The Santa Barbara officer was dedicated and disciplined in everything. His lean muscular body was indicative of his many hours in the police gym and his careful choice of food. His brain was stimulated with daily doses of crossword puzzles, Sudoku, and chess games, which he never lost.

"No conclusions, but I have excluded everyone except those on these sheets." Blake flipped through the papers. "With the exception of Ms. Farrell, and the soprano, Michelle Woodhouse, all had the means and opportunity. The motive to kill Myers remains a mystery. There were three murders and I have made the assumption that the Chambers and Sommers' homicides are connected, but don't know if there were two killers or one. I can't see how the Myers case is connected to the others, but it may be. I am certain that his killer lives at The Wind and Sea. Let's start with his case. I've interviewed all the possible persons of interest three times and have boiled the list down to eight men and three women, as you can see on the chart. I'll start with the women.

"I made a copy of my interview notes for you. Here's yours." McGee passed eleven sheets to Ferguson. "All of them attended the talent show and are young and strong enough to race to the third floor, kill Myers, and return to the Great Hall in fifteen minutes. I'll summarize as you read through the notes. Let's start with his wife, Carrie Boswell."

Woody flipped though the papers until he found the right one. Blake settled back in his chair and read his notes on Boswell to refresh his memory.

"Carrie and Arnold were married in 1995 by a judge in Los Angeles. Both were married before; she had a son, he had a daughter who lives in Oakland and hates him, but her alibi for the time of his murder checked out. This second marriage didn't amount to much. They led separate lives and were never seen socially together either at The Wind and Sea or elsewhere. She is a successful writer of steamy novels and scandalous biographies of famous people. She's writing one now on Deborah Farrell."

"I know she's given me unflattering tidbits about Farrell's many escapades. Nothing relative to Myers," Woody interjected, but he said nothing about her unwanted sexual advances.

"She was Roman Catholic but never attended church. He was a non-practicing Jew who immigrated to this country from England in the early sixties," Blake said as he laid down the sheet. "I can't find any motive for her wanting to kill him. I'm sure they had a prenuptial agreement and in California she could have received a divorce by just filing for one."

"Is he the only Jew at The Wind and Sea?"

"No, there's one other, Rose Marie Dentz," Blake answered, and then smiled. "And so far as I know, there are no Nazis there either."

Woody raised his head. "How about Gunther Krause? He came to this country from Germany in 1957."

."If I remember correctly, Myers had a slight accent. Check with British immigration. Maybe England was just a stopover," Woody suggested.

"I will. I've eliminated Carrie as a suspect. Arnold was an embarrassment, but maybe a good lover. She could have divorced him, or murdered him in an easier way than running up three floors and pushing him down a staircase.

"Next is Rose Marie Dentz, psychologist to the stars. She knew Myers only as a fellow member of the Breakfast Club. She thought he was a dimwit and teased him constantly, but she felt sorry for him and regretted her taunting afterward. Gunther Krause and she have become an item, but I don't know how hot and heavy their romance is," McGee said.

"Rose Marie is professionally well-known and several of the residents of The Wind and Sea have used her services, including Deborah Farrell."

"Did you ask her why Farrell needed her services?" Woody asked.

"Yes, but she wouldn't divulge it—protected doctor-client information—but she did tell me that her first visit was in 1965."

"Very interesting," Woody said as he immediately began to scribble.

"Dentz was sitting at one of the front tables at the talent show and as she is five foot nine and a little overweight, easily identified. I have eliminated her as a suspect but she is one of just a few who are acquainted with people in two of the murder cases, Myers and Farrell."

"Did she ever meet Mark Chambers?" Woody asked.

"I asked her that and she said to her knowledge, no," Blake answered.

"The last woman on my person of interest list is Mary Lee Hopkins, school teacher, atheist, and probably communist," Blake said. "She keeps herself in shape by running four miles a day and working out at the local gym. She's seventy-three now and entertains Francis Pisano regularly. If any woman could run up three floors and handle Myers, it's her. She also teased Myers with gusto at the Breakfast Club."

"Any connection with Hazel Sommers or Mark Chambers?"

"No, except she was a school teacher in the Brentwood School District when they all lived there. But they had no children in her school so I can't find a connection."

Woody looked at his watch. "I have an appointment with Ms. Farrell at four. It's about three-thirty so I don't have time now to go over the men persons of interest."

Blake grabbed the remaining sheets. "Here, take these with you, study them, and call me," he said.

Woody left with a knot in his stomach. He didn't relish the upcoming interview with Ms. Farrell and drove slowly. Karen O'Brien greeted him at the door and led him to the living room where Ms. Farrell and her attorney waited.

"Good afternoon, Detective. May I introduce you to my lawyer, Stuart Millheiser?" she asked.

They sat at the table, and Millheiser—not happy for being dispatched to Santa Barbara from Sir Basil's office on such short notice—immediately went on the defense. "Detective Ferguson, I advised Ms. Farrell against meeting you. We have nothing further to add, and I believe you are infringing on my client's privacy."

"I'm sorry you feel that way, Mr. Millheiser. This is a courtesy call to advise Ms. Farrell of new information we have, giving her a chance to explain, if she can. I could have made her drive down to Hollywood."

Deborah smiled. "Thank you, Detective, please proceed."

Woody sighed; he hoped her lawyer wouldn't make a fool out of him. "Ms. Farrell, on August 13, 1978, you told Detective Matteson that you were with a Hazel Sommers on August twelfth, the day that your husband, Mark Chambers, was murdered."

"Yes, I remember that nice man and that's what I said. And if I remember correctly, Detective Matteson got the same answer from Mrs. Sommers."

"Yes, he did at first before Mrs. Sommers became confused as to the date," Woody said.

"Well, did she agree finally on the date," Millheiser pointed out.

"Yes, on the twelfth," Woody agreed.

"Then, Detective, what's your problem? Why are you here?"

"Because, Mr. Millheiser, Mrs. Sommers was confused. Ms. Farrell was at her house on the eleventh, not the twelfth. We have Mrs. Sommers' 1978 calendar confirming that date and the testimony of a Ms. Logan that on the twelfth of August 1978, Mrs. Sommers was at her house all day with two other women." Woody was so nervous he nearly choked on the last sentence.

Deborah collapsed in her chair and Millheiser rushed to the sink for water.

Woody remained silent while Millheiser and Karen ministered to the stricken woman. After five minutes, Deborah recovered, but was pale and obviously upset.

"As you can see, Detective Ferguson, Ms. Farrell is in no condition to continue. I'll be in touch."

Woody said good-bye to Farrell and handed Millheiser his card. "I wouldn't wait too long to call me, Counselor. The district attorney is anxious to resolve this case."

Stuart Millheiser sat beside Deborah. "This is serious, Deborah," he said, concern etched on his face. "Now you not only don't have an alibi, but you lied to them. Do you have any answer to this problem?"

"I truly thought I was at her house on the twelfth. Maybe I was confused, but so was Hazel."

"If you weren't there, where were you on the day your husband was murdered?"

She lit a cigarette and sipped her water. "I don't remember."

Chapter 28

Requiem

Except for the few residents involved, there was little interest in the murder investigations swirling around the community. The "White Virgin" episode created quite a stir, both on and off the campus. Its solution disappointed those who fervently anticipated further visits and perhaps the "second coming," but delighted the majority who knew it was a hoax and hated the disruption caused by the crowds of onlookers. They were sorry for Sandra Garfield and hoped she would prevail in the ongoing lawsuit.

Old and frail Maude Perkins was forgiven for her transgressions. Chris Fowler, also feeling sympathy, let her remain at The Wind and Sea providing she had psychiatric help, which Rose Marie Dentz volunteered to provide.

The residents even lost interest in the Myers murder. Outside of being a member of the Breakfast Club, Arnold didn't participate in any resident activity. Few knew him and those that did were derisive.

General Fredrick Sutherland had been ensconced in that "cuckoo's nest," the Alzheimer's ward, euphemistically named "The Garden," but every once in a while he reappeared. Mostly, he caused amusement by commanding anyone near him to stand and salute a senior officer, but once he caused management a major problem. All sequestered patients needed exercise and when the weather allowed, caregivers took them for walks around the campus. On a beautiful, warm April day, Sutherland's caregiver escorted him on such an excursion. About one hundred feet from the Alzheimer's unit and toward the main gate, the general pointed to a winter mum bush. Thinking it would be a nice gesture, the caregiver left Sutherland standing and walked to pick a blossom for him. After snipping it she turned around to hand it to him, but he had disappeared.

Chris organized a search party to scour the campus—nothing. If he wasn't within the community fences, then he was outside them; the worst

168

nightmare an executive director could have. Lawsuits would be forthcoming from a stranger if the patient caused harm to him and from his family if the inmate was injured.

The police and the TV networks were called and they promised to do what they could. The general was not found by nightfall and Fowler spent the night cruising the neighborhood. His job was on the line.

By noon the next day a police cruiser stopped at the lobby door. A disheveled executive director rushed to meet it. A burly officer gently pulled a man out of the back seat. "Is this your truant?" he asked.

"Yes, thank you," Chris answered. "Where did you find him?"

"Sleeping on a bench in Aliso Park. It was cold last night and he was dressed only in a pajama top and cotton pants and slippers. The officer brought him back to the station to find him a blanket and give him some food. Poor guy. We had the word about your missing patient so after he was warm and fed we brought him here."

"General, what did you think you were doing?" Chris asked.

Sutherland saluted sharply. "Going to inspect the troops, sir. To see if they had everything they needed."

Living in a retirement community was like playing the children's game of "pretend." Nearly everyone at The Wind and Sea had had spouses and lived important, busy lives situated in large, comfortable homes surrounded by friends and family. These attributes now were different. Many husbands or wives had departed this life, the apartments were small, friends and family were gone. But the game of "pretend" made the changes bearable.

When The Wind and Sea opened, all the new residents extended themselves to make new friends. Now four years later, these acquaintances had become close dimming and eclipsing the memories of longtime friends lost through death or distance. It was sad to lose longtime friends and even more heartrending to have death terminate a meaningful new friendship. The average age of the residents was eighty-two. The insurance company's actuarial tables indicated that the mix of males and females now living at The Wind and Sea had a life expectancy of seventy-eight. Insurance companies became successful by relying on those tables, which soon proved their accuracy, making retirement life even more bittersweet.

Dee Leif, the poetess, after a three-year battle, succumbed to breast cancer. Her husband joined the single men. Bill Hastings, after shooting his best score, bought a round of drinks in the 19th Hole and suffered a fatal heart attack. His wife soon moved to be close to her daughter.

This was the "Greatest Generation" that had been challenged by the Great Depression and World War II. They had won those battles; they would be undaunted by sickness and death. There were parties to attend, romances to celebrate, and card games to be won.

Chapter 29

Epidemic

Every resident at The Wind and Sea was vaccinated each October against influenza, which struck in the winter months in Southern California. The first few month of 2000 were cruelat The Wind and Sea. All residents were in the high risk group for influenza. In addition, many suffered from chronic lung disease such as asthma or emphysema, heart disease, chronic kidney disease, anemia, or a compromised respiratory system. Their risk was multiplied, putting them in extreme danger.

J. C. Wellington was the first victim of this scourge. His body was racked with aches and pains with alternating chills and high fever and loss of appetite.

He was taken to the Santa Barbara Cottage Hospital where he expired. One by one the residents and the staff were stricken. The intensive care center at The Wind and Sea soon filled. Sir Basil sent his personal physician to take a sick Deborah Farrell to the St. Francis Medical Center.

Soon all four of the local hospitals were full as the epidemic ran wild, in the general public as well. Nearly everyone at The Wind and Sea was seriously ill and the authorities quarantined the institution. No one was allowed in or out.

Uncontrolled bowels and vomiting were two other ramifications of this disease and the reduced staff was unable to coup with cleaning up the mess. Soon the place stank; it was a hellhole. Michelle Woodhouse, the soprano, died, and it was two days before her body could be removed. All of the county and city health personnel were taxed to the limit—overwhelmed by the sheer magnitude of this vicious enemy. The Wind and Sea was on its own. Sir Basil tried to send a rescue team of doctors, nurses and workers to help, but the National Guard stopped them at the gate. He was allowed to offer only gauze masks and medical supplies.

Chris Fowler was infected, but insisted on making daily inspections to do what he could. Early one morning he discovered a scene so macabre and horrible it sent him screaming into the street. Four healthy women had sat down for a game of bridge in apartment 122 in the early evening. When he visited next at two in the morning all were seriously ill and struggling for breath. Three died within a week. This horrendous virus attacked the lungs, shutting off life-giving air.

Not to be denied Sir Basil obtained a court order to send in his special team with food and fresh water. They isolated the few remaining healthy persons into the top floor of the independent building. The first floor housed the most seriously ill. The less sickly were transferred to the second and third floor where cots were added to each room. The staff stayed on the fourth floor and in the cottages. The dead were removed immediately and taken to one of the over-crowded morgues in Santa Barbara and Ventura counties. Soon, temporary morgues were established in several abandoned warehouses; coffins were hastily built of plywood.

This virulent strain of flu didn't spread across the country evenly, but was isolated in pockets across the nation, with Southern California being affected the worst. Medical authorities concluded it was brought into the Los Angeles Harbor aboard a freighter from China which was also experiencing a SARS pandemic.

Gradually, the scourge abated and by the middle of March no new cases were reported. Emergency wards were closed, and the residents returned to their apartments and cottages. Thirteen residents of The Wind and Sea had died; ninety-percent had been seriously infected. Authorities tried to ascertain why this community was so viciously attacked. No conclusion ever was forthcoming, but the nearness of a chicken farm and the visit of a contingent of planners from China sent to study retirement communities, were noted as possible causes.

As the community emerged from disaster, Sir Basil and Chris Fowler were elevated in the minds of the residents. The camaraderie felt by the residents for one another now extended to the staff and Sir Basil. Together they had fought the enemy and survived. They were brothers. One for all and all for one.

Enrico Di Donoto also became a hero. When everyone was so sick, he distributed joints of marijuana to all that wanted them. They helped relieve the pain of the disease both physically and mentally. The smell of the weed's smoke masked the odor of the uncontrolled bodily functions brought on by the flu.

The smell of marijuana was so unique it would be detected immediately now that the place was clean. Enrico had an idea and took it to Fowler. "Chris, many men and some women enjoy smoking cigarettes and cigars and marijuana joints. They enjoy this habit and it's not harmful to anyone else, but the smoke will smell up the halls and rooms. Let's take one of the apartments, you have several not occupied, and convert it into a smoking room. I'll equip it with the latest venting system that will remove all the smoke and odor. It's expensive, but it will be my pleasure to provide it. I'll also buy a pool table and a poker table. What do you say?"

Fowler thought for a few minutes, and then went to his personal bathroom. After returning he looked Enrico in the face. "Officially, here's what I can do without getting permission from headquarters. If you'll pay for everything, I'll let you use one of the unoccupied rooms, probably 442, as a rumpus and smoking room. I'll agree to tobacco smoking and marijuana, too, if I can't smell it. Just be sure your venting system gets rid of that odor and I'll let everyone know when I'm coming to that room. One other thing, be sure you do the remodeling legally with all the necessary building permits and insurance policies, okay?"

"More than okay; I'll get going immediately," Enrico said. As he was leaving he turned and asked, "By the way, would you like a few joints?"

Chapter 30

Recovery

By the end of March, things were getting back to normal at The Wind and Sea. The large flag at the main gate flew at half staff, and Memorial services for the thirteen dead residents were held in the Great Hall. Chris Fowler returned from a few days off ten pounds thinner; and his once-tanned face was now a gray pallor. All of the rooms had been steam cleaned and new furniture replaced those badly stained pieces.

The resident's *esprit de corps* heightened. They had met a deadly foe and won. A sense of comradeship and loyalty to The Wind and Sea was strong. It no longer was "us against them," but rather "one for all and all for one."

The Great Hall had a full schedule. Soloists, string quartets, a chorale group, and even a full orchestra came and did their part to revive an embattled community. The Santa Barbara Opera Company performed *Cavalier Rusticana* to an enthusiastic audience, who loudly applauded and vented the air with many "bravos."

The residents knew that Deborah Farrell had donated a lot of money for the extra nurses and medical supplies and she was a big hero. Even Sir Basil received much praise for his efforts—he'd ignored the cost and did what he could to alleviate the suffering.

Victory was achieved but the cost was high. The occupancy rate was now down to eighty percent. The cost for damage and replacement of assets would be in six figures, and the residents were worried that this burden would be theirs. Rumors spread that Sir Basil had given up and would sell The Wind and Sea to the highest bidder.

As soon as they were able, romantic couples began to see each other again. Gunther Krause and Rose Marie Dentz surprised everyone by announcing their engagement, with the wedding to follow in late spring. Here were two large people in their eighties acting like they were in their twenties. "Remember your age, Gunther; you don't want a heart attack," one wag advised. These two took the jokes about their relationship in stride and suggested in return that everyone else was jealous of their late-in-life virility.

Mary Lee Hopkins and Francis Pisano's relationship was treated differently. No one teased these two. Mary Lee was an ex-school teacher and had experience in handling tough, unruly boys. She always gave residents more than they delivered and soon they learned to stay out of her area of authority. Pisano was a quiet and private man with worldly experience whom no one wanted to test. If, as everyone assumed, Mary Lee was an innocent, old maid before meeting Pisano, she now was viewed as an experienced senior, college coed cheerleader—and she smiled more.

Roger Palmer advised The Wind and Sea that he would not be returning and to please list his cottage for sale. He would be living with his wife at her New York address.

An election was held and Mary Lee Hopkins became the new president of the executive council, replacing the late J. C. Wellington. Enrico Di Donoto became the vice-president. Many residents were fearful of this "hammer and anvil" team. She would be too abrasive, and he, too scary. This management would challenge the establishment, and all the gains made during the last year would be forfeited. Their fears were unfounded. Mary Lee didn't write a manifesto for the oppressed residents, she became conciliatory and friendly and management reciprocated.

This euphoria was to last only a short time. Two events were about to overwhelm The Wind and Sea that affected everyone from Sir Basil to the cleaning ladies.

*   *   *   *

"We dodged a bullet," Sir Basil told his officers, Frank Carter, and the investigator, Omar in the conference room at his headquarters in Los Angeles. "In costs, loss of income, damages, and cleanup, the epidemic left a price tag of about two million dollars. It took a much higher toll on the residents— thirteen dead. Frank. I trust our insurance will cover us against any lawsuits for mismanagement."

"It will, Sir Basil, unless somewhere in our chain of command someone did something stupid. Anyway, so far so good," the lawyer answered.

"Those are good people we have there at The Wind and Sea. I'm very fond of them. They won't sue frivolously."

Watts, Quinn and Turner looked at one another and smiled. They knew who he was talking about when he mentioned fondness.

"Let's get a crew up there as soon as possible and get the community whole again. My projection had us breaking even in about two years. Now, my guess is it will take about five, but we'll stay with the six percent rate increase per year. We can't afford to increase the vacancy rate. You notice that Goodwin Oliver is not here. I've terminated our president for malfeasance and promoted John Watts to take his place. Congratulations, John."

Everyone applauded and slapped John on his back; he was very popular.

"I'm told a smoking room has been added at Enrico Di Donoto's expense and marijuana is the most popular flavor. I trust Enrico; he'll keep this activity under control." Sir Basil turned a sheet of paper face down on the table, and studied the next one. "Omar, you can cross J. C. Wellington off your list of those to be investigated. The poor fellow didn't survive the flu. What else do you have for us?"

Omar stood and read from his notebook. "First, the news that I just received—Paul Ostrow and his wife, Yvonne, have left. They're paid up and didn't leave a forwarding address."

Sir Basil jerked to attention. "Wasn't he the man who had his face bandaged?"

"Yes, supposedly from a car accident," Omar explained. "But I'm sure it wasn't, and he hadn't had a plastic surgeon work on him either, in my opinion. It was a mask to hide his identity. Evidently, there's no reason for him to continue this charade, but Ostrow may have fit somehow in another situation I'm exploring involving Gunther Krause. In my guts, I have new knowledge about Gunther's past activities and I believe that somehow they had something to do with Myers' death."

Everyone in the room quit talking; Frank Carter lifted his pen.

"Gunther came to this country in 1957 and went to work for a New York bank. In 1965 he took a leave of absence and was gone for two years. He often talks about South America and I assume that's where he went. Why South America? Germans, especially the Nazis, flocked there after the war to escape war crime prosecutions. Perhaps he went to visit family or friends there. Let me digress for a moment.

"As you know I speak four languages including Lebanese and Hebrew. When I lived in Lebanon, I met Isaac Stein, an officer in the Mossad, the Jewish intelligence agency, which is said to be the best in the world. Anyway, I translated for him when he was interrogating suspected Lebanon terrorists. Isaac and I became good friends. He's now assigned to the United Nations in New York. Two weeks ago, he contacted me and I flew back there to spend a few days with him. I asked if he had ever met a Gunther Krause. His eyes sparkled and he became quite animated.

"'Gunther's a great man' Isaac had said. 'He went to Argentina in 1965 to visit relatives that had fled the horrors of Germany. I met him through a member of his family. He spoke Spanish fluently with them, so I asked him to work with us. Five years before, we had captured the big fish, Karl Adolph Eichmann, packed him off to Israel, and hanged him for unspeakable brutality. But there were dozens more smaller fish hiding in Argentina and Gunther helped us tremendously in tracking them down. Give him the credit for bagging Ernst Kohler, Hans Steiger, and that butcher, Rudolf Bergman.'"

Omar wiped the sweat from his face. "Gunther stayed two years to help them, and then returned to the U. S.—California—to start his real estate business."

Sir Basil stroked his moustache. "So Gunther is a Jew—he looks like a poster German. Why suspect him of wanting to kill another Jew?"

Omar took a sip of water. "Isaac Stein told me the Mossad and Gunther were also hunting Jews who had helped the Nazis. Many Jews were blonde with blue eyes, had non-Jewish names, and pretended they were Christians to save themselves from the death camps. These Jews were cowards, and to save their own skin, identified other Jews, those who had escaped Nazi notice. Isaac said that Gunther really stayed to capture one Wilhelm Kleiner, a Jew who had betrayed him and sent him and his family to the infamous Majdanek camp in Lubin, Poland. His wife and two small children were gassed. We never found Kleiner but heard that he had immigrated to the United States."

They all sat stunned at the conference table. "My God, what a burden to carry around all these years. Hatred is so debilitating," Sir Basil commented. "Omar, are you saying that Arnold Myers was Wilhelm Steiner and that Gunther discovered his real identity and had his revenge?"

"Yes, Sir Basil, I am."

"Then turn everything you have over to Lieutenant Blake McGee. I hate to do this to Krause, but we have information that belongs to the police. This case will be resolved sooner than later."

Sir Basil then grabbed Omar's arm and led him to a far corner of the conference room. "Omar, Maude Perkins was our mole at The Wind and Sea, wasn't she?"

"Yes, Sir Basil, but she died in the flu epidemic."

"Don't replace her." Sir Basil looked directly into the investigator's eyes. "I mean it, Omar, No more spying."

"Okay, boss, I agree. Also, we've lost Abby. He's working for Enrico Di Donoto now."

"Omar, are we still getting kick-backs from that Indian gambling casino?"

"Yes, Sir Basil." Omar checked his notebook. "About twenty thousand a month."

"Stop it, and I mean immediately. That's pimping and I don't want to be part of that despicable enterprise."

Exhausted, Sir Basil sat back down. He looked ten years older than his seventy-seven years. "There's nothing on the agenda that's needs immediate attention. Let's go home."

He started to rise and shake everyone's hands, but instead slumped back into his chair. "Stay a few minutes, Frank. I need to talk to you," he whispered to his lawyer.

After the others had left, and in a soft, low voice, Sir Basil said, "Frank, I'm worried about Debby. L.A.'s new district attorney, Nigel Fairbanks, wants to become governor. He needs to win a gold-plated case; I think he's going to reopen the Mark Chambers' murder case. She doesn't have an alibi any more and now can't remember where she was on that fateful day. It's all circumstantial, but it could be convincing. Tell me about Stuart Millheiser; is he really a solid criminal defense lawyer?"

Frank stood and walked over to his old friend and wrapped his arms around him. "I wouldn't have recommended him to you, Sir Basil, if I didn't think he was the best. I don't believe he's ever lost a case."

"I love that woman and want to live with her. I can't do that if she's in jail."

"That won't happen, my dear friend. I guarantee it," the lawyer said.

For the first time since his days at Eton, the tall, knighted Englishman openly cried.

Chapter 31

Mea Culpa

Lieutenant Woodrow Ferguson hadn't slept; today would be the worst day of his life. No eggs or bacon for breakfast; coffee would be all he could keep down. He shaved carefully, looking long and hard at himself in the mirror. *You bastard*, he thought.

He arrived at his office, picked up the necessary papers, and, without speaking to anyone, jumped into the passenger seat of an unmarked car. Uniformed officer, James Gilmore, drove and Sergeant Murphy sat in the back. He tried not to think about the task at hand during the ninety-minute drive to Santa Barbara and concentrated on the beautiful spring day, the sparkling ocean, the green hills, and the California poppies that were in full bloom.

Much too soon for Woody, they arrived at The Wind and Sea gate, were admitted, and drove to the intended building. Ferguson strolled to the door and rang the bell.

Steve answered the door. "Hello, Woody. What's up?"

"I'm sorry, Steve, but you are under arrest for the murder of Hazel Sommers. You have the right to remain silent. Anything you say can and will be held against you in a court of law—"

"Forget Miranda, I know my rights," Matteson said indignantly.

"I also have a court-ordered warrant to search the premises." Woody presented the document to Steve.

"Gilmore, you take the bedrooms and living room. Murphy, take the rest. You know what to look for," Woody ordered. "And Steve, I'll have to cuff you."

"Should I get my lawyer?" Steve asked in a barely audible voice.

"That's up to you," Woody answered.

"As old friends, can you tell me what you have?"

178

"Steve, you know I'm not supposed to talk to my prisoners about an impending case. I'm just a foot soldier—the messenger. The district attorney will want to interrogate you as soon as we get back to my precinct. I strongly urge you to have your lawyer present at that time. I know only what I put in my report."

"Can't you at least tell me what you reported?" Steve begged.

Woody stalled. He knew he shouldn't say anything, but his old friend was in mental anguish and he wanted to offer some relief. "Only Captain Milford and I knew that Sommers was murdered in her house. Everyone thought she was killed where they found her on the vacant lot. A few days ago you stated to me, unequivocally, that she was killed in her house and that's where tooth fragments would be found. Only the murderer knew those facts."

Steve became animated and tried to swing his manacled hands. "Hell, Woody, that was just an educated guess. No one would knock out her teeth and acid wash her fingers out in the open in full sight of everyone. Her house was the logical place to do it."

"They didn't think so twenty years ago," Woody stated.

"Hell, they didn't think about anything. It was a terrible investigation."

"Convince the district attorney. I'm sorry, Steve, but I can't say more."

"These cuffs are very uncomfortable. Can't you remover them?" Steve said, shaking his hands. "I give you my word I'll say right here."

"Sure. Give me your car keys and stay in the living room," Woody said, gently taking the cuffs off as Steve handed him his keys.

Steve sat back on the sofa and read a magazine while Woody checked with his men. He then came back and sat with Steve. Three hours later, Murphy and Gilmore approached Woody.

"Look what we found," Gilmore said. He laid a service .38 caliber handgun on the table.

Murphy put down a gallon-sized paint can and an eight-by-ten framed black and white photograph. "These are what you wanted, right?"

Woody nodded. "Steve, pack your necessary toiletries and a change of clothes. Let's go."

"Want to drink a beer first?" Steve asked.

The men looked longingly at Woody, but he shook his head. "No thanks. We're on duty."

Traffic had increased, and for two hours, Gilmore drove, Murphy slept, and Steve and Woody were deep in their private thoughts. After arriving in Hollywood, Woody booked his prisoner and escorted him back to a cell. He checked the accumulated notes and made a few calls, then went back to Steve. "An assistant district attorney will be here tomorrow at eleven o'clock," he advised his old friend. "You should have your attorney here then, too."

Carter Hall, Steve's attorney arrived an hour early to talk to his client in the interrogation room. Clarence Atkinson, the young assistant D.A. came at eleven. He was a nervous young man who had an indefinable accent from somewhere in Kentucky. Woody and a court reporter joined them.

"What is my client charged with?" Hall asked.

"Murder in the first degree of one Hazel Sommers."

"Based on what evidence?" Hall demanded.

"Opportunity, means, and motive," Clarence answered, moving not only his lips, but also his head, which bobbed up and down. "Opportunity—his whereabouts were unknown during the twenty-four hours prior to the discovery of Sommers' body. Means—because he had the gun that killed her, and motive because for some reason he was trying to protect Ms. Farrell."

Woody looked down at the table, but Hall looked sharply at Steve when the gun was mentioned; Ferguson knew what Atkinson knew.

"You found Lieutenant Matteson's service revolver. It didn't kill anyone," Hall replied.

He had been waiting for this opportunity, and wore a cockeyed smirk on his face. "True, but the gun Juan Hernandez used to rob that convenience store was the one that killed Mrs. Sommers. He stole it from Matteson's cottage."

"He didn't remember where he found it," Hall exploded.

Clarence liked having the answer and sticking it to an adversary. "Oh yes he did, later. Tell them, Lieutenant Ferguson."

"I called Juan a few days ago. He remembered one picture you had on your wall, Steve, a photograph of three L. A. police officers. You, Steve, stood with the other two kneeling in front of you. The officers pointed their revolvers at the photographer. It frightened Juan and he remembered it. We recovered that photograph from your garage. Also, a couple of months ago, before we captured Juan, your walls were covered with pictures. After the store robbery and Juan's testimony about the pictures, you removed all of them and painted the walls to cover the nail holes and fade marks. We found a partially used can of paint from your garage that matched the new paint."

Clarence waved Woody aside and continued. "Besides Captain Milford and Woody, only the murderer knew the homicide took place in the Sommers home and that there were tooth fragments there. One other fact, you said the ground around the body was well raked. It was when you left it, but there were only traces of the raking when our crime scene people arrived because the ground had been trampled on by the police, newsmen, and sightseers. And one other thing; you were the last person to see Sommers alive."

"No, I wasn't!" Steve shouted. "I visited her on August fifteenth. Holli Logan talked to her on the sixteenth. Ask her."

"We have. You visited on the fifteenth. Sommers talked to Logan on the morning of the sixteenth and then you came back that night and killed her." The assistant D.A. pounded the table triumphantly.

"That's enough for now. I would like to talk to my client alone," Carter Hall said.

"Fine, but the hearing in front of the judge takes place tomorrow afternoon. He'll be binding you over for trial and we'll be asking that your client be remanded without bail."

Clarence Atkinson was so pleased with himself he stopped just short of imitating Tarzan's triumphant bellow. He controlled himself with curt graciousness, "You may use this room. Call the guard when you're finished. Good afternoon."

After Clarence and Woody left, Hall removed his coat and hung it over the back of a chair. "All they have is the gun; the rest is circumstantial, but that damn gun is all they need," he advised.

"I didn't murder her—it was self-defense," Steve declared.

"You'd better tell me all about it." Hall plucked a pen from the inside pocket of his jacket.

"Mark Chambers was murdered on August twelfth. Deborah Farrell said she was with Hazel Sommers on that date as an alibi. I visited Sommers on the fifteenth at her home in Brentwood. At first she confirmed Farrell's alibi for the twelfth. Then she became confused and couldn't remember whether it was the twelfth or eleventh. Finally, she said she was positive it was the twelfth. I left and went back to my office thinking the matter was closed.

"Sommers called about two p. m. on the sixteenth and wanted to see me again that night at six. I arrived on time and we sat at that little table in her den. She apologized, and then stated that she had talked to her friend, Holli Logan, and now she was sure that Farrell was at her house on the eleventh, not the twelfth. That date was critically important to this case so I wanted her to be sure. I initiated an argument with her, stating that I thought she was mistaken. Our verbal exchange became heated and she swore and pounded the table. 'You think I have dementia, don't you,' she said.

"'No, I believe you're confused,' I replied.

"'God damn you,' she yelled and reached over to the lamp table next to where we sat, opened a drawer and pulled out the Browning .22 caliber pistol, and pointed it at me. I reacted and grabbed the barrel of the gun. We wrestled for a moment; she was unbelievably strong. One of us pulled the trigger and the bullet hit me in the fleshy part of my upper right leg. I finally got control of the gun as a second shot hit her in the chest. Honestly, I don't know whether I pulled the trigger or she did. As she fell away from me, she grabbed the gun—my finger had remained on the trigger—and a second shot hit her. I just reacted the way I was taught. The last thing I wanted to do was to hurt her. It was either self-defense or an accident."

Hall stopped writing and looked at Steve. "It was, but can we prove it?" He looked back down at his notes. "Go on, what did you do next?"

"I believed that if Sommers disappeared, Farrell's alibi for the twelfth would hold-up. Holli Logan would think that Hazel had left for a few days and wouldn't go to the police to change the date. Her disappearance had nothing to do with the Mark Chambers murder. Holli never put the two together until after DNA tests proved that the Pink Daffodil was Sommers.

"I hated to do it, but I had to make the body unidentifiable by removing and breaking her teeth and acid dipping her fingers. Otherwise the authorities would blame Farrell for Sommers' death."

"Why?" Hall asked. "Why did you care if Farrell had an alibi? If she was guilty of the murder of her husband, she should be punished. Why didn't you act like a police officer should?"

Steve hung his head; tears rolled down his face. His whole body seemed to shrink as he stared, not at, but through his lawyer. "Because I loved her. I began loving her the first time we met and it increased with every visit. She is so lovely, so vulnerable, and so ephemeral. She needed protection against all the barbs and thorns of this world. I would be her knight in shining armor. Then maybe she would recognize me and love me in return. That's all I wanted."

"You risked everything and she doesn't even know you exist."

"I know. It sounds crazy. My wife died years earlier. We were deeply in love. For three years I was lonely and miserable. I looked at no other woman and then Deborah came into my life. I was struck by a bolt of lightening."

Hall hugged his client. "You poor bastard; I'm sorry."

A guard rapped on the door. "How much longer, Counselor?"

"Ten minutes," Carter answered. "Go on, Steve."

"I wanted to localize any collateral damage so I moved the table and laid her on that crocheted rug that was underneath it. I found some swimming pool acid in the garage and poured some in a bowl and soaked her hands in it. I took the blood-stained rug behind the garage and washed it in the Clorox I found and left it in the garage hoping it wouldn't be recognized as the rug from the den.

"After searching for tooth fragments, I wrapped the body in a sheet and put it in the trunk of my car along with a rake from the garage and a pink daffodil I took from a bunch in the kitchen. I think maybe Deborah brought her the flowers on her last visit. I drove until I found a deserted lot about two miles away. I didn't want to just dump her. I wanted her to look as nice as possible so I raked an area, laid out the body properly, left the daffodil in her hand, said a prayer for her, and left. It was now about two a. m. on the seventeenth of August." Steve was exhausted as he finished and sat with his head in his hands.

"That may be a true story, but the prosecutor is not going to believe it and it will be difficult to sell to a jury," Hall surmised. "It wasn't premeditated so the state will go for second-degree murder but that's fifteen years to life. You don't deserve that. What you're really guilty of is obstruction of justice. It was either self-defense or accidental death, which, if proved, would get you off free, but it's just your word and I don't think a jury will buy either plea. If only we had something they wanted, we could plea bargain. Everything is plea bargained these days; nobody wants the time, cost, and uncertainty of a trial."

Steve, who had been completely detached and feeling sorry for himself, suddenly came to attention. "You want a bargaining chip, Counselor?"

"Yes, something—anything."

"I've had this stored in my conscious for over twenty years. It's been eating at me and now is the time to use it."

"Go ahead; I'm interested," Carter said. "I'll get another ten minutes from the guard."

For the next ten minutes Steve told his lawyer what had happened twenty years previously and who was involved.

Hall clapped his hands together. "Fantastic! That's platinum plated. I can't wait to lay it on that peacock, Clarence. He's going to run screaming to his boss, that jerk, Nigel Fairbanks."

Hall phoned Clarence Atkinson the next morning. "It would be a good idea if we meet one more time before the hearing this afternoon."

"Why?" the assistant district attorney asked. "He owned the gun that killed her—first-degree murder."

"Don't you want to know what really happened, and how, or do you want to appear unprepared before the judge," Carter said. "Let's keep it off the record for the time being. No recorder."

Clarence hesitated, and then talked to someone in the D.A. office. "Okay, I'll be there at eleven. I hope I'm not wasting my time. Don't want to short change the taxpayers, you know."

He arrived on time, then sat down like a potentate waiting for oblations. "I'm ready. Now tell me what really happened, but don't insult my intelligence."

Steve was prepared and began. "You were right. Mrs. Sommers called me and asked that I return, she said she made a mistake and wanted to set the record straight. She was nervous and distraught. She was difficult to understand; she may have been drinking. In frustration I asked, 'Well, what date did she come over here? Was it the eleventh, the twelve, or the thirteenth?' Maybe I was a little too rough because I must have scared her. She reached over to the lamp table next to where we were sitting, opened the drawer and pulled out the Browning.

"I tried to grab the gun, but she was unbelievably strong. She resisted, and pulled the trigger. The bullet struck me in the upper part of my right leg and bled Type-A blood on the rug. I thought she was going to kill me and I tried to again take control of the gun. In the tussle the trigger was pulled twice and I don't know whose finger was on the trigger, but both shots hit her in the chest and she died. It was self-defense."

Atkinson laughed and clapped his hands enthusiastically. "Marvelous, send the script to Hollywood; maybe its Oscar material."

"It was self-defense or an accident. What motive did Matteson have for murdering her? He never met her before the fifteenth. Why would he want to harm her? The judge will want to know. I think he'll buy our story. It makes better sense," Hall said.

"Maybe, but what about the cover up, knocking out the teeth and acid washing the fingers. If it was self-defense why not just leave the story to the authorities?" Clarence asked.

Carter conferred with Steve for five minutes, then spoke. "My client doesn't agree with me but gave me the authority to accept a charge of 'obstruction of justice,' no jail time."

Clarence laughed so hard he choked. "Let's just go and see the judge and stop wasting my time," he said after he gained control.

"Your boss, Nigel Fairbanks, is a good friend of Justice Roger Palmer, isn't he?" Carter asked coyly.

"Yes, they were in the same law partnership."

"And Fairbanks will be running for governor of California on the Republican ticket next fall, won't he?"

"Yes, and he'll win in a landslide."

"And Justice Palmer is heading his campaign and is his chief fundraiser. Isn't he?"

"Yes Mr. Fairbanks is proud to have such a distinguished man in charge of his campaign."

Carter had him hooked and now started to reel him in. "Justice Palmer can't head up your campaign or any thing else if he's in jail, can he?"

The smile disappeared and a twisted mouth shouted, "What the hell do you mean? You could be sued."

"Not by the judge. Do you remember Deborah Farrell's trial in 1979? The one that Judge Palmer stopped because someone tampered with the jury— a little dark man with stringy hair?"

"Yes. We had that trial won before the tampering."

"Now listen carefully, you little sycophant, Judge Roger Palmer hired that little man to talk to the jurors and get the trial stopped. And we know where that little man is and he will testify for us and identify your precious judge as the man who paid him to bribe the jurors." Carter relished every word.

"Why would such a distinguished man stoop to such a trick for the murder trial of a woman he didn't know?" Clarence shot back.

"Because that worthy man was in love with the woman on trial," Carter whispered in the prosecutor's ear.

"I don't believe you—you're bluffing," a frightened attorney gasped.

"Bluffing are we? You go to Judge Palmer and tell him what we offered. Then tell him that this little man with stringy hair goes by the name of Paddy; he has a tattoo of a naked lady on his right bicep that does the bump when he flexes his muscle. Tell Palmer Paddy has a lisp, and he used to be a snitch for Lieutenant Matteson, and is very loyal to him because Matteson saved him from prison once."

"To give you time to contact Judge Palmer, who is in New York, I suggest you talk to our judge and get a delay. After you talk to Palmer, talk to Nigel and see if he doesn't agree with our offer—obstruction of justice, no jail time—and let's add no fine either. Steve will do six months community service."

"Damn you, Hall. Matteson kills a woman and you want him to go free."

"Right, Clarence; that's exactly what we want and we're sure your boss will agree. Justice must be served."

The smile widened on the face of the suddenly animated Steve Matteson. "Mr. Atkinson, when you contact Judge Palmer ask him what body and paint shop repaired his right front fender. It's important."

After Clarence stormed out of the interrogation room, Carter Hall asked, "What was that all about?"

"Sir Basil made a presentation at The Wind and Sea a few weeks ago," Steve answered. "Afterward, he walked Deborah back to her cottage. Roger Palmer followed them and I followed him. I saw him peeping through Farrell's bedroom window and in a few minutes leave mad as hell. I looked and saw what had upset him; Sir Basil was making love to Deborah. The judge had been her steady boyfriend until Sir Basil showed up. When Sir Basil left for Los Angeles, he said a big car followed and forced him off the road near Ventura. He plunged down an embankment into the ocean and was damn near killed. I know, but can't prove that big car was driven by Judge Palmer. I wanted the judge to know. It will help him make up his mind to tell Nigel what to decide on my punishment."

Hall pulled his jacket off the back of the chair. "Steve, why did you keep that gun? That was a stupid thing to do."

"I know. I had a deep fascination for it. It mesmerized me. You know, after the incident, I resigned from the force, changed my first name, and moved to Santa Barbara. I wanted to distance myself from what I had done and yet I kept the gun. I can't explain it."

Chapter 32

So Close and yet so Far

Omar sent the information about Gunther Krause overnight to Blake McGee. He read it twice and then took another look at his Krause interview. "Now I know why Myers was afraid of Paul and Yvonne Ostrow, Rose Marie Dentz, and Gunther Krause. They were all Jews—his worst nightmare. Blake contacted the British Immigration Service and without too much difficulty, it located Wilheim Kleiner's file. Kleiner must carefully have covered his work for the Nazis because there was no mention of anything in the file that would have attracted attention from the War Crimes Commission.

The wartime Nazi authorities listed him as Lutheran, unfit for military service, and assigned as a train switch operator in Berlin. Without checking further, Western Germany's government in Bonn in 1952 accepted this report and the British government did too.

Kleiner emigrated to England in 1952 and three months later fled to Argentina as an ordinary seaman on a freighter. England at that time was checking all immigrants for any possible connection to the Nazis and evidently he became fearful.

McGee also asked the British authorities to check on an Arnold Myers. It discovered that an Arnold Myers had emigrated from Argentina in 1960 and left for the United States in 1962 where he was granted citizenship five years later.

McGee called and reported everything to Woody Ferguson, starting with Omar's package. "Arnold was a very savvy guy. He conned both the Bonn and British governments. He didn't go directly to Argentina from Germany because Mossad would be looking at that escape route, so he slipped into the country as a British seaman. Then guessing that any Nazi hunters would be checking Argentina civilians going directly to the U. S., he went back to

England and then two years later into the United States. When trying to escape it's best not to travel in a straight line."

"I believe Sir Basil's man, Omar, cracked your case wide open," Woody remarked. "Gunther was sick the night of the murder and had no alibi, he had a dozen objects in his apartment that could have been used as the murder weapon, and he had a motive. You won't get a better suspect than Gunther Krause."

"I'm going to call Gunther, tell him what I know, and hope he will add to it," Blake said.

"Okay, remember Arnold was brutally murdered and Gunther is big and strong," Woody said. He didn't mention Steve Matteson's case.

Two days later, Lieutenant McGee called and made an appointment with Krause. Sergeant Malloy went with him. It was a lovely spring day when Santa Barbara was unsurpassed. A gentle breeze from the ocean subdued the heat from the sun. Everything growing burst forth with the colors of a rainbow, and the redness reflected off the tile roofs added energy to the blues, greens, and yellows of the abundant plants. Everything was so boisterous, so cheerful, so filled with vivacity, so perfect. *God is in his heaven and all is right in the world*

Except everything was not all right in Blake's world. He liked Gunther Krause and hated what he had to do.

"Hi, Mr. Krause. Remember me? I'm Lieutenant Blake McGee, Santa Barbara police," he announced as the door opened. "Sergeant Malloy will be taking notes."

Krause was dressed casually, but wore a long-sleeve sport shirt on this hot day in April. "Is it again about the Myers murder?" he asked.

"Yes, I'm afraid it is," Blake answered with a hardened overtone.

"I have nothing to add to my last testimony. I was sick and alone with no alibi but stayed in my room all night. I had no motive to kill that pitiful man. Would you like some coffee or something stronger, Lieutenant?" Gunther asked as he stood to get the drinks.

"No thanks," Blake answered as he looked into the sorrowful brown eyes of a man who had suffered too much. "But you do have a motive, Mr. Krause. A powerful one. Wilheim Kleiner, alias Arnold Myers, caused the torture and deaths of your wife and two small children."

Gunther staggered and almost fell as he slipped back into his chair. He buried his face in his hands. "I've lived with that horrible secret a long time, Lieutenant, almost sixty years. But I didn't kill him. I've wanted to do to him what the Nazis did to me and my family, but I didn't."

"Mr. Krause, we know most of what happened, but not all. We know that Kleiner—Myers—left Germany in the fifties, paused briefly in England, then worked his way to Argentina on a freighter, and changed his name to Arnold Myers. He then returned to England for a couple of years and immigrated to the U. S. We know that in 1965 and 1966 you worked with the Israeli intelligence agency, Mossad. You went to Argentina looking for Myers, but missed him by a few years. How did you catch up with him at The Wind and Sea?"

"The Mossad. It has had a team tracking him since the sixties. They finally found him in Hollywood. One of its agents recognized him when he was on a television talent show reading his poetry. They tracked him to The Wind and Sea, and advised me and I moved here too. I had requested that Mossad allow me to be present when it captured him."

"But you killed him instead—you and the Ostrows, Paul and Yvonne. They were Mossad, weren't they?"

"Yes, but killing him was not in their plans. They wanted to capture him and send him back to Israel where he would be tried in open court, where the entire world could see what a monster he was, and then hang him."

"Tell me, please, what he did to you."

Krause was a worldly, sophisticated man with bright intelligence and insight. He was a courteous, gentle man who seldom smiled. A melancholy sadness was deeply ingrained in his psyche, but when asked about his distant past on this warm, beautiful day, memories forced a full smile to blossom on his face.

"Have you ever been to Lubec, Germany, Lieutenant?"

"No, Mr. Krause, I haven't."

"Go when you get a chance. It's a small, ninth-century town on the Baltic; it's Hansel and Gretel, Disneyland. Flowers painted on the little houses, men in their lederhosen pants, women in their colorful aprons. A comic opera sort of town, toy soldiers, everyone singing . . . . We had a small house by a river. We had a dog, Hugo, and my little boy, Franz, who was two, and I played with him near the river. My one-year-old daughter, Klara, stayed home and helped her mother, Terese. We were so happy for two years—then Kleiner." The smile left to be replaced with hateful scowl.

"I was the assistant manager of our family bank in Lubec. The war had started, but so far the Nazis hadn't bothered us. Krause is not especially a Jewish name and we didn't openly practice our Jewish religion. I gave special attention to the German officers who patronized the bank. I spoke four languages and offered my services to the German army, which they used from time to time.

"Wilheim Kleiner came into the bank, looked around, introduced himself to me, and left. A few days later he returned and asked for me. He said he wanted to open an account, but had never dealt with a gentile bank. He was obviously Jewish and I assured him his money would be safe. The third time he came he again asked for me. He wanted to attend a Jewish service because it had been a long time since he had. We were having one at my house on the next Friday night and I invited him. He came and I introduced him to other men. Two days later the Gestapo came to our houses and hauled us away to the infamous Majdanek prison camp in Lubin, Poland. I was the only survivor of this group. The American army saved my life, because when it arrived, I weighed only ninety pounds."

McGee went to Krause and patted him on the arm. After a few minutes of silence McGee asked, "Your prison identifying numbers are tattooed on the inside of your arm, aren't they, and that's why you wear those long-sleeved shirts, even in the summer?"

"Yes, and did you notice that Myers had no numbers on his arm?"

"No. I wonder if the medical examiner, Jake Conroy, found any?"

"He couldn't," Gunther quickly added. "He didn't have any—the bastard. He sent thousands of Jews to their untimely deaths in those prison camps and not a mark on him." Gunther stopped and the tears flooded from his eyes. "My poor babies, my poor babies," tumbled from his mouth as he recoiled from the horror of his memories.

"I believe the court will be lenient with you, Mr. Krause. No man could take what you did without retaliating."

"But Lieutenant, I didn't kill him."

McGee shook his head. "You waited two years before acting against Myers, why?"

"The problem was transportation. Paul Ostrow was a Mossad agent. His head was bandaged to hide his real identity. I don't know his real name, but I know he's a major in the Mossad. Eighteen months ago he and his wife, with my help, were going to kidnap Myers and smuggle him onto an Israeli steamer making a special trip to L. A. for that purpose. Something happened and the steamer trip was canceled. Since the first of the year, we've been waiting for an Israeli diplomatic group to arrive in Los Angeles. We were going to dope Myers and take him to that group, who had a passport and other papers for him, but they've been delayed. Since Myers was killed, Paul and Yvonne have been waiting orders for another assignment. It came last week and they disappeared."

"A jury won't believe that you could live for two years near the monster that murdered you wife and children without revenge. No man could restrain himself that long; I couldn't. Your only hope is to get the Ostrows to return and confirm to the court what you have told me."

"They can't; Israel won't let them. The two countries have diplomatic ties. Kidnapping a citizen of the United States and taking him to Israel to be executed would cause serious damage between these two friendly nations. They have to do their jobs, and I'll just have to take my chances, alone."

McGee banged the table with his fist. "It's not fair. After all you've been through because of this horrible creature and now he comes back from the grave to inflict more pain. Damn it."

"You have the right to remain silent," McGee read from a piece of paper. "If you say anything it may be used against you in a court of law. You have the right to have an attorney—"

Gunther waved his arm. "Don't bother, Lieutenant. I know my rights; I'll be all right. I hope the food here doesn't go to the dogs. Tell Rose Marie I love her and will miss her."

"I will, Mr. Krause. I'm sorry but I'll have to cuff you."

"That's okay, Lieutenant. You're my only chance. Find the killer; I'm counting on you."

"I'll do my best, but unless you're he—" McGee grabbed Gunther's cuffed hands and gave them a squeeze. "My heart says you're innocent, but my policeman's head knows you are guilty. In your shoes, I would have strangled Myers the first time I realized who he was. I promise you, I'll keep my eyes open. But now I'll have to start from scratch. It'll take time."

"I survived in a Nazi death camp for four years. Your prison will be a picnic. Take your time—but find him," Gunther said with a smile as he was being led to the police car.

Chapter 33

The Arrest

Glorious spring days were an elixir to the residents of The Wind and Sea. The pains of arthritis were less sharp, the walkers and crutches were lighter and the food tasted better. The new landscapers had selected, planted, and cultivated exactly the right mix of ferns, flowers, and trees; every living flora on the campus was luxuriant. The chefs were inspired, the management gracious, and the residents content with their memories and lives. There were exceptions: four inhabitants were hospitalized with serious ailments, six were in the intensive care unit, one placed in The Garden, and another had finally succumbed to the ravages of breast cancer. But even the sorrow felt for these unfortunate few was modified by this most glorious weather and the sight of the bursting floral rainbows seen everywhere.

"Old age isn't so bad," one elderly man said.

"But youth is much better," his friend replied, pointing to two college boys cavorting with bikini-clad coeds.

In the distance, the dark blue ocean changed gradually to turquoise near the shore where the never-ending waves churned the water into white foam before depositing it on the sandy beach. Brave surfers challenged the big waves. Usually the ocean won these bouts, but a few golden boys conquered the big swells and triumphantly rode them to shore. Southern California beach culture considered vanquishing a big wave equivalent to winning the Masters or landing on the Moon.

The news about Detective Steve Matteson and Gunther Krause consumed the campus. They were both well liked and respected. Steve had donated his services in solving the "Lady in White" and the identity of the kleptomaniac. He always helped the widows with their daily problems—computers and

TVs, sticky windows, and leaky faucets—and never refused when asked to eat dinner with three or more single women.

Gunther was admired for his work on the dining service committee. He'd fought successfully for resident's rights and was most appreciated. Until his recent close association with Rose Marie Dentz he too had made himself available to accompany the elderly ladies to dinner and to the occasional dances. The Los Angeles Times, which was subscribed to by many of The Wind and Sea residents, featured the Pink Daffodil case, and the *Santa Barbara News Press* headlined the Myers murder. All the residents subscribed to one or the other.

Krause was questioned at the police station, and released, but told to stay in Santa Barbara County. Los Angeles had an Israeli consulate and the D.A.'s office contacted it to verify the status of the Ostrows. The consulate knew nothing, but suggested the Israeli ambassador in Washington might. Krause had to wait for the outcome of that inquiry.

Detective Steve Matteson was charged with "obstruction of justice" and the judge set his bail at $250,000. L.A. newspapers condemned the district attorney, stating that the brutal killer of Hazel Sommers should have been charged with "murder in the second degree." Nigel Fairbanks, the Los Angeles District Attorney, was walking a fine line. He had to protect Roger Palmer, but he also needed all the convictions possible in highly publicized cases.

This magnificent weather was wasted on Sir Basil when he and Stuart Millheiser visited Deborah Farrell late in the afternoon. Deborah took one look at their faces and suggested cocktails; Sir Basil eagerly accepted, but Millheiser declined.

"Karen," Deborah said. "You know how Sir Basil likes his martini. Please make one for me too."

Sir Basil wearily sat in a big upholstered chair near the fireplace while Millheiser opened his briefcase and removed some papers, but remained standing.

"Not good news, Ms. Farrell," he began.

"Not more questions from that young detective, please," she protested.

"Worse, I'm afraid." Worry lined Millheiser's face. "The election is coming and the district attorney—wannabe governor—Nigel Fairbanks, needs a big highly publicized win. I'm afraid he will reopen the Mark Chambers' case."

Deborah had removed her shoes and sat reclined in a corner of the sofa with her bare feet curled beside her. "What do they have now that they didn't have before?" she asked.

"Most importantly, you had an alibi before, you don't now. We'll learn what else they have in 'discovery.' Think hard, Ms. Farrell. Where were you on the day your husband was murdered?"

"I've tried, Mr. Millheiser. It was twenty-two years ago and I don't remember. I thought I was at Hazel Sommers' house. I asked her and she confirmed that I was there. Now the police have evidence that I wasn't with her on the twelfth of August. I don't understand. If I wasn't with her, I don't remember where I was."

"Was this Hazel a ding-bat, sort of confused?"

Deborah thought for a moment then her face broadened into a big smile. "Yes, yes she was. Usually she was late and often missed meetings because she had the wrong dates."

"Will your other friends agree that maybe she was suffering from dementia?" Millheiser asked, intently looking at his client.

"Yes, definitely yes. One of us always would call her the night before a meeting to remind her of the time and place of any affair," a rejuvenated Deborah said, realizing a lifeline had been thrown to her.

"Did she have a nickname?"

"No, but everyone knew she was unreliable. Someone once called her 'Hazel the *fazeable.*'"

"That's a lousy pun, but if they file against you, we can use it." Stuart smiled for the first time.

The phone rang and Karen answered it. "Mr. Millheiser, it's your office," she announced.

The lawyer walked to a small table in the living room, listened for two minutes then said, "Yes, I'll get back to you in a few minutes, thanks." He walked back to a chair next to the sofa. "That bastard Fairbanks has made his move. He's filed first-degree murder charges against you, Ms. Farrell. Detective Ferguson is giving you the choice of where you want to be arrested, here, or at the police station. I suggest you do it here. Have that local reporter for the *Santa Barbara News Press* present and as many of your Wind and Sea friends as possible. I want to put a spin on this event before Fairbanks has a chance."

Millheiser called his office and gave them instructions. A few minutes later they returned the call.

"Detective Ferguson will be here in ninety minutes. That'll give us plenty of time," Stuart said.

Sir Basil called Jeff Grainger, and the office of the local TV station. Ms. Farrell and Karen phoned all of the ladies Deborah had invited to her coffee klatch and they were asked to contact as many others as they knew.

As soon as Woody entered the campus he knew this would not be a simple arrest. Hastily drawn signs were thrust in front of his car as it crawled through a crowd of residents. "OUR DEBORAH HAS SUFFERED ENOUGH," one sign demanded. "LEAVE OUR LADY ALONE," and "GO BACK TO LOS ANGELES," were others.

A hundred people or more blocked the streets around Deborah's cottage. Woody and Sergeant Murphy parked and walked the rest of the way through an unfriendly crowd. Woody knocked on the door, and a sullen Karen opened it without any greeting. She escorted them to the living room where Deborah and the two men were waiting. "I'm sorry, Ms. Farrell, but I have my orders. You are being arrested for the murder of Mark Chambers, your husband, on August 12, 1978. You my remain silent, but if you speak it may—"

Millheiser stepped in front of Deborah. "Detective, I'm Stuart Millheiser, Ms. Farrell's attorney. I'll take Ms. Farrell to your headquarters."

"I'm sorry, Counselor, but Ms. Farrell must remain in my custody." Woody peered around Millheiser to Deborah. "I'm sure your lawyer will be able to get you out on bail, Ms. Farrell."

"Yes, thank you. Karen will bring my things in the car with Sir Basil and Mr. Millheiser."

As soon as the door opened, the crowd assembled outside cheered. The TV cameras rolled and Jeff and his cameraman took notes and pictures. The TV man had brought an extra microphone and thrust in front of the lawyer's face. Millheiser grabbed the mike and began, "Dear friends, of one of the loveliest ladies living today, Deborah Farrell, you are witnessing the most flagrant violation of simple human rights that I have seen in my thirty years as a defense attorney. Nigel Fairbanks, the District Attorney of Los Angeles County is running, as you know, for governor of this great state of California. He needs a big win; he hasn't had one for a long time. In fact, he just made a big mess of the Pink Daffodil case.

"Ms. Farrell just happened to be in the wrong place at the wrong time. She was put through this ordeal once before, more than twenty years ago. The state had no evidence against her then and it has none now. But this arrogant man, Fairbanks, doesn't care. His ego won't let him. Punishing her may get him some votes, he thinks. I assure you that Ms. Farrell is not guilty of any crime, let alone murder. I will punish Mr. Fairbanks in court and I ask you to deny him what he wants most, the reason for this farce—the governorship of California. Thank you."

Deborah held Sir Basil's arm as he led her to the car. She waved and smiled at everyone with tears rolling down her cheeks, and they blew kisses back to her. Everyone waved as the two cars slowly drove through the gates of The Wind and Sea.

All the residents were outraged that one of them, a lovely, but fragile lady, could be plucked from their midst and subjected to such a degrading humiliation. One person's discomfort exceeded the others.

Chapter 34

The Trial

Deborah Farrell's trial began five years after O. J. Simpson's and the ramifications were eerily similar. Both cases had collateral victims: Ron Goldman's charged to Simpson and Hazel Sommers' to a man trying to help Farrell. Both murders happened in Brentwood, California and both trials were to determine if one spouse killed the other. There was one big difference: Simpson's trial was held in downtown Los Angeles; Farrell's would be in West Los Angeles—largely white and affluent.

The large, fifty-seat bus from The Wind and Sea would make the daily trip to the courthouse for a long as the trial lasted. The residents provided a large rooting section and hoped their presence would help their distressed sister survive this cruel ordeal.

After two weeks of jury selection, voir dire, five white women, three white men, two black women, and a Hispanic man and woman were seated. The trial started on October 19, 2000 with Nigel Fairbanks for the prosecution, assisted by Clarence Atkinson, and Stuart Millheiser for the defense with Frank Carter by his side. The egos and expertise of both lead attorneys were well known; no one expected a dignified trial. The judge was the Honorable Russell Standiford, a no nonsense Swede, who was the biggest man in the courtroom, and who once won a wrestling match with a grizzly bear. Both lead attorneys were aware of his reputation and would try to deport themselves accordingly.

"Mr. Fairbanks, your opening remarks, please," Judge Standiford said, then banged his gavel. He had the reputation of breaking more gavels than all the other judges on the Superior Courts combined, averaging three gavels per trial.

"Thank you, your honor." Nigel first faced the judge, then turned toward the jury. "Ladies and gentlemen of the jury, we all know the defendant. For

over thirty years she was the leading lady of the silver screen and the stage—
beloved by all. In 1979, the State of California charged Ms. Farrell with the
murder of Mark Chambers, her husband at the time. The prosecution had
completed their case when Judge Roger Palmer declared a mistrial because a
person or persons unknown offered bribes to the jury to vote for acquittal."

Fairbanks referred to his notes, then continued. "The defendant had the
means—her gun was used to kill Mr. Chambers. She had the motive; her
husband was having an affair with a younger woman, and he was stealing
money from her. And she had the opportunity because she has no alibi. She
claims she doesn't remember where she was on that fateful day when her
husband was murdered.

The D. A. paused nd made eye contact with several of the jurors before
continuing.

"For twenty-two years, the police have diligently worked on this case.
State and local police have searched; private investigators have been employed.
Even some federal agencies have been involved. The result of all this time
and energy—nothing. Deborah Farrell remains the only viable suspect. In
addition to the damning evidence I will introduce, we have witnesses that will
reveal the defendant's frame of mind, and her compulsive, demanding nature
that gets what it wants when it wants it.

"Concentrate on the evidence; don't let Mr. Millheiser sidetrack you into
Hollywood's make believe world and I know you will reach a verdict of 'guilty
as charged.' Thank you."

Judge Standiford looked at Stuart. "Mr. Millheiser, your opening
statement, please."

Stuart nodded to the judge, then turned to the jury. "Ladies and gentlemen
of the jury, my statement will be short. I will rebut all charges made by the
prosecution. I will cut them to ribbons."

Stuart walked closer to the jury box, and in a confidential tone, softly
said, "This case was tried over twenty years ago and ended in a mistrial. The
prosecution's evidence was smoke and mirrors then, as it is now."

Stuart stepped back a pace, and in a loud, angry voice shouted, "I'll tell
you why this district attorney, Nigel Fairbanks, has resurrected this case."
He paused as all the jurors waited attentively. "Because he is a politician and
wants to be the governor of our great state. A conviction of this great lady,
in his one-track mind, would bring him recognition and votes. You are too
intelligent to fall for his little game of deception. Thank you."

"Motion to strike, your honor," Fairbanks shouted.

The Wind and Sea rooting section cheered and clapped. Judge Standiford
jumped to his feet with gavel in hand, but when he looked at this group of
spindly, bent people in their eighties and nineties, he gently rapped on his

desk. "Spectators, please remember you are guests of this court. I will tolerate no demonstrations.

"The motion is granted. The jury will disregard the defense attorney's remarks. I believe this would be an excellent time for the noon break. Please be in your seats at two." His gavel hit his desk one second later.

Millheiser took Deborah by the elbow. "The California Club is at the next block, and I'm a member. I think the walk would do us good. We'll have lunch there and talk over a few things. Oh, and the bartender makes a good martini."

Fifteen minutes later, the two lawyers, Sir Basil, and Deborah were seated in one of the club's private dining rooms.

Nothing about the case was discussed during the cocktails or light meal, but as the dishes were being carted away Stuart began. "Deborah, I have their witness list. Detective Matteson, that's no surprise. Mimi St. Cheree?"

Deborah dabbed her lip with her napkin. "Twenty years go, she was my hairdresser. I'm surprised she's still around. She must have been in her forties then, but looked twenty years younger."

"Maria Vega?" Stuart asked.

"I don't remember. Give me a minute." Farrell walked around the room and finally a smile appeared. "One of my housekeepers. I remember now."

"Did you treat her right? Does she have any reason to want to hurt you?"

"I did. We got along fine. I even gave her a month's bonus when I moved. I can't think of anything she could say that would hurt me."

"Holli Logan is on the list. She's there to kill your alibi. That's a big worry."

Stuary looked up. "How about Dr. David Morris?"

"Oh my God. He was my gynecologist," she murmured as her face contorted into a grimace. "They can't make him testify against me, can they?"

"Anything that was said about your medical condition in private between you two is protected—doctor-patient privilege," Stuart answered. "Anything you want to tell me about him?"

"No, not now." Her eyes suddenly expressed all the sadness in world.

"Did you have any kind of a relationship with him outside of doctor, patient?"

She looked directly at Sir Basil. "Yes. For a short time he was my lover. But it was in 1973, a year before I knew Mark."

"Please review that period in you mind. Tell me anything that might be relevant to Marks's murder."

She nodded and turned her head away from Sir Basil. "It was a short affair and meant nothing to either of us."

Stuart gave Deborah a minute to collect herself. "There are two more names: Gerald H. Timson and Thomas Warner."

"Timson was my private investigator who discovered Mark was cheating on me, and Thomas Warner, an accountant who found out that my dear husband was stealing from me. Both testified in the first trial. Read the transcript—they'll have nothing new to add."

"The police reported that there were no forced entries. How did the perpetrators gain entrance both times—first, to rob you, then again to kill your husband? Either you or Chambers gave someone a key, or a lock was picked, but its been too many years to check for that. Did you ever loan anyone your key?"

Deborah shook her head. "No, never."

"This is going to be a major problem." Millheiser looked intently into Farrell's eyes, hoping to determine the truth.

The people from The Wind and Sea were out in front of the courthouse. When Deborah arrived back from lunch, cheers from the group could be heard as far away as First and Grand. She waved and blew kisses to her well-wishers as she proudly sashayed inside.

Exactly at two, the judge cantered toward his bench. His size was awe inspiring as he dwarfed his bench and all the men standing near him. "Call your first witness, Mr. Fairbanks."

"Thank you, your honor. The prosecution calls Mimi St. Cheree."

A small, pert woman waltzed toward the witness chair smiling at everyone. Her body was perfectly formed. She was in her sixties, but face lifts and body tucks transformed her to a forty-year-old. She wore a short, tight skirt and a revealing blouse. Her cropped blonde hair accentuated dark blue eyes and full red lips. The men noticed every wiggle of her derrière and every rise and fall of her full breasts. They sighed with pleasure when she finally sat down.

After the witness was sworn in, Fairbanks began. "Do you know the defendant, Ms. St. Cheree?"

"Yes indeed, Mr. Fairbanks. Twenty some years ago, I owned a little hair salon in Brentwood. Ms. Farrell came in each week to get her hair set and have a manicure."

"She was good customer?" he asked.

"The best. Always on time and a good tipper."

The rooting section clapped, but a scowl from the judge silenced them.

Fairbanks pressed on. "Did Ms. Farrell ever say anything about her husband, Mark Chambers?"

"Oh yes. She didn't like him. Said he was a drunk and a skirt chaser. A no good son-of-a-bitch was how she described him."

"Was she upset with him every week?"

"No, but often."

"Now, Ms. St. Cheree, please be sure of your answer. Did Ms. Farrell ever threaten to harm her husband?"

Her brain was not asked to think often, but Mimi made an outward appearance of trying to make it work. "Once she said she hoped his new sport car would run off a cliff. Another time she said he was the worst mistake she'd ever made and wished he would drop dead. Oh, I remember now, it was just about a month before Mr. Chambers was murdered. Ms. Farrell was so angry when she came into the shop, she was shaking. I asked her what was wrong and she said. 'My god damn husband, he's impossible. If I had a gun, I'd shoot him right between his bloody eyes. I've got to get rid of him.'"

The spectators buzzed; nearly everyone turned and talked to his or her neighbor. The Wind and Sea group stoically looked straight ahead in silence.

Fairbanks held up his right hand. "Thank you, Ms. St. Cheree. Your witness, Counselor."

The district attorney smiled at the jury and walked back to his table. Stuart Millheiser quickly reached the witness chair, smiling broadly and shaking his head as he walked.

"Ms. St. Cheree, a beauty shop is like a men's barber shop or a bar. It's a place where people go to relax and say crazy things, isn't it? Where they gossip and release all their frustrations."

"I guess so, Mr. Millheiser, because my clients do say ridiculous things. Last week Mrs. Hines said her husband didn't appreciate her cooking and she was going to bake him some dog food to see if he could tell the difference."

"Do you believe she actually did that, Ms. St. Cheree?"

"No, she was just talking."

"Women like to say critical things about their husbands. A beauty shop is just the place where they have an audience, and they know nobody takes them seriously. Nothing will happen, no matter what they say, correct?" Stuart asked.

Mimi laughed. "Right, Mr. Millheiser. In fact, last week Mrs. Jones said that if her husband didn't put down the toilet seat after taking a pee she was going to hire an electrician to wire the seat and give him a shock every time he lifted it."

"Ms. St. Cheree, did you ever hear any of your clients praise their husbands?"

She looked at her hands. "A short time ago, Mrs. Jones congratulated her husband. She said that after four children her husband finally learned how to feed a new one without choking him."

"Ms. St. Cheree, it's just a game with your clients. It's a forum where each woman tries to outdo the other in criticizing their second-rate husbands. It's a way to generate sympathy."

"Yes, yes, Mr. Millheiser. Some of things they say are out of this world, but they really don't mean them. It's just their way of passing the time while waiting for their hair to dry."

"Thank you, Ms. St. Cheree. Your witness, Fairbanks, for any redirect."

Fairbanks rushed to the witness. "But Ms. St. Cheree, have you ever heard any of your clients repeat what Ms. Farrell said, quote, 'If I had a gun I'd shoot him right between his bloody eyes.' Unquote?"

Mimi thought for a moment. "No, I haven't."

Nigel's spirits rose, Stuart's sank. But then Mimi's face brightened. "But I once heard Mrs. Claremont say, 'I wish my husband were triplets. Then I could hang one, shoot one, and stab the third in five places.'"

The judge joined the spectators in laughter as Fairbanks trudged back to his table.

The next two witnesses for the prosecution were from the first trial and repeated their testimonies. Gerald Timson said that Farrell's husband Mark Chambers took a Ginger O'Conner to the Hilton Hotel in Beverly Hills where they enjoyed room-shaking sex. Thomas Warner, the accountant detailed how Chambers stole $120,000 by forging Ms. Farrell's signature.

Stuart Millheiser didn't bother to cross-examine.

After Warner's testimony, the judge adjourned the court for the day. Deborah and Sir Basil took a cab, and joined the attorneys back at their office for briefing and a drink.

"We had a good day. You can joke about anything you said to Ms. St. Cheree. Timson and Warner were used to show motive, but I'll reverse any impression they had on the jury when I question you, Ms. Farrell. Get a good's night sleep; tomorrow may be tougher."

The judge entered the courtroom exactly at nine the next day, and the prosecution called Maria Vega.

A slim, attractive, Mexican-American woman in her fifties walked to the witness chair. Her abundant black, curly hair complimented her brown eyes and skin.

"How were you employed by Ms. Farrell, Ms. Vega?" Fairbanks asked the witness, after smiling broadly at the jury.

"I cleaned her house, helped at parties, and took care of the pets."

"Did you live in the house?"

"Yes, everyday except Thursdays. They were my days off." Her dark eyes flashed as she answered.

"The murder of Mr. Chambers and the robbery three months earlier both happened on Thursdays, so you were not there, were you?"

"No." She blessed herself and murmured, "*Gracias, madre de Dios.*"

Maria was upset, and the prosecutor was overly concerned. "Would you like some water, Ms. Vega?"

"No, thank you. I'm all right."

"I understand your fright, Ms. Vega. If you had been in the house and the person with the gun saw you, well, you might have been killed." The D.A.'s concern was overwhelming.

"Doesn't it seem strange that the house was empty on both days? It's like the perpetrators knew that it would be." An all-knowing smile followed the remark.

Millheiser rolled his eyes. "Objection, your honor. Argumentative."

"Sustained. The jury will ignore that last remark."

Fairbanks nodded and continued. "Now, Ms. Vega, about a month before the murder you spotted something in the kitchen pantry, didn't you?"

"Si, yes."

"What was it? Do you remember?"

"A gun, Mr. Lawyer."

"A gun?" Nigel exploded. "Your employer reported to the police that her gun had been stolen three months before. Are you sure it was a gun? Was it like this one?" He walked back to his table, retrieved Prosecution's Exhibit 2, returned, and showed it to the witness. "This is a .38 caliber Smith and Wesson and is the gun that killed Mr. Chambers," he said quietly.

"I don't know, Señor, all guns look alike to me. I hate them. My brother was killed by one."

"Take another look, Ms. Vega. Did the gun in the pantry look like this gun?"

"Objection. Asked and answered," Stuart angrily shouted.

"Overruled. The witness may answer."

"Yes, they were similar," she answered, visibly upset.

"Thank you, Ms. Vega. One more question. Did you report seeing the gun to Ms. Farrell?"

"I don't remember. I don't think so."

"Thank you, Ms. Vega. Mr. Millheiser will want to ask you some questions. Your witness, Counsel."

Stuart stood and addressed the judge. "Your honor, the defense asks for a twenty minute break. The prosecution, in discovery, forgot to inform us about this gun. We need time to prepare."

"I believe we all need a break. Granted. You may step down, Ms. Vega," the judge agreed.

The Wind and Sea people walked to their parked bus. They knew that Jim, the driver, had brought liquid refreshments and ice.

Twenty minutes later, Maria was back in the witness chair and the defense attorney held something in his hand. "Ms. Vega, did you touch the gun in the pantry?"

"Yes, Mister. I was cleaning the pantry and I had to lift and move everything."

"This is the murder weapon. Lift it and then this lift this gun. Was the gun in the pantry light like my gun or heavy like the murder weapon?"

Maria lifted first one gun, then the other. "I think more like your gun, Mr. Millheiser."

"Now, Maria, do you see this wheel in the middle of the gun that rotates like this?" Stuart spun the cartridge holder on the murder weapon.

"Yes, Mister."

"On the gun I brought, this wheel doesn't rotate. It's part of the gun. Did the wheel on the gun you saw rotate?"

"I don't know; I didn't try. But I think the gun in the pantry looks more like your gun."

"Thank you, Ms. Vega."

"No redirect, your honor," Fairbanks said.

"Your honor, this is offered as Defense Exhibit 1, a toy barbeque pistol, used to put out flames that flare up from fatty meat." Stuart handed the toy gun to the bailiff and walked back to his table.

"Call your next witness, Mr. Fairbanks," the judge ordered.

A pudgy, five-foot-nine-inch man with wispy hair, wearing glasses, and appearing to be in his seventies, walked slowly to the witness chair. His face was expressionless, but his brown eyes flicked from side to side.

"State your name and address please," the clerk said.

"Doctor David Morris, The Wind and Sea in Santa Barbara."

"Your honor," Fairbanks began. "Dr. Morris is a reluctant witness. The State had to subpoena him. I ask for permission to treat him as a hostile witness."

"Granted."

"Dr. Morris for how long have you known the defendant?"

"For thirty-five years."

"As friends or as her doctor?"

"Both," Morris answered succinctly.

"Were you intimate?"

"Objection," Stuart shouted. "Their personal relationship is none of Fairbank's business."

"It is, your honor. Goes to motive."

"The witness may answer," the judge decided.

"I refuse to answer because it would violate the doctor-patient privilege," Morris insisted.

"Your honor," a now agitated prosecutor said. "This privilege is reserved to protect the privacy of what is done and said by a doctor or his patient during the treatment of an ailment and in the privacy of the doctor's office. Sex is not a treatment for an ailment."

"Are you a sex therapist Dr. Morris?" the judge asked.

"No, Judge, I'm an OB/GYN."

"Then you will have to answer Mr. Fairbanks' question."

"Yes," Morris answered, looking at his hands.

Okay, you were her lover. Were you also her OB/GYN?"

"Yes."

"Did you deliver any babies, perform abortions, or medically treat Ms. Farrell in any way."

Millheiser jumped up at the same time as Morris shouted. "Go to hell, you bastard."

A second later Stuart said. "Objection. These questions directly violate the doctor-patient privilege."

"Your honor," Fairbanks shouted above the roar in the courtroom. "Carrie Boswell just had a best-seller published. 'Deborah, the Goddess.' In it, on page 232, the author states that Ms. Farrell has had at least two abortions and one child. These events are public knowledge, so not protected."

Milheiser jumped to his feet. "Judge, having statements published in a sleazy book does not make them true. There's a best-seller in the book stores that claims the president of the United States is an alien."

Standiford shouted, "Order, order!" He slammed his gavel on his desk, breaking it and sending the big part of it thirty feet into the courtroom. "Damn it, Sit down and be quiet. The objection is sustained. The conversation between a doctor and his patient in the privacy of the doctor's office is privileged. Move on, Mr. Fairbanks."

Fairbanks took a drink of water and combed his curly hair with his fingers. "Dr. Morris, both you and Ms. Farrell live in The Wind and Sea Retirement Community, don't you?"

"Yes."

"Isn't it common knowledge that Roger Palmer was Ms. Farrell's lover for a long time and now a Sir Basil Rathbourn is?"

"I don't know or care, Mr. Fairbanks, and I believe you need medical help. You are obsessed with sex. Have you been deprived all of your life?"

The courtroom exploded. The Wind and Sea contingent were louder than any other group. "Give him hell, Morris," they shouted in unison.

Ten minutes later, order was restored. "Mr. Morris, did you know the victim, Mr. Chambers?" Fairbanks asked.

"Yes, we are both members of the same tennis club."

"Were you ever in Chambers' Brentwood home?"

"Once, maybe twice at cocktail parties," he answered, glaring at the prosecutor.

"Been there alone?"

"I don't remember, maybe once."

"Have a key?"

"No, someone let me in."

"Husband at home?"

"Go to hell, you pervert," Morris shouted.

"Not responsive, your honor."

"Answer the question, Dr. Morris," the judge ordered.

"Yes, I went there to meet him. Probably about a tennis club event."

Fairbanks paused, looked at the witness, and then said, "No more questions at this time, your honor."

"Be ready at nine tomorrow, Mr. Millheiser, for your cross-examination," the judge quickly said. "Court is adjourned."

"What was Fairbanks trying to accomplish with Doctor Morris?" Sir Basil asked later as they sat having a drink in Millheiser's office.

Stuart Millheiser thought for a moment before answering. "I believe two things mainly. First, he wanted to muddy your reputation, Ms. Farrell."

"Deborah, please."

"He wanted to knock you off the pedestal people have put you on. He floated the idea that you had many lovers and abortions. You were a loose woman and therefore capable of murder. He knows the members of the jury like you and want to set you free. He has to get one or two of them thinking you're not the goddess they thought you were and could commit murder.

"Secondly, goes to motive. You fell in love with one of your numerous lovers and wanted to get rid of your husband."

"How're you going to handle Morris in cross?" Sir Basil continued.

"He wants to help. I'll just have to feel him out."

The next morning Deborah made a special effort to greet personally as many fellow residents as possible.

"We love you," many shouted.

"I love each and every one of you," she replied. "Thank you for your support."

Doctor Morris was in the witness chair ready when the judge told Mr. Millheiser to begin.

"How many abortions have you performed, Dr. Morris?"

"I don't know exactly, but probably around four hundred."

A collected sigh escaped from the spectators.

"What kind of women get abortions, doctor?"

"All kinds. Young teenagers—having a child would ruin their young lives and handicap the baby; older women with surprise pregnancies; women who are too old to raise a child; women who were abandoned by their husbands; or single women who can't support a child."

"Doctor, after the abortion, how do these women feel?"

"Depressed, sometimes suicidal."

"Doctor, you have had many years experience with women and their problems. Hypothetically, let's say Ms. Farrell had had an abortion. How would that experience have affected her?"

"She would have been devastated. She loves children and life and would resist the taking of a life in every way she could."

The courtroom erupted in a roar of support for the defendant. "Please let me add," Morris stood and looked directly at Fairbanks. "I resent Mr. Fairbanks using me as an instrument to smear Ms. Farrell."

The judge didn't try to control the storm of support that blew through his court. After ten minutes, he banged his gavel and told Millheiser to continue.

"I have no further questions for this witness, your honor."

"Mr. Fairbanks, call your next witness," the now smiling judge ordered.

"Holli Logan, your honor."

This sixty-five-year-old creature looked stunning in a short tailored suit. "I can't believe she's a lesbian," Sir Basil said. "Look at those legs; they're spectacular. My God, what a waste."

With her head held high she sashayed to the chair and winked at the judge.

"Ms. Logan, Hazel Sommers was a good friend of yours?"

"Yes, Mr. Fairbanks, my closest." She crossed and uncrossed her legs.

"Let me show you Prosecution's Exhibit 2, a 1978 calendar that belonged to Mrs. Sommers. Do you recognize it?"

"Yes, she left it with me just before she was killed. I've had it in my possession for over twenty years."

"Now look at the date, August twelfth, and read what is written on that date by Mrs. Sommers."

Holli looked closely. "It says 'party time at Holli's.'"

"Will you please tell the jury what that means?"

"Yes. I had a few ladies over, including Hazel, to discuss a fundraiser for the tennis club. Afterward, we had a few drinks and let our hair down—party time."

"So Mrs. Sommers was with you all day on the twelfth of August?"

"Yes, all day and into the night."

"Thank you. No more questions. Your witness, Counsel."

"No questions at this time, your honor."

"The prosecution calls Detective Steven Matteson."

After he was sworn in and gave his name and address, the prosecutor asked him the same questions asked at the first trial, twenty-one years earlier. He identified the murder gun as belonging to Ms. Farrell, but stolen three months earlier; stated that the murder was on August 12, 1978, and that he had interviewed Ms. Farrell on the thirteenth and Hazel Sommers on the fifteenth.

"Detective, you have admitted killing Mr. Sommers, the Pink Daffodil?" Fairbanks asked.

"Yes, it was self-defense as you well know." Steve's body tensed and coiled as if to strike.

Although this news had been published, the admittance stunned those crowded in the courtroom.

"Now, Detective, when you interviewed Ms. Farrell she stated that she was with Mrs. Sommers at the time of her husband's murder. Was that confirmed by Mrs. Sommers?"

"At first she did, but then seemed confused and thought it might have been the eleventh. She looked for her calendar but couldn't find it. Then at the end of my visit she stated that it was the twelfth positively," Steve said, looking at Deborah.

"But we now know she was wrong, don't we?" the D.A. asked.

"Yes, if we are to believe Ms. Logan."

"What do you mean? Are you suggesting that Ms. Logan is lying?" Fairbanks' act of incredulity was perfect.

"At the time, Mrs. Sommers said Ms. Farrell was with her on the twelfth. Now twenty years later, this calendar shows up showing something different. I don't trust old evidence, hidden for twenty years. If she was confused during my interview on the fifteenth, she might have been confused when she made that entry into her calendar."

"Forget the calendar. On the day of the murder she was with Ms. Logan and not with Ms. Farrell. The defendant, Deborah Farrell, has no alibi for that date," a visibly upset prosecutor said.

"How do you know?" Steve's angry retort made Fairbanks take a step backward.

"I have no further questions for this witness," the prosecutor said, and walked away. As he reached his table he added, "The prosecution rests, your honor."

Steve slowly lifted himself out of his chair. He took a step and staggered, but recovered immediately and smiled to the jury. He didn't take the shortest route, but one that took him by the defense table. When he reached it, his left leg buckled and he fell to the floor by Ms. Farrell's chair. He pushed himself up, said a few words to her and walked back to the spectators section.

"This court is adjourned for the day," Judge Standiford announced. "Will you be ready with your first witness tomorrow morning, Mr. Millheiser?"

"Yes, your honor."

"Stuart, I'm tired and don't feel well," Deborah said in a loud, raspy voice. "A nap at the hotel will cure everything. We can talk later."

"We've gone over your testimony several times. You'll be all right. Rest and be ready for tomorrow. Try to remember where you were on that day. It's of vital importance."

The next morning was windy and cold, but the faithful from The Wind and Sea arrived ready to encourage their queen. Some used canes, others walkers and two used the automatic lift on the front door to drop their wheelchairs to the sidewalk level. The "gray power" brigade was ready to charge.

"The defense calls Deborah Farrell," Millheiser announced as soon as the judge gave him the signal.

"How are you this morning, Ms. Farrell?" her attorney asked.

"Fine, just fine. Thank you."

She didn't look fine. She was pale; her skin looked like old parchment and there were dark circles under her eyes. She looked vulnerable and helpless. But she was beautiful, a fragile goddess dressed in a white, pure silk suit with intricate Battenberg lace in an exquisite design. The pants delightfully complimented the top.

"Ms. Farrell, it's a shame you have to put up with this ordeal again. The judge in the first trial stopped the proceedings and we all thought that would be the end. But this district attorney, for his own personal reasons, has seen fit to do it all over again."

"Objection, objection."

"Sustained," the judge said. "A caution, Mr. Millheiser."

Millheiser ignored the judge. "Ms. Farrell, let's cut right to the chase and save the jury valuable time, shall we?"

"Yes, I'm sure they would appreciate that. I know I will."

"Before a jury can convict an accused of murder in the first degree they must decide beyond a reasonable doubt that the defendant had the means, the opportunity, a motive or motives, and that the action was premeditated. Are you all right; shall I get you a glass of water?"

"No, Counselor, I'm fine, please continue."

"You had a gun, the means?"

"Yes a .38 caliber Smith and Wesson revolver but it was stolen three months prior to the murder and reported to the police. An expensive watch and jewelry were also taken."

"What about the gun your maid Maria Vega found in the pantry?"

Deborah laughed and then coughed. "That was a water piston that my husband used when he barbecued."

"So much for means; you didn't have any—the gun was not available to you at the time of the murder. Now let's study motive. The prosecution states you murdered your husband because he was cheating and stealing from you."

"That's ridiculous. I knew for a long time he was a cheat and a thief. I filed for divorce two months before the murder. In California, a no-fault state, I would have received my divorce and have been rid of him. I had proof of his philandering so there would have been no alimony. Why should I take the risk of killing him?"

"Why indeed, Ms. Farrell? Now how about opportunity. Where were you on the day your husband was murdered, August 12, 1978?"

"I told the investigating officer I was with a friend, Hazel Sommers, but now I realize I was confused. I was with her on the eleventh not the twelfth."

"Where were you, Ms. Farrell?"

She began to cry uncontrollably and the judge stopped the proceedings for five minutes. "Can you proceed, Ms. Farrell?" he finally asked.

"Yes, your honor, thank you. This experience has been buried so deeply in my subconscious that until last night I have been unable to retrieve it. Suddenly I remembered, crystal clear, I did have an abortion. I was fifty-three at the time and much too old to raise a child, and my doctor told me that because of my age the baby would not be healthy and would probably have Autism or Down syndrome.

Silence permeated the courtroom. The spectators were concerned for the defendant. How dare the prosecutor subject her to this ordea?

"After the procedure, I asked the doctor for the fetus. I took it and buried it in one of the most beautiful spots in the world, the Dana Point Headland. Any of you that have been there will agree with me, I'm sure. The headland is a big rock outcropping that extends about a half-a-mile into the Pacific. It's about a thousand feet high and from the top, looking to the north, you can see the waves crashing on the sand all the way to Laguna Beach. To the south Dana Point and San Clemente are visible and to the west Catalina Island, twenty miles distant sparkles in the sun surrounded by the deep blue of the ocean. It's nearly untouched with its own flora and fauna.

"Right on the top, I dug a little hole and buried my poor baby. I haven't been there in over twenty years. The last time was on the day my husband was killed."

She spoke softly, but everyone heard because no one talked or moved. They intensely listened and were touched by this tale of grief.

Stuart Millheiser had expected her to say she didn't remember where she was on that day. Though in shock, he didn't show it. After a few minutes he asked, "Is there anyone who can corroborate this sad story, Ms. Farrell?"

"Yes. After I had buried my child, I stood there appreciating the magnificent sight. Suddenly, a man came and stood besides me. 'Isn't this the most beautiful spot in the world?' he asked. I agreed and we talked to each other for awhile. I told him my name and he said his was Bill something. I don't remember his last name."

"What did he look like," the attorney, who was flying blind, asked.

"He was young, in his thirties, sandy hair and a scraggily beard. About one hundred and fifty pounds and a little taller than me—five foot nine or ten. Oh, and he had a mole just under his left ear. We talked for thirty minutes, then he left."

Millheiser, still confused and afraid he would make a mistake, decided to wait and hear what Fairbanks asked. "No further questions. Your witness, Counselor."

Fairbanks couldn't believe his good fortune. This would be the most effective cross-examination he had ever made. *What a concocted cock and bull story they've hatched.*

"Ms. Farrell, I agree. Let's keep it simple and save time, but first let's talk about something that really bothers me. I have reread the police report of your robbery. It states there was no visible sign of a forced entry. Every window, every door was locked tightly. Who had keys to your house?"

"Just my husband and me."

"Did you or he loan or give a copy to anyone?"

"I didn't."

"Then how did the robber or robbers and the murderer get in?"

"If you don't know, how should I?"

"Then either you or Mr. Chambers are the only ones who could gain entrance to the house."

"Objection. Conclusion not warranted by the evidence," Millheiser shouted.

"Sustained."

Fairbanks stared at her for a moment then asked, "Did you or your husband make a claim against the insurance company for the loss of a watch and jewelry?"

"No, they weren't insured."

"Then your husband, Mark Chambers, had no motive to steal the watch and jewelry or the gun to kill himself."

"I guess not."

Fairbanks flexed his muscles and became belligerent. "You, Ms. Farrell, are the only person who had access to the house and had a motive—hate. You staged a phony robbery, reported the gun stolen, and then used it later to kill your husband."

"I had no motive. I didn't want him dead. I just wanted him out of my life. A divorce would have done that."

"Shear, blind hate is a powerful motive and I believe you hated your cheating, lying, crooked husband."

"Objection, argumentative."

"Sustained. The jury will disregard that last remark by the prosecutor."

"So you could have had the means, the gun, and the motive, hate. Now let's discuss opportunity, an alibi. You lied about your first one, didn't you?"

"No, I was confused and mistaken."

"Okay, let's talk about the second one. After trying for years you just happened to remember last night where you were on the day of the murder, amazing."

"Life is full of amazing events, Mr. Fairbanks."

Fairbanks spread his arms in disbelief. After a knowing smile to the jury, he continued.

"Do you really expect this intelligent jury to believe your Hollywood script about a man with a mole who just happened to be in a remote place at exactly the time you needed?"

"I hope so. It's the truth."

The D. A.'s smile turned to a scowl and he thundered, "It's a fairy tale, out of whole cloth. It's good, but without corroboration, it's worthless. I don't think this jury believes in fables."

"Objection. God damn it, Judge, he's sermonizing, making statements. He knows better."

"Sustained. Mr. Fairbanks, save these conclusions for your final argument and Mr. Millheiser, watch your language."

The audience became restless. They were angry at Fairbanks.

"I have no further questions for this witness, your honor."

"Mr. Millheiser, do you wish to redirect."

"Yes, Judge, I do. Ms. Farrell did you kill your husband?"

"No."

"Did you rob you own home and steal the murderweapon?"

"No."

"I have no more questions, your honor."

"Who is your next witness, Mr. Millheiser?"

"I don't have one, your honor."

"Tomorrow is Saturday. We will reconvene on Monday at nine. Will there be any rebuttal, Mr. Fairbanks?"

"No, your honor."

"Then have your final argument ready, counsel."

They took a cab back to the lawyer's office. "You took me by surprise. How in the world did you come up with your alibi? Without corroboration it won't fly, but it's better than nothing. Why didn't you pass it by me before the trial began?" Stuart asked after they had settled into their chairs.

"I thought you would try to talk me out of it."

"I would have. I don't believe the jury believed it. Frankly, I don't; maybe that's the reason you didn't tell me. It's too transparent."

"I thought you would say that," she said with a quirky little smile.

Coffee was served. Milheiser nervously paced the floor as Deborah sat quiely and relaxed.

"I didn't cross-examine a few of their witnesses because there was nothing to refute. They want to vote for you, Deborah. The jury won't convict if I can put reasonable doubt in their minds. The unforced entry into the house twice on the maid's day off and your lack of a believable alibi bothers me. But that's all circumstantial and reasonable doubt should carry the day. Probably a hung jury. The body language of jurors number three and number nine are bothersome."

"No, I couldn't go through another trial. Please, no hung jury," Deborah sobbed.

The bus arrived early on Monday. Ten-foot signs on both sides of the bus read, "WE LOVE OUR DEBBY."

Everyone expected this would be the last day of testimony and they hoped the jury would make a quick 'not guilty' decision.

Rico was the bookie and accepted bets on the outcome. He made the odds. A hung jury was the favorite, five-dollar bet on it made you two, your five back plus two. Five dollars on not guilty earned six, and five on guilty earned eight.

Before his final argument, Stuart told Debby, "I believe this alibi is a mistake. It's unbelievable and will hurt you."

Debby smiled and shrugged her shoulders. "We'll see," she said. "Good luck, Stuart," was her final remark as he started to walk toward the jury. His closing statement was short and succinct. He told the jurors that the prosecution had no evidence she'd committed the murder. Their case was all circumstantial. The police investigated the robbery and found it was caused by person or persons unknown. She had no motive and had an alibi. He almost choked when reviewing her alibi, but said, "She doesn't have to prove where she was; the prosecution has to prove that she was at the murder site."

He then affirmed what the judge had said in his instructions. "If there are reasonable doubts, you must acquit." After thirty minutes he thanked them and sat down.

Fairbanks was full of fire and brimstone. "The gun theft was staged, she had the means. She hated her philandering husband, she had the motive. Her alibi was pure fiction, as everyone in the courtroom knew, and there was no forced entry. Therefore, the perpetrator was either her husband or her, and he didn't commit suicide."

"He's good," Stuart said. "Frankly, I'm worried. That damn alibi. I believe the judge made some mistakes and we could get a reversal on appeal. It's in the hands of the defense gods."

As Fairbanks was making his last statement, a middle-aged man walked into the courtroom. A hush started at the door and grew in intensity until he reached the defense table where he leaned over and talked to Millheiser.

Chapter 35

The surprise witness

The judge glared at the intruder. He had planned to adjourn for the afternoon after the prosecuter had finished making his closing remarks. But now his many years of experience on the bench told him something extraordinary was about to happen and instead of reaching for his gavel he relaxed in his chair.

As soon as the prosecutor finished his closing remarks, Millheiser jumped from his chair. "Sidebar, your honor," he shouted. Fairbanks slowly followed Stuart to the judge's bench. "A most important witness has just arrived."

"What's his name?" the judge asked.

"William, Bill, Munson, my client's alibi."

"I object," Fairbanks said. "His name wasn't on their witness list. This is all cheap theatrics. The phantom witness appears at the last minute; it's just a 'B' movie script."

"Mr. Munson is a solid citizen, well known in San Diego, and a decorated war hero," Stuart added.

The judge thought for a few minutes. "I'll allow his testimony. You may have all the time you need to prepare a cross-examination, Mr. Fairbanks."

"Your honor, I believe this to be a gross miscarriage of justice, maybe cause for reversal."

"Are you threatening me, Mr. Fairbanks?"

"No, your honor, just reminding you of a possible result of your decision."

"Proceed with your witness, Mr. Millheiser," an angry judge said.

"Your name and address please," the bailiff asked.

"William B. Munson and I live at 1221 Hacienda Street in San Diego."

The calm witness settled into his chair and crossed his legs. "Mr. Munson, what do you do?" Milheiser asked

214

"I'm a test pilot for the navy at Mira Mar."

"Have you ever met or talked with me before today?"

"No."

"Have you ever met or talked to the defendant?"

"Yes, about twenty years ago."

"Would that be on August 12, 1978?"

"Yes, exactly."

Millheiser now realized he looked at a ten-carat diamond. He wanted to ask the right questions before the prosecutor had a chance to do so. "How can you be so certain?"

"I'd driven from San Diego to Santa Ana on navy business. On the way home, I noticed the Dana Point headland and wanted to study it. I met Ms. Farrell on the top and we talked for about thirty minutes. After we parted, I continued to drive home. Just after San Clemente, the car directly in front of me blew a tire and crashed into the middle divider. I ploughed into him and totaled my new Mustang. I'll never forget that day; I loved that car."

"How are you certain that the lady you met that day is the defendant, Ms. Farrell?"

Munson looked at the witness for a few seconds before answering. "I had seen her in the movies. I never forgot her; how could I? She hasn't aged at all."

Fairbanks helpless at his table became apprehensive as he sensed danger. Was the defense springing a trap?

"What prompted you to come to this courtroom today to testify for her?"

"A TV news program last night. I recognized her immediately and remembered meeting her on the headland. I wanted to help her by telling the truth and confirming her alibi."

"Please describe yourself?" an eager attorney asked.

Munson shrugged. "An average guy. Five foot ten, one hundred-sixty pounds, brown hair, and in good shape for a fifty-two-year-old."

"Do you have a mole under your left ear?" Stuart immediately realized this was a stupid question.

Now Milheiser became nervous. If the witness answered no, Farrell was in trouble.

The witness laughed then quickly answered. "Yes. She remembered my little gem, didn't she?" He turned to show the mole to the attorney and the jury.

"One more question. When you talked to the defendant, what time was it?"

"After lunch, around two or three o'clock."

Milheiser wanted to dance and clap his hands but controlled himself.

"Thank you, Mr. Munson."

"Are you ready to cross, Mr. Fairbanks?"

"Yes, your honor, we'll do it now, but we will investigate this witness to make sure he is what he says he is. If we find he is not, we'll expect this court to act."

"Noted, please continue," the judge curtly said.

The district attorney asked several questions about the August twelfth meeting between Farrell and Munson. His answers further confirmed that there had been such a meeting.

"Do you know the penalty for perjury, Mr. Munson?" Fairbanks asked.

"Yes indeed, Counselor. There's no way that I would lie to this court and jeopardize my career or pension. I'm not stupid," Munson fired back.

"You're excused," an exasperated prosecutor said.

"This trial has been completed. I will state my instructions to the jury this afternoon. The jury will begin deliberations tomorrow." The judge's gavel banged and in a relaxed manner he recited sections of the criminal code, explaining each carefully.

At four, the weary residents piled back on the bus. They hoped the jury would make a quick decision the next day. The journey back and forth to Los Angeles had now become an ordeal.

At the same time, two men climbed into a booth at Manuel's Cantina on Olivera Street in downtown Los Angeles. "We're far enough away. I don't believe anybody here will recognize us," the younger man with the mole under his left ear said.

"Thank you. You were superb. She was trained to learn lines quickly, but you were equally good; even I believed you," the other man in his seventies said. "I should be writing movie scripts."

"I owed you," the first man said. "I was drunk and speeding with the commander's wife in the car. You stopped me in your patrol car and could have taken me to jail. I would have been disgraced and my naval career ruined. But you escorted me home and didn't give me a ticket. I hope I have repaid you."

"You have, my friend. I thank you and Deborah Farrell thanks you," the older man said.

They enjoyed their margaritas. Thirty minutes later, the man with the mole said, "I have to go. With this traffic it will take two hours to get to San Diego. Sometime you must tell me how you signaled her that you wanted to have a meeting."

"I will, dear friend. Soon, I hope."

The next morning, the courtroom was packed and a huge crowd had gathered outside. Fortunately, the bailiff had set aside fifty seats for The Wind and Sea residents. Promptly at nine, the judge entered, addressed the jury for a few minutes, then sent them to the room where they would deliberate the case and reach a decision.

"I don't know how long they will take," Stuart said. "My office is a more comfortable place to wait. The bailiff will call me. The weather is good and it's only a ten minute walk."

Two hours later, the call came and they nervously hurried to the courthouse. "The speed of their decision means the jury ignored all the testimony except the last alibi. They either believed it or not."

They were in their seats as the jury foreman gave the bailiff a slip of paper. He delivered it to the judge, who glanced at it before returning it to the bailiff.

"Has the jury reached a decision?" the judge asked.

"Yes, it has, your honor." The foreman turned toward Deborah and smiled.

"Not guilty," he said in a loud, clear voice.

Chapter 36

The Cruise

Hoping they would be celebrating after the verdict, Jim had loaded the bus with liquid refreshments for those who wanted them. Everybody joined in the revelry and the bottles were empty by the time the bus reached Agura.

The good news spread quickly and the whole campus staged a rally in the courtyard—the same as those they'd experienced sixty years earlier in college, except there were no goal posts to take down.

Farrell's good news was just the beginning. Detective Blake McGee received a letter from the Israeli Ambassador in Washington.

Lieutenant Blake McGee
Santa Barbara Police Department
Dear Sir:
I have received your letter dated August 14, 2000 about the possible presence of Mossad agents at The Wind and Sea. Be advised that it is not the policy of the Israeli government to place intelligence agents on the sovereign soil of its friends. There are none in the United States.
Cordially,
Hosea Isaacs, Secretary
Israeli Embassy

Blake called Gunther and gave him the news. "I don't believe the Israeli secretary, but I understand his position. I know they didn't come to kill Myers, but to kidnap him, probably with your help. He wasn't kidnapped and there's no evidence that you killed him, therefore, I'm not charging you with anything, Gunther, but until this murder is solved you will continue to be a person of interest."

"Thanks, Blake. I'll do what I can to help you solve this murder."

Steve Matteson also received good news. The Los Angeles County's District Attorney, Nigel Fairbanks, formalized Steve's plea bargain. He agreed that Detective Matteson killed Hazel Sommers in self-defense and Matteson admitted to altering the evidence by removing teeth and obliterating the fingerprints of the victim, which is obstruction of justice. He was sentenced to probation for a period of one year.

The fifty bus riders took credit for the verdict and formed a club they named the Gray Panthers. Their slogan was "Don't Mess with the Gray Panthers" and their goal was to raise money for various local charities. The women would read to neighbors who were visually impaired or baby-sit for single mothers. The able men would help on the nearby playgrounds by being assistant coaches for the Little Leagues or acting as tutors.

Sir Basil hosted a party in the Great Hall. There was an open bar and the food was catered. He brought Diggy Quinn, Larry Turner and John Watts with him to act as hosts and dance with the single women. Everyone who was well enough came. The Wind and Sea was one happy place; everyone felt twenty years younger.

In late November, Deborah Farrell wanted to show her gratitude and announced the *piece de resistance*, a ten-day, round trip, Christmas cruise to Puerto Vallarta, Mexico and back. All residents were invited, thirty-six residents accepted, the others declined because they had holiday commitments, infirmities, or fear of sea sickness.

She gave each of the participants a slick, colorful flyer designed by a Hollywood friend of hers. The bright orange sun on it illuminated a white cruise ship on a deep blue ocean and the map of Mexico with the trip's ports-of call, Mazatlan, Manzanillo, Puerto Vallarta, Cabo San Lucas, Ensenada, and Los Angeles noted. The cruise would leave Los Angeles on December 24, 2000 and return to L. A. on January 3, 2001.

Anticipation for this fun event ran wild, especially for those residents (mostly single women) who had never sailed before. Gunther Krause and Rose Marie Dentz decided to openly share a stateroom as did Mary Lee Hopkins and Francis Pisano. Jeffrey Grainger talked his boss into paying for his voyage so he could cover the story. "There'll be many human interest stories that our readers will enjoy," he convincingly told his editor. He would share a stateroom with Steve Matteson. Even after writing a scathing book about Deborah, Carrie Boswell had the nerve to accept an invitation. She would share her room with Virginia Wellington, the widow of J. C. All of the resident's staterooms would be on deck six. Deborah would share her three-bedroom suite with Sir Basil on deck nine and Karen would occupy one of the other bedrooms.

The happy vacationers and their luggage filled two buses. After three and a half hours of beastly traffic, they arrived at Pier 82, Port of Los Angeles, Cruise-ship section.

"Isn't she beautiful?" Deborah pointed to the *Wanderer*'s 490 feet of gleaming white steel.

The residents agreed as they stood around a mountain of baggage and pointed theirs out to the waiting stevedores. Ordinary seamen escorted them to their stateroom where they instructed the travelers how to operate the room functions—TV, air-conditioning, wall safe, and sliding door.

In the 1920s and 30s, hordes of well-wishers stood on the dock as the great ocean liner departed. Serpentine and confetti floated in the air, and bands played enthusiastically. Now those traditions were gone—there were no crowds, serpentine, confetti, or a band at Pier 82—but the residents' excitement peaked when the ship's deep-throated horn blasted a farewell to Los Angeles. To them this was not just another cruise-ship, it was the Queen Mary sliding through the Hudson River bound for London in 1929. They traveled first class, dressed in ermines and pearls and rubbing elbows with Dukes and Earls.

Their nineteen staterooms ran consecutively on the port side of deck 6. The group of people on the starboard side had arrived earlier and was already partying. A bearded, young man wearing glasses dressed in the ship's complimentary bathrobe, with a glass held high in one hand and the bottle of champagne in the other, bumped into Carrie Boswell as she opened her door to see what all the noise was about. "Grab a glass, mate," he said. "Let me give you a splash."

She took one look at this crazy Aussie with a tattoo on his chest and a scar over his right eyebrow and said, "Absolutely." She couldn't believe her luck and dashed into her room to get one provided on the shelves near her refrigerator.

"My name is Jake Plumber, from Sydney. By the way, are you eating with anyone?"

"I was, but she can eat with someone else in our group. We have a big one."

"I noticed. They're older, but you must be a young chaperone."

"Well, thank you. I'm older than you, but know how to have a good time. My name is Carrie Boswell."

He looked her over from her feet to the top of her head. "Age is only an attitude and yours is at the thirty-five level. Right mate? See you at seven, 'okay,' as you Americans say."

Dress was casual, and the group went to dinner in their travel clothes. At seven, they started to flock to the main dining room, the Crystal Room, and grouped together in tables of six or eight—everyone except Carrie who sat at a table for two with Jake.

"I can't believe Carrie, in their seventies, snapping up a man fifteen years younger," Gail Jenkins said.

"I can," Tom replied with lecherous smile. He knew he would be getting into trouble with his wife, but he couldn't resist saying, "This will be a short trip with no time to teach the basics. His antennas told him she was experienced, *tempus fugit*"

"Oh, Tom, you're disgusting. He's just being nice to her, she's lonely. They'll have dinner a dance or two and go to bed," his wife said.

Gunther laughed so hard he choked until he turned red. "You're right, Gail. Dinner, two drinks, and then bed, but on the starboard side."

Tom jumped to his feet, inspired. "Time is short; let's throw our room keys into a hat and swap wives."

The men laughed, the women hissed and Gail threw a hard roll that hit Tom directly on his forehead.

"Just kidding. Can't you take a joke?" He rubbed his head.

The next day was Christmas, a full day at sea, and formal dress. At three p.m. the mandatory life-jacket drill was held. Few put them on properly. In fact, some were on backward, but the happy-go-lucky crew laughed and turned them around.

The *Wanderer* had four dining rooms. Beside the Crystal Room there were *Antoine's* for French cuisine, *Eastern Longitudes* for Asian food and the *Ristorante Capri* for Italian delights. Deborah Farrell and Sir Basil were asked to sit at Captain Alfredo Romero's table in the Crystal Room. All tables received drinks before dinner, three different wines with it, and a choice of three different soups, followed by a selection from four different salads— all served with panache. A duet of lobster and filet mignon was nearly everyone's choice for his or her main entry, followed by an unlimited selection of desserts and cheeses.

"Oh my God, Captain, how do you keep so slim and fit?" Deborah asked the smiling skipper.

"We Italians have the perfect genes for good food, wine, and women," he answered as he kissed her hand. "I'm from Genoa. Columbus had them and so do I. It's in the soil."

The *Wanderer* docked at Mazatlan on December 26. Located on Mexico's Gold Coast, this village was the closest Mexican resort to the United States. Nicknamed the "Pearl of the Pacific," Mazatlan offered everything for the America tourist. For golfers, courses by Lee Trevino and Trent Jones. For those in love, perfect weather and ten miles of stunning Pacific beachfront with picturesque churches and historic buildings.

Ms. Farrell had cocktail parties for groups of six or eight in her suite. After they had returned from exploring Mazatlan, she invited Amy and Glen Thompson, Chauncey and Latisha Talbot, and Enrico and Francesca Di Donoto.

Chauncey related some of his experiences for the government sailing on very primitive vessels in the Indian Ocean and the China Seas. "As you know, the Chinese are great gamblers and they would lay odds on anything and everything: how many dolphins would be seen in a day; how much distance would be covered and even if the ship would be attacked. The food was terrible; a day without stomach cramps was a miracle."

"That's exceptionally interesting, Chauncey. Please, sometime tell me more," Deborah said.

"I'm writing a book about those days. You'll get a copy."

"Speaking of gambling," Rico said. "Slick is making a fortune at Black Jack."

Slick, Tom Jenkins, was a dealer in Las Vegas at several of the casinos; Black Jack or twenty-one was his game. There the casino used two to six decks for the game to prevent the pros from counting the cards. On this ship, the casino used only one because nearly all of the people aboard were amateurs. "Slick's in Seventh Heaven. With one deck he can count the face cards and know with some degree of certainty how the cards will fall. He'll own this ship by the time we reach L.A. Don't anybody alert the pit boss and spoil his fun."

"In Vegas, if they catch anyone counting, they throw them out of the casino," Sir Basil commented. "That would be pretty fatal out here."

"I have news," Deborah said. "Denise, my niece, is flying to Manzanillo and will meet the ship there tomorrow. She'll use our other bedroom."

The next day the ship docked at Manzanillo at eight. As soon as the ship was cleared by port authorities, Deborah and Sir Basil had a taxi drive them thirty-five miles to the airport where Denise's direct flight from Los Angeles would arrive at nine. The plane was an hour late, and collecting luggage and clearing customs took another hour, but the three happy people arrived back at the ship in time for Bloody Mary's and lunch.

After lunch they joined fellow residents to go sight-seeing in Manzanillo, a major beach resort and self-proclaimed "sailfish capitol of the world." It hosted a yearly sailfish fishing tournament. Manzanillo, Mexico's second largest port, was also well-known internationally for deep-sea fishing and the green flash phenomenon during sunsets.

At five, Deborah and Sir Basil, with Denise's help, hosted David Morris, Gunther Krause and Rose Marie Dentz, Lucille Sutherland, Virginia Wellington, and Steve Matteson.

This was the first time that Deborah and Steve had been together since the trial and both were eager to talk. Denise, knowing the situation, cornered Steve on the patio and called for her mother to join them, and then left the two to talk.

"You saved my life. I could never thank you enough," Deborah said as she squeezed Steve's hand.

"I stared at you from the witness chair and moved my lips, hoping to interest you," he explained.

"I knew you were trying to make contact."

"Exactly. Then when I stumbled near you, I hoped you would lean over so I could tell you that I had an alibi for you."

"I thought you would approach me in some way and it was perfect. How did you think of it on such short notice?"

"Oh, it wasn't short. I've been working on it for a long time. I saved Bill Munson's career a long time ago and we've been friends ever since. He kept saying he owed me so I gave him a chance to pay me back."

"Why did you take such a chance? You don't even know me."

Steve looked longingly at her and held both of her hands. "Oh, but I do. I've known you since that first trial. I tried to help you then and I'm glad I finally got the chance." He hesitated and a tear appeared in the corner of his eye. "You needed me and I wanted so desperately to help . . . because I love you. I know it's hopeless, you have another, but I can't help it. I'm hopelessly in love with you."

She gasped and quickly walked to the bathroom. "Something wrong with Deborah?" someone asked.

"No," Steve said. "She got a tickle in her throat and needed a drink of water."

Deborah returned in five minutes and joined the others.

David Morris usually was a polite, but dull dinner partner, but this afternoon he was quite agitated. He'd drunk two large, gin martinis rapidly and was now nursing his third. Heart doctors talked about heart problems and dentists discussed bicuspids and molars, but the part of the female body that OB/GYNs deal with usually precluded discussion. But today Dave had to tell two off-color jokes about it.

"Denise, may I ask how old you are?" he asked in a loud voice.

"Of course. I was born in sixty-four, so that makes me thirty-six," she answered.

"Damn, life is so unfair. My poor Katherine, dead at twenty. She would have been forty-four last week. I would have been a grandfather. Damn that bastard, damn," David muttered.

"Come on, David. I'll walk you back to your stateroom. You've had enough party for one day," Steve said.

"No, I'm staying. Debby, you want me to, don't you?"

"No, she doesn't, pal. You're going to go and sleep it off," Steve said as he hoisted the smaller man on his shoulders and carted him off.

"I'll be back, leave the hatch open as they say in the navy," Steve remarked as he carried the now comatose body down the passageway.

The next day, December 28, the ship docked at the port-of-call everyone had been eagerly anticipating. Puerto Vallarta, where the movie "The Night of the Iguana" was filmed and Richard Burton and Elizabeth Taylor began their torrid love affair that burnt its way through six continents and two marriages. Before the film, it was a small, dusty village. Now its Bay of Banderas was lined with resorts and hotels for American tourists anxious to enjoy fun-in-the-sun while surfing, whale watching, golfing, or simply drinking Margaritas.

Denise was enjoying her first vacation from her husband, Jack, since the birth of their daughter, Janet—named after her aunt. Denise co-hosted the last of the two cocktail parties for the remaining Wind and Sea residents as the *Wanderer*'s itinerary called for a two-day stay at Puerta Vallarta.

The ship sailed at six p. m. on the night of December 30 and headed for Cabo San Lucas. Cabo for decades had a reputation for world-class sport fishing, especially for marlin. To satisfy American demand, top golf course designers competed to make Cabo the golf Mecca of Baja, California. Gunther, Rico, and several other Wind and Sea residents chartered a boat and spent the day angling for marlin, sailfish, and swordfish. They donated their catch to the chef.

The *Wanderer* blasted its horn at six and pulled anchor for Ensenada. The crew prepared for New Year's Eve. Deborah and Steve smiled at each other, but avoided long conversations. He now was embarrassed by his expression of love, but happy she knew how he felt. Deborah was glad he did because she too felt affection for this man who had risked so much for her.

David Morris drank only moderately at the succeeding parties, but stayed aloof, particularly from Steve.

At seven, the wind suddenly changed direction. The zephyr-like eastern winds now it blew from the northwest at increasing velocity. By 7:30 p.m., it was near gale strength and the ship began to roll and pitch. The weather had been near perfect and this was the first experience that most of the residents had of rough water. At first they laughed as they wobbled from side to side in the passageways, but by dinner time, many stayed in their rooms.

On formal nights, The Wind and Sea contingent had stayed together, ate in the Crystal Room, danced in the Starlight Ballroom, attended the show, and except for those few that went to the casino, retired. Tonight, their last big party night, Deborah asked that after dinner they all come to the Horizon Lounge for a farewell get-together. "It will be our party, with a dance band, caviar, and champagne. Something we'll remember forever," she explained.

The six-course dinner began at eight with champagne and ended at midnight with a toast to 2001 and the singing of "Auld Lang Syne." In between courses, the ten-piece band played all the beloved songs of the forties and fifties. It was the most sumptuous meal, served in the best manner in the grandest venue that any had experienced. The tired partygoers longed for their beds, but all were determined not to disappoint Deborah. They dragged their exhausted bodies to the Horizon Lounge for one more drink as the winds increased and the ship was now rolling ten degrees.

By 1:30 a.m., only a sober David Morris, Deborah and Steve remained. Everyone else had trickled back to their staterooms. The only crew members up and about were on the bridge or in the engine room. The wind now howled at fifty miles per hour as the ship's pitching and rolling made it difficult to walk.

Steve leaned toward Deborah. "I'm so happy that horrible ordeal is behind you. It's wonderful to see you happy again."

"You two think you're so smart. That pathetic alibi fooled the stupid jury, but not me," Morris suddenly snarled.

Steve jumped up and lunged for David.

David reached inside of his tuxedo and pulled out a revolver, and pointed it at him.

Deborah screamed.

"Shut up, you bitch. With this howling storm, no one can hear you."

"What do you want?" Steve demanded.

"I want revenge and I'm going to get it, so don't try anything, Detective. This gun is loaded with .38 shells and I know how to use it." David waved the gun.

"Revenge for what?" Deborah asked. "I haven't done anything to you."

"Never did anything? You dumb bitch; you just murdered my beautiful daughter, that's all."

She shook her head. "I never met your daughter."

The ship rocked and rolled. Deborah and Steve grabbed the table, and Morris clutched it with his left hand.

"You're worse than a street whore. You let me make love to you; said you cared, and then a month later you get engaged to that bastard, Mark Chambers. He was my daughter's fiancé, for God's sake. You didn't care. He was just another pair of pants to share a bed with. But Katherine was crushed. When he told her he was leaving her, she jumped into her new car, revved it up to a hundred miles an hour, and crashed it into a tree. All because you couldn't keep your god damn hands off him.

Deborah's body tensed as she convulsively screamed. A shocked Steve raised his fist and inched his body toward the aggressor.

"Don't move. I'll blow your head off." Morris waved the pistol at Steve. "You're not going to get any help; the passengers are all in bed and the crew is elsewhere fighting the storm."

The Horizon Lounge was on the eleventh deck. A double door aft led to a promenade deck where the athletic passengers exercised. Twelve trips around the deck equaled a mile. The pitching increased to fifteen degrees. Steve looked at the sea, and a few seconds later, as the ship's stern tilted upward, he saw the starry sky. Sooner or later this violent gyration would throw David off balance toward the down side and Steve could jump him from the up side—he hoped.

Dave snickered, which turned to a belly laugh.

"What's so funny?" Steve asked.

"You cops; you had everything backwards. You thought dear Deborah left a key somewhere for an accomplice to find, to rob the house, and then murder Mark. Just the opposite. Mark made a copy and gave it to me to do both. For two months we met at the tennis club to plan this caper. He told me how much he hated you, Deborah, and then I told him I did too. 'Let's kill the bitch,' he suggested one afternoon. 'She's divorcing me. I won't get anything afterward, maybe there's something in her estate for me if we're married when she dies.'"

Deborah threw up her hands. "Nothing. That nobody would have received zilch," Deborah screamed above the howling wind.

David lost his balance, then steadied himself. "The first break-in was planned to get your gun. I was supposed to leave after I'd killed you and the police would suspect the robbers. But you lucked out. You were at Hazel's on August eleventh and supposed to be home on the twelfth, but you weren't. Where were you? You certainly were not at Dana Point talking to that navy character. That was pure bullshit. Where were you?"

Debby looked down at her hands and shook her head. "I just don't remember."

"Well," David continued. "Mark showed up later to find your body, and grief stricken, he would have called the police, but there was nobody. He was infuriated and started to curse me. I hated him, too, and was going to kill him later, so I took the opportunity presented, shot him and left the gun to incriminate you. Two for the price of one."

"You killed Arnold Myers, too, didn't you?" Steve asked as he shifted his position.

David licked his lips. "Had to. I was his wife's obstetrician and on a visit he met my daughter, Katherine, with her fiancé, Mark Chambers. At the talent show he bought one of the pictures showing Deborah with her husband and recognized him as the same man who was with my daughter. I saw the immediate change in him and I knew he knew I'd killed the man who had caused my daughter's death, the bastard. I heard him say he was going for a cigarette, so I rushed upstairs, put the 'Out of Order' sign on the elevator, and waited for him. My daughter loved croquet and I kept her set. A mallet from it was the perfect tool to crush his head—short handle, heavy head."

The ship plunged and Steve leapt toward David, but the distance was too far and David adjusted in time to fire. The shell hit Steve in the abdomen. He screamed and fell, writhing in pain to the floor.

"Did you know, dear Debby, that killing someone in international waters and throwing the body overboard is the perfect way to commit murder? No jurisdiction, no body, no witness. There's no government to investigate, and the ship certainly doesn't want anything to do with the crime. It's just a perfect way to get rid of someone, and that's what I'm going to do now. First with you and then I'll come back and get him."

A crying Deborah pounded her assailant with her little fists as he lifted her pushed the door open, and carried her onto the wet, rolling deck against a now sixty-mile-an-hour gale.

Steve struggled to stand, but soon collapsed back on the carpet. Deborah screamed and continued to kick and beat on her determined assailant with her ebbing strength." You demented bastard," she yelled

David had her near the top of the railing, when a bearded man blew through the same door with his pistol drawn. "Drop her," he yelled.

David couldn't or didn't want to hear, and continued to lift the panic-stricken woman. From twenty feet away the person fired and two bodies fell to the deck, one in shock and the other dead.

The bearded man fired twice more in the air to get attention, and a deck officer came running. They carried the two bodies back to the lounge and laid them next to Steve.

The bearded man with the scar and tattoo smiled at Steve. "Don't you recognize me, mate?" Steve took a close look. "Well, I'll be damned. Lieutenant Blake McGee of the Santa Barbara police— welcome aboard." Steve wrapped his arms around his friend.

They introduced themselves as policemen to the officer and briefly explained what had happened. "I'm Lieutenant Paolicelli and this is beyond my rank. He's going to be mad, but this is one for the captain; I have to get him out of bed. First, I'll ring the doctor and get him up here. He'll bring paramedics to take you and the lady down to sick bay. You're not bleeding too badly; our doctor can take care of it. Lt. McGee, stay here till I get back."

After the officer left, Steve spread his arms, begging for an explanation.

"We're having 'Pioneer Days' in Santa Barbara in two weeks and for about a month I've let my beard grow," McGee said. "After I decided to infiltrate Farrell's party, I added the phony tattoo and scar."

"What about romancing Carrie?" Steve asked. "Pretty hot stuff."

"Actually, she recognized me and I asked her to play along with my plan. I didn't tell her much, but I told her it was important. She's a great old gal."

"When did you know it was Morris?" Steve inquired.

"Before you did. When I interviewed the suspects a few weeks ago, something about Morris bothered me. I told Chris Fowler, the executive director, that I wanted to go through David's and Farrell's units after you all had left for the ship. He approved my request and as soon as you departed at noon, I entered Morris' apartment. On the top of his baby-grand piano was an eight-by-ten picture of his daughter, Katherine and her fiancé. It must have been her last picture. Pictures of her at various ages were in the other rooms. In Farrell's den was the picture that Woody Ferguson told us about; Farrell with her fourth husband, Mark Chambers. An electric shock went through me as I studied it. Mark Chambers was the fiancé; they were the same man. He jilted Morris' daughter, and she then committed suicide. Morris hated Chambers and killed him and he hated Farrell who now was in mortal danger.

"My captain talked to the cruise line and ordered me a ticket; I packed and had a driver bring me down to the ship."

"What about tonight?" Steve asked.

"Morris hung around when he shouldn't have and I guessed he was planning to do something to Ms. Farrell tonight. It was late, nearly everyone was in bed and there was a storm blowing—a perfect night for mischief. Carrie had been drinking, and I had to carefully escort her down five decks, tuck her in bed, and then climb five decks back to the Horizon Lounge. Fortunately, I got there just in time."

The medics arrived and took Steve and Deborah to the fourth deck hospital. A grumpy Captain Romero strolled into the lounge with Lieutenant Paolicelli and sat next to Blake, who knowing that the captain would have a major decision to make, carefully detailed the events of the night and the history behind them.

Romero thought for a moment and then made his decision, "We can't stop at Ensenada. If the Mexican port authorities learn of the murder, they could tie up the ship for a week. We skip Ensenada and land at Los Angeles day after tomorrow."

McGee assembled and briefed The Wind and Sea group the next morning. Ms. Farrell has recovered; she'll be with us for dinner. Steve was lucky, the bullet went completely through a fleshy part of his abdomen, in and out, and didn't hit anything vital. He'll have to stay in the hospital for a few days in Los Angeles." He paused and smiled. "Didn't we have an exciting and wonderful trip?"

After the cheers, drinks were ordered and Deborah Farrell was toasted. "The best I've ever had," Mary Lee said and everyone agreed. "If I live to be a hundred, nothing will beat it."

Epilogue

August 2009

The ivy now covered the walls completely, the multi-colored azalea plants were windowsill high, the trees and hedges were full and tall, and the daffodils, roses, petunias on the campus had thrived and were abundant. The bougainvilleas bursting with magenta-red color covered the trellises over the walkways. Loving care, plenty of water, and the Santa Barbara sun had been kind to the flora at The Wind and Sea during the last ten years. The same warmth and passing time were not so kind to the people of this community.

Gunther Krause and Rose Marie Dentz maintained their separate apartments, but in all other ways acted like a married couple. They ate together, traveled together, and presumably, slept together. Rose Marie donated her time and expertise to consoling the residents, mostly women, who suffered from grief, depression, or loneliness.

In 2003, Gunther contracted Type I diabetes and needed daily shots of insulin. He dieted, exercised and lost twenty-five pounds, and was able to keep the disease under control. As business and the other activities of his life became less important, his interest in the holocaust increased. Dormant memories of his young wife and two children flooded back into his mind. He joined the Simon Wiesenthal Holocaust Center in Los Angles and became a docent, serving two days a month.

He was a member of the Breakfast Club, helped the kitchen prepare better food, but most importantly became a mentor to Executive Director Chris Fowler, and helped him become a wonderful and caring manager. Chris had a chance to become an officer of the corporation, but turned the opportunity down to remain with his friends, the residents of The Wind and Sea.

Blake McGee became nationally famous as the cop who had cracked a twenty-two-year-old murder case. He was soon promoted to chief of detectives and in 2004 was elevated to Santa Barbara's chief of police. At the same time, he received his law degree from the University of California at Santa Barbara. In 2008 President George Bush asked him to come to Washington and become an assistant to the Attorney General. The Pink Daffodil case was linked to the Mark Chambers-Deborah Farrell murder case and Woodrow Ferguson received credit for solving that twenty-two-year-old case. He was promoted to the rank of captain in the Los Angeles Police Department.

Jeffrey Grainger garnered literary fame when his collection of short stories titled, "Elders at Play" became number six on the non-fiction best-seller list in the New York Times. The feature stories were the two murders and the travails of the White Lady, but many of them were from the notes he took on the cruise.

Enrico Di Donoto's wife, Francesca, was diagnosed with terminal, stomach cancer with two months to live. This tough, often brutal, criminal man became a tender caregiver. He attended to her every need and desire during the day and night.

"Why, Reverend Thompson? Why is she subjected to this suffering? She has always been a loving, giving person; never hurt anybody. Me now, I deserve it. God should be punishing me. I have hurt many people. The Ten Commandments, I've torn them to shreds. Yet I'm healthy and she's in terrible pain. Why? Is God punishing me through her?"

Glen hugged the bigger man. "That question has been asked through the ages. No one, including me, has found the answer. Life is so unfair. Some are born smart, beautiful and rich. Others come into this world brain damaged, disfigured, and poor. Maybe God is neutral in this world. He doesn't become involved in which side wins wars, or which team wins ball games, or who is sick or healthy. This world is ours to nurture or destroy. Maybe he's keeping score and the ones that act in accordance to his dictates in this world are rewarded in the next. I do know that when I do something nice for someone, I feel better."

Francesca died and Rico vowed to become a paragon of virtue and helpfulness. Forest fire destroyed his marijuana patch, but he continued to supply those that needed the weed for medical purposes. All of the frail old women could count on him to take them shopping or fix a faucet or change a lightbulb. He donated money to the local Boys and Girls' Club and acted as a deacon for Glen Thompson's services.

In 2006, Sir Basil retired from the board of The Retirement Communities of the West. John Watts, the current president replacing Goodwin Oliver, was promoted to that position. Sir Basil moved to cottage number eight in 2006, was eighty-three, and in good health until he fell and broke his right hip. The operation was successful, but the rehabilitation was slow and painful.

Although he had a full-time nurse, his next-door neighbor, Deborah Farrell, checked on him daily and made sure he was given the best.

She was eight-one, but retained the allure of a much younger woman. Her fragile beauty remained: her eyes suggestive, her hair luminous, and her body firm. Their fondness and desire for each other remained strong, but suppressed by their physical disabilities. They held hands while listening to classical music and the songs of their youth. She read to him, they played cards and games, and Sir Basil told her the marvelous stories of his wild youth.

Both would have been happy and contented to continue living this idyllic life, but Sir Basil contacted pneumonia and was taken to a hospital where he died whispering her name. Anticipating his demise, Sir Basil had told Deborah that he wished to be buried in his family cemetery in Yorkshire, surrounded by his ancestors that first were laid to rest in this hallowed earth in the eleventh century.

Karen O'Brien had married Woody Ferguson and Deborah Farrell was now alone with her memories and pictures—but not for long. Two days after Sir Basil's body was flown to England, there was a knock on her door; Steve Matteson had come to pay his respects.

"I'm so glad you came," she said as she held his hand a little longer than necessary. "I owe you so much for all you have done for me."

"I've wanted to see you, but with Sir Basil here, I thought it best to keep my distance," he shyly answered.

"I'm very lonely now. I hope you will come often."

"Dear lady, I would love to be at your doorstep at dawn and go home at dusk." His longing was apparent to her and cherished.

"Steve, you are a good-looking man, ten years younger than I, but that's what I enjoy. My most lonely times are in the middle of the night. Would that fit into your schedule?"

The hair stood up on the back of his neck. *My God, is my wildest dream possible?*

Only twenty percent of the retirees who had initiated The Wind and Sea were left. Soon they would be gone. This generation, who had made its mark on the world, was marching on to that great beyond. The "Baby Boomer" generation was replacing them, filling the vacated apartments and cottages. Martinis and Scotch on the rocks were being replaced by coffee latte and wine tasting. "Swing music" giving way to "Rock and Roll." Nothing would ever be the same, except that in time the "Boomers," too, would realize The Wind and Sea would be their last stop.

The Appendix

The Wind and Sea is a fictional institution, but it is representative of the better retirement communities that are being built all over the world and particularly in the western part of the United States.

The author of this book, after fifty years in the business world, retired and now lives with his wife in "The Covington," a continuing care retirement community operated by the Episcopal Home Communities and located in Aliso Viejo, California. Life at The Covington was the source for many of the story lines and characters of the "The Last Stop."

Many of the leaders of the "Greatest Generation" live at The Covington, including doctors, lawyers, college professors, a world-class scientist, a judge, a museum director, and dozens of successful businessmen.

The Covington was especially blessed with residents who had mastered the English language. The weather, beauty, and closeness to Laguna Beach and the Orange County Performing Arts Center drew them to this "campus." A snippet of their lighter prose and poetry is included below for the reader's enjoyment.

Betsy Schulman

Mother, grandmother, widow; UCLA graduate, English teacher, story-teller, and poetess extraordinary. Resident in Cottage # B-6.

I Don't Want To Go There

There are no trees on Mars. I don't want to go there!
No tree-houses, no swings, hanging from leafy limbs,
No forests, deer, no bears,
No orchards hung with apples, plums and pears,

I don't want to go there!

There is no shade on Mars, bring sun-block SPF 62,
And even that won't do. You'd have to have a tent
And who wants to bring a tent that might be rent
In two, by howling Martian winds?
I don't want to go there

There are no books on Mars, unless you bring your own.
And who could read a book in all that sand and dust and
Glare?
Reading when your tent might tear—any second.
You'd hang onto the flaps and pray your book won't blow away
I don't want to go there.

I have no friends on Mars, no folks, no girls, no boys,
No neighbors, not a pet. No barking dogs, no noise! And yet,
I do love music. Could I live without Scarlatti,
Pavarotti, and mornings at the Met?
I don't want to go there.

I like the color red. It's a change from blue and green.
There are things up there I've never seen, I guess
Away from all this earthly toil and stress—
No guns, no traffic jams, no cars, no WARS (so far.)
Well, maybe—someday— I'd like to go to Mars.

An American Grandma Gives Osama Some Sound Advice

Osama Bin Laden, where are you?
Come out, give up. Say you're wrong!
You're causing so much confusion
In the land of the brave and strong.

Don't you know that nobody likes you?
Your sisters pretend they don't know you
They're ashamed of the way you behave.

You've trashed their place in society,
And well, they just wish you would shave.

Your grandma must surely be weeping;
Whatever went wrong she can't guess.
You were an adorable baby,
And now—you are really a mess!

Resign from Al Qaeda, Osama,
Face the music. You're on the skids.
Make it up with your wife. Settle down! Get a life!
Spend some quality time with your kids.

Dancing the Hukilau

"Won't you come and dance the Hukilau with me?" the little girl said in her fake grass skirt, holding out her hands pleadingly.

How could I refuse? She was part of a local Sunday school group sent to entertain us following a luau lunch at The Wind and Sea. As she took me onto the stage, my recalcitrant feet dragged a bit and my arthritic knee made mild protest. *You know you really shouldn't do this.* It grated. But I didn't listen to this sound advice because the child was so appealing, and besides, I liked to dance. Soon I was swaying, floating my hands off to the side ad singing, "Oh, I'm going to a hukilau. To a huki-huki-huki-hukilau."

Mama always said I danced as soon as I walked. I don't recall this but I do remember being in a Maypole dance when I was seven and going the wrong way. I was joyfully unaware of ruining the whole pattern, skipping and humming along until I saw my teacher's anguished expression and her wild gestures to turn back. Which I did. And I found myself with a short bit of ribbon while the other kids were still weaving with their longer ribbons. But I gamely danced on and ended being woven into a tight little knot.

When I was nine, Mama decided I should spend my twenty-five dollars Grandpa sent me for Christmas on tap-dancing lessons. My mother thought these dancing might improve my poise and grace, and get me exercising instead of reading all day. I learned the buck-and-wing and a few other steps. Every evening at home I tapped across the kitchen linoleum, showing my family what I had learned. My loving parents applauded my efforts, but my brothers looked bored. All too soon the money ran out. This being the Depression time, I had to give up tapping. Daddy pried the metal taps from my black, patent-leather dancing shoes, which I wore to Sunday school for the rest of the year.

Endangered Species Komodo Dragons

If you've never seen a Komodo Dragon—don't
bother!
He is a great, gross, slobbery cobber,
With a strong desire to chomp on your gizzard
And besides, he's really only a lizard!

He's nine feet long and three hundred pounds,
On Komodo Island he abounds.
He rolls all around in sand and clover,
And his breath is enough to knock you over.

He'll eat anyone; wife, child or mother.
He's socially one mean, mixed-up brother!
Morally challenged and just plain crazy,
And most of the time he's downright lazy.

Because he's so fat, you might think he can't run,
But he's swift as a greyhound, when he wants
To have fun.
Such as chasing a poor little cat till it cries,
Then he—don't look!—Not for innocent eyes!

His home is an island, all rocky and hot.
But a fun, happy place? No, it is not!
Watch out for the kids. Don't tan on the sand,
Or all they might find the next day— is a hand.

So if someone invites you to go to this place,
Tell them you're busy, and keep a straight face.
Say, "I'm terribly sorry, it may sound banal,
I've a date with my dentist for a root canal."

Life with Boxes

Gradually, gradually, the boxes are dwindling. Boxes containing all my possessions, all my precious things— the detritus of more than seventy years of living and accumulating.

I thought I had rid myself of all the unnecessary stuff before moving down to The Covington. I winnowed through my clothing; heartlessly discarding beloved garments I hadn't worn for years. But wait! They—in the new place—won't have seen my pink pantsuit. Better keep that. And the khaki jacket with all the pockets, so useful for bird watching. Surely I'll need this! The piano had to go. No room for that in my new small cottage in the retirement community.

At last the sorting, discarding, recycling, and giving away is done, leaving me with only basic furniture and dozens of boxes of assorted objects and papers. All carefully labeled: liv. room, den, kitch, bath, guest rm, and bdrm. and placed accordingly in the center of each room by movers.

Life becomes a matter of living with boxes, stepping around boxes, and emptying boxes. But where to put everything? Towels and sheets must be rolled up and stacked in a tiny linen closet in my bathroom. The kitchen reveals only two reachable shelves in all the nice army of cupboards. Were they expecting long-armed Amazons here?

Never mind. I do my best. I stack things away and promise myself I'll organize better another day. Each empty box is a triumph. I smash it, (*"Take that,"* I say.) and stack it out by the trash cans.

Sorting through the papers is really the worst. Why does my accountant insist I must keep tax records for seven years? Surely five will do. Or three? My lawyer sends me huge folders with letters instructing me to "keep these forever." Forever? Am I, like Scrooge with his moneyboxes, to stagger through Eternity with boxes dragging behind me, mine filled with legal papers? Give me a break!

At last I am down to the cartons of framed photos of children, grandchildren, and even great grandchildren. I have hung as many as possible on walls. The rest must go into the garage. Oh yes, and that huge box of slides of all my travels, and that box of diaries of the same, and that box of— Oh well! Some day, when I have time, I'll clean out the garage of all the boxes.

The Ivory-Billed Woodpecker

They found me! I've been discovered!
By now everyone knows.
I've barely recovered from my shock.
And I'm in the throes
Now I must warn the flock.
Of a giant bird watch.
For twenty-six years I've managed to escape
Birders are all around,
In kayaks, a pair.

Whispering, "Hush, there he goes!"
It wasn't fair.

I'd just popped out for an acorn or two.
Life will never be the same.
One had a camera.
One can never go back
He didn't even say "cheese."
And undo the damage,
Took my picture as fast as you please.
That's just the price of fame.

*   *   *   *

Diana Lycette

Mother, grandmother; lives with her husband, Bill, and a haughty cat.

Smith College, Univ. of Wash, leader of writers groups, published author of short stories, novellas and children's books. Resident: Cottage # 3.

Enquiring Minds

Do you run into a lot of questionnaires these days? Often it's a polite patient voice on the telephone at dinner time. "We're conducting a survey. Could you spare a few minutes of your time?"

How can you say no to that disembodied unknown trying to make a living at home by invading time and space at your home? You find pathetic images flashing across your mental screen: a young mother, one eye on a child, the other on her check-list, her eyes growing farther apart with each phone survey she completes; a man in a wheelchair dialing with a pencil clinched between his teeth.

"Sure," you say agreeably, to dispel these chilling pictures. "Go ahead, ask me."

You swallow dry chunks of half-chewed dinner and brace yourself for what you know is coming: a quest for your opinions. The caller usually begins with hypothetical scenarios, subjunctive and conditional. "If the election was held today, would you cast your vote for A or B?"

There it is, the dreaded decision. Ever facetious, you are tempted to reply, " It's not so much a vote I would cast for A, more like a good-sized rock or maybe a dead fish— and I never heard of B."

Well, you can't say that. Shape up. Behave like a responsible citizen, even if you have to lie.

Next the caller may want input on questions of "community infra-structure." All you want is input of what used to be hot food.

Silence on the line. I grab a carrot to sustain life while the caller pauses to see if a miracle will happen and I will come up with a proper response. Finally she sighs and says, "I'll just check 'none of the above.'"

I sense her disapproval. Another wish-washy, uncommitted, uninformed, uninvolved respondent, crunching carrots instead of ideas.

Even more threatening is the survey taker who probes beyond politics to pry into matters of the soul. Where do you stand on capital punishment? On drunk driving? On that saddest of decisions, abortion? Should women be encouraged to stay home and be homemakers, whatever that is, or to make lives for themselves, whatever the cost? Should we make war in the desert, draw a line in the sand and defend it with our marines, backed up by our unlikely allies, the draperied Saudis and the born-again Russians? If the present has become so exceedingly surreal, what can the future hold?

The surveyor grows impatient. You begin to feel a relentless pressure to perform. You can't just mutter, "No opinion," and escape into a mound of cold potatoes.

What do you mean, "No opinion?" Don't you read, don't you listen, don't you care? Did you just arrive here, a hapless and exhausted fugitive from outer space?

That's it, a reprieve! I am an alien; my enormous wings are molting. I just stopped by for a little rest. I have seen all sides to your universe, all sides to your questions. I see the guiltless, grasping fetus waiting to make its claim, waiting to live. I see the nauseated mother who wants a life too, and not that one.

I see soldiers who volunteered to serve, to train, to shoot. Some of them are raring to go—they want in. Others want out. Others just want some clean socks. If they don't fight a small war now, will the Big One come later?

"Come on," says the voice. "What is your opinion? Do you want freedom or slavery, life or death, yes or no?"

"Put down," I say firmly. "Put down, please, that I am strongly in favor of clean socks."

Domestic *Pas de Deux* with Toast

"You still mad?" he asked.

"I'm not mad," she said, frowning at her husband in his pajamas, the ones with tiger stripes.

He turned a page of the morning newspaper. After the rustle of newsprint, there was silence. He peeked at her over the headlines. "Then why do you look like that?"

"Well, I certainly do apologize for the way I look. You should be used to it by now."

More silence. A page turned. He persisted. "Is it what happened at the Gordons yesterday? Are you still stewing about that?"

"I don't stew," she informed him. "You were impossible of course."

He set the paper down. "This toast is stony cold," he remarked. "Stony cold, and there's no marmalade. Why are we always running out of things?"

"Did you put marmalade on the grocery list, like you're supposed to? No-o, so it's your fault." She got up and marched into the kitchen, though a really impressive march was difficult since the kitchen was no more than five steps away from the table. She opened and closed cupboards dramatically. After a moment she was back with an armload of items capable of being spread: boysenberry jam, honey in a squeeze bottle shaped like a teddy bear, peanut butter, and a bent tube of anchovy paste. She plunked them down on the table, resisting the impulse to align them in a pleasing alphabetical array. "Here," she said. "By the way— you've been messing with my spice cabinet again. Can't find a thing there after you're done with it."

He ignored her offerings and stood up. "Spice—that's it! I'll have cinnamon toast." He skirted the table and escaped into the kitchen. His voice crept around the doorway. "What do you mean I was impossible? I was just having a little fun."

She sniffed. "You know how the Gordons idolize that cat. They'll probably never speak to us again."

His voice came plaintively from the depths of a cabinet. "I can't find the cinnamon. Are we out of that too?"

She maintained a dignified silence while small jars and cans were tumbled about. Finally, he returned bearing a tin of cinnamon and the sugar bowl. "Ah," he said with a grin. "This makes me feel like a little kid again."

"You are a little kid," she observed. "Anyway, you act like one. You and your teasing."

"That cat of theirs started it," he said defensively. "He always wants to chew on my shoe laces."

"That's no excuse. The minute we go over there you start fooling around with Tigger, getting him all excited. The same way you act with the grandchildren rolling on the floor. You give those children such a case of the giggles, they don't calm down for a week. And then you teach them those awful limericks."

"That's poetry. I thought you were in favor of poetry."

She wasn't impressed. "Was it poetry to chase Tigger around the yard till he ran up a tree? And what you yelled definitely wasn't Shakespeare."

He sprinkled sugar liberally, so that showers of it fell off the toast when he bit into a piece. "I didn't yell," he mumbled around the toast. "Not very much."

"And you shouldn't have thrown things."

"Well, the silly cat ran and I got excited."

He stuffed in the last of the toast and licked his fingers. "The Gordons over-reacted. You will admit that. There was no need to call the fire department. Tigger was going to come down from that tree. Cats always do."

"Not when you set fire to the tree."

"That was an accident," he insisted. "I just tapped out a few pipe ashes and the next thing I knew . . . ." He drew an outline of mounting flames in the air. "Besides, when things started getting out of hand I did try to smother the flames with that old towel."

"Too bad it had paint thinner on it."

He tried changing the subject. "Did you ever notice how Jane Gordon's voice gets really shrill when she loses control? Regular fishwife."

"You mean when you tossed the burning towel into the carport and burned up their entire bin of recyclable grocery bags?"

"Too bad they were plastic. Such a smell."

There was a moment of silence as they recalled the events of the previous day. Giggles erupted from both ends of the table.

"You know," he said. "I think I'll have another piece of the cinnamon toast. You want one?"

"As long as you're up," she concluded. "And for once, would you please remember, the cinnamon goes back on the shelf after the chervil but before the cloves."

"Got it," He said agreeably. "*Before* the chervil, *after* the cloves."

*   *   *   *

Ruth Cushingham

Renaissance woman and graduate of Pomona College where she studied all of the arts: drawing, painting and sculpture. Organic gardening and writing poetry are her current passions. A few of her hundreds of poems are included. Mother and grandmother, widow; a resident in apartment # 431.

Where are my Keys

What shock when I see I have lost it!
I had it right here in my pocket.
My key ring so valued and needed
Is gone . . . and I feel so defeated.

I've looked everywhere, but it's plain
That can't be true, or the same
Would come into view,
I could hand it to you.
My search would be through and be ended.

I traced back in time to each action,

Recalling each part of the fraction.
Most puzzles have answers specific;
This problem's a headache terrific.

At night out of sight, I still dream it
It seems to be found, I have seen it!
But when I awake,
One turn my thoughts take
Is to look in some place and find it.

How long can this searching go on?
Is my mind the thing that has gone?
I'm leaving this line still unwritten
'till I find out with what I am smitten.

God wants me Physically Fit

I have a glimmer
Of my being slimmer
But maybe there's reason for weight.

Aged bones lack the padding
It sadly is lacking
It slides to the side when you sit.

Mobility's there:
Still now you take care.
If you fall you might call your fall fate.

Movement is agile
But bones become fragile
I slow down, aware not to slip.

They Don't Make Mirrors Like They Used To

When she looked in the mirror,
It was with dismay
An array of worn wrinkles
Had wandered her way.

On a place that now looked
Like an aged-old crone,
The flesh falling loosely
The muscles lacked tone.

And her frame not the same,
For old bones bore new weight.
She's explaining, proclaiming
The dreadful mistake.

This reflection's the wrong one,
A person unknown!
Pray take her away,
Make her leave me alone.

People Watching

Oh there's a blond with hair real long.
A foreign, fat man chomping chips.
A dashing fashioned lady walks
While swaying, swinging her slim hips.

Big curly black has turned his back
On winsome couple walking by.
With cane in hand a lame old man
Recalls the days when he was spry.

Small babe is laid down in car seat,
When changed a bottle makes it fed,
Its cries subside when it can eat,
Soon settled; now asleep in bed.

Some strangers' names exchanged are lost,
Quick promises only made soon fade.
Held cell phones buzz, but at a cost;
So loved, no private calls relayed.

The clatter of the chatter looms;
With mental ear muffs, ears I gird.
More people pause, they fill the rooms,
Shrill noise of boisterous boys heard.

Good bet I'll stretch; my knees are numb,
I rise and walk as legs allow,
It's no surprise eyes see me come,
For I'm what they are watching now.

*　　*　　*　　*

John H. Dilkes

Born April 29, 1911 in Ilkeston, Derbyshire, England. Served in West Africa in WW II and immigrated to the U.S.A. in 1982. Poetry is his main passion followed by soccer, cricket, billiards, and ballroom dancing. At 97, he is the community's elder statesman and lives in apartment # 227.

Then Came the Dawn

The sun rose up from out of the sea,
It was dazzling with beauty and light.
The golden beams reveal the ecstasy,
Of a beautiful morn, radiant and bright.

Waves could be heard on the sandy beach
Shimmering cool at the early dawn.

Birds, moving swiftly, chirp in noisy screech,
Skin divers, silently sway on high waves borne.

A new morn is signaled on the coast
Before some locals have left their bed,
The night watchman's ready for his toast
And a good hot drink will do him stead.

The policeman, out on his beat
Returns from the hazard of the night
To his home he goes a hasty retreat,
He's had a busy time stopping youths in fight.

So soon, traffic will be stop, go, stop,
All types of vehicles join in the race
To rush to business, office or shop
Everyone's looking for the parking space!

The Retirement Home

I had looked around for many a day,
To find a retirement where I could stay.
When I found a wonderful brand new home,
Could find peace there, now no need to roam.

The Covington, name of my new abode,
Has lifted me from quite a heavy load.
There is wonderful food, I must admit,
René, the French chef is a perfect fit.

Everything here is just simply first-class
Quality building hard to surpass.
Comfort the key note, as a home should be,
Come visit, you'll be happy what you see!

The swimming pool is quite an attraction,
That brings some residents to quick action.
The exercise room now is quite updated,
With gadgets for the sophisticated.

The library is such a splendid show,
Wonders been performed—this we know.
The splendid indexing can save much time,
Should not be better, it's simply sublime.

The executive council has worked so well,
It has gained ground, in a limited spell.
With McGuire and Steele leading the way,
Their guidance clear, will help members stay.

Heads of departments have coped quite well,
They will be much wiser as time will tell.
The staff have co-opted in splendid style,
Full accommodations reached were worth while.

Today we rejoice, we conclude the first year,
Let's celebrate and all be of good cheer.
Nothing succeeds like success we are told,
So raise your glasses, rejoice and be bold.